REMARKABLE TRIALS,

INCLUDING, AMONGST OTHERS,

THE

CELEBRATED CASES

OF

EUGENE ARAM.
MARCHIONESS BRINVILLIERS.
JONATHAN BRADFORD.
COLONEL FITZGERALD.
LORD AND LADY SOMERSET.
DR. DODD.
CAPTAIN GOW.
ELIZABETH CANNING.
THE TWO PERREAUS.
JOHN THURTELL.

DUCHESS OF KINGSTON.
MONSIEUR D'AUGLADE.
THE REV. MR. HACKMAN.
EARL FERRERS.
HENRY FAUNTLEROY.
RICHARD PATCH.
JOAN PERRY & HER TWO SONS
MRS. BROWNRIGG.
DICK TURPIN.
WILLIAM CORDER.

———

"TRUTH IS STRANGER THAN FICTION."

LONDON:

PUBLISHED BY GEORGE VICKERS, STRAND;

AND SOLD BY ALL BOOKSELLERS.

1851.

LONDON;
STEWARD AND SNOW, PRINTERS,
WATER STREET, STRAND.

CONTENTS.

THE INVISIBLE AVENGER;

OR,

GUILT'S FATAL CAREER.

I.—EUGENE ARAM.

"My gentle lad, what is't you read—
Romance, or fairy fable?
Or is it some historic page
Of kings and crowns unstable?"
The young boy gave an upward glance,—
"It is 'The Death of Abel.'"—Hood.

THE remarkable name of Eugene Aram, belonging to a man of unusual talents and acquirements, is unhappily associated with a deed of blood as extraordinary in its details and the manner of its discovery as any in our Calendar of Crime. Assuredly it affords one of the most striking examples even amongst those marvels which have been recorded of God's revenge against murder.

The reading world is well acquainted with this village tragedy, as represented in Bulwer's novel. But the story is one of those singular events where real life seems more romantic than romance itself. It touches every chord that vibrates in sympathy with scenes of mystery and terror; and calls into exercise that deepest-rooted principle of curiosity which leads us to the study of great crimes, as aberrations of our moral nature, to which no one knows how soon, if the mind be shaken from its balance by some unusual temptation, he may himself be subjected. The murder so long concealed, so unaccountably brought to light,—the scene at St. Robert's Cave, the trial, the defence,—make it seem as if the Genius of Romance had snatched the pen of History for a moment to relieve her details by this frightful episode, when the story has to be related. Who can peruse the particulars of the terrible tale, without realising to their mind's eye the schoolmaster in the court at York—so subtle, so self-concentred—equal, as he said himself, to equal fortune—watching with inward agony but outward calmness the progress of the evidence against him; and then rising to deliver his celebrated defence, which convinces no one by its sophistries, and yet leaves on the mind a mingled feeling of admiration and horror? No portraiture of the kind can be more impressive than the real Aram of history. From the surface of common life his original character is projected in bold relief—a compact and consistent whole; his strong intellect playing into the hands of his evil principle; his courage enabling him to realise his plans—his constancy to bear their consequences. Fiction can add nothing to the effect of such a character. But to the story :—

There was, in the year 1744, one Daniel Clarke, a shoemaker by trade, belonging to Knaresborough, in Yorkshire; a clever man at his calling and in general esteem, having

No. 1.   B a good share of business. His trade increasing, and his establishment, by addition of apprentices, being enlarged, he at length thought of wedlock, paying his addresses to Hannah Olding, an exciseman's daughter, to whom he was in due time united. With this young woman he obtained a considerable dowry,—the sum being not less than £300.

It happened, however, that although Clarke's business seemed to be in a flourishing condition at the time of his marriage, and he bore a fair character, he yet had already formed an intimate acquaintanceship with Eugene Aram and one Richard Houseman, both residing also in Knaresborough. Aram was at this period well-respected, and indeed esteemed, by the better sort of people of the neighbourhood. He was a man of learning, and fitted in an extraordinary degree, in fact, for the duties of a schoolmaster. He was always of a studious habit, and tradition even now points to a beautiful spot, on the banks of a mill-stream, in the neighbourhood of his father's residence, where, in his boyhood, book in hand, he would wile away many hours of the summer's day in deep thought. Though but immediately of humble birth,—his father having been gardener to Sir Walter Blacket, of Newby, in the county of York,—yet his family had been of the middle gentry, the origin of which he could trace up to the reign of Edward III. Through the general estimation in which he was held, and the uncommon abilities and extensive learning which he possessed, he was regarded with more respect than persons in the same station of life with him are usually held in similar localities to that in which he was found at the date in question. His manner of living and outward deportment had been blameless for years. He was upright and fair in his dealings, and was remarkable for his show of tenderness and humanity, upon which he much prided himself to the last. So far did he seem to be endowed with the milk of human kindness, that, as a schoolmaster, he seldom inflicted corporal punishment upon his pupils, and when he did so it was with apparent reluctance. At the same time he was considered, by those who thought they knew him best, as a sceptic in matters of religion, being in the habit of making light of sacred things in argument, and even of the distinctions in virtue and vice.

Richard Houseman was a flax-dresser, who also bore a fair reputation in Knaresborough, having been for many years regarded as an open-hearted, industrious, and inoffensive person; nor was it without exciting marvel, when the conduct of the several parties mentioned came to be better known, that he could ever have been prevailed upon to have a hand in the heinously wicked deeds with which he became connected. In relation to Clarke, he had long professed the warmest friendship and a remarkable degree of brotherly affection, being ever ready to do him a substantial service. So much was this the case, that at the time of the shoemaker's disappearance he was very considerably in Houseman's debt for money lent.

It would appear that about the period of Clarke's marriage, Eugene Aram had begun to exercise an extraordinary control over the devoted man. Naturally enough, to all appearances, the shoemaker was honestly congratulated on his union and the circumstance of obtaining with the young woman such a sum of money as might prove of great service in the way of his business. The pair of friends were now very much together, the conversation generally turning upon the opportunity which Clarke had to become rich, and to make a genteel figure in the world; a result for which, it was said, the tradesman yearned with great eagerness and anxiety. Certain it is, that he was so wrought upon as to fall into the snare of thinking his credit was already vastly increased, and that none who were at all acquainted with him in Knaresborough would object to trust him for goods to any amount.

But what was Clarke to do with goods thus obtained? And how was it possible for him to keep possession of them without paying their full price? Aram was at once ready with a scheme, into which the other rushed, and it was this,—that as, with the reputed increase to his fortune, and the obvious propriety of setting himself and young wife handsomely up in the world, he could be at no loss to get goods sent to his house, first by one, then by another, and next by a third, &c., he was to make the best use of his time in this way, and that as soon as he had collected a rich assortment, he was to decamp and quit the country altogether. As for the goods, the safest method would be for the shoemaker to leave them in Aram's custody, who would take care in good time to have the whole transmitted to Clarke under a fictitious name, and that he, the schoolmaster, would soon join his friend, and thereafter they should spend their days in ease and abundance.

Extraordinary, surely, must have been the credulity and simple nature of Clarke, nor less wonderful the cajollery and fascinating power of Aram, in order to bring such a scheme into operation. However, the shoemaker was deluded into the villanous design, setting about its execution in a resolute style. There was scarcely a shop in all Knaresborough where he had ever before dealt, but was now marked to furnish some portion of its contents. Even such as were comparatively strangers to him he was directed by the principal mover to victimise, throughout the neighbourhood as well as in the town. It seemed to be a matter of little consideration what sort of articles could be got. Accordingly, in the list of things thus fraudulently obtained, cambrics, velvets, saddlery, blankets, silver plate, jewellery, and watches figured, no dealer having scrupled to furnish whatever was named by the hitherto unimpeached and now well-married Daniel Clarke. Considerable sums of money were also borrowed by the agent of evil, the whole, including property and solid cash, amounting to a rich acquisition, although how much never seems to have been accurately ascertained; many of the articles thus surreptitiously obtained having been secretly conveyed to Aram, or by the two villains to a place named St. Robert's cave, a dismal and unfrequented spot adjoining to the Nid, a stream near Knaresborough.

Notwithstanding the great quantities of things which had been collected in the manner mentioned, the craving Aram was still unsatisfied, persuading his accomplice and tool that it was the more portable and valuable articles upon which they should fix their minds, such as silver tankards, spoons, and other precious gear in small bulk, which goldsmiths would furnish, and tavern-keepers trust in loan; so that there was a second draught made, the occasion and excuse mentioned by the shoemaker being a stylish wedding dinner which he was to have. The plot again succeeded, so that abundance of goods was collected.

A day or two before the departure of Clarke, Aram and Houseman being in company with him, something dropped which let the flax-dresser into the secret of the shoemaker being about to leave the country. Houseman upon this spoke of the money which he had lent to his friend Clarke, being the sum of twenty pounds, when an arrangement was gone into as to the manner in which the debt was to be paid, viz., in leather. From this moment, too, it appeared, Houseman was drawn into the system of villany practised by the other two. At last the important night arrived, being the 7th of February, 1744, when having met, at a late hour, it was proposed by Aram that they should take a walk, in order to come to some settlement as to the further disposal and secreting of Clarke's goods. It afterwards appeared that a fourth individual was in company with the party on that awful night,—one Henry Terry having been suspected as the person, although his identity was never satisfactorily proved. After that night Clarke was never again seen alive. The man was soon missed, and from his known intimacy with Aram and Houseman a suspicion arose that they might be concerned in the frauds which had so largely been practised. Search was accordingly made for the goods, some of which were found at Houseman's, and others dug up in the schoolmaster's garden. No plate, however, was met with, so that it was believed Clarke had carried this wholly off with him.

There was not at first the slightest suspicion entertained of the shoemaker having been murdered, nor until all means of discovering him failed. Neither could the suspicion of robbery be brought home even to Houseman, whilst Aram seems to have been in a short time acquitted from the imputation by most people. And yet a doubt of the schoolmaster's honesty, and even of his innocence relative to the missing man's life, was harboured by some; and as the lingering doubt appeared deeply to wound a mind which professed itself to be wondrously proud and susceptible, his withdrawal from the place was not thought at all unaccountable.

Eugene Aram, having gathered his valuables together, left Knaresborough, without acquainting a single soul of his intentions. London, as the safest place of refuge, was pitched upon by him. Here he began to make a showy use of the money and effects he possessed; in a manner, too, which would have been quite unsuitable in the quarter which he had left. In short, he became the gentleman; dressing well, and keeping genteel company, to which he found access, by means of his learning, his extensive knowledge, and the captivating manners which he could well put on.

Having left his wife behind at Knaresborough, he bethought himself of having a fresh one; and fixed his eyes upon a beautiful young lady, who bore the outward appearance of having a competent fortune. It so happened, however, that the wily and penetrating Aram was in this instance at fault in regard to the true character and qualifications of the girl, she being no other than the mistress of a gentleman from Leeds, who was sojourning in the metropolis. The late schoolmaster was fascinated by the wanton, bestowing upon her many presents, and offering to make her his wife; and that he was not married to her, must be imputed to the sting and horror of conscience, which kept him in continual dread of meeting with his merited deserts.

Being, as he daily was, one afternoon on a visit to take tea with the girl at her lodgings, the gentleman from Leeds chanced to drop in, and was not, it may be naturally supposed, wholly pleased at finding his young lady so familiarly engaged with another than himself. However, he restrained his displeasure, behaving with civility to Mr. Aram during the time. The late schoolmaster's face, he thought, was not altogether unknown to him, so that he resolved to put his suspicions to the test. Returning to the girl's apartments shortly after the departure of her new lover, the gentleman questioned her concerning the same, to which she answered that she believed him to be a person in good circumstances, that he seemed to have plenty of money, and that he was paying his addresses to her in an honourable way. The gentleman, however, although he could not disapprove of her wish to form an honourable connection with another, expressed his doubts with regard to the rank and wealth of her ardent wooer, advising her to be very cautious what steps she took. To confirm her the more in what he said, he told her, if she followed his advice, she might, he imagined, soon satisfy herself with regard to his position in life, suggesting certain queries that she might put to him at his next visit,—such as what countryman he was? whether he had not lived at Knaresborough, in Yorkshire? whether he had not known one Daniel Clarke of that town? and whether the shoemaker was in London at the time, or if he knew what had become of him? "The answer which your wooer will give to these questions," said the gentleman, "will convince you, I anticipate, that something lies couched under them, and that he is neither wholly unembarrassed in his circumstances or mind."

Aram paid his daily visit as usual to the young woman, who had promised, and was quite prepared to put him to the suggested tests. He was more than usually gay and assured, prosecuting his suit with renewed fervour; when, at length, on telling her that he was not altogether free of inquietude on account of the gentleman whom he had seen when last in her presence, she took occasion, although carelessly, and without any apparent distrust, to go into the contemplated examination.

She began by inquiring in what part of England he mostly resided; to which his answer was that he generally spent a month or two in London every year, but that his estate and place of residence was in Essex.

"Did you never live in Yorkshire, sir?" inquired she, "at a place called Knaresborough?" At this he seemed a little confounded, and began to hesitate, saying, No; he never lived there, although he had been at the place more than once, for a few days on business.

She here began to see plainly that her questions troubled him, and determined to pursue the interrogations a little further, asking him whether he was not acquainted with one Daniel Clarke, of the town mentioned, and if he knew what had become of him,— whether he was with him in London, or not? Here Aram's confusion became great; he was in consternation, his whole frame becoming visibly shaken; so that the girl felt convinced that her gentleman from Leeds had some very cogent reasons for setting her upon questioning her wooer in the manner he had. To the last questions the schoolmaster gave most unsatisfactory and faltering responses, saying that he never knew any such man at Knaresborough, and consequently could give no account of him, and therefore offered no information whether he was in town or not. He had indeed, on second thought, seen such a person in or about Knaresborough, and heard of his being advertised in the papers; but who or what he was, and what had become of him, he could say nothing. But why should she be so particular in her inquires about so low a creature as a shoemaker? Here, however, he fancied that he had overshot himself, so that quickly recovering his thoughts, he added, "A shoemaker I think he was described in the papers." To this the girl carelessly replied, she had no great reason for her curiosity, but had been desired by the gentleman that he had seen when they were at tea the evening before, to put the questions.

"He desire you, Madam!" exclaimed the still more confounded lover, "pray what countryman is he?"

"Oh! he is of Leeds," was her reply, "and he thought he was acquainted with your person; but since it proved a mistake on his part, there need be no more said about the matter."

The mistake, though of little consequence to the frail girl, was not so unimportant to the conscious Aram, for every footstep he now heard on the stairs, caused him to cast most anxious glances towards the door, dreading, no doubt, the appearance of his evil genius. He, therefore, took his leave of the fair one much earlier than had been his custom, assuring her that matters of business called him away, but that he should have a long interview with her next day. That day, however, never came; nor could the gentleman from Leeds, though he made the most diligent inquiry for Aram, ever obtain the least tidings of him.

Having been living in the profuse manner already mentioned, the sham Essex gentleman's ill-got wealth, no doubt, soon became much abridged; so that at length he must have felt himself compelled to resort to his old and more regular calling, although he was not again heard of by any one who had previously been acquainted with him, until he was found to be at Lynn, in Norfolk.

It might have been mentioned earlier that when Aram became at first suspected of being an accomplice with Clarke in that person's nefarious and fraudulent transactions, a process had been granted from the Steward of the Honour of Knaresborough, to arrest him for a debt due to one Norton, which was done with a view to detain Aram until such time as a warrant could be had from a justice of peace, to take him up for being concerned with the shoemaker in cheating people out of their goods. Contrary, however, to the expectation of every person—he being then thought very poor—he paid what he was arrested for, besides a considerable mortgage upon a house of his near Ripon.

Aram's departure from Knaresborough seems to have put a stop to any further examination into his connection with Clarke; for nothing of striking importance was discovered of the ill-fated shoemaker's murder until the 1st of August, 1758, which was upwards of thirteen years from the time of the man being missing. At this latter date, however, it happened that a labourer, employed in digging for stone to supply a lime-kiln, at a place called Thistle-hill, near Knaresborough, having at the edge of the cliff dug about half a yard deep, found an arm-bone, and the small bone of the leg of a human skeleton. In proceeding further with his spade, he discovered the whole of the bones belonging to the body, which, by their position, seemed to have been put in double. This remarkable occurrence being quickly rumoured throughout Knaresborough, gave grounds for suspecting the skeleton to be that of Daniel Clarke, and the more so as there had been no other person missing in that neighbourhood for more than sixty years. The strangeness of the event excited people's curiosity greatly, and led to a strict inquiry into all its particulars; a coroner's inquest was held thereon, one of the first persons examined being the wife of Eugene Aram, whom he had deserted and left behind him at Knaresborough.

This woman had indeed frequently given hints of her suspicion that Daniel Clarke had been foully dealt with, and she now spoke out more plainly than ever. Her testimony was to this effect: Daniel Clarke, she said, was an intimate acquaintance of her husband, and that they had frequent transactions together before the February of 1744; and also that Richard Houseman was often with them. Particularly that on the 7th of February, about six o'clock in the evening, Aram came home when she was washing in the kitchen; upon which he directed her to put out the fire, and make one up-stairs. She accordingly did so. About two o'clock in the morning of the 8th of February, Aram, Clarke, and Houseman came to Aram's house together, and went up-stairs to the room in which she was, where they remained for about an hour. Her husband asked her for a handkerchief for Dickey—meaning Richard Houseman—to tie about his head; and she did as requested. Clarke then said, "It will soon be morning, and we must get off." Upon this they all three went out, while she observed that Clarke had a sack or wallet upon his back, which he took along with him, but whither they went she could not tell. She next stated that about five o'clock of the same morning, her husband and Houseman returned, but that Clarke did not return with them. Her husband came up-stairs, and desired to have a candle that he might make a fire below. To which she objected, saying, there was a good one in the room above, where she then was. Aram answered, that "Dickey was below, and did not choose to come up-stairs." Upon which she asked, what they had done with Richard Clarke? To this her husband gave no answer, but desired her to go to bed, which she refused, saying, "You have been doing something bad." Aram then went down with the candle. She felt desirous to know what they were about below, and was going to proceed down-stairs, when she overheard Houseman say, "She is coming." To this her husband replied, "We'll not allow her." Houseman then said, "If she does come down she'll lett." "What can she lett?" replied Aram; "poor simple thing! she knows nothing." To which Houseman replied, "If she tells that I am here, it will be enough." Her husband then added, "I will hold the door to prevent her from coming." Houseman then whispered, "Something must be done to prevent her letting," and pressed him very much; saying, "If she does not lett now, she may at another time." "No, no," returned her husband; "we will coax her a little until her passion be off, and then take an opportunity to shoot her." Upon which Houseman seemed satisfied, subjoining, "What must be done with her clothes?" Upon this it was agreed that she should be allowed to lie in her clothes where she was shot. She hearing this discourse, was much terrified, but remained quiet until near seven o'clock in the same morning, when Aram and Houseman went out of the house. Upon this she went down-stairs, and seeing there had been a fire below, and all the ashes taken out of the grate, she went and examined the dunghill; and perceiving ashes of a different kind than usual to be upon it, she searched amongst them, and found several pieces of linen and woollen cloth, very nearly consumed, which had the appearance of belonging to wearing apparel. When she returned into the house from the dunghill, she found the handkerchief she had lent Houseman the night before; and looking at it, beheld some blood upon it, about the size of a shilling. Upon this she went to Houseman's house, and showed him the pieces of cloth, saying she was afraid they had done something bad to Clarke. Houseman then pretended that he knew nothing about what she said or meant. From the above circumstances she stated, in conclusion, that she believed Daniel Clarke had been murdered by Houseman and her husband, on the night described.

Mr. Philip Coates, of Knaresborough, brother-in-law to Daniel Clarke, said—He had known him from a child, and that he was with him on the 7th of February, 1744, about nine o'clock at night, and that Clarke promised to call upon him in the morning. But he not calling, he went to Clarke's house, where he was told he had gone to Newall to his wife. On the 10th of February, Mr. Coates went to Newall to seek Clarke, but could not hear of him, nor ever did, though he had been advertised for some time. He also said that a week or ten days before Clarke was missing, he received a large sum of money, but that no money was remaining at his house on his being missed.

Several additional criminating particulars were elicited from other witnesses at the inquest. Houseman was present at the examination by order of the Coroner, and was observed to feel very uneasy, discovering what were considered as signs of conscious guilt, such as trembling, turning pale, and faltering in his speech. Upon the skeleton being produced, he was requested to take up one of the bones, in observance of a superstitious custom of making such as were accused of murder to touch some part of the body found and supposed to have been foully dealt with. Houseman obeyed, and on taking up the bone, unwittingly dropped these words: "This is no more Dan Clarke's bone than it is mine." The observation immediately struck all who heard it as being significant, and led to closer and further questioning of the man,—his answers convincing the Coroner that since the flax-dresser was so positive the bones before him were not those of Dan Clarke, he could give some account of him. Being told so, and pressed hard upon the point, he at length answered that he could produce a witness who had seen Daniel Clarke upon the road, two or three days after he was missing from Knaresborough. Accordingly this witness—one Parkinson, was sent for, who said that he himself had never seen Daniel Clarke after the 7th of February, although a friend of his (Parkinson's), told him he had met a person like Clarke; but that, as it was a snowy day, and the person had the cape of his great coat up, he could not speak positively as to his identity. This, instead of proving satisfactory, increased the suspicion against Houseman, as being either the murderer, or an accomplice in the murder of Clarke. He was therefore arrested, and re-examined before William Thornton, Esq.; and here he confessed as follows:—

That he was in company with Daniel Clarke the night before he went off, which he believed might be on a Thursday, in February, 1744; that the reason of his being there with him was upon account of some money, viz., £20, which he had lent Clarke, and which he wanted to get again of him, and for which he then gave him some goods that took up a considerable time in carrying from Clarke's house to his, viz., from eleven—the hour at which he went to Clarke—till same time the next morning; that the goods he took were leather, and some linen cloth, which, as soon as he had possessed himself of, and also a note of the prices he was to sell them at, he left Clarke in Aram's house, with Aram and another man, unknown to him; that Aram and Clarke immediately after followed him out of Aram's house, and went into the market-place with the other unknown person, which the light of the moon enabled him to see; that he did not know what became of them after that. He utterly disavowed that he came back to Aram's house that morning with Aram and without Clarke, as was asserted by Mrs. Aram, except along with Clarke, as already told. Further, that he did not see Clarke take any wallet, plate, or things of value along with him when they came out of Aram's house the last time, early in the morning; admitting, however, that some time after Clarke was missing, Mrs. Aram came to him in a passion, and demanded money of him, saying he had money of her husband's in his hands, and that she pretended to show him some shreds of cloth, asking him if he knew what they were? to which he answered that he did not know. In conclusion, he entirely denied that he ever had been charged with the murder of Daniel Clarke, till by Mrs. Aram in her examination before the Crown,—disavowing all knowledge of the dreadful deed.

Being asked if he would sign his deposition, his answer was, that he chose to decline doing so for the present, for that he might have something to add, and, therefore, wished to have time to consider of it.

As he declined signing the above statement made by him, it was presumed he had something more to divulge, and therefore was committed to York Castle the following morning. At Greenhammerton, on the road to York, he conducted himself in such a manner as to show he had been concerned in the murder, or that he knew of it, and also that he was desirous of making a confession on his arrival at York. Being come to the immediate neighbourhood of Micklegate, and made acquainted that Mr. Thornton was then passing by, Houseman expressed a desire to speak out; and having been taken into the parsonage house of the place, before Mr. Thornton, he confessed:—

That Daniel Clarke was murdered by Eugene Aram, late of Knaresborough, on the morning of the 8th of February, 1744; that he went with them, having been asked to do so, to a place called St. Robert's Cave, near Grimblebridge, where Aram and Clarke stopped, and there he saw Aram strike Clarke several times over the breast and head, and saw him fall as if dead, upon which he came away and left them; that whether Aram used any weapon or not to kill Clarke, he could not tell, nor did he know what was done with the body afterwards, although he believed that Aram left it at the mouth of the cave; for that, seeing Aram do the deed, he (Houseman) made off, and got to the bridge end, where, looking back, he saw Aram coming from the cave, who had a bundle in his hand, but did not know what it was; that upon this he hastened back to Knaresborough, without either joining Aram or seeing him again till the next day; and that from that time to the moment of his examination, he (Houseman) had never held any conversation whatever with Aram. Afterwards, however, Houseman added that Clarke's body was buried in St. Robert's Cave, and that he was sure it was still there, but desired that it might remain till such time as Aram might be taken. He said also that Clarke's head lay to the right, in the turn, at the entrance of the cave.

On Houseman's commitment to York Castle, proper persons were appointed to examine St. Robert's Cave, where, in accordance with his confession, was found a skeleton of a human being, the skull lying as he had described. No time was lost in endeavouring to find out Aram, who at length was discovered at Lynn, in Norfolk, where he was usher in a school, and thence brought to Yorkshire, his examination taking place before Mr. Thornton, the same justice of the peace who had already deeply interested himself in this memorable case. Aram then made a statement which was to the following effect:—

That he had been well acquainted with Daniel Clarke, but utterly denied having any connexion with him in those frauds with which the shoemaker stood charged, at or before the time of his disappearance, which must have been about the 10th of February, 1744, the period at which he,—Aram,—was arrested by process for debt: that it was at that date he first heard of Clarke being missing; that he remained in Knaresborough some space of time after this, without molestation, and then removed to Nottingham, to spend a few days with his relations, thence going to London : and that he remained in the metropolis till he went to Lynn. He admitted that he might have been with Clarke in the February mentioned, but did not recollect having been with Houseman and Clarke on the 7th much less of being in their company after two o'clock in the morning, nor at Grimblebridge, nor near a place called St. Robert's-Cave, nor that he knew anything of Clarke's being murdered; nor that he came home on the morning of the 8th of February, 1744, at five o'clock, with Houseman; nor that he made a fire for them in his own house.

Aram, however, declined to sign these declarations, that he might have time to recollect himself better, Mr. Thornton, meanwhile, thinking it proper to make out his commitment to York Castle. Two officers, Barker and Moor, were accordingly ordered to convey him to prison, and had actually proceeded some distance on the road thither, when he requested to be taken back to the Justice of Peace, when he proceeded to state and confess—That he was at his own house the 7th of February, at night, when Houseman and Clarke came to him, with some plate, both of them going for more several times, of which goods Clarke was endeavouring to defraud his neighbours: that he could not but observe that Houseman was all that night very diligent to assist Clarke, and that such was Houseman's business that night, and not the signing of any note as pretended by Houseman : that Henry Terry, then of Knaresborough, was as much concerned in abetting the said frauds, as either Clark or Houseman : that Terry took the plate in a bag, while

Clarke and Houseman took the watches and other things of value, carrying them toge-ther to St. Robert's Cave, and there beating most of the plate flat: that it was thought too late in the morning of the 8th of February, for Clarke to go off any distance, and that, therefore, he staid in the cave till the night following, as he believed; they having sent him victuals by Terry, he being considered the most likely person to do this without sus-picion, as he was a shooter, and might go there under the pretence of shooting: that the next night, in order to give Clarke more time to get off, Terry, and Houseman, and him-self, went down to the cave, but that he, Aram, did not go in, or see Clarke at all, staying outside to watch at a little distance lest anybody should surprise them: that he believed they beat some plate, for that he heard a noise of the kind, continuing in the cave for about an hour, after which they came out, telling him that Clarke was gone off: that he then observed they had a bag, which he took in his hand, and found that it contained plate: that on asking why Clarke did not take the plate along with him, Houseman and Terry replied, that they had bought it of him, as well as the watches, and that they had paid him with what would be less cumbersome than the articles they had purchased. After adding other similar statements, calculated to represent Houseman and Terry as principals in the frauds, and also as having been with Clarke at a later period than even he himself had been, he signed the declarations, and was then conducted to York Castle, to await the opening of the next assizes.

From what Aram stated there was reason to suspect Terry as having been an accomplice in the murder, so that he was also arrested and committed to the Castle. Bills of in-dictment were forthwith preferred against the three; but as the prosecutor could not be fully supplied with witnesses for the immediately ensuing circuit of the criminal judges, the trials were postponed till the Lammas Assizes,—the proceedings having been also dropped relative to Terry, for want of evidence against him.

On the 3d of August, 1759, Richard Houseman and Eugene Aram were brought to the bar. The former, however, having been acquitted, he was received as witness against Aram, the school-master, when he deposed:—

That in the night between the 7th and 8th of February, 1744, about eleven o'clock, he went to Aram's house. That after two hours spent in passing to and fro between their several houses, to dispose of various goods, as well as to settle certain notes con-cerning them, Aram proposed to Clarke first and then to him (Houseman) to take a walk out of the town. That when they came within six or eight yards of St. Robert's Cave, he found that Aram and Clarke were quarrelling. That he saw Aram strike Clarke several times, upon which the latter fell, and he (the witness) never saw him rise again. That he did not observe any instrument in Aram's hand, and knew not that he had any. That after this, without offering any interposition, or giving any alarm, he left them, and returned to his house. That the next morning he went to Aram's house and asked what business he had with Clarke last night, and what he had done with him? Aram replied not to these questions; but threatened him, if he ever spoke of his being in Clarke's com-pany that night,—vowing vengeance, either by himself or some other person, if he men-tioned anything relating to the affair. Such was the sum of Houseman's testimony at the trial of Aram.

A Mr. Beckwith was next called, who deposed that Aram's garden had been searched, owing to a vague suspicion that he might have been an accomplice in the frauds of Clarke. That parts of clothing, and also some pieces of cambric which he had sold to Clarke a little while before, were found here.

A third witness was the watchman, Thomas Barnet, who stated that about one in the morning he saw a person come out from Aram's house, who had a wide coat on, with the cape about his head, who seemed to shun him. That upon this he went up to him, and put by the cape of his great coat, and perceived it to be Richard Houseman; and that he contented himself thereafter with wishing him a good night.

The officers who executed the warrant for the arrest of the schoolmaster were next examined, who dwelt on some expressions dropped by him before he arrived at Knaresborough. They stated that he at first denied, when they went into the school-room, at Lynn, knowing anything of Daniel Clark, or even of the town to which he had belonged; but that he corrected himself after a little time, and even admitted that he had some knowledge of St. Robert's Cave.

The skull of the skeleton found in the cave was next produced, there being on its left side a fracture, from the nature of which it was considered that the stroke producing the same could not have been made but by some blunt instrument; the piece having been beaten inwards, and could not be replaced but from within. Mr. Locock, the surgeon, who produced the skull, gave it as his opinion, that no such breach could proceed from natural decay; that it was not a recent fracture by the instrument with which it was dug up, but seemed to be of many years' standing.

Such made the chief part of the testimony against Aram, the criminatory evidence closing with the exposition of the mute witness—the skull of the deceased! And now it was that the prisoner was asked, in that peculiarly thrilling and awful question—What he had to say in his own behalf? Till now, Eugene had not changed his posture nor his countenance. His dark and piercing eye had, indeed, for one instant fixed on each witness that appeared against him, but quickly dropped its gaze again upon the floor. Now, however, a faint hectic flushed his cheek, when he seemed to gather and to concentrate himself for the defence. He glanced round the court as if to see what had been the impression created regarding him, and commenced that remarkable defence, still extant, and still considered as wholly unequalled from the lips of one defending his own, and such a cause.

"My Lord, I know not whether it is of right, or through some indulgence of your lordship, that I am allowed the liberty at this bar, and at this time, to attempt a defence, incapable and uninstructed as I am to speak. Since, while I see so many eyes upon me, so numerous and awful a concourse, fixed with attention, and filled with I know not what expectancy, I labour not with guilt, my lord, but with perplexity. For having never seen a court but this, being wholly unacquainted with law, the customs of the bar, and all judiciary proceedings, I fear I shall be so little capable of speaking with propriety in this place, that it exceeds my hope, if I shall be able to speak at all.

"I have heard, my lord, the indictment read, wherein I find myself charged with the highest crime, with an enormity I am altogether incapable of; a fact, to the commission of which there goes far more insensibility of heart, more profligacy of morals, than ever fell to my lot, and nothing possibly could have admitted a presumption of this nature, but a depravity, not inferior to that imputed to me. However, as I stand indicted at your lordship's bar, and have heard what is called evidence adduced in support of such a charge, I may humbly solicit your lordship's patience, and beg the hearing of this respectable audience, while I, single and unskilful, destitute of friends, and unassisted by counsel, say something, perhaps like argument, in my defence. I shall consume but little of your lordship's time; what I have to say will be short, and this brevity, probably, will be the best part of it.   However,   tis offered with all possible regard, and the greatest submission to your lordship's consideration, and that of this honourable court.

"First, my lord, the whole tenour of my conduct in life contradicts every particular of this indictment.   Yet I had never said this, did not my present circumstances extort it from me, and seem to make it necessary.   Permit me here, my lord, to call upon malignity itself, so long and cruelly busied in this prosecution, to charge upon me any immorality, of which prejudice was not the author.   No, my lord, I concerted not schemes of fraud, projected no violence, injured no man's person or property.   My days were honestly laborious, my nights intensely studious.   And I humbly conceive my notice of this, especially at this time, will not be thought impertinent or unseasonable; but at least deserving some attention,—because, my lord, that any person, after a temperate use of life, and series of thinking and acting regularly, and without one single deviation from sobriety, should plunge into the very depth of profligacy, precipitately and at once, is altogether improbable and unprecedented, and absolutely inconsistent with the course of things.   Mankind are never corrupted at once; villany is always progressive, and declines from right, step by step, till every regard of probity is lost, and every sense of all moral obligation totally perishes.

"Again, my lord, a suspicion of this kind, which nothing but malevolence could entertain, and ignorance propagate, is violently opposed by my very situation at the time with respect to health, for but a little space before I had been confined to my bed, and suffered under a very long and severe disorder, and was not able, for half a year together, so much as to walk.   The distemper left me indeed, yet slowly and in part; but so emaciated, so enfeebled, that I was reduced to crutches; and was so far from being well about the time I am charged with this fact, that I never to this day perfectly recovered.   Could then a person in this condition take anything into his head so unlikely, so extravagant?   I, past the vigour of my age, feeble, valetudinary, with no inducement to engage, no ability to accomplish, no weapon wherewith to perpetrate such a fact; without interest, without power, without motive, without means.

"Besides, it must needs occur to any one, that an action of this atrocious nature is never heard of, but, when its springs are laid open, it appears it was to support some indolence, or supply some luxury, to satisfy some avarice, or oblige some malice; to prevent some real or some imaginary want.   Yet I lay not under the influence of any one of these.   Surely, my lord, I may, consistent with both truth and modesty, affirm thus much; and none who have any veracity, and know me, will ever question this.

"In the second place, the disappearance of Clarke is suggested as an argument of his being dead; but the uncertainty of such an inference from that, and the fallibility of all conclusions of such a sort, from such a circumstance, are too obvious, and too notorious to require instances.   Yet, superseding many, permit me to produce a very recent one, and that afforded by this Castle.

"In June, 1757, William Thompson, for all the vigilance of this place, in open daylight, and double ironed, made his escape; and notwithstanding an immediate inquiry set on foot, the strictest search, and all advertisements, was never since seen or heard of. [The skeleton of William Thompson was found on Saturday, the 8th of July, 1780, behind the Old Court House in the Castle of York, near the foundation, and about three feet from the wall, with double irons on, having lain there *twenty-three* years.   It was supposed that he got on the top of the Old Court House, by the assistance of a ladder which stood there, had dropped down the wall, and was killed in so doing.   As nothing but nettles and other weeds grew in the place where the bones were found, it was seldom gone into by any person.] If, then, Thompson got off unseen, through all these difficulties, how very easy was it for Clarke, when none of them opposed him? But what would be thought of a prosecution commenced against any one seen last with Thompson?

"Permit me next, my lord, to observe a little upon the bones which have been discovered. It is said, which perhaps is saying very far, that these are the bones of a man; it is possible, indeed they may be; but is there any certain known criterion, which incontestibly distinguishes the sex in human bones? Let it be considered, my lord, whether the ascertaining of this point ought not to precede any attempt to identify them.

"The place of their deposition too, claims much more attention than is commonly bestowed upon it. For, of all places in the world, none could have mentioned any one wherein there was greater certainty of finding human bones, than an hermitage, except he should point out a church-yard; hermitages, in times past, being not only places of religious retirement, but of burial too. And it has scarce or never been heard of, but that every cell now known contains, or contained, these relics of humanity; some mutilated, some entire. I do not inform, but give me leave to remind, your lordship, that here sat Solitary Sanctity, and here the hermit or the anchoress hoped for that repose for their bones, when dead, they here enjoyed when living.

"All this while, my lord, I am sensible this is known to your lordship, and many in this court better than I. But it seems necessary to my case that others, who have not at all, perhaps, adverted to things of this nature, and may have concern in my trial, should be made acquainted with it. Suffer me then, my lord, to produce a few of many instances, that these cells were used as repositaries of the dead, and to enumerate a few in which human bones have been found, as it happened in this in question; but, to some, that accident might seem extraordinary, and, consequently, occasion prejudice.

"1st, the bones, as was supposed, of the Saxon St. Dubritius, were discovered buried in his cell at Guiscliffe, near Warwick, as appears from the authority of Sir William Douglas.

"2nd, The bones, thought to be those of the anchoress Rosia, were but lately discovered in a cell at Royston, entire, fair, and undecayed, though they must have lain interred for several centuries, as is proved by Dr. Stukely.

"3rd, But our own county, nay, almost this very neighbourhood, supplies another instance; for in January, 1747, was found by Mr. Stoving, accompanied by a reverend gentleman, the bones in part of some recluse, in the cell at Lindholm, near Hatfield. They were believed to be those of William of Lindholm, a hermit, who had long made this cave his habitation.

"4th, In February, 1744, part of Woburn Abbey being pulled down, a large portion of a corpse appeared, even with the flesh on, and which bore cutting with a knife; though it is certain this had lain above two hundred years, and how much longer is doubtful; for this abbey was founded in 1145, and dissolved in 1538 or 9.

"What would have been said, what believed, if this had been an accident to the bones in question?

"Farther, my lord, it is not yet out of living memory, that a little distant from Knaresborough, in a field, part of the manor of the worthy and patriotic baronet who does that borough the honour to represent it in Parliament, were found, in digging for gravel, not one human skeleton only, but five or six, deposited side by side, with each an urn placed at its head, as your lordship knows was usual in ancient interments.

"About the same time, and in another field, almost close to this borough, was discovered also, in searching for gravel, another human skeleton; but the piety of the
same worthy gentleman, ordered both pits to be filled up again, commendably unwilling
to disturb the dead."

The reader, who will remember that it is a great principle of the law, that no man
can be condemned for murder unless the body of the deceased be found, will perceive
at once how important was the point of defence which the prisoner had been arguing by
means of the instances cited. After the enumeration of such remarkable cases, he
burst forth in the following strain :—

"Is, then, the frequent discovery of bones in such places forgotten, or industriously
concealed, that the discovery of those in question may appear the more extraordinary?
Extraordinary—yet how common an event! Every place conceals such remains. In
fields, in hills, in highway-sides, on wastes, on commons, lie frequent and unsuspected
bones. And our present allotments for rest for the departed, is but of some centuries.

"Another particular seems not to claim a little of your lordship's notice, and that of
the gentlemen of the jury; which is, that perhaps no example occurs of more than
one skeleton being found in one cell; and in the cell in question was found but *one*;
agreeable, in this, to the peculiarity of every known cell in Britain. Not the invention
of one skeleton, then, but of two would have appeared suspicious and uncommon.

"But then, my lord, to attempt to identify these, when even to identify living men
sometimes has proved so difficult, as in the case of Perkin Warbeck, and Lambert Sym-
mel, at home, and of Don Sebastian abroad, will be looked upon, perhaps, as an attempt
to determine what is indeterminable. And I hope too, it will not pass unconsidered here,
where gentlemen believe with caution, think with reason, and decide with humanity, what
interest the endeavour to do this is calculated to serve, in assigning proper personality
to those bones, whose particular appropriation can only appear to eternal Omniscience.

"Permit me, my lord, also very humbly to remonstrate, that, as human bones appear
to have been the inseparable adjuncts of every cell, even any person's naming such a
place at random as containing them, as in this case, shows him rather fortunate than
conscious prescient, and that these attendants on every hermitage only accidentally
concurred with this conjecture. It was a mere casual coincidence of words and things.

"But it seems another skeleton has been discovered by some labourer, which was full
as confidently averred to be Clarke's as this. My lord, must some of the living, if it
promote some interest, be made answerable for all the bones that earth has concealed,
and chance exposed? And might not a place where bones lay be mentioned by a person
by chance, as well as found by a labourer by chance? Or is it more criminal accidentally
to name where bones lie, than accidentally to find where they lie?

"Here, too, is a human skull produced, which is fractured; but was this the cause, or
was it the consequence of death,—was it owing to violence, or was it the effect of
natural decay? If it was violence, was that violence before or after death? My lord,
in May, 1732, the remains of William, Lord Archbishop of this province were taken up,
by permission, in this Cathedral, and the bones of the skull were found broken; yet
certainly he died by no violence offered to him alive, that could occasion that fracture
there.

"Let it be considered, my lord, that upon the dissolution of religious houses, and
the commencement of the Reformation, the ravages of those times both affected the
living and the dead. In search after imaginary treasures, coffins were broken up,

graves and vaults dug open, monuments ransacked, and shrines demolished. Your lordship knows that these violations proceeded so far, as to occasion Parliamentary authority to restrain them; and it did, about the beginning of the reign of Queen Elizabeth. I entreat your lordship to suffer not the violences, the depredations, and the iniquities of those times to be imputed to this.

"Moreover, what gentleman here is ignorant that Knaresborough had a castle, which, though now in ruins, was once considerable both for its strength and garrison. All know it was vigorously besieged by the arms of Parliament; at which siege, in sallies, conflicts, flights, and pursuits, many fell in all the places round it; and where they fell were buried; for every place, my lord, is burial earth in war; and many, questionless, of these yet rest unknown, whose bones futurity shall discover.

"I hope, with all imaginable submission, that what I have said will not be thought impertinent to this indictment; and that it will be far from the wisdom, the learning, and the integrity of this place, to impute to the living what zeal in its fury may have done; what nature may have taken off, and piety interred; or what war alone may have destroyed, alone deposited.

"As to the circumstances that have been raked together, I have nothing to observe, but that all such circumstances have been frequently found fallible and frail. They may rise to the utmost degree of probability, yet are they but probability still. Why need I name to your lordship the two Harrisons, recorded by Dr. Howell, who both suffered upon circumstances, because of the sudden disappearance of their lodger, who was in credit, had contracted debts, borrowed money and went off unseen, and returned again a great many years after their execution? Why name the intricate affair of Jaques du Moulin, under King Charles the Second, related by a gentleman who was counsel for the crown? And why the unhappy Coleman, who suffered innocent, though convicted upon positive evidence, and whose children perished for want, because the world uncharitably believed the father guilty? Why mention the perjury of Smith, incautiously admitted King's evidence, who, to screen himself, equally accused Faircloth and Loveday of the murder of Dunn—the first of whom, in 1749, was executed at Winchester, and Loveday was about to suffer at Reading, had not Smith been proved perjured, to the satisfaction of the court, by the surgeon of the Gosport Hospital?

"Now, my lord, having endeavoured to show that the crime laid to my charge is altogether repugnant to every part of my life; that it is inconsistent with my condition of health about that time; that no rational inference can be drawn that a person is dead who suddenly disappears; that hermitages were the constant repositories of the bones of the recluse; that the proofs of this are well authenticated; that the revolutions of religion or the fortune of war, has mangled or buried the dead; the conclusion remains, perhaps, no less reasonably than impatiently wished for. I, at last, after nearly a year's confinement, equal to either fortune, put myself upon the candour, the justice, and the humanity of your lordship, and upon yours, my countrymen, gentlemen of the jury."

The prisoner ceased, and the painful and choking sensation of sympathy, compassion, regret, admiration, all uniting, all mellowing into one fearful hope for his acquittal, made themselves felt throughout the crowded court.

It, no doubt, was expected that Aram, in his defence, would have remarked upon the evidence adduced against him, especially of Houseman, whose testimony, most certainly, in many particulars afforded ground for exposure and contradiction. The prisoner, however, so haughtily glanced over the immediate testimony of this witness, as could only be accounted for as being the natural result of a disdain that belonged essentially to his calm and proud character, or as the result of his consciousness of guilt. The truth, however, was, that the defence had been drawn up long before the trial, and that he seemed never to have entertained before-hand a suspicion of the fidelity of his confederate. At all events, whatever the general feeling of the audience might be as regarded Aram's share in the murder, there was one present whom the harangue—so memorable for its ingenuity and eloquence, too ingenious, indeed, for innocence,—did in no degree move with a belief that it was true or worthy of credit, and this was the judge.

It is much to be regretted that we have no minute and detailed memorial of the trial, except only the prisoner's defence. The summing up of the judge was considered, at that time, scarce less remarkable than the speech of Aram; he stated the evidence with peculiar ease, and at great length to the jury. He observed how the testimony of the other deponents confirmed that of Houseman; and then, touching on the contradictory parts of his story, he made them understand, how natural, how inevitable was some such contradiction in a witness, who had not only to give evidence against another, but to refrain from criminating himself. There could be do doubt but that Houseman was an accomplice in the crime ; and all, therefore, that seemed improbable in his giving no alarm when the deed was done, &c., &c., was easily rendered natural, and reconcileable with the other parts of the evidence. Commenting next on the defence of the prisoner,—who, as if disdaining to rely on aught save his own genius or his own innocence, had called no witnesses, as he had employed no counsel,—and eulogizing its eloquence and art, till he destroyed their effect, by guarding the jury against that impression which eloquence and art produce in defiance of simple fact, he continued that Aram had yet alleged nothing to invalidate the positive evidence against him.

Every one who is at all accustomed to attend upon criminal trials is well aware how great and sudden is sometimes the change in the minds of the jurors, which the summing up of the judge produces ; and in the case in question, the effect was like that of magic. That fatal look of a common intelligence, of a common assent, was exchanged among the doomers of the prisoner's life and death as his lordship concluded. They found the prisoner guilty without leaving the court, and he who was to announce to Eugene Aram the number of hours he had to live, put on the black cap.

In the startling records of crime and punishment, there is no more striking feature than the veil of obscurity which the Great Ruler of Events occasionally permits the offender to throw over his crime. Apparently the offender is forgotten, the suspicion for ever swept out of men's minds, and the transgressor is secure. Years intervene. The notion of undisturbed impunity has obtained full possession of the criminal's imagination ; he is not only unmolested, but his condition and circumstances seem to afford tokens of enviable fortune and real prosperity. He defies detection, and proudly exults in that the world shall never know of him that which he knows of himself. But on a sudden the scene changes ; when wrapped in his fancied security most strongly, the eye of justice opens its light upon him, and an outraged law demands and receives its victim.

Aram received his sentence in profound composure ; he even maintained a dignified unmovedness of aspect—the self reliance, it seemed, of a soul collected in itself. No forced or convulsive effort, vainly masking the terror or the pang ; no mockery mimicking contempt for others, but rather as daring fate than defying the judgment of men. He appeared to wrap himself in the independence of a calmed spirit, rather than the disdain of a despairing heart.

Aram, who became so remarkable for his erudition, was almost entirely self-taught, and his progress in learning merits notice: mathematics, at an early period of his age, engaged his attention, and he soon understood quadratic equations, and their geometrical construction. Prompted by an irresistible thirst of knowledge, he determined to make himself master of the learned languages; he got and repeated fragments of Lilly's grammar by heart; he next undertook Camden's Greek Grammar, which he also repeated in the same continuous manner. Thus instructed, he entered upon the Latin classics, and at first would pore over five lines for a whole day, rather than be baffled in translating and construing them, never, in all the painful course of his reading, leaving any passage till he thought he perfectly comprehended it. Having perused all the Latin classics, both historians and poets, he went through the Greek Testament, and then applied himself to Hesiod, Homer, Theocritus, Herodotus, Thucydides, and the Greek tragedians. He next, and with indefatigable diligence, while at Knaresborough, acquired the Hebrew tongue; he lost no opportunity of making improvement in the most difficult enterprises. He attained a knowledge of history and antiquities, and also of heraldry and botany; few plants, either domestic or exotic, were unknown to him. Beyond and amid all these, he ventured upon the Chaldee and Arabic, but had not time to make any great advances in the latter. He found the Chaldee easy enough, on account of its connexion with the Hebrew. He also investigated the Celtic, as far as possible, in all its dialects; began collections, and made comparisons between that, the English, the Latin, the Greek, and even the Hebrew. He had made notes, and compared above three thousand words together, and found such a surprising affinity, that he was determined to proceed through the whole of all these languages, and form a comparative Lexicon upon a new and most comprehensive plan. He was also far from being a contemptible poet. With this vast stock of learning, acquired without the assistance of a master, with his extraordinary talents and perseverance, what might Eugene Aram not have become in the career of honour, innocence, and virtue? What might he not have achieved? But alas! how frightfully was his wonderful course of study arrested by enormous crime! how fatally did he blot his trophies with guilt! with what unlooked for and fell certainty was the brilliancy of his genius, and the apparent sunshine of his life, quenched!

Aram's sentence was a righteous one, and he submitted to it with a wonderful stoicism. The morning after he was condemned, he confessed the justice of his doom to two clergymen, who had a licence from the judge who tried the cause to attend him, by declaring that he murdered Clarke. Being asked by one of them, what his motive had been for the terrible deed, he answered that he suspected Clarke of having an unlawful commerce with his wife; that he felt persuaded at the time when he committed the murder he did right; but since that period he had thought it wrong. The excuse thus made, however, was greatly suspected of being false, not merely because of his having so avariciously conducted himself, but because of the insinuation thrown out against his wife, who was known to be an industrious and deserving poor woman, whom he ever treated cruelly.

In the course of his interview with the clergymen, Aram said, " Pray, what became of Clarke's body, if Houseman went home (as he said upon my trial) immediately on seeing him fall?" One of the clergymen replied, " I'll tell you what became of it; you and Houseman dragged it into the cave, stripped and buried it there;—brought away his clothes and burnt them at your own house;" and to this construction he gave his assent. He was asked whether Houseman had not earnestly pressed him to murder his wife, for fear she should discover the business they had been about on the night of the terrible tragedy. He hastily replied, " He did, and pressed me several times to do it."

This was the substance of what passed with Aram the morning after the trial; and he promised to make a more ample confession, it being also generally believed that he would have disclosed everything that remained in mystery regarding the matter which preceded the murder. But he prevented any further discovery by the attempt which he made upon his own life, shortly before the hour appointed for his execution. When he was called from his bed to have the irons taken off him, he would not rise, alleging he was very weak. It was found that he had cut his arm in two places with a razor, which he had concealed for some time before. By proper application, however, he was brought to himself, and though weak, was conducted to the place of execution, where, being asked if he had anything to say, he answered, No. Immediately after his death and being cut down, his body was conveyed to Knaresborough Forest, and hung in chains pursuant to his sentence.

On the table in the cell from which he was taken to the scaffold, was found a paper, containing the following reasons for his attempt upon his own life:—" What am I better than my fathers? To die is natural and necessary. Perfectly sensible of this, I fear no more to die than I did to be born. But the manner of it is something which should, in my opinion, be decent and manly. I think I have regarded both these points. Certainly no body has a better right to dispose of a man's life than himself; and he, not others, should determine how. As for any indignities offered to my body, or silly reflections on my faith and morals, they are (as they always were) things indifferent to me. I think, though contrary to the common way of thinking, I wrong no man by this, and hope it is not offensive to that Eternal Being that formed me and the world ; and as by this I injure no man, no man can be reasonably offended. I solicitously recommend myself to the Eternal and Almighty Being, the God of nature, if I have done amiss. But perhaps I have not, and I hope this thing will never be imputed to me. Though I am now stained by malevolence, and suffer by prejudice, I hope to rise fair and unblemished. My life was unpolluted, my morals irreproachable, and my opinions orthodox.

"I slept soundly till three o'clock, awaked, and then wrote these lines :—

> "Come, pleasing Rest, eternal Slumber fall,
> Seal mine, that once must seal the eyes of all ;
> Calm and composed my soul her journey takes,
> No guilt that troubles, and no heart that aches ;
> Adieu ! then sun, all bright like her arise,
> Adieu ! fair friends, and all that's good and wise."

These lines, found along with the other paper, were supposed to have been written by Aram just before he cut himself with the razor. It was also generally believed that, although he laboured to vindicate suicide, and made a profession of superiority to vulgar notions, or what the world might say of him, yet that his motive for the attempt upon himself was the fear of shame ; also that he was anxious to convince all who spoke of him when he was no more, that moral purity as well as mental greatness was his.

It is but justice to add, however, that all the authentic anecdotes of this extraordinary person, represent him as being habitually gentle in manner and conduct. A clergyman (the Rev. Mr. Hinton) said, alluding to the later period of the murderer's life, that he used frequently to observe Aram, when walking in the garden, stoop down to remove a snail or worm from the path, to prevent its being trod upon. Mr. Hinton conjectured that Aram wished to atone for his crime by showing mercy to every animal and even the meanest creature ; but the fact is that there are several anecdotes to show that he was equally humane before the crime was perpetrated. Such are the strange contradictions of the human heart ! One particular more :—the late Admiral Burney was a scholar at the school at Lynn, where Aram was an usher, subsequent to the murder of Clarke. The admiral stated that the usher was beloved by the boys, and that he used to discourse to them of murder, not occasionally, but constantly.

II.—EARL FERRERS.

In the whole annals of British criminal jurisprudence, there never has been greater public excitement created perhaps than by the trial of Lawrence Shirley, fourth Earl Ferrers. Nor was the extreme interest experienced on that occasion other than what might well have been expected. The fact of a peer of the realm being brought to the bar of justice, charged with a capital crime, which had no relation to state or political affairs, was a most extraordinary occurrence ; and when it is considered that a very strong impression was experienced in many quarters, that the accused was a person who could not be regarded as in possession of the faculty of reason—that he was insane—it cannot be a matter of wonder that an unusual interest should prevail respecting the issue of the proceedings which were instituted against that nobleman.

Lawrence Shirley, Earl Ferrers, Viscount Tamworth, was descended from a family which held considerable rank and large estates in Lincolnshire, Northamptonshire, Derbyshire, and Warwickshire, before the Conquest. Many of them bore arms, and received especial honours from their prince, particularly from Henry IV. and Henry VIII. In the year 1615, Sir Henry Shirley married Dorothy, the youngest of the five daughters and heiresses of the Earl of Essex, the unfortunate favourite of Queen Elizabeth. Robert, the son of Sir Henry by his lady, having distinguished himself in the Royal army for Charles I., was afterwards confined by Cromwell in the Tower, where he died. His second son, Sir Robert, who was born during his father's confinement—his elder brother being dead—succeeded to the estate and title; and, in 1677, was summoned to Parliament by the title of Lord Ferrers of Charley, a title that had been borne by Robert Devereux, the last Earl of Essex of that family, upon whose death it became extinct, but thus was revived in the grandson of Dorothy, his youngest daughter. This nobleman had many considerable posts under Charles II. and King William III.; and, on the 3rd of September, 1711, was advanced by Queen Anne to the title of Earl Ferrers, Viscount Tamworth. He died in 1717, leaving three sons, the eldest of whom succeeded to his estate and title, who, dying without issue in 1729, they devolved on Henry, his next brother and heir, who dying unmarried, his title and estate descended to his nephew Lawrence, the unhappy Earl Ferrers, of whom the following account is given. His Lordship's uncle, from whom he derived his title, had been put under restraint by the authority of a statute of lunacy that was obtained against him; and after a short return of reason, relapsed into incurable madness, in which state he continued till his death. Lady Barbara Shirley, his Lordship's aunt, was also a lunatic, and confined as such.

Lawrence Shirley himself had unquestionably so far a tincture of the family disorder as to be subject to sudden causeless and outrageous bursts of passion. He often walked hastily about the room, clenching his fists, grinning, biting his lips, and talking to himself, without having any assignable cause to ruffle his temper, and without being under the influence of liquor. He would sometimes talk to himself many hours after he was in bed; and he was known to entertain most unfounded suspicions of those about him; to go about secretly armed; to be frequently absent when he was spoken to; to make mouths in the looking-glass, spitting upon it, and using gestures that, by those who saw him, were thought to be indications of madness.

In September, 1752, he married the youngest daughter of Sir William Meredith, whom he treated with great brutality, though she was of the most mild and amiable disposition. He was also almost constantly on bad terms with every one of his relations. About four years before his memorable trial, his irregular sallies became more frequent than ever, which was imputed to an unhappy quarrel with his lady. The quarrel was indeed carried so far, that she was separated from him by an act of Parliament; and it was also ordered by the same act, that a person should be appointed to receive the income of his estates, and apply it as the act appointed. He at this period seemed to Mr. Geostry, an eminent attorney, who had been accustomed to transact business for him, to be so much disordered in his mind, that that gentleman declined being farther concerned for him.

About a year and a half before his trial, having been on a visit to the Earl of Westmoreland, Lord Ferrers quarrelled with Sir Thomas Stapelton, and went, with manifest disorder in his countenance and deportment, to Mr. Geostry, proposing to publish an extravagant advertisement in all the papers, tending to challenge Sir Thomas, and to post him for a coward if he did not give him satisfaction; yet he was at the time perfectly sober. Now, the outrage he had committed at Lord Westmoreland's was, by his relations, considered as so much the effect of lunacy, that a consultation was held to take out a commission of lunacy against him. From this, however, they were deterred, by considering that, as his intervals of sanity were long, it was probable he would be able to defeat them; and that, if the court should refuse a commission, the Earl might sue them for *scandalum magnatum,* upon which the damages would be very great.

His lordship sometimes lodged and boarded at the house of one Williams, an innkeeper, and his behaviour being such as deterred persons of rank from associating with him, he kept low company, among whom he indulged himself in many extravagances, and it was the common opinion of all the neighbours that he was mad. For example, when he had ordered coffee, he would frequently drink it out of the spout of the coffee-pot; he used to threaten to break the glasses, to force open Mrs. Williams's bureau, and to throttle her if she opposed him; and these freaks he frequently had when he had drank nothing that had the least intoxicating quality in it. He is said to have lamented his fits of lunacy to one Philips, at whose house he was about to lodge, ten years before the date of his trial, with a view of cautioning the people, and that they might not be affronted at his behaviour. During all this time, however, he managed his affairs with great acuteness and penetration; he was even t'ought by his attorney, Mr. Geostry, to know so well what he was about, that he suffered him to perform several legal acts that were necessary to cut off an entail, which, if he had considered him as a person *insane,* he neither ought, nor, as it is said he declared, would have suffered him to perform.

When his rents were ordered to be paid to a receiver, the nomination of the party was left to himself; and he appointed Mr. John Johnson, a person who had been taken into the service of Lord Ferrers' family in his youth, and was then his lordship's steward; hoping, probably, that he should have sufficient influence over him to have procured some deviation from his trust in his favour. But the earl soon found Mr. Johnson would not oblige him at the expense of his honesty, and from that time he seems to have conceived an implacable resentment against him; nor is it difficult to conceive that envy of position to a man so haughty, impetuous, and irascible, as was his lordship, would produce such an effect. He, from this time, spoke of his steward in opprobrious terms, saying he had conspired with his enemies to injure him, and that he was a villain. With those sentiments he gave him warning to quit an advantageous farm, which Mr. Johnson had under his lordship; but finding that the trustees under the act of separation had, already, granted him a lease of it,—this having been promised the steward by the earl himself, or his relations, his lordship felt disappointed and offended, and probably from that period meditated a more cruel measure. Still he thought proper to dissemble his malice to the man, as being the most proper method in order to facilitate the gratification of revenge; so that poor Johnson was deceived into an opinion that he never was upon better terms with his lord in his life, than at the very time he was contriving to destroy him.

Lord Ferrers at this period lived at Stanton, a seat about two miles from Ashby de la Zouch, in Leicestershire; and his family consisted of himself, Mrs. Clifford, who lived with him, and four daughters, together with five servants,—an old man and a boy, and three maids. Mr. Johnson lived at the house belonging to the farm which he held under his lordship, called the Lount, about half a mile distant from Stanton.

On Sunday, the 13th of January, 1760, the earl went to the Lount, and after some discourse with Mr. Johnson, ordered him to come to him at Stanton, on the Friday following, the 18th, at three o'clock in the afternoon. His lordship's hour of dinner was two, and soon after that hour, Mrs. Clifford being in the still-house, the earl came to her, telling her that she and the children might take a walk. Mrs. C——, who seemed to have looked upon the words as an order to go out, prepared herself and her children accordingly, asking whether they might not go to her father's, which was not far off, to which his lordship assented, saying that they might stay till half an hour after five. The two men servants he also contrived to send out of the way, so that there was no person in the house but himself and the three maids.

In a very short time after the house was thus cleared, Mr. Johnson came and was let in by Elizabeth Burgeland, one of the maids. He asked if his lordship was within, and was answered in the affirmative, saying that the Earl was in his room; upon which the steward proceeded thither, and knocked at the door. Hereupon his lordship opened the door, and ordered him to wait in the still-house. After Mr. Johnson had been there about ten minutes, the earl came out again, and calling him to his own room, went in with him, and immediately locked the door. When they were thus locked in together, his lordship first ordered the steward to settle an account, and, after a little time, produced a paper, purporting, as he said, to be a confession of his villany, requiring the devoted man to sign it. Johnson refused, and expostulated, and his lordship then drawing a pistol, which he had charged and kept in his pocket, no doubt for the purpose, presented it, bidding him to kneel down. The poor man then knelt down upon one knee, but the earl cried so loud as to be heard by one of the maids at the kitchen door, " Down on your other knee, declare that you have acted against Lord Ferrers; your time is come, you must die!" and then immediately fired. The ball entered the body of Mr. Johnson at a vital part, yet he did not drop, but rose up and expressed the sensations of a dying man, both by his looks and by such broken sentences as are usually uttered on such desperate occasions. Upon this, though the Earl seemed at first determined to fire at him again, finding that he did not fall prostrate, he was yet forced out of that resolve by involuntary remorse, or a sudden feeling of pity, on beholding the dreadful and instantaneous change in the countenance of his victim. He opened the door and came out of the room, where he had been shut up with the unhappy steward about half an hour; and the report of the pistol having frightened the women into the wash-house, he called out, " who is there?" One of the maids answered him, when he ordered her to find one of the men, and another to assist in getting Mr. Johnson to bed. At this time his lordship was perfectly sober, and having despatched a messenger to Mr. Kirkland, a surgeon who lived at Ashby de-la-Zouch, he went back where he had left Mr. Johnson with the maid, and asked him how he found himself. The unhappy victim answered that he found himself like a dying man, and requested his lordship to send for his children. His lordship consented, and a messenger was despatched to the Lount, to tell Miss Johnson that she must come to the hall immediately, for that her father was taken very ill. Upon her arrival she soon learned what had happened, his lordship sending one of the maids with her up to the room into which her father had been removed, immediately following himself.

Mr. Johnson was in bed, but did not speak to his daughter. Lord Ferrers pulled down the clothes, and applied a pledget, dipt in arquebusade water, to the wound, and soon after quitted the room. From the time the dreadful deed was perpetrated the earl continued to drink porter till he became drunk. In the meanwhile the messenger that had been sent for the surgeon, having at length found him, at a neighbouring village, about 5 o'clock, brought him to Stanton. On Mr. Kirkland's arrival, Lord Ferrers told him that he had shot his steward, but that he believed he was more frightened than hurt; that he had intended to shoot him, and that he was a villain, and deserved to die. " But," added he, " now that I have spared his life, I desire you will do what you can for him." His lordship at the same time desired the surgeon that he would not suffer him to be seized, declaring that if any one should attempt it he would shoot them. Mr. Kirkland, who prudently determined to say whatever might keep the earl, who was in liquor, from any further outrage, told him that he should not be seized.

The patient complained of a violent pain in the bowels, and the surgeon preparing to search the wound, his lordship informed him of the direction of it, by showing him how he held the pistol when he fired it. The ball was found to be lodged in the body, at which the earl expressed great purprise, declaring that he had tried the pistol a few days before, and that it carried a ball through a deal board, near an inch and a half thick.

Mr. Kirkland then went down stairs to prepare some dressings, and Lord Ferrers soon after again left the room. From this time, in proportion as the liquor, which he continued to drink, took effect, his passions became more tremendous, and the transient fit of compassion, mixed with fear for himself, gave way to gusts of rage, and the predominance of malice. He again went up into the room where Johnson was dying, and pulled him by the wig, calling him villain, and threatening to shoot him through the head. The last time he went to the poor man, he was with great difficulty prevented from tearing the clothes off the bed, which he attempted with great fury, that he might strike him.

A proposal was made to the earl by Mrs. Clifford, that the dying man might be removed to his own house; but he replied, " he shall not be removed, I will keep him here to plague the villain." Many of these expressions were uttered in the hearing of Miss Johnson, whose distress in such a situation it is easier to conceive than describe. Yet even after his lordship's abuse of her father, he told her that if he died he would take care of her and the family, provided they did not prosecute.

When the earl went to bed, which was between eleven and twelve o'clock at night, he told Mr. Kirkland that he knew that he could, if he would, set the affair in such a light as to prevent his being seized, desiring he might see him before he went away in the morning, and declaring that he would rise at an early hour. Mr. Kirkland, in pursuance of his plan, told him he might go to bed in safety, and to bed he went.

The surgeon, even for his own personal sake, was very solicitous to get the patient removed, because if he died where he was, contrary to the assurances he had given his lordship, he had reason to think his own life would be in danger. As soon, therefore, as the earl was in bed, the surgeon sent and informed Mr. Johnson that he would take care he should be removed with all expedition. He accordingly went to the Lount, and having fitted up an easy chair with two poles, by way of a sedan, and procured a guard, he returned about two o'clock, and carried the dying man to his own house, without it appearing to add much to his distress; and here he lingered till nine next morning, when he expired.

As soon as Mr. Johnson had breathed his last, the neighbours set about seizing the earl. A few persons armed set out for Stanton, and as they entered the hall-yard, they saw his lordship going towards the stable, as they imagined, to take horse. He appeared to be just out of bed, his stockings being down, and his garters in his hand, having probably taken the alarm immediately on coming out of his room and finding that his victim had been removed. One Springthorpe, advancing towards the earl, presented a pistol and required him to surrender; but his lordship putting his hand to his pocket, the man imagined he was feeling for a pistol, and stopped short, being probably intimidated; thus suffering Lord Ferrers to escape back into the house, where he fastened the doors, and stood upon his defence. The people who had come to apprehend him beset the mansion, the number increasing rapidly. In about two hours his lordship appeared at a garret window, and called out—"How is Johnson?" Springthorpe answered, "He is dead;" upon which the earl insulted him, called him a liar, and swore he would not believe anybody but Kirkland. Upon being again assured he was dead, he desired the people might be dispersed, and said he would surrender; yet almost in the same breath he desired the multitude might be let in and have some victuals and drink; but the issue was that he went away from the window swearing he would not be taken.

The people, however, still continued around the house, and about two o'clock of the day, after his lordship had appeared at the garret window, he was seen by one Curtis, a collier. He was then armed with a blunderbuss, two or three pistols, and a dagger; but Curtis, so far from being intimidated by supposing he had a pistol in his pocket, marched up boldly to him, in spite of his blunderbuss and all; when the earl seemed to be so struck with the cool and determined resolution of the brave fellow, that he suffered himself to be seized without making the slightest resistance. And yet, the moment he was in custody. he declared he had killed a villain, and that he gloried in the deed.

His lordship was carried from his manor to a public-house at Ashby de la Zouch, where he was kept till the Monday following, during which interval the coroner's inquest had sat upon the body,—the jury bringing in a verdict of Wilful Murder. From Ashby de la Zouch, the earl was sent to Leicester gaol, and from thence, about a fortnight afterwards, he was brought, in his own landau and six, under a strong guard, to London, where he arrived on the 4th of February, about noon, dressed like a jockey, in a close riding frock, jockey boots and cap, and a plain shirt. Being carried before the House of Lords, and the verdict of the coroner's inquest being read, he was committed to the custody of the black rod, and ordered to the Tower, where he arrived about six o'clock in the evening, having conducted himself, during the whole journey and at his commitment, with great calmness and propriety. He was confined in the Round Tower, near the drawbridge; and warders were constantly in the room with him, and one at the door. Two sentinels were posted at the bottom of the stairs, with one upon the drawbridge, with their bayonets fixed; and from this time the gates were ordered to be shut an hour sooner than usual.

Mrs. Clifford and her four young daughters, who had come up with the earl from Leicester, took a lodging in Tower-street, and for some time a servant was continually passing with letters between them; but at length this correspondence was permitted only once a day. During his confinement he was moderate both in regard to his drinking and eating. His breakfast was a half pint bason of tea, with a small spoonful of brandy in it, and a muffin; with his dinner he generally drank a pint of wine, and a pint of water; and another pint of each with his supper. In general his behaviour was decent and quiet, except that he would sometimes start, tear open his waistcoat, and use other gestures, showing that his mind was disturbed. Mrs. Clifford came three times to the Tower, but was not admitted to see him; his children, however, were allowed to be with him some times.

On the 10th of April, having been a prisoner in the Tower two months and two days, his lordship was brought to his trial, which took place before the peers, in Westminster Hall; the Lord Keeper, Lord Henley, acting as Lord Steward. After the usual preliminaries, the earl was placed at the bar by the deputy governor of the Tower, having the axe carried before him by the gentlemen gaoler, who stood with it on the left hand of the prisoner, with the edge turned from him. His lordship, when he approached the bar, made three reverences, and then fell upon his knees at the bar.

"Your lordship may rise," said the Lord High Steward.

The prisoner rose up, and bowed to his Grace, and to the House of Peers. The compliment was returned him by his Grace and the Lords.

Proclamation having been made for silence, the Lord High Steward spoke to the prisoner as follows :—

"Lawrence, Earl Ferrers, you are brought to this bar to receive your trial, upon a charge of the murder of John Johnson; an accusation, with respect to the crime, and the persons who make it (the grand jury of the county of Leicester, the place of your lordship's residence), of the most solemn and serious nature.

"Yet, my lord, you may consider it but as an accusation ; for the greatest or meanest subject of this kingdom (such is the tenderness of our law), cannot be convicted capitally, but by a charge made by twelve good and lawful men, and a verdict found by the same number of his equals at least.

"My lord, in this period of the proceedings, while your lordship stands only as accused, I touch but gently on the offence charged upon your lordship; yet for your own sake, it behoves me strongly to mark the nature of the judicature before which you now appear.

"It is a happiness resulting from your lordship's birth and the constitution of this country, that your lordship is now to be tried by your Peers in full Parliament. What greater consolation can be suggested to a person in your unhappy circumstances, than to be reminded that you are to be tried by a set of judges, whose capacity and penetration no material circumstances in evidence can escape, and whose justice nothing can influence or permit.

"This consideration, if your lordship is conscious of innocence, must free your mind from any perturbations that the solemnity of such a trial might excite; it will render the charge, heavy as it is, unembarrassing, and leave your lordship firm and composed, to avail yourself of every mode of defence that the most equal and humane laws admit of.

"Your lordship, pursuant to the course of this judicature, hath been furnished with a copy of the indictment, and hath had your own counsel assigned; you are therefore enabled to make such defence as is meet for your benefit and advantage ; if your lordship shall put yourself on trial, you must be assured to meet with nothing but justice, candour, and impartiality.

"Before I conclude, I am, by command of the House, to acquaint your lordship, and all other persons who have occasion to speak to the Court during the trial, that they are to address themselves to the lords in general, and not to any lord in particular.

"Lawrence, Earl Ferrers, your lordship will do well to give attention while you are arraigned on your indictment."

The earl having been arraigned, the case of the Crown was stated by the Attorney-General, Charles Pratt, afterwards Lord Camden, in a speech which has been regarded as a model for an address on the part of the prosecution. Two or three of the learned gentleman's observations shall alone be cited here. "My lords," said he, near to the

opening of his speech, " as I never thought it my duty in any case to attempt at eloquence where a prisoner stood upon trial for his life, much less shall I think myself
justified in doing it before your lordships; give me leave, therefore, to proceed to a
narrative of the facts."

The narrative of the Attorney-General was, in substance, as has already been given in
the preceding account. In conclusion the learned gentleman said :—"These are the
circumstances which attended this horrid murder. I have opened them faithfully from
my instructions. The case is rather stronger than I have made it. The witnesses are
to acquaint your lordships whether I have opened the case truly. If the evidence comes
out as I have represented it to your lordships, then your lordships' sentence must be
agreeable to law. The noble earl at the bar must be found guilty. If he has any defence, God forbid that he should not have a fair opportunity of making it. Let him be
heard with patience. The prosecutors will be as glad as your lordships to find him
innocent."

The trial continued till the 18th. The fact charged, however, was easily proved. In
defence, the earl himself examined several witnesses to prove his insanity, managing his
case in such a manner as showed a perfect recollection of mind, and an uncommon understanding. It was with a most delicate and affecting sensibility that he mentioned
the situation of being reduced to the necessity of attempting to prove himself a lunatic,
in order that he might be deemed and held innocent of a murder. The paper which his
lordship put in at the conclusion of the evidence which he had adduced relative to his
insanity, and which contained his defence, was read by the clerk, and ran as follows :—

" My Lords,—It is my misfortune to be accused of a crime of the most horrid nature.
My defence is, in general, that I am Not Guilty : the fact of Homicide is proved against
me by witnesses who, for aught I can say to the contrary, speak truly.

" But if I know myself at this time, I can truly affirm I was ever incapable of it
knowingly : if I have done and said what has been alleged, I must have been deprived of
my senses.

" I have been driven to the miserable necessity of proving my own want of understanding; and am told the law will not allow me the assistance of counsel in this case,
in which, of all others, I should think it most wanted. The more I stand in need of
assistance, the greater reason I have to hope for it from your lordships.

" Witnesses have been called to prove my insanity—to prove an unhappy disorder of
mind, and which I am grieved to be under the necessity of exposing. If they have not
directly proved me so insane as not to know the difference between a moral and an im-
moral action, they have at least proved that I was liable to be driven and hurried into
that unhappy condition upon very slight occasions. Your lordships will consider whether
my passion, rage, madness (or whatever it may be called), was the effect of a weak or
distempered mind, or whether it arose from my own wickedness, or inattention to my
duty. If I could have controlled my passion, I am answerable for the consequences of
it; but if I could not, and if it was the mere effect of a distempered brain, I am not
answerable for the consequences. My lords, I mention these things as hints—I need
not, indeed I cannot enlarge upon this subject: your lordships will consider all circumstances, and I am sure you will do me justice. If it be but a matter of doubt, your
lordships will run the hazard of doing me injustice, if you find me guilty. My lords,
if my insanity had been of my own seeking, as the sudden effect of drunkenness, I should
be without excuse. But it is proved, by witnesses for the crown, that I was not in liquor.

Mr. Kirkland, who drank and conversed with me, in order to betray me (Mr. Attorney-General may commend his caution, but not his honesty), represents me the most irrational of all madmen, at the time of doing a deed which I reflect upon with the utmost abhorrence.

"The Counsel for the Crown will put your lordships in mind of every circumstance against me; I must require of your lordships' justice to recollect any circumstance on the other side. My life is in your hands; and I have everything to hope, as my conscience does not condemn me of the crime I stand accused of, for I had no preconceived malice, and was hurried into the perpetration of this fatal deed by the fury of a disordered imagination. To think of this, my lords, is an affliction, which can be aggravated only by the necessity of making it my defence. May God Almighty direct your judgments and correct my own!"

The Solicitor-General, the Hon. Charles Yorke, afterwards Lord Chancellor, made a long and elaborate reply on the part of the Crown, in relation, especially, to the prisoner's defence of insanity. Alas! that defence proved unavailing, the Peers unanimously finding the Earl guilty; and having been brought up for judgment on the 18th, and been called upon to say why sentence of death should not pass, he thus addressed the court through the clerks, declaring, as will be found, that he had been adverse to advance the plea of insanity, and that he had done so only to gratify his friends:—

"My lords, I must acknowledge myself infinitely obliged for the fair and candid trial your lordships have indulged me with. I am extremely sorry that I have troubled your lordships with a defence that I was always much averse to, and has given me the greatest uneasiness, but was prevailed on by my family to attempt it, as it was what they themselves were persuaded of the truth of; and had proposed to prove me under the unhappy circumstances that have been ineffectually represented to your lordships.

"This defence has put me off from what I proposed, and what perhaps might have taken off the malignity of the accusation; but as there has been no proof made to your lordships, it can only be deemed at this time my own assertion, but that I must leave to your lordships.

"My lords, I have been informed of this intention of the family before; and your lordships, I hope, will be so good to consider the agony of mind a man must be under, when his liberty and property are both attacked. My lords, under these unhappy circumstances, though the plea I have attempted was not sufficient to acquit me to your lordships, according to the laws of this country, yet I hope your lordships will think that malice, represented by the counsel for the Crown, could not subsist. As I was so unhappy as to have no person present at the time of the fatal accident, it was impossible for me to show to your lordships that I was not at that instant possessed of my reason.

"As the circumstances of my case are fresh in your lordships' memories, I hope your lordships will, in compassion to my infirmities, be kind enough to recommend me to his Majesty's clemency.

"My lords, as I am uncertain whether my unhappy case is within the late act of Parliament, if your lordships should be of opinion that it is, I humbly hope the power of respiting the execution will be extended in my favour, that I may have an opportunity of preparing myself for the great event, and that my friends may be permitted to have access to me.

"If anything I have offered should be thought improper, I hope your lordships will impute it to the great distress I am under at this juncture."

The Earl received sentence to be executed on Monday, the 21st of April, and then to be anatomised; but in consideration of his rank, the execution of the sentence was respited till Monday, the 5th of May. George II. is reported to have said, when applied to that the punishment might be altered from hanging to beheading, "No, he has done the deed of the bad man, and he shall die the death of the bad man."

During the interval between the condemnation and the execution, Lord Ferrers made a will, by which he left £1,300 to Mr. Johnson's children; £1,000 to each of his four natural daughters; and £60 a year to Mrs. Clifford for her life. This will, however, being dictated after his conviction, was not valid; yet it was said that the same, or nearly the same, provision came to be made for these several parties.

In the mean time a scaffold was erected under the gallows at Tyburn, and part of it, about a yard square, was raised some eighteen inches above the rest of the floor, with a construction to sink down upon a signal given, the whole being covered with black baize.

On the morning of the 5th of May, about 9 o'clock, the earl's body was demanded of the keeper of the Tower by the Sheriffs of London and Middlesex. His lordship being informed of this, sent a message to the sheriffs, requesting that he might go in his own landau, instead of the mourning coach that had been provided by his friends; and his request being granted, he entered his carriage, drawn by six horses, with Mr. Humphries, chaplain of the Tower, who had been admitted to his lordship that morning for the first time. The landau having been conducted to the outward gate of the Tower, was there delivered to the sheriffs. Here Mr. Sheriff Vaillant entered the carriage of his lordship, expressing his concern at having so melancholy a duty to perform; whereupon the earl said, "I am much obliged to you, and take it kind that you accompany me."

His lordship was dressed in a suit of light-coloured clothes, embroidered with silver, said to be his wedding suit; and soon after Mr. Vaillant entered the landau, he said, "You may perhaps, sir, think it strange to see me in this dress, but I have my particular reasons for it." The procession then began in the following order:—A very large body of the constables for the county of Middlesex, preceded by one of the high-constables. A party of horse-grenadiers, and a party of foot; Mr. Sheriff Evrington in his chariot, accompanied by his under-sheriff, Mr. Jackson; the landau, escorted by two other parties of horse-grenadiers and foot. Mr. Sheriff Vallant's chariot, in which was his under-sheriff, Mr. Nicols; a mourning coach and six, with some of his lordship's friends; a hearse and six, which was provided for the conveyance of his lordship's corpse from the place of execution to Surgeon's-hall.

The procession moved so slow, that his lordship was two hours and three quarters in his landau; but during the whole time he appeared perfectly easy and composed, though he often expressed his desire to have it over, saying, that the apparatus of death, and the passing through such crowds of people, were ten times worse than death itself." He told the sheriff that he had written to the king, to beg that he might suffer where his ancestor, the Earl of Essex, had been executed, and was in the greatest hopes of obtaining that favour, as he had the honour of quartering part of the same arms, and of being allied to his Majesty, and that he thought it was hard that he should die at the place appointed for the execution of common felons." The King's observation in reference to the matter has already been cited.

Mr. Humphries took occasion to observe, that the world would naturally be inquisitive concerning the religion his lordship professed, and asked him if he chose to say anything upon that subject. To which the earl answered, "that he did not think himself accountable to the world for his sentiments on religion; but that he always believed in and adored one God the Maker of all things; that, whatever his notions were, he had never propagated them, or endeavoured to gain any person over to his persuasion; that all countries and nations had a form of religion by which the people were governed, and he looked upon who ever disturbed them as an enemy to society. That he very much blamed Lord Bolingbroke for permitting his sentiments on religion to be published to the world. That the many sects and disputes which had arisen about religion, had almost turned morality out of doors,—that he could never believe what some sectarians taught, that faith alone will save mankind; so that if a man, just before he dies, should say only, I believe, that *that* alone wold save him."

As to the deed and crime for which he suffered, he declared that he was under particular circumstances, that he had met with so many crosses and vexations, he scarce knew what he did; and most solemnly protested "that he had not the least malice against Mr. Johnson."

When his lordship had got to that part of Holborn which is near to Drury-lane, he said, " he was thirsty, and should be glad of a glass of wine and water;" but upon the sheriff stating to him that a stop for that purpose would naturally draw a greater crowd around him, which might probably disturb and incommode him, yet that if his lordship still desired it, it should be done,—he most readily answered, " that is true, I say no more, let us by no means stop."

When they approached near the place of execution, his lordship told the sheriff that there was a person waiting in a coach near there, for whom he had a very sincere regard, and of whom he should be glad to take his leave before he died; to which the sheriff answered that if his lordship insisted upon it, it should be so, but that he wished him, for his own sake, to decline the interview, lest the sight of a person for whom he had such a regard should unman and disarm him of the fortitude he possessed. To which the earl, without the least hesitation, replied, " Sir, if you think I am wrong, I submit;" and upon the sheriff telling his lordship that if he had anything to deliver to that person, or any one else, he would faithfully do it, his lordship delivered to him a pocket-book, in which was a bank-note, and a ring, and a purse with some guineas, in order to be delivered to that person, which was done accordingly.

The landau having reached the place of execution, the earl alighted from it, and ascended upon the scaffold, with the same composure and fortitude which he had displayed from the moment he quitted the Tower. Soon after he had mounted the scaffold, Mr. Humphries asked his lordship if he chose to say prayers ? which he declined ; but upon his asking him if he did not choose to join with him in the Lord's Prayer ? he readily replied he would, for he " always had thought it a very fine Prayer;" upon which they knelt down together upon two cushions, covered with black cloth, when his lordship with an audible voice very devoutly repeated the Prayer, afterwards with great energy uttering this ejaculation, "Oh God, forgive me all my errors,—pardon all my sins."

The earl then rising, took his leave of the sheriffs and the chaplain ; and after thanking them for their many civilities, he presented his watch to Mr. Sheriff Vaillant, which he desired him to accept of; and signified his desire that his body might be buried at Breden, or Stanton, in Leicestershire, He then called for the executioner, who immediately came to him, and asked him forgiveness; upon which his lordship said " I truly forgive you, as I do all mankind, and hope myself to be forgiven." He then intended to have given the executioner five guineas, but, by mistake, put them into the hand of the executioner's assistant, upon which an unseasonable dispute arose between the unfeeling wretches, which Mr. Sheriff Vaillant instantly silenced.

The executioner then proceeded to do his duty, to which the earl with great resignation submitted. His neckcloth being taken off, a white cap, which he had brought in his pocket, being put upon his head, his arms secured by a black sash, and the cord put round his neck, he advanced by three steps to the elevated part of the scaffold; and standing under the cross beam that went over it, which was also covered with black cloth, he asked the executioner, " am I right?" Then the cap was drawn over his face, and upon a signal given by the sheriff,—for the earl upon being asked declined to give one himself,—that elevated part, upon which he stood, instantly sank down from his feet, leaving him entirely suspended. For a few seconds his lordship struggled, but was soon released from the agonies of death by the pressure of the executioner.

From the moment of the earl's ascending the scaffold until his execution, was about eight minutes; during which his countenance was not observed to change, nor his tongue to falter.

The accustomed time of one hour being past, the coffin was raised up to receive the body, and being deposited in the hearse, was conveyed to Surgeon's Hall, to undergo the remainder of the sentence. A large incision was made from the neck to the bottom of the breast, and another across the throat; the lower part of the belly was laid open, and the bowels taken away. It was afterwards publicly exposed to view in a room up one pair of stairs at the Hall; and on the evening of the 8th of May it was delivered to his friends for interment.

The following lines were said to have been found in his lordship's apartment :—

> " In doubt I liv'd, in doubt I die,
> Yet stand prepar'd the vast abyss to try,
> And undismay'd expect eternity."

The conviction and execution of Lawrence, Earl Ferrers, have been regarded as presenting a striking example of the impartial majesty of the English law, and of the purity of its administration; and yet there can be but little doubt, that at the present day, the deed for which he suffered would have been held as that of an insane person, and consequently not been visited with the extreme penalty which overtook his lordship.

Earl Ferrers was, in the opinion of all who knew him, a person of a violent spirit, and, as such, had committed many outrages. His behaviour to his lady was habitually so brutal, that a separation was effected by Act of Parliament. On his trial, it was proved that he had long been beset with unfounded suspicions of plots and conspiracies, unconnected ravings, sudden starts of fury, denunciations of unprovoked revenge, frantic gesticulation, and a strange caprice of temper. Lunacy was hereditary in his family; a solicitor of reputation had renounced his business, on the full persuasion of his being disordered in his brain; a physician, skilled in this branch, pronounced him insane; and one of the peers declared from his seat, that he looked upon him as a maniac, and that if some effective step was not taken to divest him of the power of doing mischief, he did not doubt but that they should have occasion to try him for murder; and the prediction was uttered even previous to the time of his separation from his lady. In short, as has been well remarked by one of England's historians, the madness of Earl Ferrers appeared in his conduct, and not in his conversation,—his arguments and observations being very rational, even when his behaviour was frantic. And as if, at the hour of death, to show to his countrymen the cruelty of this judgment, he dressed gaily for the occasion. The earl's case is therefore in any sense a most melancholy one; unless, indeed, it may be regarded as having served an important purpose, seeing that it has been made use of by some of the most eminent writers on the medical jurisprudence of insanity, and has helped to those more enlightened and philosophic views which are entertained by the ablest inquirers into the subject of mental derangement.

A case similar to that of Earl Ferrers is mentioned by Pinel, the celebrated French writer on the " Medical Jurisprudence of Insanity," under the head of Moral Mania, and where a different course was adopted with the party :—" An only son of a weak and indulgent mother was encouraged in the gratification of any caprice and passion of which an untutored and violent temper was susceptible. The impetuosity of his disposition increased with his years. The money with which he was lavishly supplied, removed every obstacle to the indulgence of his wild desires. Every instance of his opposition or resistance roused him to acts of fury. He assaulted his adversaries with the audacity of a savage; sought to reign by force, and was perpetually embroiled in disputes and quarrels. If a dog, a horse, or any other animal offended him, he instantly put it to death. If ever he went to a *fête* or any other public meeting, he was sure to excite such tumults and quarrels as terminated in actual pugilistic encounters, and he generally left the scene with a bloody nose. He, however, when unmoved by passion, possessed a sound judgment. When he became of age, he succeeded to the possession of an extensive domain. He proved himself fully competent to the management of his estate, as well as to the discharge of his relative duties, and he even distinguished himself by acts of beneficence and compassion. Wounds, law-suits, and pecuniary compensations were generally the consequences of his unhappy propensity to quarrel. But an act of notoriety put an end to his career of violence. Enraged with a woman who had used offensive language to him, he precipitated her into a well. Prosecution was commenced against him; and on the deposition of a great many witnesses who gave evidence to his furious deportment, he was confined in the Bicetre."

The medical remark upon this case is, that there was something more than the unrestrained indulgence of strong passions, though no doubt, the passions of this person were naturally remarkably strong and active; the understanding, though sound, was incapable of restraining their impulses, for the reason that they were excited by disease, and therefore beyond its controul. The constant excitement of passions already too much developed by means of a vicious education, led to that condition of mind in which the healthy balance of the effective and intellectual faculties was destroyed,—in other words, to moral mania.

Having noticed this French case, a few incidents may be added to what has already been mentioned regarding Earl Ferrers' ungovernable passion.—At the Derby races, in 1756, he ran his mare against a military friend's horse for *fifty pounds*, and was the winner. After the race, he spent the evening with some gentlemen, and in the course of conversation the Captain—who had heard that his lordship's mare was with foal—proposed, in a jocose manner, to run his horse against her at the expiration of seven months. Lord Ferrers felt so affronted by this circumstance, which he took it into his head had arisen from a preconcerted plan to insult him, that he quitted Derby at three o'clock in the morning, and went immediately to his seat at Stanton Harold, in Leicestershire. He rang his bell as soon as he arrived, and, a servant attending, he asked if he knew how the Captain came to be informed his mare was with foal. The servant declared he was ignorant of the matter, but the groom might have told it; and the groom being called' he denied having given any information respecting the subject. Previously to the affront presumed to have been given on the preceding evening, Lord Ferrers had invited the Captain and the rest of the company to dine with him as on that day, but they all refused their attendance, though he sent a servant to remind them that they had promised to come. His lordship was so enraged at this disappointment, that he kicked and horse-whipped his servants, and threw at them such articles as lay within his reach.

Some oysters had been sent from London, which not proving good, his lordship directed one of his servants to swear that the carrier had changed them; but the servant declining to take such an oath, the earl flew into a rage, stabbed him in the breast with a knife, cut his head with a candlestick, and kicked him on the groin with such severity, that he was under the surgeon's care for several years afterwards.

Lord Ferrers's brother and his wife paying a visit to him and his countess at Stanton Harold, a casual dispute arose between the parties; and Lady Ferrers being absent from the room, the earl ran up stairs with a large clasp-knife in his hand, and asked a servant whom he met, where his lady was. The man said, "In her room," and being directed to follow him thither, his lordship ordered him to load a pair of pistols with bullets. This order was complied with; but the servant, apprehensive of mischief, declined priming the pistols, which the earl discovering, swore at him, asked him for powder, and primed them himself. He then threatened that if he did not go immediately and shoot his brother, he would blow his brains out. The servant hesitating, his lordship pulled the trigger of one of the pistols, but it missed fire. Hereupon the countess dropped upon her knees and begged him to appease his passion; but in return he swore at her, and threatened her destruction if she opposed him. The servant now escaped from the room, and reported what had passed to his lordship's brother, who immediately called his wife from her bed, and they left the house, although it was then two o'clock in the morning.

Now, assuredly such a madman should not have been allowed to go at large. It must be conceded that most generally his fury arose from the excitement of drinking, and, probably, on the night in question, he had drank to intoxication. Nevertheless, the confinement of a similar place to that of the Bicetre should have been his, in order to prevent him from perpetrating such a deed as sent him to the gallows.

III.—ELIZABETH BROWNRIGG.

ELIZABETH BROWNRIGG, about twenty years before her trial for horrid cruelties inflicted upon her poor apprentice girls, had lived as a servant in a family in Prescott-street, Goodman's fields; and it was while in this situation that James Brownrigg, who had served his time to a plaisterer and house-painter in the same neighbourhood, married her. Soon afterwards they settled at Greenwich, where he carried on business for himself; about five years after they removed to London.

The family of the Brownriggs increased very rapidly, for they had sixteen children, but of whom only three were living at the period of their mother's trial. Mrs. Brownrigg, meanwhile, had learnt midwifery, and had been appointed by the overseers of the parish

of St. Dunstan-in-the-West, to act as midwife to the poor women in their workhouse, in which capacity she was said to have acted with great skill and humanity. She was also a faithful wife, and a tender, affectionate parent.

It appeared, from the date of her trial, to have been about four years previous to that period when James Brownrigg took the house in Fetter-lane, where the cruelties were perpetrated; and at this time he kept a horse, and had a lodging near to Canonbury-lane, Islington.

In the month of February, 1765, Mary Mitchell, a poor girl of the Precincts of White Friars, was bound an apprentice to Brownrigg, by the overseers, and was then nearly fourteen years of age. About three months afterwards, Mary Jones was also bound apprentice to Brownrigg, by the Governors of the Foundling Hospital, being also about the age of 14.

It appeared that the poor girls were at this time treated with great cruelty; what in particular were Mitchell's sufferings did not transpire, but the cruelties which Jones endured were very great. For example, Mrs. Brownrigg used to lay down two chairs on the kitchen floor, in such a manner that the seat of one might support the back of the other; then she would fasten the girl down, sometimes naked, and sometimes with her clothes pulled over her head; and thus tied down, the apprentice was whipped by the savage woman till strength failed to wield the weapon. On other occasions, when the young creature had been washing the rooms or stairs, her mistress would find fault with her work, and taking the girl up in her arms, would plunge her head in the pail of water that stood by.

No. 3.   D

By such treatment the girl received many hurts in different parts of her body, particularly on the head and shoulders, from the edges of the pail; besides being kept in continual terror by threats of drowning, Mrs. Brownrigg often calling on Mary Mitchell to fill her a tub of water for that purpose. Where the latter girl slept at this time was not explained, but Jones's berth was in a hole under a dresser, in the same room with the master and mistress, and facing the foot of their bed. This room happened to be level with the shop, the door of which opened into the street; and one Sunday morning, as the girl lay silently deploring her miserable condition, and ready to die in consequence of the brutal treatment to which she had been subjected, together with dreadful apprehensions of the future, she cast her eye upon the key of the shop door, which hung against a post, and perceiving that Mr. and Mrs. Brownrigg were both fast asleep, she had resolution to make one effort for liberty and life; and rising very softly, she was fortunate enough to steal into the street, without discovery.

This happened after she had been bound about eight weeks, in the month of July. When she got into the street she was at a loss where to go; she had no home but the Foundling Hospital, and thither she did not know her way; however, she asked of every one she met, and, at last, of a man, who was so kind as to show her to the gates. She was instantly admitted; and, having told her story, and showed her wounds and bruises, one of which was upon her eye, and had so injured it, that for some days it was feared she would have lost it, the following order was made by the governors:—

"That Mr Plumptree, the hospital solicitor, do write to James Brownrigg, a painter in Fetter-lane, who had a child, Mary Jones, apprenticed to him by this corporation, and acquaint him, that if he does not forthwith make satisfaction for the abuse to the said child, this corporation will prosecute him with the utmost severity."

What particular steps were taken by the parties in consequence of this order does not appear, but soon after Brownrigg was summoned to attend the Chamberlain of London, before whom the matter was settled, and the girl discharged from her apprenticeship.

Mitchell was now left alone, and continued patiently to drudge and to suffer till about the middle of the February following, when she had served about one year of her time, and then she also found means to run away. She was, however, found in the streets by Brownrigg's youngest boy the same day, and brought back to her confinement, and the renewal of the barbarities to which she, too, had been subjected. From this time, she was never suffered to stir out of doors, having been frequently tied up and whipped naked.

About the same date, Mary Clifford, a third apprentice, was bound to James Brownrigg, by the overseers of White Friars precinct. She was a month upon liking or trial, and during that period was well treated, eating and drinking as the family did. At length she was bound, and now a sudden change took place in the poor girl's condition, Mrs. Brownrigg commencing her system of infernal cruelty, frequently beating the friendless creature over her head and shoulders, sometimes with a walking-cane, sometimes with a horsewhip, and at other times with a hearth-brush.

It was this girl's misfortune, either by natural weakness or bad nursing when an infant, to wet the bed, and for this reason she was ordered to lie on a mat, in a place called the cellar, which had been a coal-hole, and was described as a cold, dark place, about as big as a closet, under the stairs. The mat, however, after some time, was taken away, and a sack, with a little straw in it, substituted in its place; sometimes there was nothing but a few rags, and sometimes the bare floor beneath her. As to covering, she had sometimes her own most scanty clothes, sometimes a bit of blanket, and frequently she was quite naked. It does not appear that she had any other food than bread and water, nor had she enough even of this afflicting allowance of the imprisoned.

Once, when she was famishing for hunger, she broke open a cupboard where victuals were usually kept, but found none; and once, when she was fainting with thirst, she pulled down some boards to come at water. For the first of these crimes she was made to strip naked, and continued to wash naked a whole day, being every now and then beaten with the stump end of a riding whip; for the other offence, a jack chain was put round her neck, and the end fastened to the yard door: it was strained as tight as it could be without choking her; and when she had passed the day in this condition, she was sent down into the cellar when it grew dark, with the chain still on her neck, and her hands tied behind her, to pass the night, without bed or covering, in the cellar.

It was common for both the girls, Mitchell and Clifford, to go about the house quite naked; for Brownrigg being, by their indentures, obliged to find them clothes, frequently ordered them to be taken off, upon discovering any little rent, hole, or other sign that they were wearing out. Mitchell, in particular, scarcely ever had stockings, nor, generally, had she anything upon her person but an old rag of a waistcoat, which did not cover her behind. But, as the Brownriggs were tried for their cruelty to Clifford, and Mitchell was the principal evidence, little appears concerning the latter girl of a particular nature; sometimes, however, she was locked up with the other victim of this fiendish mistress in the dark and damp cellar, to pass the night, both being constantly imprisoned in that dismal cell from Saturday to Sunday night, while the family were at their country lodgings in Islington; and during all such times they had no sustenance but a piece of bread, for water itself was not added or allowed. The return to town of their master and mistress the girls dreaded more than death.

The office of gaoler seemed to have been in general performed by the eldest son, though sometimes the prisoners were locked up by others, once in particular, by Benham, an apprentice boy, who in his examination swore, that when he locked them in, Clifford was quite naked.

The girls were so often and so savagely whipped and beaten, that their bodies, especially their heads and shoulders, were nearly one entire scab, the skin being broken afresh as fast as it healed; for Mrs· Brownrigg never left off whipping till she drew blood. A writer in the "Gentleman's Magazine" relates that Mittchell declared to an acquaintance of his, that sometimes, after they had been whipped, the blood which streamed from their wounds formed puddles underneath them where they shivered and crouched in the cellar.

In order to inflict the monstrous punishments, the first expedient in Mrs. Brownrigg's system was to strip the girls quite naked, and then tie their hands up to a water·pipe that was carried along the kitchen ceiling. This pipe, however, at length gave way, so that a staple was driven into the ceiling by the husband, at his wife's desire; and the cord with which their hands were bound, was fastened to the iron.

Clifford was also sometimes beaten with cruelty by the son, John. He one day ordered her to put up a bed, which she attempted to do, but was not able; upon which he beat her with the buckle-end of a leathern belt, till she was covered with blood, and then he put up the bed himself. This wretch also found her at another time naked and bleeding, having been tied up and whipped by his mother; yet in this condition, the tigress having ordered him to continue the barbarity which her own physical strength could no longer prosecute at the time, the fit son of such a diabolical mother did as he was requested, and performed the horrid office.'

Some acts of cruelty were also spoken to on the trial of Mrs. Brownrigg, which were of another kind; for she would frequently fix one of her hands on each of the cheeks of the girls, and bring them down their faces with such sudden and extreme force, as to make the blood start from their eyes. Mitchell having complained to a female lodger,— the only one who appeared to have been in the house during Clifford's time, of ill-usage, —of the cruelties she endured, the woman, upon some disagreement with the mistress, reproached the savage with the subject of the girl's complaint; upon which Mrs. Brownrigg ran to the girl, and driving a pair of scissors into her mouth, cut her tongue in two places.

The account of what happened on the day when a most frightful attack was made upon Mary Clifford, with its most important results, is in substance as follows :—

On Friday, the 30th of July, 1767, about ten o'clock in the morning, Mrs. Brownrigg having threatened the girls all the week, went down into the kitchen, and tied Clifford up, as usual, to the staple. Her head and shoulders were then very sore, but scabbed over in many places. Yet, notwithstanding the state in which the poor, helpless victim was in, her tyrant lashed and belaboured her with a horse-whip, in the presence of Mitchell, till the blood copiously followed the strokes. She was at length let down and ordered to wash, naked and wounded as she was; and while she was stooping down to the tub, her mistress struck her over the head with the but-end of the whip. Five times during that dreadful day was she tied up, still naked and bleeding,—still covered with old wounds: five times whipped and beaten as long each time as the monster who inflicted the torture had strength of arm to wield the instrument of punishment. Mary Clifford's sufferings were drawing near a close, for she was now mortally wounded, especially by the tremendous blow which she had received with the but-end of the whip, when stooping down to the tub to wash, as well as her feeble fingers could do, the gore from her face and person.

One cannot but pause here and marvel that there should have existed among the human species a wretch, who, instead of nourishing and showing kindness to young friendless creatures of her own sex, could thus commit such outrages against humanity,—finding gratification in cruelty and torturings which would seem to be purely diabolical,—a woman, too, who had given birth to a numerous family, of most of whom she had been bereft by death. It is also scarcely possible to avoid feeling amazed that such barbarities should have been so long perpetrated without a public discovery being made of them. Indeed, so improbable were the facts, just as were lately those in the case of the Sloanes, that nothing short of the most positive and the clearest evidence could cause them to be credited. Who could have believed that two girls of the age of from thirteen to fifteen years, in such a metropolis as London, and such a densely-inhabited neighbourhood as Fetter-lane, should have continued to suffer as Mary Mitchell and Mary Clifford did, for two years, without disclosure or escape? Let it never then be hastily concluded, on any other deplorable occasion which may occur, that because an alleged barbarity is improbable and monstrous, it is therefore not to be searched into. To return to the narrative :—

Mrs. Brownrigg had now arrived, as it would seem, at the climax of her barbarity ; or, rather, her career of wanton and unparalleled cruelty had been brought nearly to its end ; for a discovery of the whole was on the eve of being made.

Mary Clifford had received her most deadly treatment on the 30th of July, but crept about the dismal place of her imprisonment till the 4th of August, when her deplorable state was thus brought to light :—

The poor girl's father about four years before had married a second wife. He, however, deserted the woman, upon which she delivered up the child to the parish, and went into Cambridgeshire. She was absent when the girl was bound apprentice, but at length returned to London. Having now learnt to whom Mary was bound, she went twice to Brownrigg's, anxiously inquiring after the poor creature, but was both times answered by the apprentice boy that no such person lived there. After several such ineffectual efforts, both by herself and persons she sent, Brownrigg, the husband, absolutely denying that any such girl was in his house, he threatened the stepmother with sending her before the Lord Mayor for being troublesome. Upon this the disappointed and vexed woman went away, but as she was going, Mrs. Deacon, the wife of a baker that resided next door, called her in, and asked what was the matter. Upon hearing the story, Mrs. Deacon said that her family had frequently heard cries, groans, and moanings issuing from Brownrigg's premises; that she suspected there were apprentices there who were cruelly beaten; and that she would do her utmost to make further discoveries,—taking the stepmother's address in order to send for her if necessary.

About this period Brownrigg, the husband, having been concerned in a sale at Hampstead, bought a hog, and had it driven home to his house. The hog was kept in a covered yard, where there was a skylight, and this it was found necessary to open, in order to let out the smell which proceeded from keeping the animal in so confined a place. The removal of the skylight gave Deacon's family an opportunity of seeing what passed in Brownrigg's yard, and they were now upon the watch. It happened that the apprentice, William Clipson, being on the 3rd of August at a two pair of stairs window which looked down on the skylight, saw the dying girl, her head, back, and shoulders being uncovered; she was also bloody, and cut in a shocking manner. Clipson immediately went down to the one pair of stairs window, and crawled out of it upon the leads over the yard, where, laying himself across the skylight, he had a fuller view of the poor victim. He spoke several times to her, but received no answer. He then, to attract her notice, dropped two or three small pieces of mortar, one of which falling upon her head, she looked up, and attempted to speak, but could only utter a groan. This was overheard by Mrs. Brownrigg, but without pity, for Clipson in his evidence said she spoke to the girl in a sharp manner, and asked what was the matter with her; the lad then drew back out of sight, and acquainted the Deacons with what he had witnessed.

Intelligence was soon conveyed to the stepmother, who, next day, came with the overseers of the precinct; they went into Brownrigg's house, and Clipson with them. They inquired for Mary Clifford, but Brownrigg, the husband, answered that she was in Hertfordshire attending one of the children who had the hooping-cough. Clipson then said he had seen her in a deplorable condition the day before, upon which Brownrigg swore by God she was not in the house. Mitchell was produced, but the baker's apprentice insisted she was not the girl he had seen; and Mr. Grundy, one of the overseers, then sent for a constable, and searched the house, but without success.

Upon examining Mary Mitchell, her cap was found to be bloody, her head wounded in many places, and her shoulders covered with the scabs of wounds that were healing. Mr. Grundy perceiving how this girl had been treated, carried her away to the workhouse, wholly regardless of Brownrigg's blustering, who said that she was his apprentice, bidding the overseer remove her at his peril.

When they came to take off her boddice, which was of leather—and she had no shift —it stuck so fast to the wounds that the skin and scabs came away with it. After she was removed, and was assured that she should return to her tormentors no more, she began to give an account of the barbarous treatment she had so long endured, declaring at the same time that Mary Clifford was in Brownrigg's house, for that she had parted with her just before she was herself produced. Mr. Grundy, not doubting the truth of the poor girl's statement, went back to Brownrigg, telling him he would carry him before a magistrate on suspicion of murder; he also sent for a coach. Some of Brownrigg's neighbours now came about him and offered bail; a lawyer also was sent for, who endeavoured to intimidate the overseer and constable. Grundy, nevertheless, continued resolute in his purpose, saying he would answer at the proper time for what he was doing, and that as the crime which Brownrigg was taken up for was murder, no bail could be accepted of. Matters taking this turn, instead, as before, of being in Brownrigg's favour or it being his interest to conceal his victim, the girl was produced, that it might be made known she was alive. The son, therefore, by the father's order, brought her from a cupboard under the beaufet in the dining-room, where she had been hidden.

"No words," says John Wingrave, in his published narrative,—one of the constables engaged in the case,—"can so powerfully describe the shocking appearance which this miserable object made, as the silent woe with which every person present was struck at the sight of her, and the execrations which instantly followed against those who had reduced her to such a miserable condition." Her head was swollen to nearly the double of its natural size, and her neck so much, as that she could neither speak nor swallow. Her mouth stood open, and the surgeon who examined her deposed that she was *all one wound from the crown of her head to the sole of her foot,*—that her shift stuck to her body, that she was in a high fever, and that her wounds were beginning to mortify from neglect. The girls had been first of all examined at the workhouse; but were next sent to confront Brownrigg before a magistrate. Mary Clifford could only utter a *yes* or a *no* to the questions put to her; and this in a manner that was scarcely intelligible,—the loss of the power of speech appearing to have been occasioned by the wounds in the glands of her neck. Both girls were next conveyed to Bartholomew Hospital; Brownrigg being sent to prison. His wife and son had made their escape.

On the 9th of August, Mary Clifford died, and the coroner's jury brought in their verdict of Wilful Murder against James Brownrigg, and Elizabeth, his wife. The eldest son, John, was included in an advertisement for apprehending the principal criminals.

Intelligence was soon obtained that the mother and son had taken places in the Dover stage, by the names of Hartly. The information was true, though they did not think it safe to undertake that journey. It was also afterwards known that they had got into a hackney-coach in Jewin-street, which set them down in East Smithfield, and that they took a lodging in a bye street, near Nightingale-lane; here they lived on bread and water,—being afraid to stir out to purchase other food,—until the 11th, when in Ragglane they purchased some apparel, lest the description given in the advertisement of their clothing might lead to a discovery. They lodged one night at a place that was not ascertained, but next day took a lodging at a chandler's shop in Wandsworth. On the 15th of August, the chandler meeting in a newspaper with the advertisement, he was immediately struck, owing to a variety of circumstances, with the idea that his lodgers were the persons described. Next day he went to town, and lodged information accordingly. The skulking pair of miscreants were without delay brought to town in a coach, having been previously identified by their former neighbour, Mr. Deacon, and others.

The accused were many times examined, and on the 9th of September bills of indictment were found, not only against the father and mother, for the murder of Mary Clifford, but the son also. The trial took place upon Saturday, the 12th, and lasted six hours; the evidence being the same in substance with the preceding narrative. Mrs. Brownrigg was found guilty, but her husband and son were acquitted of the murder; they were, however, detained to take their trial for misdemeanour.

Though these people lived in credit, and Mrs. Brownrigg had a watch and some other trinkets, which she carried off with her, yet in prison her distress was so great, that she was obliged to borrow a few halfpence of a woman who was a prisoner in the same cell with her. The vast crowd that waited in the yard of the Sessions' House during the trial testified their joy by a shout when she was convicted; and such was the indignation which was felt at the horrid, deliberate, and persevering cruelties of which she was proved guilty, that had the crowd got hold of her person, they would certainly have torn her to pieces.

Those romances of real life, in which human suffering and the being convicted of crime form the principal features, are continually, or at least with very short intervals, taking place and enacted at the Old Bailey of London. Here it is that guilt is made manifest, and punishment awarded upon a wide scale. One, indeed of the most important reforms of recent years, has been what may significantly be termed the distribution of speedy justice. Month after month invariably, the same scene is now-a-days to be witnessed at the Old Bailey, and in the vicinity of those solid and dismal granite walls which line a long extent of one side of the street; for here the famous courts of criminal justice are held,—the Sessions' House, or, as it was formerly called, the Justice Hall, being divided only by a broad yard from the prison of Newgate, with the history of which and of its successive inmates, the tribunals alluded to are so intimately connected.

This large scene of actual and regularly recurring romance, never fails to present to the accurate and reflecting observer, a field teeming with subjects for affording an insight into human life and character of very greatly diversified kinds and hues. How various the classes and the objects of those constituting the multitudes who congregate at this spot! How distinct and different their motives, feelings, and habits!

Witnesses against and for the unhappy,—too often the hardened,—accused ones, who are many; deeply interested relatives; and not a few thieves of every gradation, anxious to know how it is to fare with their associates within doors, mingle with that motley crowd, where, after all, the blue-coated people of the police force predominate, each some way concerned with one or more of those who are to stand their trials. Merchants and professional men fretful at the loss of time to which they are subjected, and still uneasy on account of the uncertainty when their testimony may be wanted; farmers utterly from home; country louts wholly puzzled at what they behold; small tradesmen in their Sunday garb; and costermongers who are no way particular how they look—these co-mingle in the ever fluctuating and changeful groups,—there being besides no lack of women folks, chiefly of the inferior orders, and no sparing of sharp-visaged attorneys to boot, ever surrounded by groups of eager questioners, or gliding from place to place, bearing with them an obvious sense of self-importance, as if each were not only an oracle of law, but as if the distribution of justice in a great measure was entrusted to him. In short, the scene which is every day presented during the sitting of the sessions at the Old Bailey is such as can be witnessed no where else; being on all occasions suggestive principally of circumstances and conditions of a painful and melancholy nature to those who are not familiar with them; and yet found calculated to arrest the passer-by and the thoughtful.

Such are the spectacles which,—for at least eight days out of every month in the year,—have been witnessed, from about nine o'clock in the morning till night, in the immediate vicinity of the Sessions House, ever since 1834, when the act was passed for the establishment of a Central Criminal Court. *Central*, it may well be called, seeing that here are tried offences and crimes of every class and kind, from treason down to the pettiest larceny, committed within the City of London, the County of Middlesex, and all those parts of the adjoining counties which lie within a certain sweeping distance of the metropolis,—thus including no inconsiderable portion of the entire population of England.

The judges of the Central Criminal Court are the Lord Mayor, the Lord Chancellor,—such is the order in the Act,—the judges who sit in the Courts of Queen's Bench, Common Pleas, and Exchequer at Westminster,—the Aldermen, Recorder, and Common Serjeant of London. Of these the Recorder and Common Serjeant are, in reality, the presiding authorities at a great proportion of the cases brought here for trial,—a judge of the law only assisting occasionally,—when for example unusual legal points are involved, or when conviction affects the life of the prisoner. As to juries, they are summoned indiscriminately from London and from the neighbouring districts over which the sphere of the court extends;—this Central tribunal being divided into two courts, both sitting at the same time, for the greater expedition of business; that business being in no essential different from what is transacted in the Courts of Assize throughout the country, except as regards the vast amount of prosecutions which here take place. Accordingly, although there be nothing very peculiar to witness or to impress the eyesight on entering the Old Court, for instance,—that being the chamber to which the ideas of those who have sedulously perused the Newgate Calendar must be rivetted,—yet when the multitude is considered of those who here stand trembling between life and death, or who, at least, are for a time kept in suspense whether imprisonment or liberty is to be their destiny—whether transportation to a penal colony, or the enjoyment of the freedom of their native land,—a glance of the interior of such a chamber, even when unoccupied by the judge and jury, cannot fail to awaken a throng of thought of the gravest and most arresting character. There, in that large square and unadorned apartment, the eye travels from the extended bench with its desks for the judges, to the dock under the gallery to which the accused are brought through a covered passage from a neighbouring gaol, and from which so many have passed back to the cell of the condemned, to be next brought forth to stand under the fatal beam. There you behold the witness-box, where so many have vainly sworn hard oaths to rescue the guilty, and where, too, so many timid and humane ones have reluctantly given testimony that fixed the doom of their fellow-beings. The box for the jurors is on the other hand,—those men whose duty it is to weigh and to pronounce upon the most conflicting evidence, and whose verdict is irrevocable. The very green-baized table, though denuded of its loads of law books, and rows of gentlemen with flowing gowns, and powdered wigs, has a mute language that speaks to the mind. But it is needless further to pursue these silent tokens, seeing that Elizabeth Brownrigg has just been conveyed from the criminal dock from the gaze of a crowded court with the sentence of death ringing in her ears, responded to and re-echoed with cheers from the dense masses without; sending with each shout and reverberation a deeper knell to her bosom,—such knells indeed, as can only be exceeded by those of a guilty conscience and the dread of a more terrible doom which the judge of all the earth will pronounce upon every impenitent transgressor.

Sentence of death had been pronounced against the convict, and her body ordered to be given up for dissection.—The following are extracts from the Ordinary of Newgate's account of the barbarian's behaviour both before and after her commitment to Newgate. In spite of all his best endeavours, his mildest and most pathetic means to convince her of her awful position, she stood out for a while in her hardihood At length, however, she became greatly agitated, and began to acknowledge her crimes, often crying out for God's mercy for having so cruelly murdered "that innocent child." She made open confession of her guilt, also that "She had for years feared God, and walked in his ways; had not only the forms of Godliness, but experienced much delight in the service of religion; that she attended public worship at every opportunity; and when she had a family of small children was constantly, for several years, at the early Sacrament at Bow-church, and habitually read prayers in her own family; but that she had lately neglected the same, frequently breaking the Sabbath, and that having forsaken God, he had permitted her heart to become hardened and to fall into those sins for which she was justly prosecuted."

After her conviction she seems to have lost no opportunity of confessing her crimes, and the justness of the condemnation which doomed her to die. On the morning of execution, continues the Ordinary, when she was brought into the Press-yard she seemed much resigned, and joined me for some time in prayer, crying "Lord deliver me from blood guiltiness." Her husband and son had been permitted to see her, and with them she continued for upwards of two hours, being much in prayer. She expressed great concern about her two younger children, when her husband assured her, that if he should be released from his confinement, he doubted not of being able to provide for them. "She then took a last farewell of them," says the Ordinary, "and shortly after was put into the cart to be conveyed to the place of execution (Tyburn). In my way there, my ears were dinned with the horrid imprecations of the people. One said to me, 'He hoped I should pray for her damnation, and not for her salvation.' Others exclaimed, 'That they hoped she would go to hell, and were sure the Devil would fetch her soul.' This unchristian conduct greatly shocked me; and I could not help exclaiming, 'Are these the people called Christians?' She being weak, desired me to acquaint the spectators that she acknowledged her guilt, and the justice of her sentence."

The punishment of the father and son for the misdemeanour was a period of imprisonment. In the *Gentleman's Magazine*, for 1783, there is the following short paragraph:

"Brownrigg, whose wife was executed some years ago for cruelty to her apprentice girl, threw himself out of a two-pair of stairs window (Thursday, June 5th), and was killed on the spot."

———

To the account of Mrs. Brownrigg's treatment of her apprentices might be added a considerable number of cases similar or analogous to it, which have occurred not only prior to the perpetration of the heinous and hideous crimes of which she was found guilty, but of a later date,—nay, of yesterday, so to speak. The enormities of the Birds and the Sloanes are of too recent occurrence, and the horror and loathing which agitated the public mind on the discovery of the monstrous cruelty of these inhuman miscreants too near to us, to allow of any further notice of them in these pages. It is gratifying, however, to learn that the legislature has in the course of the present session turned its attention to the subject, and that an act has been passed that will tend to the prevention of such atrocious barbarities for the future.

The trial of Mrs. Elizabeth Branch, and her daughter, Mary Branch, at the Assizes held at Taunton, on the 31st of March, 1740, cannot be so familiar to the reader as the very modern ones to which reference has now been made, and may therefore be appropriately cited.

Mrs. Branch w the youngest daughter of a gentleman of considerable fortune at Philips Norton, he county of Somerset. She was born in 1687, with a shapely formed tooth in ;um, as the account published at the period of her trial has it, the singular precocic cumstance being regarded as significant of a disposition naturally fierce and barbarous. When but a child, and still more flagrantly as she grew up, she manifested a cruel spirit, not only taking apparent delight in tormenting and killing such animals as she could thus use with impunity, but in imposing punishment upon her playfellows, whenever she could or dared to use them so; and by the time she arrived at womankind, the servants around her became the victims of her savage dealings. At this time of life, however,—having been much blamed by her parents for allowing her inhumanity to get so much influence over her, admonishing her to abandon her brutality, and warning her besides, that unless she cultivated better principles and exemplified a more amiable temper, she would never recommend herself to a wooer,—she suddenly evinced a great improvement both of manners and of feeling; curbing her ferocious passions, and manifesting inclinations more fitting her sex. At length she got not only a wooer but a husband, a Mr. Branch, who was a farmer at Hemmington. Yet it required but a very short time after their union for the poor man to discover that he had married a very fiend, for she not only began to display her wonted perversity, moroseness and barbarity to those over whom she considered herself to possess an irresponsible authority, but, as came to be alleged, she rendered the entrapped man's condition so miserable, as to hasten his death.

It was quite a practice for her to beat her servants with great severity, and to keep them whole days without food. It was also a part of her system to turn them out of doors in the coldest nights, without paying them their wages. Thus it was that she conducted herself; and the reason why her barbarities did not at once come to light, and expose her to severe censure and proper punishment was this—that Mr. Branch, being a good-natured and well-meaning man, used to pay the servants their wages when so discharged unknown to his wife, making them also all the amends in his power for the injuries, of whatever kind, which they had sustained. At length he died, leaving the widow and his daughter his whole estate, which amounted to about three hundred pounds a year. And now, henceforth, the virago could get no one to serve her who had any knowledge of her character. The consequence was, that she was obliged to hire strangers, strollers, or any poor person's child that was glad to get employment of any sort and any where. And what was rather remarkable, not only did she take pleasure in her barbarities, or at least practise them habitually, but she took care to train up her child to the same taste for inhumanity to the dependent and helpless, so that her daughter ere long became also a proficient in monstrous cruelty to her kind and sex. But the career of these wretches was to have a limit, the particulars of which may be learned from the summary of the judge who tried them, and which was to the following effect :—

Elizabeth Branch the mother, and Mary Branch the daughter, said he to the jury, have been arraigned for the murder of Anne Butterworth, their servant maid, on the 4th of

November last, at Kew House, Kennington. Anne Somers, the principal witness for the prosecution, tells you that she saw the prisoners beat and pinch the deceased, and whip her with saplings till she ran with blood; and that one of the prisoners took off the deceased's shoe, and beat her therewith about the hips and the seat of the body; and then she, Mary Branch, did throw a pail of water on the deceased, with the view as she pretended to cool her, and afterwards fetched salt and salted the wounds therewith. The evidence says, that the prisoners were at that time in the parlour, as well as the deceased, and that the former got sticks and brooms, both falling upon the poor girl in a savage manner, and that the salt was brought out of the kitchen for salting the seat of the deceased with. She also tells you that she went out a milking, and that on her return she found her two mistresses sitting by the fire in the parlour, and the deceased lying before the fire; that she said to Mrs. Branch, Anne Butterworth is dead; that her mistress called the deceased by a dirty name and had her put into a bed,—she, witness, having been obliged to lie down with the dead body all night, and that the deceased was privately buried, it being alleged by the prisoners that the poor girl died suddenly. Now, this evidence is partly positive as to the fact, and partly circumstantial; and you will find, gentlemen, that though the witness did not see the prisoners directly kill the deceased, yet on her return she found the deceased dead, and the prisoners in their defence say, there was nobody else in the house at that time,—so that it follows from these circumstances that they must have been the cause of the death. The surgeon who examined the body of the deceased, after it had been taken out of the grave,—for she was buried in the dead of night, without the neighbours, who were desirous of seeing the corpse, having an opportunity of doing so,—says that the blows the deceased received in her forehead were inflicted in her life time,—and he gives you a very good reason for so saying, telling you that wounds given in a plethoric state will be livid and blackish, and that there must have been a vast effusion of blood, from the appearance of some of the wounds, these being pale and of a cherry colour; also that the wounds must have been given in life, whilst the blood was in circulation; for, says he, when that is ended no blow or bruise will make such alterations in the colour of the flesh. This, gentlemen, is the substance of the evidence for the prosecution, and if you credit the testimony of Anne Somers, you will find the prisoners guilty. They, indeed, in their defence tell you, that the deceased was sent by them to a neighbouring place for some barm; that she stayed long of the errand; that they said some harsh words to her on her return; and that having on her head a pail of water, she fell over the sill of the door, bruised herself, thereafter falling into a fit, and dying suddenly. And then they contradicted themselves, for they tell you that some malicious persons had wounded the deceased in the forehead, when the body was taken out of the grave. But what the jury is to have particular regard to in the defence of the prisoners, is that part of it wherein they acknowledge having struck the deceased, saying that if they did hurt or were the occasion of the girl's death, it was not designedly, but accidentally. Now, gentlemen, if you shall be of opinion that the prisoners accidentally killed the deceased, then you will bring in a verdict of manslaughter. Still, I must tell you that you are to weigh and consider well the circumstances together; and to bear in mind that if it was a manslaughter, it was done hastily at one blow only. It might be that the prisoners had no design of killing the deceased when they made the first attack upon her; but the circumstances show that they deliberately and with many aggravating barbarities continued till they killed the deceased, if you credit the evidence. And if you so credit the testimony for the crown, you will bring in a verdict of guilty."

One circumstance came out on the trial of the two women, which found a parallel in the case of the Sloanes, of recent notoriety. In punishing a servant boy, they had, for a nuisance he committed, made him eat his own excrement.

After about an hour's deliberation, the jury returned into court with a finding of guilty, whereupon sentence of death was pronounced upon both prisoners. At the place of execution Mrs. Branch spoke as follows to the people :—

" You who are masters and mistresses of families, to you I speak in a more especial manner : let me advise you to take care that you never harbour cruel, base, and mean thoughts of your servants, as that they are your slaves and drudges, and that any sort of usage, be it ever so bad, is good enough for them. These and such like were the thoughts that led me to use my servants as slaves, vagabonds, and thieves; it was these thoughts that made me spurn and despise them, and led me on from one degree of cruelty to my fellow mortals to another. Keep your passions in due bounds, let them not get the mastery over you, lest they bring you to this ignoble end." Having declared, as on her defence, that she did not desire to murder her servant, she then added :—" Another caution I would give you, parents, is this, that you take care to suppress in your children the first appearance of cruelty and barbarity. Nothing at this moment grieves me so much under this dreadful shock, as that I have by my example and by my command, made my own daughter guilty with me of the same crimes, cruelties, and barbarities ; and that thereby I have involved her in the same punishment and ruin with myself. I beg of you to pray for me unto God, that my sins may be forgiven me, and that I may be received into mercy."

It must have been a dreadful spectacle, as it is a woful consideration, that a mother should have brought her own offspring to such an ignominious and violent end. One cannot but be deeply moved on reading what the young woman said, as soon as her parent had ceased :—" Good people !" cried she, " pity my unhappy case, who young was trained up in the paths of cruelty and barbarity ; and take a warning by my unhappy end, to avoid like crimes. You see I am here cut off in the prime of life, in the midst of my days. Good people, pray for me ! pray for me !"

The mother, the account adds, went up the ladder first, and the daughter after her. The execution took place at an early hour of the morning, and in all probability, but for this circumstance, the populace would have endeavoured to pull them to pieces, so greatly incensed was all the country round about against these inhuman murderers.

IV.—MARCHIONESS OF BRINVILLIERS.

UPON a fine morning in autumn, towards the end of the year 1665, as was not unusual in such weather, a number of people had collected upon that part of the Port Neuf which descends towards the Rue Dauphine. Immediately their attention was directed to a close carriage, the door of which one of the police endeavoured to open ; while of four assistants that were with him, two stopped the horses, as the others seized the coachman. The carriage-door having been forcibly opened, a young officer in a cavalry uniform jumped out, closing the door quickly after him, though not so speedily as to prevent the bystanders from observing a female upon the back seat, who appeared by the care with which she strove to conceal her features to be anxious to avoid observation or recognition.

The cavalry officer at once demanded, in an indignant and imperious tone, upon what authority the carriage had been so violently and rudely arrested? and had in return, in the first place, the question put to him, "Are you the Chevalier Gaudin de Sainte-Croix?" Having acknowledged that he was the individual mentioned, a *lettre de cachet* was shown him; and having at a glance perceived that the signature of the minister of police was attached to it, he submitted to the authority, only with a haughty bearing and as much composure as he could assume, insisting that the lady should no longer be made the object of an impertinent curiosity on the part of the bystanders, and that she should be allowed to proceed on her way without further molestation. No objection being felt to this request, the carriage drove on, while the prisoner, with all possible expedition, was conducted to a cell in the Bastille, where a feeble light sometimes penetrated, but fresh air never.

The chevalier was, according to the report of some, the natural child of a French noble, but, in the belief of others, the son of poor parents, a circumstance which he regarded with such reluctance that he preferred a titled illegitimacy. As to his present rank in the army, he was a captain in the regiment of Tracy, and was, in respect of age, about twenty-eight or thirty years. He was handsome in person, with an expressive and intellectual countenance; a boon companion and a gallant officer; was very susceptible of the tender passion; apt to be jealous, were it but concerning a mistress; and prodigal as a prince, yet without an income. Towards the year 1660, while serving in the army, he had formed an acquaintanceship with the Marquis de Brinvilliers, then a colonel in the regiment of Normandy. The similarity of their ages and professions, of their tastes and principles, tended to bind them the more intimately together, so that upon the return of the army, the marquis presented the chevalier to his young wife, and he became domesticated in the family. This intimacy was productive of consequences by no means rare in the higher circles. The marchioness was at the period in all the splendour of her beauty. Her figure was small, but exquisitely modelled. Her features were charmingly delicate and most regular; and what was very remarkable, she had such a command over the expressions of her countenance, that she could render them proof against manifesting any internal emotion, or to speak her mind with passionate power. Sainte-Croix and this lady became, from the first, mutually attached. As for the marquis, he either did not see the truth, or did not care for the fact; betraying no jealousy, but pursuing a course of most reckless extravagance and profligacy, at length involving him in such embarrassments, that his young wife, who no longer loved him, but had abandoned herself to the chevalier, demanded and obtained a separation. At the time of her marriage the marquis possessed an income of thirty thousand livres, and to this she brought a dowry of two hundred thousand in addition, besides what might accrue to her from any hereditary possessions. Her name was Marie Madaleine; she had two brothers and a sister, and her father, M. Dreux D'Aubray, was *lieutenant civil* of the Chatelet at Paris. Such was the position of some of the more prominent persons in the history of the romance in real life into which we are entering.

Having quitted her husband's house, and observing no further restraint, the marchioness lived openly in the society of Sainte-Croix, a system of conduct which, being authorised by the daily examples of the French aristocracy of that period, in no degree appeared to affect the marquis, who continued his ruinous career without evincing the slightest concern relative to his wife's proceedings. But it was otherwise with her father, who felt shocked at her conduct, affecting as it did his reputation; and therefore he obtained the *lettre de cachet*, authorising the arrest of Sainte-Croix, wherever he might be found.

Accordingly, he was sent to the Bastille in the manner and at the time already mentioned, exchanging the society of the beautiful young lady for that of another personage, who figures to some extent in the present tragedy.

As the story of the Marchioness of Brinvilliers is told by M. Alexander Dumas, in his "Crimes Célèbres," a dramatic scene occurred in the cell to which the chevalier was confined, immediately after finding the bolts harshly grate upon his ears that were to bar him from liberty. By means of the faint rays of light that reached the gloomy abode, his eye alighted upon a ghastly form in the same apartment, being that of another prisoner, who, on hearing the curses which Sainte Croix bestowed upon those who had torn him from his pleasures, and blasphemies upon the Deity for permitting the like, at the same time inviting the aid of every power, whatever it might be, that would restore him to revenge—presented himself, and proffered his best services to the maddened captain. On St. Croix demanding who and what he was that so promptly volunteered his help, the answer received was to the effect, that his fellow prisoner was no other than the Italian Exili, a man not only fearfully celebrated throughout France, but Italy, on account of his numerous murders by means of poison, of which, however, it had been found impossible to procure sufficient proof to convict him, and consign him to capital execution. Exili had come from Rome to Paris, where, as in his native country, he soon attracted the notice of the police; and here, although the legal evidence was defective, yet that of a moral nature was held to be sufficient to authorise his imprisonment for a time in the Bastille. To the companionship of such a being was the chevalier doomed; the governor of the prison being unaware that he was thus yoking together two demons. As the lively French writer just named observes, the character of Sainte Croix, by its good and evil qualities, its strange combination of virtuous and vicious principles, had now reached such a crisis, as was most likely to determine the mastery of one or other of these incentives, and when, had an angel of light met him in his path, he had probably been conducted to heaven, whereas a fiend encountered him, and he was led downward to destruction. At first the chevalier shuddered on coming into contact with the notorious Italian, but the repugnance soon passed away, on listening to the man who was one of the most skilful masters for making scholars of willing pupils; in fact, Exili was no common practitioner—he was an adept in poisoning. To him murder had become an art; he had reduced it to fixed principles, and such was the eminence in its exercise that he had attained, that he seemed to pursue it less from interest, than a love of experiment and excitement.

It is probable enough that Sainte Croix at first was appalled by the representations of the Italian, although such a man could not but be anxious to obtain the means of terrible revenge which the revelations and the co-operation of such a fell adherent promised. This, however, appears to be certain, when, after about a year's association as prisoners, first one and then the other of the pair were liberated, the chevalier had so profited by the experiments and teachings of Exili, that he thought himself to be nearly as well initiated in the science of murder as was his tutor. He was acquainted now with powders and liquids, of some of which it is the property to consume by slow degrees, and of others to be so rapid in their effects that they strike d   '·· the lightning, without time for the victims to lend utterance to their agony. He   ome to cherish an interest in the terrible game which was to place the lives of all who came near to him, or into whose society he might insinuate himself, within his resistless power. He re-entered the world not only thirsting for revenge, but feeling that it would be sweet and gratifying.

Soon after the release of the teacher and the taught, apartments were hired for Exili, the cavalier having been the first that was liberated, for the Italian was to pass as the dependent of the other. Whether the Marchioness of Brinvilliers had visited her paramour during his imprisonment or not is unknown; but it is certain that after his liberation they were more intimate, if possible, than before, although past experience had taught them the necessity of more caution. Meanwhile, it was resolved between them to make an early trial of the science acquired by the chevalier, and M. D'Aubray, the father of the marchioness, was selected by the guilty lovers for the first victim. Were he dead, the daughter would be freed from a rigid censor and the opponent of her infamous passion; while her losses, through the extravagance of her husband, would be repaired in consequence of the inheritance of a portion of her father's property. But a blow thus struck must be a decisive one; so it was arranged that the poison should first be tested upon another. Accordingly, one morning, when her maid, Françoise Roussel, entered her room after breakfast, the marchioness gave her a slice of ham and some preserved gooseberries. The poor girl, without suspicion, eat of what she had thus received; but hardly had she done so, when she became ill; however, she recovered, and the marchioness, in consequence, immediately received from her paramour another and a more efficacious poison.

The period for the experiment arrived. M. D'Aubray was to pass the vacation at his villa of Offemont, his daughter offering to accompany him, which circumstance helped to strengthen his belief that she had broken off all connexion with Sainte Croix. Offemont was a place well adapted for the perpetration of the crime. Situated in the forest of Aigne, about four leagues from Compeigne, poison might do its work before succour could be obtained. M. D'Aubray set out with his daughter and a single servant. Never had the marchioness before bestowed such sedulous attention upon her parent as now. Now, too, she availed herself of her extraordinary power over her emotions. Ever by her father's side, sleeping in the room adjoining, taking all her meals with him, incessant in the most delicate attentions and the kindliest offices, allowing none to wait upon him but herself, yet amid all these tender assiduities, with her dreadful project ever in her thoughts, how is it possible to figure to oneself a more deceptive fiend,—a more smiling demon? It was while manifesting this outward affection and gentleness, yet cherishing an infernal design, that she one day presented to her parent a poisoned soup. He received it fondly from her hands, she with soothing attention watching him as he partook of it; and upon her face of alabaster no trace appeared of that awful anxiety which must have compressed her heart. Then when he had taken the soup, she received without the slightest apparent emotion the cup from his hand, and retired to her adjoining chamber, listening and awaiting the result. The effect was speedy; she heard the cries and groans of her father, and hastened to him.

The emotions of the marchioness betrayed the deepest anxiety, which her father, amid his cruel sufferings, endeavoured to alleviate, by assuring her it was merely a sudden and transitory illness, for which he was averse to call in medical skill. At length, however, the symptoms growing more alarmingly violent, he yielded to his daughter's entreaties, and gave orders all owed for a physician. He came at eight the following morning, but being only enabled to judge of the indisposition from the account given by M. D'Aubray and his daughter, he pronounced it to be a fit of indigestion, prescribed accordingly, and returned to Compeigne. The marchioness now never quitted the patient. Her bed was removed into his room; she alone tended him; and thus it was that she most narrowly and incessantly watched the progress of the terrible malady which she had brought upon her parent.

The physician returned in the morning; M. D'Aubray was worse; for though the vomitings had ceased, the internal pain was more excruciating than before,—a strange heat seeming to consume his bowels. To remove to Paris was now proposed, in order to obtain the best advice and assistance; but the patient had become so weak that it was doubtful whether he would be able to bear the fatigues of the journey. The marchioness, however, was most earnest for the removal, and her father acceded to the proposal, reclining in the carriage with his head resting upon her bosom during the journey. Everything had proceeded to her wish. The scene was changed; the physician who had seen the earlier symptoms would not witness the final struggles or the agonies of death; and in tracing the progress of the illness, no one would be present to speak. Thus the thread of inquiry had been broken, and its shreds were now too far apart to be reunited. M. D'Aubray continued to grow worse and worse but reached Paris alive, where he expired after an agony of four days, in the arms of the weeping murderess, upon whom with his last breath he bestowed blessings and heaped thanks for her unexampled tenderness to him during his last illness. No one dreamt a suspicion of the parricide; no examination of the body took place; and the tomb closed upon the murdered one without anything more remarkable attending the departure of the worthy man than what attaches to the decease of the grey-haired after a short illness, excepting the apparently deep grief, which for a time refused to be soothed, of her who destroyed him.

The objects which had begun to be contemplated by the marchioness and her paramour were not yet fully attained. She had got rid of a rigid censor and a vigilant eye; and Sainte-Croix had got his revenge in some measure slaked. But M. D'Aubray's will did not realise all the expectations of the guilty lovers; the greater part of his property descended to his two sons; and hence the daughter's fortune was but slightly increased. Meanwhile the chevalier still pursued his extravagant course of life, and needed money. He had a steward and three footmen, beside a carriage and equipages; and as he was young, handsome, and an acquaintance of some distinguished people, as well as the accepted lover of the stately Marchioness of Brinvilliers, tradesmen and others did not particularly inquire into his revenue.

After the lapse of the usual period of mourning the marchioness and Sainte-Croix openly resumed their intercourse. Her brothers now remonstrated through the medium of the younger sister, then in a Carmelite convent, the marchioness at the same time hearing that her father had enjoined on them the duty of her moral guidance. Her first crime she found to be almost fruitless. She had hoped to free herself from the remonstrances of her parent, and to share his fortune; yet her inheritance barely sufficed to pay her debts, while the father's censures were continued by her brothers, the elder of whom was president of the civil tribunal, and could separate her again from her lover: the younger was a Parliamentary counsellor, whose influence was not slight, and might be used to curb her in if she proved obstinate. Now these inconveniences were to be remedied, according to the tactics which the guilty lovers had fixed upon. One of Sainte-Croix's footmen, named Lachaussée, quitted his service, when, through the influence of the marchioness, the man was taken into the employ of her brothers. But this time, the better to avoid suspicion, it was determined on to make use of a poison less rapid in its action than that which had destroyed the father. They recommenced their operations. The marchioness was regarded as a charitable lady, ever ready to relieve

DESGRAIS THROWING OFF HIS DISGUISE.   [*See page* 54.

the distressed, and to share with the Sisters of Mercy the attendance upon the sick, to whom she sent wine and medicine at the hospitals. Hence it caused no surprise to see her at the Hotel Dieu, distributing biscuits and preserved fruits to the convalescent. One month after this she re-visited the hospital, to inquire after some patients in whose welfare she was much interested. She was informed they had suffered a relapse, that fresh symptoms had presented themselves, that a deadly languor overcame them, beneath whose influence they gradually wasted away. Of its cause the doctors at the institution could tell her nothing ; they said the disease was unknown, defying their utmost skill. Again, at the expiration of a fortnight, she made more inquiry : some of the patients were dead, others still lingered in hopeless agony, mere animated skeletons, whose only signs of life were the voice, sight, and breath. Within two months all were dead to whom she had administered biscuits, dried fruits, &c., medical skill having been equally foiled upon their examination after death, as it had been in their treatment while living. Such success was most encouraging to the marchioness and her paramour ; and Lachaussee, who was still in the service of the brothers of the murderess, received a command to fulfil his mission.

It was about this time, namely, the beginning of April, 1670, that the brothers of the marchioness went to spend the Easter holidays in the country, Lachaussée accompanying them. The day after their arrival a pigeon pie was placed on the table at dinner ; seven who partook of it were soon taken ill ; three who had not were unaffected. Singular enough, those on whom the poison took the strongest effect were the two brothers : perhaps they were known to be partial to the dish mentioned. Here, as before, all medical aid proved powerless. They returned to Paris, both so changed that they seemed to have been the victims of a protracted and most painful illness.

The marchioness was at this time residing in the country, where she remained during the illness of her brothers. At the very first consultation all hope of saving the life of the president was relinquished by the physicians. His case was similar to that of his father. For the three last days of his life he complained as if a fire were constantly raging in his chest, the flames of which were indicated by the aspect of his eyes, these continuing terribly animated even kindled up when death had obtained the mastery over the rest of his body. He died on the 17th of June, 1670. Suspicions were excited, and a post mortem examination took place, but the doctors would not affirm the death to have occurred from other than natural causes. At the end of the next three months the other brother died, many of his symptoms having been similar to those of the predeceased, though the destruction had made slower progress. He was subject to violent paroxysms of mind besides those of his body, that allowed him no repose, which additional symptom may in part be accounted for, in the extreme eagerness to be assured of the malady which carried off the other two of the family, the anxiety about the real cause of their deaths, and the desire yet to defend his own life. But at length he sunk under the subtle poison, of whose ravages, however, as yet, no certain evidence could be obtained. With regard to the minister of the guilty and murderous lovers, the man Lachaussée, so far was suspicion from alighting upon him, that the counsellor left him a sum of one hundred crowns, in consideration of his attentions.

Events of such a strange nature, so frequent and fatal in one family, could not always escape suspicion. True, no conjectures hitherto were levelled towards the marchioness or her lover, the former going into mourning, and the other pursuing his course of extravagance as before; and now it was said he must have discovered the philosopher's stone. In society he had made acquaintance with many of the nobility, and formed friendships with men of fortune, amongst the latter of whom was Reich de Penautier, a millionaire, the receiver-general of the clergy, and treasurer of the estates of Languedoc,—one of those people with whom all things succeed; and who seem by the power of money to give laws to creation. Penautier was connected in business with his head clerk, who died suddenly of apoplexy, an event which was known to him before the man's family were made acquainted with it; all papers relative to their partnership disappearing, so that the widow and her children were left wholly destitute. The clerk's brother-in-law commenced an inquiry upon some vague rumours as to the cause of the man's death, but the relative who so unseasonably stepped forward, himself died suddenly also. Penautier, the friend of Sainte-Croix, rich as he was, and at the head of lucrative offices, still longed for other appointments, one of these having been held by a personage of the name of Saint Laurent, with whom Sainte-Croix had also not only formed an intimacy, but to whom he recommended one of the three grooms already alluded to, whose name was George. The chevalier's old servant was not long in the employ of Saint Laurent before the latter was taken ill; the symptoms in every respect resembling those of M. de Aubray and his sons, but terminating much more rapidly in death. Penautier now stepped into the vacant office, no doubt handsomely rewarding Sainte-Croix. But as suspicion was entertained by the new made widow of foul play having been used for the removal of her husband, the body was ordered to be opened. Upon learning what steps were to be taken, George, Sainte-Croix's old servant, disappeared without requiring his wages, greatly strengthening the doubts which were at first entertained by the widow. To render the suspicions relative to the runaway still deeper, an abbé, a particular friend of the deceased, aware of the sudden disappearance of George, happened to meet the man some days after in a street near the Sorbonne. They were both on the same side, and a hay-cart which was passing at the time stopped up the way. George, who at this moment recognised the abbé, rushed beneath the waggon in a crouching posture, at the risk of being crushed to death as it proceeded, and passed through below it, thus escaping from the mere sight of a person whose presence recalled at once his crime, and made him tremble for its retribution.

At the instance of Madame de Saint Laurent, active search was made for George, but the fellow escaped. Meanwhile rumours of so many strange and unexplained deaths were widely circulated in Paris; in the gay saloons of which their frequent discussion gave Sainte-Croix no small degree of inquietude. No suspicion as yet rested upon him as being in any way connected with the sad events, but precaution, he felt, was most necessary; so that he bethought himself of obtaining a situation, which would place him beyond the reach of rumour and of danger. A vacancy was about to occur in the king's household, of which the purchase-money was one hundred thousand crowns; and although without any known income, it was stated that he was about to give this sum. Still, he pursued his chemical experiments in an obscure part of the city, while his proper place of residence was in the street *des Bernardins.* Yes, his manipulations in regard to the preparations of subtle poisons were conducted with all possible secrecy; a just retribution, however, being at no great distance. Already he was so ill, although ignorant of the cause, that unable at length to quit his dwelling-house, he had got a furnace brought to him, that he might still continue his experiments. He was at this time engaged in researches into the nature of a poison so subtle, that its mere emanation was fatal. He had heard of the poisoned napkin that the eldest brother of Charles VII. had used, whilst playing at tennis, and tradition had related to him the history of the gloves of Jeanne d'Albert. These were secrets which, though now lost, Sainte-Croix hoped to recover. It was amid these fearful occupations, at the moment when bending over his furnace, watching, no doubt, the deadly operation approach its greatest intensity, that the glass mask worn by him as a protection against its fumes, went to pieces, and the agent or accomplice of so many murders, by means of his fell knowledge and preparations, was struck down as by a thunderbolt. His wife—for the villain was a married man,—surprised that he remained an unusually long time in his laboratory, repaired thither, and found him lying extended and quite lifeless, near to the furnace, the fragments of the glass mask round him. It was impossible for her to conceal the circumstances of his death; the servants had seen the body and could reveal the facts. The proper functionary was, therefore, required to put everything under seal; thus insuring a proper scrutiny into the affairs and conduct of the deceased.

The tidings of the chevalier's death flew rapidly abroad, for he had been a public character, and the report was that he was about to purchase an important place at court. Lachaussée was amongst the first who heard of his death; and this fellow knowing that the rooms of his former master were in possession of the authorities, he made the most anxious endeavours to obtain hold of some money and papers, which he declared to belong to him, but received for answer that he must wait the removal of the seals. Nor was Lachaussée the only one who became seriously alarmed by the death of Sainte-Croix; for the Marchioness of Brinvilliers, to whom the secrets of the fatal cabinets now sealed were familiar, no sooner heard of the sudden death of her paramour, than she hastened to the functionary who had set his seal to the places and things referred to; and, although it was late at night, requested an immediate interview, and desiring that a particular casket should be given up to her. Her entreaties were unavailing, although she offered fifty louis for the article. No time was now to be lost; she set out immediately from her mansion, in the street Neuve Saint-Paul, to her country-house, and thence proceeded to Liege, where she took refuge in a convent.

At length the necessary functionary and his officers proceeded to look over the property and articles which had been under the authoritative seal, one of the first objects which arrested their attention proving to be the very casket that the marchioness had been so eager to get into her possession,—that same eagerness having aroused an unusual curiosity to ascertain the nature of its contents. It was about a foot square, upon opening of which a half-sheet of paper appeared, entitled "My Will," whereon the most positive injunctions were written that the casket with its contents should be conveyed to the marchioness at his death; but that if her decease should precede his own, that the whole should be burnt, "inasmuch as whatever it contains belongs to her alone, and that there is nothing in it of any use to another." The paper also bore an order and injunction in the following words: "There is a packet, directed to M. Penautier, which should be delivered up." Such an opening increased the interest of the scene, and the inventory was proceeded with in silence.

A number of most carefully sealed up packets were met with, several of them containing strange chemical mixtures, others poisons; phials were found containing remarkable liquids, and other singular substances also presented themselves. There was a small box in which was a kind of stone, designated "the infernal stone;" also a packet endorsed— "to be burnt in case of my death," in which were thirty-four letters, said at the time to be in the handwriting of the marchioness; also another packet in which were twenty-seven pieces of paper, each endorsed—"Many curious secrets." Besides these and similar extraordinary objects and descriptions, two bonds were found, one from the marchioness, the other from Penautier; the former corresponding in date with the death of M. d'Aubray the father, the latter with that of Saint Laurent, the difference of money amount showing that, according to the tariff of Sainte Croix, parricide was more expensive than a mere common assassination. At the moment of his death also he had bequeathed his poisons to his mistress and his friend: he had not revelled sufficiently deep in crime, he desired to be a party in murder even after death.

The first care of the officers, after having made these strange discoveries, in the course of the inventory, was to analyse the contents of the packets, and to test them upon various animals. The following is part of the report which resulted from these proceedings :— After describing the careful preparation, subtle qualities, and fatal properties of one of the poisonous compounds, the account proceeds thus: "In water the weight of the poison commonly throws it down, or the former rises and the poison is precipitated. Fire consumes and dissipates what there is of harmless and pure, and leaves only an acrid, pungent matter, which resists its influence. The effect that the poison produces on animals is still more sensible, its malignity being uniform wheresoever it spreads, vitiating all it touches, and consuming the intestines by a violent and strange inflammation. Still, in animals, its appearance is so carefully concealed, that it cannot be detected; every part is separately endowed with life, whilst death circulates in the veins, leaving no trace behind of its existence. Every kind of test has been applied; the first by pouring some drops of the liquid found in one of the phials, in oil of tartar and sea water; and nothing was precipitated at the bottom of the vessels into which it was poured. The second, by pouring the same liquid into a sanded vessel, left no matter dry or acrid to the tongue, nor scarcely any fixed salt was found. The third was upon a turkey hen, a pigeon, a dog, and other animals; and upon dissection a small portion of coagulated blood upon the ventricle of the heart was all that could be traced of its action. Two other experiments upon a cat and a pigeon, by a white powder, gave similar results; death was in both cases gradual, but left scarcely any trace of its cause."

These discoveries and results, whilst proving the extent of Sainte-Croix's chemical knowledge, excited the suspicion that he had not gratuitously employed his art. And now the late deaths, so sudden and remarkable, occurred to all. The bonds of the Marchioness of Brinvilliers and Penautier proved the existence of covenants of blood; but as one was absent, and the other too rich and powerful easily to be reached and arrested without strong proof of their guilt, Lachausée was thought of, who had manifested such an anxiety to obtain some property which he alleged belonged to him that remained in the possession of the chevalier. Besides, the man had been in the service of Sainte-Croix for seven years, including the period of his attendance upon the brothers of the marchioness. He was brought before the proper tribunal, where he firmly denied the charges preferred against him of guilty knowledge relative to his late master's proceedings and property. According to the barbarous law of the period, there being a deficiency of proof otherwise, Lachaussée was put to the torture, a mode of examination which was employed when the judges, not being convinced, desired to obtain direct proof from the avowals of a culprit, prior to their passing sentence; and also after judgment had been given, with a view to discover the prisoner's accomplices.

The man underwent these terrible proceedings, which in his case was that of the *boot*, a process which consisted in placing each limb of the prisoner between two wooden boards, and then compressing them together by a ring of iron, after which wedges were driven down the wooden frames. The ordinary torture was four, the extraordinary eight wedges. At the third wedge, Lachaussée declared he was ready to confess. The torture was thereupon remitted. He was placed upon a mattress, and being unable to speak, he requested half-an-hour to regain sufficient strength to do so.

Upon his recovery, the wretch admitted his guilt, at the same time declaring that Sainte-Croix and the marchioness had employed him to poison her brothers; adding that the chevalier had intended to poison the sister-in-law of the marchioness, the wife of one of her brothers, viz., the president of the civil court. Lachaussée was condemned to be broken alive on the wheel, and there to expire. By the same decree the marchioness was condemned to have her head cut off. The Italian, Exili, the principal in one sense of all this evil, with whom Sainte-Croix had for a long time kept up an intimacy,—thence acquiring much, if not most of the chemical skill which he turned to such direful purpose, disappeared like another Mephistophiles after the destruction of Faust, and no one heard more of him. Thus we have arrived at the close of the First Act of the dreadful drama; we now enter upon the Second, in which the Marchioness of Brinvilliers is by far the most prominent character, being meanwhile within a sanctuary, the convent at Liege.

Although the marchioness was in a convent, it appears that she had by no means renounced certain earthly indulgences. She soon became reconciled to the death of Sainte-Croix, whom she had loved so much as at one time to threaten suicide on his account, and appointed as his successor a person named Theria, of whom, however, beyond his name, no information remains. Meanwhile, as every new discovery made relating to her intimacy with the deceased chevalier, and their mutual proceedings, the more deeply implicated her, it was resolved to pursue her even into the retreat where she conceived herself in safety. Yet this was an undertaking of great difficulty, and requiring the utmost address. Desgrais, one of the most active of officers, offered to take the conduct of the commission. He was a handsome man of about thirty-six or thirty-eight years of age, whose appearance in no way betrayed his employment; assuming all characters with equal ease, associating with every grade of society, under his disguise, from the most miserable beggar to the greatest lord. His offer was accepted. Accordingly he departed for Liege, escorted by a body of archers, and furnished with a letter from the king, addressed to the Municipal Council of Sixty, by which Louis XIV. reclaimed the marchioness. The council, upon the perusal of the demand, ordered her to be delivered up to Desgrais. This was much, yet not enough for the purpose desired; for he dared not arrest the marchioness in the convent for two very important reasons,—first, because, if made acquainted of his intentions, she might readily find concealment in some of the cloistered retreats known only to the superiors of the establishment; and secondly, because an attempt of this kind in so religious a city as Liege, would be considered a profanation, and might lead to some popular excitement, by means of which she might be enabled to escape with triumph.

Desgrais now considered what disguise he should assume, and thinking that of an abbè the least likely to excite suspicion, he presented himself at the gates of the convent as a compatriot returning from Rome, who was unwilling to pass through Liege without paying his respects to a lady so distinguished by her accomplishments and misfortunes as the marchioness. Desgrais put on all the manners of one of patrician family; and, flattering as a courtier, adventurous as a hero, charming alike by his vivacity and his self-reliance, this visit failed not to secure for him the invitation to pass another. He was not slow to take advantage of the favour; he returned early next day, and was even more cordially received than before. Intellectual, and accustomed to good society, of which lately she had been deprived, the marchioness found in Desgrais the refined manners of her Parisian circles. The charming abbè affected to be obliged to quit Liege almost immediately; he was consequently the more urgent for another interview; and this was arranged for the next day, with all the usual forms of a rendezvous. He was of course punctual, and had been impatiently expected; but by a conjunction of circumstances, which had doubtless been created by the expert police officer himself, their agreeable conference was continually interrupted, and this, too, precisely at the moment when witnesses were most inconvenient. Desgrais professed to feel exceedingly hurt at the occurrence of these ill-timed interruptions, and spoke of the danger of both of them being compromised thereby. All this he followed up by beseeching the marchioness to grant him a meeting beyond the city, at a place where they should neither be recognised nor followed. The marchioness met Desgrais at the appointed spot, when, on taking her by the hand, he made a signal,—the archers advanced,—the lover removed his mask,— and the wretched lady was made a prisoner. The officer upon this returned immediately to the convent, produced his order from the Council of Sixty, by which he got access to the room of the marchioness, where beneath her bed he found a casket, which he immediately sealed up and brought away. When she beheld this in his hands, the sight appeared wholly to overwhelm her; but, recovering herself, she claimed from him a paper which it contained, entitled her *Confession*. The request was, of course, refused;

and as he turned to give orders to set forward directly for Paris, she endeavoured to choke herself by swallowing a pin, but was prevented. At the place where they halted in the evening for supper, the knives, forks, and everything with which self-destruction could be attempted, were removed. Whereupon the marchioness bit a piece from the glass out of which she was drinking, but was prevented from swallowing it as before. She then said to Barbier, one of those who guarded her, that if he would save her she would amply reward him, proposing for that purpose the assassination of Desgrais. This, however, the man declined, but offered to serve her in any other way in his power. Thereupon, she asked for pen, ink, and paper, and wrote the following :—

"My dear Theria,—I am in the custody of Desgrais, who is forcibly carrying me from Liege to Paris. Come and release me."

Barbier took the writing, and promised to deliver it as addressed, but instead of doing as he said, it was placed in the hands of Desgrais. Next day she sent another, acquainting her paramour that as the escort consisted of only eight persons, four or five determined men might readily defeat them, and that she reckoned upon his making the attempt. At last, anxious from not receiving any answer, nor observing any indication of an endeavour to fulfil her requests, she despatched a third, in which she besought Theria, if he were not able to attack the escort and free her, at least to slay two of the four horses which belonged to it, and to profit by the confusion this would cause, to gain possession of the casket, and destroy it, as without this she was inevitably lost. At Rocroy, the escort was met by the Counsellor Palluau, whom the Parliament had empowered to meet the prisoner on her way, and to submit her to an unexpected examination, so that being thus taken by surprise, she should not have had time for preparation. Desgrais made him acquainted with every previously ascertained fact, and also placed in his hands the casket which had been a point of such extreme solicitude to the marchioness. Palluau opened it, and found, amongst others, the paper entitled "My Confession."

This confession furnished a strange proof of the necessity which constrains the guilty, even in the most enormous cases of crime, to confide the secret either to the keeping of man or to the mercy of God. One would pronounce the preservation of such a record as she had drawn out, to be no less than a monstrous infatuation. The account was comprised in seven articles, and commenced thus :—"I confess myself to God, and to you, my Father,"—being a complete narrative of her crimes. In one of the articles she confessed to have been an incendiary; in another, to have commenced her unchaste life at seven years of age; in another, to have poisoned her father; in others to have poisoned her brothers, to have attempted to poison her sister, and to have indulged in strange and unheard of debaucheries, which she recited; the world, ancient and modern, does not seem to offer anything more disgustingly flagitious or fiendishly heinous than did this woman.

Not only in the preliminary examination by Palluau, on the way to Paris, but after her arrival there, when before the judges that sat upon her trial, the marchioness confined herself to a complete system of forgetfulness or of flat denial in her answers. For many hours together, and this on several occasions, she maintained, with the utmost respect towards the court, the proudest contempt towards the witnesses that testified against her. The evidence, however, was overwhelming, although her defence was committed to M. Nivelle, one of the most celebrated advocates of France. One female witness, for example, testified that the marchioness on a certain occasion, when rather animated after a party, said to her, showing her a little box, " See ! this is the way to avenge yourself of your enemies, and, small as this box is, it is full of inheritances." It was also sworn to that both the marchioness and Sainte-Croix had, for a length of time, always poison about them in case of arrest, and which might, of course, be in any way used as suited their views.

Even before the close of the trial, it was manifest to all who were acquainted with what had been elicited regarding the wretched prisoner, that an awful sentence of condemnation would be pronounced against her, a conclusion at which she herself could not fail to arrive when on the 16th of July, 1676, she beheld M. Pirot, doctor of the Sorbonne, enter her cell in the Conciergerie, which he did at the request of the president of the court before which she was arraigned. The considerate and humane judge, foreseeing the result of the trial, and thinking that spiritual assistance should not be withheld until the last hour, had obtained an interview with the good priest, who, although Pirot observed to the judge there were already two of the sacred order attached to the prison, and that he was hardly adequate to the task,—unable as he was to endure the sight of blood, —yet consented. The good priest was the more easily persuaded to yield to the benevolent request, on hearing the judge's assurance that, accustomed as he was to the recklessness of crime, the marchioness surpassed all that had come before him, and that she was endowed with a self-possession which had something fearful in its character.

The marchioness had just returned from the court when Pirot entered, where she had for three hours persisted in her course of denial, although the president, in reminding her of her awful situation,—appearing for the last time before a human tribunal, and so soon to be ushered into the presence of God,—had done this in a manner so touching, that the oldest judges, and those most accustomed to such scenes, shed tears. As soon, therefore, as she beheld the priest enter her prison apartment, not doubting that he came as the messenger of death, she advanced towards him, saying :—

"You come then, sir, to announce ———"

Upon this she was interrupted by one of the priests of the prison who accompanied the doctor of the Sorbonne.

"Madame," said he, "let us first commence by prayer."

They knelt together, the marchioness requesting the attendants to add for her sake a prayer to the Virgin : then at the conclusion of their supplications, she recommenced, addressing Pirot :—

"Assuredly, sir, you come at the request of the president to console me, and it is with you that I must pass the little which remains to me of life."

"Madame," replied the doctor ; "I come to administer to you all the spiritual consolation in my power. I can only wish it were not on an occasion like this."

"Sir," cried the marchioness, "we must resign ourselves to our misfortunes ;" then turning to the other priest, "Father," she continued, "I am obliged to you for this introduction of M. Pirot, and for your promised visits to me. Pray to God, I beseech you, for me. For the future I shall only address myself to your friend here, as I must confer with him on matters which admit no other hearer. Farewell, and may God reward you for the kindness you would so willingly have exercised towards me."

Upon this the priest so addressed withdrew, leaving the marchioness with Pirot, and the prison attendants, who kept as far aloof as the limits of the apartment would permit. Thus freed from listeners, and believing that her sentence had been already pronounced, she commenced a conversation with the doctor relative to it, but was answered that at present this was not the case ; adding that he did not know precisely when it would be, nor what might be the result.

"I have no anxiety about the future," she replied; "if my sentence be not yet passed it will be to-morrow. I expect it to be death; and the only hope I indulge is that of some delay between judgment and its execution; for were I led forth to die to-day, I should have but little time to prepare, and I am sensible, sir, how much need I have of more. Yes," continued she, after a pause, "the more I reflect the more I am convinced a day is far too short a respite to fit me to appear before the tribunal of my Maker, to abide His judgment, having suffered that of man."

Upon hearing her thus speak, Pirot assured her, that should even sentence of death be pronounced that day, it would not be executed until to-morrow. "Yet," added he, "though the hour of death be yet uncertain, I approve of your resolution to prepare for it as though it were declared."

It was thus the conversation for some time was carried on, the marchioness intimating her intention to confess the events of her life, being desirous, however, in the first place to ascertain the opinion of the doctor as to her innocence or guilt, and what course he would now recommend her to adopt. Pirot replied that he was well aware of the fearful crimes charged against her; and that it was impossible to hope for pardon from God, unless she revealed not only the nature of the poison, but its antidote, and also the names of her accomplices; that this reparation was due to society, and that without this, as the system might be continued, she would be accountable for the crimes by such means committed after her death; and to crime in death, added he, there is no remission of punishment: to obtain this remission, our crimes must perish first. With these sentiments the marchioness coincided; then anxiously inquired whether there were not sins of so deep a dye, so fearful in number, that the church dared not remit them; and, if the justice of heaven could enumerate, was it possible for its mercy to forgive them. Pirot upon this said, whilst his heart recoiled from her with dread and horror, that there were no sins to which mercy could not be extended; that this was an article of faith, and that she could not be a true Catholic if she doubted its truth; adding, that despair and impenitence alone were irremissible sins. The marchioness prayed earnestly for grace to receive this truth, professing her sincere belief in it, but adding, she was fearful the Almighty would withhold pardon from one so unworthy of the blessings she had enjoyed. The doctor reassured her, and it was during such conversation that he formed an estimate of her character, which estimate, together with the narrative of the last hours he spent with the wretched creature, is to be found in a MS. which he left of the particulars.

The Marchioness of Brinvilliers, according to the doctor's opinion and estimate of her, was a woman naturally brave, and endowed originally with a meek and virtuous imagination, yet seemingly indifferent to the impressions it received; her mind was active and acute; her notions clear and decisive, which she expressed with precision and brevity; she was ready with expedients in cases of difficulty, and at once resolving upon the course to be pursued; yet, withal, trifling and inconstant, impatient of repetition, which induced the doctor not unfrequently to change the subject of discourse, or reinforce it in a more varied form. She spoke seldom, but well, without study and without affectation; always self-possessed, and never misled into inconsiderate expressions. It would have been impossible, either by her conversation or bearing, to have imagined her so fearfully criminal as confession proved her to be. It is the more a matter of surprise, and wherein we must submissively bend to God, that one so blessed with a soul of a naturally elevated character, a presence of mind amid the most unforeseen events, firmness which nothing could shake, and a resolution to await and endure death if need were, could have so retrograded, and become capable even of parricide. She was of a slight figure; her hair was of chesnut colour, and very thick; the head well formed; her eyes blue, of a mild expression, and very beautiful; her skin was extremely fair; and the expression of her countenance by no means disagreeable, although not collectively alluring. Her age was forty-six, but she looked much older. Her face generally wore a placid and amiable expression; yet, at intervals, when sorrowful or excited, the emotion was testified by a look in some degree fearful; her scorn or anger were marked by a sort of painful convulsiveness. Such is the sketch which the doctor of the Sorbonne formed of the marchioness even on the occasion of his first interview with her.

In the course of Pirot's first visit to her, she bethought her that he had not attended mass, which she besought him instantly to do, in the Chapel of the Conciergerie, imploring of him to say it on her account, and in honour of the Virgin, whose intercession she might thus obtain, as Mary was her patroness, to whom, amid all her crimes and dissoluteness, she had never ceased to offer up her supplications. To this Pirot consented—the doctor, it may be remarked, from the tenour of the account in manuscript which he left, as given by Alexander Dumas, approving cordially of the wretched criminal's conceptions and practices relative to her prayers to the Virgin. Our present business, however, is not comment, but fidelity of narration. Upon the doctor's return from attending mass, he learned that the sentence of death had been pronounced, and that her hand was to be cut off. This rigorous addition to her punishment, which, however, was subsequently mitigated, induced him immediately to repair to the condemned one, who received him with much serenity, hoping that he had earnestly prayed for her, and requesting to know whether she should have the consolation of receiving the sacrament.

"Madame," said Pirot, "if you are condemned, you will then certainly be deprived of that consolation, and I should but deceive you were I to encourage such an expectation."

The marchioness shortly after contrasted her situation with that of her death, probably at Liège, impenitent, or without the expiation of her crimes upon the scaffold, expressing the regret she felt for the manner in which she had conducted herself before the judges, avowing a perfect submission to the sentence pronounced by the president, and good will towards her prosecutor, who had obtained it; thanking them both with much humility of manner, as her future welfare seemed to depend upon the infliction of the sentence. The dinner was announced. She immediately placed herself at the table along with the attendants of the prison, who never quitted her apartment, with a mind and manner as easy and unembarrassed as though she had been doing the honours of her own table. She desired the two men and the woman, who watched and attended her, to seat themselves at the board.

"Sir," said she, addressing the doctor, "you will excuse ceremony upon your account; these excellent persons have been accustomed to take their meals with me, for the sake of society, and we will now avail ourselves of it, if you have no objections." Then turning towards the woman, she added, "My poor Madame du Rus, I have been very troublesome to you for some time; but have a little more patience, you will soon be rid of me."

These and similar things she said with the most perfect self-possession and simplicity; and as those present turned aside to conceal their tears, she seemed to feel for them. Then observing that the dinner remained upon the table untasted, she invited the doctor to take his soup, apologising for its common quality. For herself she took some broth and two eggs, excusing herself to her companions for not having helped them; but pointing out also, that neither knife nor fork had been allowed her so to do."

"To-morrow," said she, " is a fast-day, and although—"

"Madame," replied the doctor, interrupting her, " if your usual food be requisite for your support, you need not be so scrupulous; for the rule of the church is not compulsory in a case of the present kind."

The marchioness promised to avail herself of the privilege if she felt it necessary, but hoped that with some slight addition to the day's fare, and the two fresh eggs she should take after *the question*, it would not be requisite.

The doctor declares that he was dismayed at her *sang froid*, and at hearing her order with perfect composure the slight addition to her usual meal.

The dinner over, writing materials were brought in, and she wrote an affectionately worded letter to her husband, saying that the marquis had always done his duty towards her so far as it was in his power, and also that their correspondence had been always continued. She requested forgiveness for her conduct, and concluded by confiding her children to his care.

"You gave me yesterday great hopes of the mercy of God," said the marchioness, the moment that the doctor returned to her next morning, he being about to take her confession, in continuance of the commencement which had been made of it on the preceding day, "but I dare not think that I can finally be saved, without the pains of purgatory. Were even my love of God much more intense than it can be, I could not expect salvation without suffering the punishment which is due unto my sins. Now I have heard that the fire of the place where the soul lingers for a time, is similar in all respects to that of hell, where the condemned remain for ever. Tell me now, I beseech you, M. Pirot,—how can the soul, which finds itself in purgatory at the moment of its separation from the body, be assured that it is not in hell?'

" Madame," replied the doctor, " God is too just to add doubt to the punishment he inflicts. At the moment of the separation of the soul, it receives the judgment of the Creator, hears the sentence which condemns, or the mercy which absolves; knows whether it be renewed in the spirit, or abides in mortal sin; whether it be in the fire that is never quenched, or the flames which endure but for a time. The sentence you will hear the moment the sword of the executioner has freed you from this life; already redeemed, you pass immediately into the presence of the blessed." The marchioness felt greatly soothed by the doctrine taught by the Sorbonne priest.

Soon after this teaching and the conclusion of her confession to the ghostly doctor, an officer arrived to read to her the sentence of the court, and to conduct her to the torture chamber, where she was to undergo *the question* or examination. With regard to the sentence, she was to undergo that of *both kinds*, in order to obtain the names of all her accomplices; she was next to make a public avowal of, and demand pardon for, her crimes before the principal entrance of Notre Dame ; to which she should be taken in a common cart, barefooted, a rope around her neck, holding a lighted torch, of about two pounds' weight; and thence be conducted to the *Place de Grève*, where she should be beheaded, her body burnt, and her ashes scattered to the winds. Another *item* in the sentence was that, of such property as she had inherited from her family, four hundred livres should be levied for masses for the repose of the souls of her victims.

Having been conducted to the torture chamber, and given over to the executioner, whom she had recognised at once, by the rope in his hands, she regarded him coldly from head to foot; but without uttering a word. Even the other terrible apparatus which was before her she surveyed with firmness; but on perceiving three buckets of water, she turned to one of the officers, not wishing to speak to the executioner, and said, " It is to drown me, doubtless, that so much water has been brought here; for surely, considering my size, you have not the purpose to make me swallow it." The executioner, without a word, took off her veil, and successively all her clothes, then placed her against the wall, and made her sit on the wooden frame of the ordinary torture, which was about two feet high. The questions as to her accomplices, &c., were again repeated, to which she replied as before, viz., denying that she had any accomplices, affirming that she knew neither in what the poisons consisted, nor their antidotes; adding, " if you will not believe my word, my body is in your power, you can torture that."

Upon this a sign was made by an officer to the executioner, who proceeded to fasten the feet of the marchioness to two rings placed before her; then turning her body backwards he fixed her hands also to two rings in the wall, distant about three feet from each other. By this the head was at the same height as the feet, whilst the body, supported by a trestle, formed a half curve, as if resting upon a wheel. Still further to stretch the limbs, the executioner gave the rack two turns, which brought the feet, before this distant about a foot from the rings, six inches nearer.

Upon the trestle, and during the racking, the horribly treated creature several times cried, " Oh! my God! they kill me, and yet I have spoken truth." Water was given, and in this manner :—The executioner had near him certain jars full of water, each containing about two pints and a half, and a vessel, like a wine strainer, being placed against the mouth of the accused, a jar-full was poured down the gullet at a time, leaving an interval for the prisoner to confess, or reply to the questions put. If denial was persisted in, jar after jar, to the number of eight, were sometimes emptied into a human creature's body, constituting the extraordinary torture. In the manner mentioned, while on the rack, water was applied to the marchioness, the barbarous proceeding being supposed to cause all the terrific and painful feelings of death by drowning ; this torture was often protracted with the most cruel art. Under such abominable treatment she soon became much convulsed, but said only, " you may kill me." But we will not go through the disgusting scene, otherwise than by saying that, although the injection of water was several times renewed, it failed in obtaining any further information from her of any consequence than that of which they were possessed at the commencement of the barbarities. The rack too, had been increased, till the ligatures at the wrists and feet were so stretched, that the flesh was cut and the blood flowed copiously.

As soon as she was unbound, the humane Pirot returned to the chamber, having obtained the permission of the marchioness to retire and say a mass, to the end that the Almighty might endow her with patience and courage to endure her fearful pains. The truth is, he felt himself utterly unable to endure the horrors of the scene which had been enacted.

"Ah! sir," cried she, the moment she perceived the doctor; " I have long desired your return, to receive your consolations. Oh! this torture has been prolonged, and has proved dreadfully afflicting to me; but now I have no more to deal with men, and God alone now will occupy my thoughts."

"And on that account," replied the priest, " these sufferings are to be considered blessings, every torture being now the means of inclining you towards heaven."

No wonder that during the period of the doctor's absence from the chamber of torture, a great change had been wrought in the appearance of the marchioness; her face, he says, being now highly flushed, though before pale; and her eyes, instead of their mild expression, gleaming with feverish excitement,—whilst her frame was overcome by fits of convulsive shivering.

After a lapse of time of some two or three hours, everything was put in readiness for the procession that was first to conduct the marchioness to Notre Dame, to make her public avowal, and thence to the scaffold, clad in the shift of criminals. Before she was placed in the cart, about fifty spectators were admitted to where she was, certain noble ladies being of the number; so that well did she exclaim to the good priest, as she held up her manacled hands, " Oh! sir, does not this appear a strange and barbarous curiosity ?" Some time after, when writhing under the indignities of popular curiosity which beset her, her visage became convulsed, her brows sternly knit, her eyes seemed to emit fire, her mouth was distorted, and for an instant the demon appeared in every feature.

It was, says Alexander Dumas, during this paroxysm, which lasted for a quarter of an hour, that Lebrun, who was close by, became so impressed by the effect, that the following night, unable to sleep, and having its reflection continually presented to his mind, made the beautiful sketch now in the Louvre, and near this another sketch of a tiger, to show that the principal traits were the same, and bore a strong resemblance to each other.

The cart in which the marchioness was to make her last journey on earth, was one of the smallest that could be obtained, bearing yet within it the signs of the low purposes for which it was used, without a seat, with only a little straw scattered about, and being drawn by a wretched horse, which seemed to complete the ignominy of the vehicle. The marchioness was made to get in first. Pirot was the next, who took his place on her right hand; and then came the executioner. His assistant was seated outside, with his back towards the other three, and his legs upon the shafts.

The procession had advanced only a few steps, when the face of the marchioness became more hideously convulsed than before, so much alarming the doctor that he earnestly besought an explanation of the cause. She raised her manacled hands towards some one who followed the cart on horseback; and as the priest grew more urgent in his wish for an explanation, she said :—

"The man who has followed the cart so closely is Desgrais, who arrested me at Liege, and who so ill-used me when his prisoner; so that I could not, seeing him thus here, overcome the emotion you have observed."

Shortly after, however, on listening to the good Pirot, who stated that the officer had but fulfilled the instructions imposed upon him, she regarded Desgrais with a mild expression, repeating a prayer on his behalf.

Having carried the lighted torch to Notre Dame, assisted by the doctor, and having read her public confession of poisoning her father and brothers, and of attempting similarly the life of her sister, the procession moved towards the Place de Grevè. Some delay having been occasioned by the crowd in the immediate vicinity of the scaffold, regarding the doctor with a calm look, she said—

"Sir, it is not here we must separate; you have promised not to quit me in life; I trust you will keep your word."

"Most certainly, madame," he replied; "death will alone part us. I will not quit you; do not disturb your mind with such a fear."

"I expected this of you," she responded; "you will be with me upon the scaffold—

near me—and now I must bid you farewell; and as that which awaits me upon the scaffold may by its awful preparations divert my mind, suffer me now to express my gratitude; for if I am inclined humbly to endure the sentence of the judge of earth, and contritely to await that of heaven, it is to you, to your care that I owe this becoming disposition of mind. All that remains for me now is to beseech your forgiveness for the anxiety and trouble I have caused;" and as tears interrupted the priest's reply, "Is it not so? you do fully forgive me."

The doctor answered her with his tears, being unable to express himself otherwise at the moment.

"You will say upon the scaffold the *De Profundis*, upon my death stroke," added she; "and a mass to-morrow for me; you will do this; you will promise me; is it not so?"

"Yes, madame," he answered, hardly able to articulate; "be composed, I will comply with every request."

At this instant the executioner went to lift the marchioness from the cart, and immediately she ascended the ladder. On the scaffold she was made to kneel before a bar of wood, which divided it; the priest knelt by her side, so as to be enabled to address her to the last. The executioner now cut off the hair which hung around her neck; and although the preparations lasted half an hour, and were at times even harshly conducted, she uttered no complaint, and gave no other signs of anguish than by the tears which silently fell. He next removed the top part of the dress she had worn from the Conciergerie, bound a handkerchief over her eyes, and desired her to hold her head erect, which she did, apparently intent only on the exhortation of the doctor, repeating at intervals the prayers he recited, when they bore immediate reference to her salvation. The executioner had meanwhile drawn from beneath the folds of his mantle a long sabre; and as, after pronouncing absolution, the priest saw he was not yet ready, he said these words as a form of prayer, which the marchioness repeated slowly after him:—

"Jesus, son of David and Mary, have pity upon me; Mary, daughter of David, and mother of Jesus, pray for me; my God, I abandon my body, which is but dust and ashes, to the wind; in the fulness of faith you will raise it once again, and reunite it to my soul. Suffer, O Lord, that my soul may re-ascend to the source whence it proceeded; from you it came, unto you let it return; and as you are of it the origin and commencement, so likewise, O Lord, be its continuance and end."

The words were hardly uttered, when the priest heard a dull heavy blow, like the sound given by a cleaver, when dividing flesh upon a block, and immediately the voice ceased. The head rolled on the scaffold, whilst the body fell forwards, supported by the rail, and so remained to the gaze of the populace, whilst Pirot stood and repeated a De Profundis. The executioner then, taking under one arm the body, and with the other hand picking up the head, threw them both immediately upon the wood pile behind the scaffold, to which his assistant immediately set fire.

"On the morrow," says Madame de Sevigné, "the bones of the marchioness were sought for, as the people believed she was a saint."

———

We append a few observations relative to the art and practice of poisoning, as the crime has obtained in various countries at certain periods. And first, it is to be remarked, that the alchemists, some centuries ago, by their continued experiments, necessarily acquired considerable practical skill in chemistry; and for a long time a great part of this knowledge was constantly devoted to the composition of the subtlest and most deadly poisons. The demand for these fearful inventions increased with the supply, and the supply in its turn with the demand, until, in many parts of Europe, the domestic comfort of every private individual was disturbed by the increasing fear of becoming a victim to the diabolical art of some secret enemy. Early in the 16th century, the crime seems to have gradually increased, till, in the 17th, it spread over Europe like a pestilence. It was often exercised by pretended witches and sorcerers, and finally became a branch of education amongst all who laid any claim to magic and supernatural arts. Popular alarm and popular love of the marvellous, established, by innumerable fables, the really frightful nature of this new and atrocious crime. Every substance, it was believed, which could be tasted, smelt, or even touched, might be made, by a skilful poisoner, the means of inflicting inevitable death. Every one has heard of the limpid and tasteless potions which destroyed life—some in the twinkling of an eye, some by gentle and inexplicable decay : of the flowers, whose scent carried a deadly vapour to the brain; of the delicious perfumes, which spread mortal languor through the air ; and of the gloves, whose touch insinuated a subtle venom through the pores.

It was in Italy that these terrible practices first appeared, that they were most commonly used, and that they were longest retained. The most superficial acquaintance with the history of that unhappy country is sufficient to show that assassination by poison was a tolerated, if not a professed, expedient among Italian statesmen in the 15th and 16th centuries. But long after the convulsions of these times had been set at rest by the establishment of something like regular governments, the same crimes continued to prevail in domestic life, and that to an incredible extent. At Rome, in particular, there reigned in succession, during the latter part of the 17th century, two notorious sorceresses, known as La Spaza and La Tofagna, who were the inventors of, or most skilful operators with, the celebrated slow poison known throughout Europe as the Manna of St. Nicholas of Bari ; and their pride in their art, or their sympathy for unhappily allied persons of their own sex, was such, that they are said to have occasionally removed obnoxious husbands, out of pure generosity.

In France and England the crime of poisoning, though occasionally practised, never became common as a national characteristic. It was, to be sure, introduced into the former country by Catherine de Medicis, who, as might have been expected from her character, was a warm and zealous patroness of whatever was Italian. In her time, Paris abounded in druggists and perfumers,—almost always, however, Italians by birth,—who professed this atrocious mystery ; and several of the great ladies and seigneurs, belonging to the court of Henry III., became infamous for their dealings with such persons.

And yet the epidemic which had become extinct, broke out again in France, about a century later than when it was introduced by Catherine de Medicis, and this with a sudden violence which all the exertions of the Government could not for several years suppress. About the middle of Louis the Fourteenth's reign, the police of Paris found reason to suspect that poisoning was becoming a common crime in private life ; and scarcely had their attention been attracted to the subject, when the domestic tragedy in which the Marchioness Brinvilliers so infamously figured stunned the nation. Her conviction and the formidable example made of her were very far from producing the intended impression. The crime of poisoning continued and increased until it became for the time more common than it had ever been in Italy. It was not confined to cases of deadly enmity or of urgent necessity. The hope of acquiring an inheritance, or of getting rid of a debt, was deemed quite sufficient ground for its commission. The Cardinal de Bonzy, for instance, incurred the darkest suspicion, in consequence of the rapidity with which certain life annuitants upon his property had died off. It was known that he had publicly " thanked his stars" for his deliverance ; and a notorious poisoner, with whom he was said to be intimate, was from that time known by the apt *sobriquet* of M. de Bonzy's *star*.

The few notorious murders by poison of persons of condition which have occurred in England, fortunately excited at the time such universal horror and indignation, as to prevent the crime from becoming fashionable or very common. The practice had, however, appeared as early as the reign of Henry VIII.; for we find that prince, with characteristic humanity, endeavouring to suppress it by enacting that persons guilty of it should be *boiled alive*; and we believe that this punishment was actually inflicted upon a London citizen's widow, convicted of having murdered her husband. The worthless Dudley, Earl of Leicester, is almost the only English statesman whom historical evidence, or even common report, has accused of the habitual use of such weapons against his enemies. Among the many dark and uncertain rumours which were current concerning the death of his unhappy countess, that which ascribed it to poison was the most generally credited. Several of his rivals at court are said to have narrowly escaped a like fate ; and his own death was believed to have been caused by inadvertently partaking of poison which he had prepared for his second wife. We shall, in the course of the present serial publication, enter at length into the case of Overbury, the atrocious murder which disgraced the next reign. Fortunate it is for the memory of James, that the ludicrous absurdity of his personal demeanour has thrown into shade the hateful and abominable vices of his ; and that the testimony of his indignant subjects has been in some measure forgotten in the good-natured ridicule of modern genius. Several other sudden deaths, which happened about the same historical period,—those, for instance, of Edward VI., Henry Prince of Wales, and James I. himself,—were attributed by vulgar suspicion to the same cause; but there appears to have existed no satisfactory proof in any of the cases, and it is certain that the practice of poisoning never became common in private life, unless, indeed, be excepted what appears to have grown of late years something like to a system of murder on the part of some of the poorer classes in manufacturing districts, where burial and such like societies are rife, and where the victims have been generally helpless children. This appalling evil, however, is likely to be suppressed by legislative measures ; at the same time that the national horror and indignation excited by the monstrous practice has been everywhere unequivocally expressed, so that there is little danger of the British character being stained through its various grades by the terrible enormity becoming prevalent amongst them.

V.—COLONEL FITZGERALD.

HENRY GERALD FITZGERALD was the natural son of the Viscountess Kingsborough's brother, an Irish noble family of honourable connection, and on the death of his father, was reared by her ladyship—her brother having died without any legitimate issue—as if he had been her own son. The youth had many things to recommend him to her attention, besides being fatherless and of an unfortunate birth. He was handsome and of noble carriage ; he became master of winning and dignified manners ; and he was endowed with a spirit capable of chivalrous enterprise and splendid action. In early life

COLONEL FITZGERALD SHOT BY THE EARL OF KINGSTON.—*See page* 78.

he entered the army, where he shone to advantage, and here in consequence of the manner in which he recommended himself, aided no doubt by strong family interest, he in a comparatively short time rose to the rank of colonel. He was also fortunate in the domestic alliance which he formed by marriage; nor were there many whose early and matured manhood gave promise of greater prosperity and felicity than did this Irish gentleman at the time that he resided with his young, handsome, and amiable spouse at Bishopgate-upon-Thames.

Lord and Lady Kingsborough were united when they were both young, and in the course of a few years had a numerous family. Naturally enough they chose the vicinity of London for their place of residence during the greater portion of the year, in preference to Mitchelstown, in the county of Cork, because of the education of their children; one of whom was the Hon. Mary King, the heroine of the present remarkable story, and whose governess had been the not uncelebrated Mary Woolstonecroft, afterwards the first wife of William Godwin, author of "Caleb Williams," &c., and mother of the wife of Shelley, the poet. It may not be altogether here irrelevant to introduce some notice of the female just mentioned, to whose care the daughter of Lord and Lady Kingsborough had for a time been entrusted.

Mary Woolstonecroft, afterwards Mrs. Godwin, was born in or near London in 1759, of poor parents, who then resided at Epping, but in course of time removed to a farm near Beverley, in Yorkshire, where she frequented a day-school in the neighbourhood.

No. 5.   F

Her early years were not passed happily, for her father seems to have been a man of no judgment, a despot in his family, and in the habit of lifting his arm in the correction of his children with recklessness. They again removed to Hoxton, near London, and next to Walworth, without, however, bettering their worldly circumstances.

In her twenty-fourth year, Mary Woolstonecroft formed the plan of conducting a school at Islington, in conjunction with her sisters,—having been herself in a great measure self-taught. In 1785 she went to Lisbon as companion to a lady, leaving to her sisters the management of the school, which soon after her return she felt compelled to abandon. She now turned to literary employment as a source of support, and published "Thoughts on the Education of Daughters." She also, in the course of years, amongst other works, sent forth her "Vindication of the Rights of Women," in which productions sundry bold or rather wild theories on the duties and character of her own sex were unhesitatingly urged. She now fell in love with Mr. Fuseli, the painter, though he was a married man; and not meeting with any return to her passion, she went to France, this being in 1792. Here, within a few months, she formed a connexion with one Imlay, an American, by whom she was afterwards abandoned. She now made two attempts at suicide, and next became attached to William Godwin, whom, after cohabiting with him for about six months, she married, in conformity with the practice of the more respectable portion of society, rather than from any moral or religious obligations which she recognised. She died in childbed in 1797. Such was the governess to whose care and guidance the Hon. Mary King had for a time been consigned;—nor can it be denied that every degree of indiscretion, and even of profligacy might be expected as the natural consequence of such principles as this governess set forth in her books and also in passages of her life. What might not be looked for from the teachings of a gifted woman of an ill-regulated mind, who could recommend *libertinism and suicide* not only by precept, but by example? But to the main story in hand:—

We have seen Colonel Fitzgerald's better side, and to all the advantage that he can properly be shown; for it lamentably so happened that his manly and attractive exterior covered a spirit which, instead of directing itself mainly and eventually to praiseworthy pursuits or truly gallant enterprizes, gave itself up to dishonourable and flagitious courses. These he pursued with rarely equalled duplicity and effrontery, and with all the fierceness of unhallowed, unrestrained passion, even to a monstrous abuse of the hospitality to which he had been so much indebted on the part of the noble house of Kingsborough, and in basest requital of that lady who had reared him as if he had been one of her own offspring, instead of being the illegitimate son of her deceased brother. Yes, in return for all this, and whilst he a married man too, was daily received at Lord Kingsborough's as a kinsman and a genuine friend, he fixed his licentious eye upon their simple and unsuspecting daughter, resolved as he was to seduce and ruin her. In fact, the manner and nature of his attentions to the young creature became so obvious that they were noticed by some of the music-teachers from whom she took lessons; and so very marked did his behaviour towards her grow in the eyes of those observant persons, that they deemed it necessary to give the young lady's parents intimation of the same. They, however, having ever been unconscious of any such villany themselves; incredulous, too, as respected the Colonel, who bore himself so fairly before them; and deeming it impossible that any being who had been so deeply benefited by them as he had been could harbour such detestable purposes as were suggested,—trusting to these presumptions and reasonings, they turned a deaf ear to the whispers, still manifesting to the reckless seducer their hospitality and confidence.

When it was that the miscreant began to exercise his ensnaring arts; how far the young creature's mind was fortified against evil by the past teachings of Mary Woolstonecroft; how long it took the Colonel to remove whatever virtuous foundation there was in the heart of the victim by his wiles, or what was the precise nature of the arguments and means by which he at last triumphed over all her scruples and repugnance to the fearful step which she took, we cannot tell. Suffice it to say that, in the summer of 1797, the Hon. Mary King suddenly disappeared from the family residence in the vicinity of London, to the dismay and horror of those nearest and who should have been dearest to her; deigning—no doubt as advised by the scoundrel who misled her—merely to leave behind her in her room a note to the effect that she had fled from her home to drown herself in the Thames. Such a terrible announcement of course stunned her parents at the first as if with a death-blow, not a moment being lost in dragging the river near to their residence. The reader need not be told that the search proved fruitless, although a shawl and bonnet which had belonged to her were found at the water's edge, which had been dropped at the spot no doubt, with the view of convincing the family that she had committed suicide. Such an impression was grievous and heart-rending; and yet a still more awful thought dwelt in the minds of some of the family, especially, it would appear, on the part of the distracted father, who being unable to discover any reason which his daughter had or could have had for destroying herself, set down her disappearance to quite a different cause. Accordingly, amongst other efforts, no means were left untried to trace her course, or the mode by which she had quitted the neighbourhood of her home; and on one occasion there seemed to be some likelihood of obtaining a clue to her retreat. There was a post-boy that came forward in answer to the advertisements and appeals which were made to the public, who stated that, at the particular period or day mentioned, as respected the discovery of her disappearance, while he was driving a gentleman to London, from the vicinity of Lord Kingsborough's mansion, his attention was arrested by a young lady, who was walking by herself, and who, from what immediately afterwards occurred, he fancied must have been at the spot and in the manner he described in the fulfilment of some previous arrangement between her and the gentleman in the carriage; seeing that his traveller, having ordered the chaise to be stopped, invited the lady to take her seat in it alongside of him, a request she hesitated not to obey, after which he drove the pair to London, but that here, after the payment of the fare, they left him, walking away arm-in-arm and disappearing from his sight.

A statement of this kind, artlessly yet circumstantially made, could not but be credited so far as it went; neither did it fail to convince Lord Kingsborough that his daughter was the female of whom the post-boy gave such an account. The agonised father thereby was strengthened in his surmise that his daughter had eloped with some one; advertisements, placards, and the offer of high rewards being widely circulated in order to lead and to tempt to a discovery of the runaway.

For a considerable time, however, these anxious efforts led to no reliable or precise information concerning Miss King's place of concealment. To be sure Colonel Fitzgerald passed not without the suspicion of having some guilty hand in the young lady's elopement; and, indeed, those who had previously lent some credence to the rumours of his too marked attentions to her while under the parental roof, grew the more assured, as the time sped, after her disappearance, that he was the person who, of all others, could give the truest account of her. Lord Kingsborough most reluctantly felt himself forced to task Fitzgerald with being a party in the distressing affair. But he, the colonel, listened to the accusation,—to its gentlest surmises even,—with such a show of natural innocence, of wounded honour, of honest indignation and horror, that his lordship found it impossible to cherish the suspicion, banishing it completely, it would seem, from his bosom. How could the generous-minded parent harbour an evil thought of one who daily, apparently with heart and soul, joined in the eagerest search for the absent, the lost one? Nay, with such a display of anxiety and zeal did he carry himself in the matter, as could only be accounted for, it was thought, by what he declared was his most prompting motive, viz., that until Miss King was found it would be impossible for him to set himself right in the eyes of her family,—in the sight of her mother,—that very lady who had been to himself, when otherwise he should have become abandoned to poverty and meanness, a very parent; that until he could confront the young lady, he should not dare to hold up his face in society or before the gaze of the world. Such, in fact, appears to have been his ardour of feeling, his assiduity of search, his deep protestations, that all suspicion of him was allayed, even on the part of those who had at one time dealt in insinuations concerning him. More closely than ever he became endeared to the afflicted parents; his sympathy for them seemed to be more intense than they could even have expected from his ardent nature; he was taken into their councils, and was their prompter to many an exertion; and for aught that could be seen or was discoverable, but for this domestic calamity, the distracted viscount and his lady never would have been led to appreciate the value of such a friend.

Such for some time was the condition of Lord Kingsborough's family, and the footing on which Colonel Fitzgerald stood in regard to them, after the disappearance of Miss King. Still the system of advertising and keeping the world awake relative to the missing young lady was followed, so that a general anxiety was experienced, and a constant speculation upheld relative to her case. Had she really committed suicide? Was it not strange, if such was the fact, that her body had never been found? Had she voluntarily eloped, and with whom? Had the marriage-tie in some measure cancelled her undutifulness to her indulgent parents? Did she live in shame? Had she been abducted by some relentless ruffian? Or was she the victim of wily seduction, and the slave of her own wilful, unhallowed passion? What more prolific theme could there be suggested for tea-table gossip—for coterie scandal—for unrestrained conjecture? The poor young thing will never be more heard of, thought some at length, seeing that all efforts, extraordinary as these have been, have failed to obtain the slightest reliable clue concerning her. Nothing short of some special providence will discover the nature of her fate; it never appearing to occur to such conjecturers that by the simplest agencies, the most unlooked for and slender circumstances, man's deepest laid schemes have often been baffled,—his most cunningly contrived secrets brought to open daylight.

It was not seldom remarked during all the uncertainty that prevailed concerning the Hon. Mary King's disappearance, that there was nothing exceedingly attractive about her, so as to render her an object of vehement admiration. She was comely enough, but by no means a young lady of rare beauty, or astonishing mental gifts. If, indeed, there was anything about her, besides her sweet simplicity and ordinary accomplishments, by which she might be specially remembered when absent, it was the circumstance of her hair, which for beauty and profusion has seldom been equalled. This, indeed, was a feature such as a poet or a painter might have made a study, and the theme of his genius; nor was the wearer of such a precious feminine gift insensible of its value, innocently enough making it the object of her culture and daily care.

So much for the personal charms of the heroine of the story, of whom all trace for a time, beyond what has already been described, was lost. One day, however, it so happened that Lady Kingsborough was giving more heed than she had often felt herself entitled to do to such proffered tales, to the statement of a girl belonging to the humbler classes, relative to a young lady of whom she had some slight knowledge, and who, she said, might be the missing party that had been advertised. Very numerous had been the calls made, with the ostensible purpose of assisting the family to the discovery of the missing damsel; these, however, having become tiresome, from the frequency with which it was observed the announcements were made, with no other end but to extort money from the advertisers. On the present occasion, however, as already stated, the distressed mother was paying heed to the story of the girl, who said that a gentleman had brought a young woman to a lodging-house in a certain part of Kennington, about the time that the placards gave out that the Hon. Miss King had disappeared from her father's house; that the same gentleman was a constant visitor; and that, although she could not give any distinct account of her features or person, yet there was one thing about her which all admired, and this was the most beautiful head of hair she had ever beheld. Lady Kingsborough could not but eagerly listen to the informant after this, and was in the act of pressing her more closely, when, all of a sudden, in walked Colonel Fitzgerald, with a new tale of his still most fruitless efforts to discover the missing daughter. "Why, this is the very gentleman," cried the girl, "who constantly visits the strange lady! He will be able to give you all the particulars about her."

Even the audacious villain, the perjured miscreant, had not the assurance and adamant effrontery to stand this assault. He rushed from the presence of his benefactress, feeling that his deception was flung to the winds, and that his character was blasted for ever. What was he to look for but vengeance from the Kingsboroughs and the scornful hate of the world. Nought for such a scoundrel was left but to die as a bravado, or as a bravado to dare mankind to do their worst, and to consign himself to the Evil One and to infamy for ever. Such, at least, appears to have been the mode of reasoning which the Colonel pursued. Nor was he slow to respond to the challenge which Colonel King, the seduced young lady's brother, sent him, calling him out to a hostile meeting. Accordingly, the duellists met on a Sunday morning, at an early hour, in Hyde Park, thus to settle the affair; Colonel King having for his second Major Wood, while the other colonel, having been unable to procure a friend, appeared alone. The particulars of the meeting will be best given in the words of Major Wood, to be found in a letter written by him at the date of the trial :—

"October 1st, 1797.

"My dear Friend,

"I shall without preface enter at once upon the affair which I mentioned to you was to take place this morning, and 'nothing extenuate, nor set down aught in malice.' Agreeably to an arranged plan, I accompanied Col. King to a spot near the Magazine, in the Park. Col. Fitzgerald we met at Grosvenor Gate, unaccompanied by a friend, which, by the way, he told me yesterday he feared he should not be able to provide, in consequence of the odium which was thrown upon his character; at the same time observing, 'that he was so sensible of my honour, that he was perfectly satisfied to meet Colonel King unattended by a friend.' I decidedly refused any interference on his part, informing him 'that had not nearer relations of the —— been on the spot, he would have seen me as a principal.' He replied 'he would try to procure a

friend,' and withdrew. I addressed him this morning, by ' Where is your friend, Sir ?, Answer (as well as I recollect)—'I have not been able to procure one : I rest assured that you will act fairly.' I then desired him to apply to his surgeon, which he immediately did, who refused appearing as a second, but said he would be within view. Colonel King was equally desirous to go on with the business. I consented. However, I prevailed upon a surgeon, who accompanied Dr. Browne, to be present as a witness that all was fairly conducted. It was no common business. I placed them at ten short paces distant from each other ; that distance I thought too far ; but I indulged a hope that Colonel Fitzgerald, sensible of the vileness of his conduct, would, after the first fire, have thrown himself on Colonel King's humanity. His conduct was quite the reverse ; in short, they exchanged six shots each, without effect. King was cool and determined ; the other, also, determined, and, to appearance, obstinately bent on blood. After the first shot, he said something to me about giving him advice as a friend. I told him I was no friend of his, but that I was a friend to humanity ; that if, after what had passed, he possessed firmness enough to acknowledge to Col. King that he was the vilest of human beings, and bear without reply any language from Col. King, however harsh, the present business then perhaps, might come to a period. He consented to acknowledge that he had acted wrong, but no farther ;—that was not enough. He now attempted to address Colonel King, who prevented him by saying ' that he was a d—d villain, and that he would not listen to anything he had to offer.' They proceeded. Colonel Fitzgerald's powder and balls were now expended ; he desired to have one of Colonel King's pistols. To this I would not consent, though pressed to do so by my friend. Here ended this morning's business—we must meet again ; it cannot end here. I have only to add, that nothing could exceed the firmness and propriety of Colonel Fitzgerald's conduct through every stage of this business.
"I am, my dear friend, very truly yours,

"ROBERT WOOD.

"P.S. On leaving the ground, Col. Fitzgerald agreed to meet Col. King at the same hour to-morrow."

The two colonels, however, were on the same day put under arrest. Meanwhile, the young lady was removed from the power of her seducer, and without loss of time conveyed to the family residence in Ireland, at Mitchelstown, it being thought that she must be there secure from any further attempts from the villain who had already done her and her house such unpardonable wrong. But the miscreant was not of such yielding stuff. He resolved, it would seem, at all hazards, again to get hold of Miss King's person, and to carry her to some quarter whence probably she might never be rescued. Nor, indeed, considering the daring of the man, the past simplicity of the young lady, and the manner in which a secret correspondence might be maintained between them, was there any absolute barrier for a time against the villain's machinations, Miss King's maid being entirely in the interest of the seducer. Fortunately, this bad girl's character and position as regarded Col. Fitzgerald was discovered, so that she was instantly thereon dismissed from the service ; but yet not before she had been the channel of opening a correspondence with him. Still the daring fellow was not driven from his flagitious purpose, but rather appears to have been more resolutely adventurous and regardless than before. The "Gentleman's Magazine" must here supply us with some interesting particulars :—

" Dublin, Dec. 12, 1797.—The colonel feeling no remorse for what he had done, and dishonouring, by the most artful stratagems, an illustrious family, had the audacity and hardihood to follow the young lady to Ireland; it is supposed, with a view to wrest her by violence from her parents, and took lodgings at an inn in Kilworth. The colonel had been there some days before his arrival at Kilworth was known, or the object of his expedition was discovered. He was observed to walk out in the night, and conceal himself in the day, and the servants at length noticed him lurking about Mitchelstown house at unseasonable hours. The intelligence having reached Colonel King (now Lord Kingsborough), who had had the duel with the colonel, and he being resolved to defeat his antagonist's project, left his father's (now Earl of Kingston) house, and went to Kilworth, where, having inquired if any gentleman was in the house, and being informed there was, he went to the apartment he was directed to that the colonel lodged in. Lord Kingsborough rapped at the door, requiring admittance; the other, knowing the voice, replied that he was locked in, and could not open the door; but, if he had anything to say to him, he would receive it in writing under the door. This enraged the young nobleman, and he forced open the door, and running to a case of pistols in the room, took one, and desired the colonel to take the other and defend himself, for that he was resolved to have satisfaction for the scheme he had formed against his sister, and which he came to this place to put in execution. On both seizing the pistols they grappled with each other, and were struggling, when the Earl of Kingston, who had been apprised of his son's departure in pursuit of the colonel, and quickly followed the young lord, entered the room, and finding them in the contest, and that his son must lose his life from the situation the colonel had him in, the earl fired upon the colonel, not, we believe, with an intent to kill him, though his aggravation was great; but the shot, however, took effect, and the colonel lost his life, but not lamented by any one who has heard of his very dishonourable conduct in this affair."

The account goes on to state some other circumstances, and says that a letter which the dismissed servant-maid carried to the colonel on her return to England, was such as " to induce him, even at the risk of his life, to make an effort to regain the young lady; and that his finances not enabling him to undertake the journey, he borrowed a sum of money of an amiable woman, who ought ever to have been most dear to him, under the pretence of making a visit to Dorsetshire. Thus accommodated, he set out for the sister kingdom, and arrived at the village of Kilworth, near Mitchelstown, the residence of the noble family, the place where the young lady was then watched with particular vigilance."

Such a fatal result to Colonel Fitzgerald's villany and Miss King's infatuation could not but produce a great sensation throughout England as well as Ireland. A trial of the surviving parties who had had a hand in the death of the seducer and lurking enemy could not be avoided, not only Colonel King, or rather Lord Kingsborough by this time, but a person named John Hartney, who had borne some part in the matter, being arraigned, at the assizes held at Cork in April, 1798, for the deed by which Fitzgerald had been cut off from the world. Both, however, were acquitted, and, in fact, neither of them had actually robbed the miscreant of his life; there being a third party who had fired the shot which slew him, viz., the Earl of Kingston, whose father,—the grandfather of Miss King,—had died in November, 1797, and the title descending to her parent. As was natural and proper, his lordship, when he came to be arraigned, demanded to be tried by his peers; so that an indictment which had been found against him as if he had been a commoner was removed by writ of certiorari into the High Court of Parliament.

His lordship's trial took place in the House of Lords, Dublin, on the 18th of May, 1798, the Earl of Clare acting as Lord High Steward on the occasion, who thus addressed the accused from the woolsack, as soon as all the preliminary formalities of the trial had been gone through :—

" Robert, Earl of Kingston, you are brought here to answer one of the most serious charges that can be made against any man—the murder of a fellow subject. The solemnity and awful appearance of this judicature must naturally discompose and embarrass your lordship. It may therefore not be improper for me to remind your lordship, that you are to be tried by the laws of a free country, framed for the protection of the innocent and the punishment of guilt alone; and it must be a great consolation to you to reflect that you are to receive a trial before the supreme judicature of the nation—that you are to be tried by your peers, upon whose unbiassed judgment and candour you can have the firmest reliance, more particularly as they are to pass judgment upon you under the solemn and inviolable obligation of their honour. It will also be a consolation to you to know that the benignity of our law has distinguished the crime of homicide into different classes. If it arise from accident, from inevitable necessity, or without malice, it does not fall within the crime of murder; and of these distinctions, warranted by evidence, you will be at liberty to take advantage."

The Clerk of the Crown then communicated the usual and following interrogatories.

" How say you, Robert Earl of Kingston; are you guilty, or not guilty, of this murder and felony for which you stand arraigned ?"

" Not guilty," replied the prisoner.

" How," resumed the clerk, " will your lordship be tried ?"

" By God and my peers."

" God send you a good deliverance."

Proclamation was then made by the serjeant-at-arms : " Oyez—oyez—oyez—All manner of persons who will give evidence upon oath before our Sovereign Lord the King against Robert Earl of Kingston, the prisoner at the bar, let them come forth, and they shall be heard, for he now stands at the bar upon his deliverance."

None replying to this appeal the peers in succession pronounced their verdict of " Not guilty, upon my honour," after which the Lord High Steward informed the accused of his acquittal by an unanimous voice, upon which the Earl of Kingston made three bows and retired.

But what became of Mary King, the fair cause of all these broils and formalities? For an answer take what we quote from " Anecdotes of the Aristocracy," by J. B. Burke, Esq., a most interesting work, extending to four volumes, for it is crammed with such anecdotes and many episodes from ancestral story, showing that there are more marvels in real life than in the pages of fiction.

" It was obvious," observes Mr. Burke, " that the late circumstances would, for a time, at least, make it painful for Mary to mingle in the circles she had been accustomed to. If she escaped positive insult, which was perhaps more than ought to be expected, still she would be subject to many unpleasant scenes from the idle and the curious, who in the obtuseness of their own feelings, might pay little respect to the delicacy of hers. Even did not these grounds for seclusion appear sufficient, still it could not be particularly agreeable for a young girl to feel, that, go where she would, every smile was at her expense, and every whisper had, in all probability, a reference to the adventures in which she had played a part so much more remarkable than pleasing. (Mr. Burke might have gone much further than he does; his remarks carry little castigation of the young lady's gross infatuation and abominable behaviour with them.) It was therefore decided by her friends to place her, under a feigned name, in the family of a Welsh clergyman, her host himself being kept in ignorance of her real quality and condition. With these simple minded people she became in a short time a great favourite. Nor was this much to be wondered at; she was young and lively, and if not a positive beauty, was yet sufficiently endowed by nature, and that nature improved by the graces of education, to maintain a superior rank in her new circle. Above all she had conversational powers of no common kind, narrating whatever she had seen, or only heard of, with a truth and vividness that, in any society, would have made her a welcome companion, but which, in the dull routine of a country life, where amusements were few, and the general intercourse extremely limited, proved as a loadstone to draw all hearts to her. It was upon this gift, moreover, that we shall find her future fortunes hinging. Carried on one day by the evident delight she gave her guests in the exercise of this faculty, and perhaps with some little secret pride that she could so move them, she plunged into the relation of her own recent adventures, with no other precaution than that of disguising the principal actors in them under fictitious titles. If on other occasions her narratives had proved so singularly vivid and full of power, it may be imagined what fire and truth she flung into her words now, when recollections of the past were giving a fresh stimulus to the feelings of the present. Her young host could not refrain from tears as he listened, and, most unusual in a man of his gentle and kindly habits, burst out into exclamations of indignant horror at the barbarity of the seducer. This warmth of sympathy on his part, so flattering to her conversational powers, and so grateful to her feelings as an injured woman, acted upon her like the sun in the fable upon the traveller, compelling her to lay aside her cloak; in the heat of the moment she no less hastily cast off all prudent reserve, exclaiming, 'I myself am the person for whom you express so deep an interest.' But the words had scarcely escaped her lips when she became sensible of her folly, and before her auditor could recover from his astonishment, added, in a far different tone, ' And now I suppose you will drive me from your roof!" Such, indeed, would have been a natural conclusion to this strange tale, but Fortune, in the case of Mary King, had written a romance of her own, and the final page was not the least wonderful in the volume: the clergyman married her.

"And had the worthy bridegroom any occasion to regret his generous affection? Not the least. They lived long and happily together; and it is not many years ago (Mr. Burke's book was published in 1849) that she died, universally respected, in the land where she had sought and found a refuge."

VI.—JOHN THURTELL and JOSEPH HUNT.

No case of secret murder ever, perhaps, created in England a greater sensation than the one we are now about to record. It was so deliberately planned, and carried out in such a cold-blooded and atrocious manner, as to distinguish it from most other enormous crimes of the kind. The parties concerned in its perpetration, too, were well known in certain circles, and were of respectable connexions and good education. Thurtell was the unworthy son of an alderman of Norwich; Hunt, a singer by profession, who seemed unlikely to engage in such an atrocity; and Probert, an accomplice, lived genteelly, and was generally respected.

The murdered man, William Weare, had been addicted to play, and connected with gaming-houses. Thurtell was his acquaintance; and in some practices of gaming had been wronged by him of a large sum of money. Hunt was also known to Weare, but not in habits of friendship. Probert, who was admitted as a witness against them, had been in trade as a spirit dealer, and rented a cottage in Gills'-hill-lane, situated in a by-quarter, going out of the London-road to St. Albans, in Hertfordshire. Probert himself was much engaged in town; but his wife generally resided at the cottage, which was fully occupied in accommodating Mrs. Probert, her sister, Miss Noyes, some children of Thomas Thurtell—the prisoner's brother—and a maid and boy servant. The deceased had been invited by John Thurtell to the cottage, to have a day or two's shooting; and he met the deceased at a billiard-room, kept by one Rexworthy, on the Thursday night previous to the murder, they having been joined there by Hunt. On the forenoon of Friday, October 24, 1823, Weare was with Rexworthy at the same place, and said he was going for a day's shooting into the country; and he went from the billiard-rooms between three and four o'clock, to his chambers in Lyon's Inn, where he packed, in a green bag, some clothes and a change of linen. He also took with him a double-barrelled gun, and a backgammon board, dice, &c. He left his chambers in a hackney coach before four o'clock, and drove to the New-road, where he went out of the coach, and returned after some time, accompanied by another person, and took the things away.

In the morning of the same day, two men, answering to the description of John Thurtell and Hunt, went to a pawnbroker's in Marylebone, and purchased a pair of pocket pistols; and in the middle of the day Hunt hired a gig, and also procured a sack and cord. They met Probert in the afternoon at Tetsalls, in Conduit-street, Bond-street; and Hunt was heard to ask him, if " he would be in it?" meaning what they, Hunt and Thurtell, were about. Thurtell drove off from Tetsalls between four and five o'clock to take up a friend, as he said to Probert, " to be killed as he travelled with him," words which Probert said he believed at the time to have been a piece of idle bravado. He requested Probert to bring down Hunt in his own gig. Probert, according to Thurtell's request, drove Hunt down in his gig, and, having a better horse, on the road they passed Thurtell and Weare. They stopped afterwards at a public-house to drink grog, at Phillimore-lodge; Hunt got out, as he said, by Thurtell's desire, to wait for him. Probert from thence drove alone to Gills-hill-cottage, in the lane near which he met Thurtell, on foot alone. He said he had done the business without his assistance, and had killed his man; and, at his desire, Probert returned to bring Hunt to the spot. Thurtell rebuked Hunt for his absence, and was answered, " Why, you had the tools." " They were no good," replied Thurtell; " the pistols were no better than pop-guns. I fired at his cheek, and it glanced off;" saying also that Weare ran out of the gig, crying for mercy, and offering to return the money he had won of him. Finding the pistol unavailing, he attempted to cut his throat with a pen-knife, and ultimately finished him by driving the barrel of the pistol into his head, and turning it in his brains, after he had penetrated the forehead. Persons who happened to be in the road, distinctly heard the report of a gun or pistol at the time, as they afterwards testified, and a noise as if of contention. Heavy and deep groans were also heard, which became fainter and fainter, till they died altogether away.

Thurtell arrived at about nine o'clock in the evening at Probert's cottage, having in his possession the double-barrelled gun, the green carpet-bag, and the backgammon-board, which Weare had taken with him from his chambers. Neither Thurtell nor Hunt had been expected by Mrs. Probert. With the former she was acquainted, but the latter was a stranger, and was formally introduced to her. They then supped on some pork-chops, which Hunt had brought with him from London. After this they went out, as Probert said, to visit a Mr. Nicholls, a neighbour of his; but their real object was to go down to the place where the body of Weare was deposited. Thurtell took him to the spot down the lane, and the body having been dragged through the hedge into the adjoining field, it was now enclosed in the sack brought by Hunt. They effectually rifled the deceased man, Thurtell having informed his companions that he had, in the first instance, taken some of the property. They then went back to the cottage again.

In the course of the evening, Thurtell produced a gold watch without a chain, which occasioned some remarks. He also displayed a gold curb chain, which might be used for a watch, when doubled; or, when single, might be worn around a lady's neck. An offer was afterwards made that a bed should be given to Thurtell and Hunt, which was to be accomplished by Miss Noyes giving up her bed, and sleeping with the children. This was refused, Thurtell and Hunt observing that they would rather sit up. Something, however, occurred, which raised suspicion in the mind of Mrs. Probert, and she did not go to bed, or undress herself. She went to the window and looked out, and saw that her husband, Hunt and Thurtell, were in the garden. They went down to the body, and finding it too heavy to be removed conveniently by them, one of the horses was taken out of the stable, and the corpse thrown across its back. Stones having been put into the sack, the whole was at length thrown into Probert's pond. Mrs. Probert distinctly saw something heavy drawn across the garden where Thurtell was, and her suspicions and fears being powerfully excited, she went down stairs and listened behind the parlour door. The parties now proceeded to share the booty, being to the amount of £6 each. The purse, the pocket-book, and certain papers which might lead to detection, were carefully burned. They remained up late; and Probert, when he went to bed, was surprised to find that his wife was not asleep. Thurtell and Hunt still continued to sit up in the parlour.

The next morning, as early as six o'clock, Thurtell and Hunt were both seen out, and in the lane together. Some men who were at work there observed them "grabbing" for something in the hedge. Thurtell observed, "that it was a very bad road, and that he had nearly been capsized there last night." Thinking that something might have been lost there, the workmen, after Thurtell and Hunt were gone, searched the spot. In one place they found a quantity of blood; further on they discovered a bloody knife, and next they found a bloody pistol,—one of the identical pair that had been purchased in Marylebone,—and it bore marks of blood and brains. The spot was afterwards still further examined, and more blood was discovered, which had been concealed by branches and leaves, so that little doubt was entertained that a murder had been committed at the spot. Thurtell and Hunt left Probert's cottage in the morning, viz., Saturday, the 25th, travelling in the gig which Hunt had come down in, carrying with them the gun, the carpet-bag, and the backgammon board belonging to Weare, these articles having been taken to Hunt's lodgings, where they were afterwards found. When Hunt arrived in town on Saturday, he appeared to be uncommonly gay. He said, "We Turpin lads can do the trick. I am able to drink wine now, and will drink nothing but wine." It was observed that Thurtell's hands were very much scratched, and some remark having been made on the subject, he stated "that they had been out netting partridges."

On Sunday, Thurtell and Hunt, with some others, spent the day at Probert's cottage. Hunt went down dressed in a manner so very shabby as to excite observation. But in the course of the day, having gone up stairs, he attired himself in very handsome clothes of the deceased, Mr. Weare.   Probert wished the body to be removed from his pond, and Thurtell and Hunt promised to come down on Monday and remove it, which they did. Hunt engaged Mrs. Probert in conversation, while Thurtell and Probert took the body out of the pond, put it into Thurtell's gig, and then gave notice to Hunt that the gig was ready.   The body was carried to a pond, at a considerable distance from the cottage, and there sunk as it had been before in Probert's pond, in a sack containing a considerable quantity of stones.   The parties who heard the report of the pistol in the lane on the Friday evening, and the discourses made by the workmen, had meanwhile led to great alarm and no small stir amongst the neighbouring magistracy.   Inquiry was set on foot, and Thurtell, Hunt, and Probert, were at length apprehended.   Strict investigation was made, but nothing at first was ascertained that could prove a murder to have been per- petrated.   The body, however, was in a few days found, Hunt having confessed where it was deposited.   As to Thurtell, it was ere long held to be clear that he it was who actu- ally committed the terrible and cold-blooded deed, while it was equally evident that Hunt and Probert were accessories to the atrocity.

On the trial, which took place early in the month of January, 1824, the officers and constables who were examined gave their accounts plainly and firmly, as persons in their line generally do; and Mr. Ward, a surgeon, of Watford, described the injuries done to the deceased in a no less distinct and intelligible manner.   When Ruthven, the Bow- street officer, was called, there was a great stir in the court, as it was known that this very active constable had in his possession several articles of great interest.   He took his place in quite a business manner in the witness box, and in the course of his examination deposited on the table a pistol, and a pistol key, the knife, a muslin handkerchief spotted with blood, a shirt similarly stained, and a waistcoat, into the pockets of which bloody hands had been thrust.   A coat and a hat marked with blood were also produced. These all belonged to Thurtell, but he looked at them with indifference.   Ruthven then produced several articles that had belonged to Weare;—the gun, the carpet-bag, and the clothes; there were the shooting-jacket, with the dog-whistle hanging at the button-hole, the half dirty leggings, shooting shoes, and the linen; and even the sight of these things had no apparent effect on either of the prisoners.

Symmonds, one of the constables, when sworn, took from his pocket a white folded paper, which he carefully undid, and produced to the court the pistol with which the murder had been committed.   The pan was open, as the firing had left it, and was smeared with the black of gunpowder and the dingy stain of blood.   The barrel was bloody, and in the muzzle a piece of tow was thrust to keep in the murdered man's brains.   Against the back of the pan were the short curled hairs of a silver sabled hue, which had been literally dug from the man's head; they were glued to the pan firmly with crusted blood.   This deadly and appalling instrument made all shudder, save the murderers, who, on the contrary, looked unconcernedly at it.

Thomas Thurtell, when called, seemed affected, but his brother, the murderer, was calm. Miss Noyes was very flippant.   Rexworthy, the billiard-table keeper, spoke of his dead friend with great decision; but the brother of Weare was truly shocked, and his sincere grief contrasted with the art and trickery of several of the hysterical witnesses.   "The landlords," says an eyewitness of the trial, "were all thoroughbred landlords, sleek, sly, and rosy.   The ostlers were *rather* overtaken, all except he of the stable in Cross-street, who told all he knew clean out.   Old John Butler, of the Bald-faced Stag, had steadied himself with heavy liquor, and he contrived to eject his evidence out of his smock frock with tolerable correctness. Dick Bingham, another hero of the pitchfork, was quite *undisguised*, and he seemed to be confident and clear in proportion to the cordials and compounds.—Little Addis, Probert's servant boy, showed uncommon quickness and a sweet manner. He was a nice, ingenuous lad. When you saw his youth, his innocence, his pretty face and frankness, you shuddered to think of the characters he had associated with, and the scenes he had witnessed. His little artless foot had kicked up the bloody leaves; he had seen the stains fresh on the murderer's clothes, and his escape from death was almost miraculous."

Mrs. Probert gave her evidence drop by drop, and not then without great *squeezing*. Every dangerous question overcame her agitated nerves, and she very properly took time to recover before she answered.—When Probert, the accomplice, was called, he was ushered through the dock into the body of the court, having been brought from prison. The most intense interest was evidently felt by all persons on his entering the witness-box, in which, indeed, the prisoners joined. Hunt stood up, and looked much agitated; Thurtell eyed the fellow sternly and composedly. Probert did not appear to be the least ashamed of his situation, but stood firmly up to answer the crown counsel, who very solemnly prefaced his examination with charging him to tell the whole truth. The face of the man was marked, you would have said, with deceit in every lineament. The eyes were like those of a vicious horse, and the lips were thick and sensual. His forehead had receded villanously in amongst a bush of grizzly black hair, and his eyes projected out of the like cover. His head and legs were too small for his body, and altogether he was an awkward, dastardly, and a wretched looking animal. He gave his account with no hesitation or shame, and stood up against the cross-examination with a face of brass; indeed he seemed to fear nothing but death or bodily pain.

Having noticed the appearance and bearing of the approver, we may here introduce a similar sketch of Thurtell, as he was seen during his arraignment.—He was dressed in a plum coloured frock coat, with a drab waistcoat and gilt buttons, and white corded breeches. His neck had a black stock on, which fitted as usual stiffly up to the bottom of the cheek and the end of the chin, and which therefore pushed forward the flesh on this part of the face so as to give an additionally sullen weight to the countenance. The lower part of the visage was unusually large, muscular, and heavy, and appeared to hang like a load to the head, and to make it drop like the mastiff's jowl. The upper lip was long and large, and the mouth had a severe and dogged aspect; his nose was rather small for such a face, but it was not badly shaped; his eyes too were small, and were buried deep under his protruding forehead, so inlaid as to defy detection of their colour. The forehead was extremely strong, bony, and knotted; and the eyebrows were forcibly marked, though irregular, that over the right eye being nearly straight, and on the left turning up to a point, so as to give a very painful expression to the countenance; his hair was a good lightish brown, and not worn after any fashion. His frame was exceedingly well knit and athletic.

It was from Probert's statement that many of the particulars which have been already given in the preceding sketch of the circumstances of the murder were directly obtained; and, however much the evidence of an accomplice is to be questioned, yet, as in the present instance, when such evidence is corroborated in its leading features by testimony and proofs drawn from other sources, it necessarily becomes important and worthy of reliance. In addition, therefore, to what has been above narrated, a few of the more striking points brought to light in the course of the approver's searching examination may be recurred to, as these were spoken to in the precise words of the witness.

Probert had dined with Thurtell, Hunt, and others at Tetsall's tavern, on the Friday, on the evening of which the murder was perpetrated. After dinner, Thurtell said to the witness, " I think I shall go down to your cottage to-night; are you going down ?" and asked me if I could drive Hunt down. I said yes. He said, I expect a friend to meet me this evening a little after five, and if he comes, I shall go down. If I have an opportunity, I mean to do him, for he is a man that has robbed me of several hundreds. He added, I have told Hunt where to stop. I shall want him about a mile and a half beyond Elstree. I took Hunt with me. When I came to the middle of Oxford-street, Hunt got out to purchase a loin of pork, by my request, for supper. When we came to the top of Oxford-street, Hunt said, " This is the place Jack is to take up his friend." In our way down we overtook Thurtell, about four miles from London. Hunt said to me, " There they are; drive by, and take no notice." He added, " It's all right—Jack has got him." Having called at several public-houses on the way, some of which Probert supplied with liquors, Thurtell and Weare had passed the other pair somewhere unnoticed. At length Probert and Hunt came to Mr. Phillimore's Lodge, which was at no great distance from the intended end of their journey. Hunt said, " I shall wait here for John Thurtell," and he got out on the road. I drove on through Radlett, towards my own cottage. When I came near to my own cottage, within about a hundred yards, I met John Thurtell; he was on foot; he said, " Hallo! where's Hunt ?" I said I left him waiting at Phillimore's Lodge for him; John Thurtell said to that, " Oh, I don't want him now, for I have done the trick." He said he had killed the friend that he had brought down with him; he had ridded the country of a villain, who had robbed him of three or four hundred pounds. I said, " Good God ! I hope you have not killed the man ?" and he said, " It's of no consequence to you; you don't know him, nor you never saw him; do you go back and fetch Hunt; you know better where you left him.' I returned to the place where I left Hunt. I said to him, when I took him up, ' John Thurtell is at my house—he has killed his friend ; ' and Hunt said, ' Thank God, I am out of it; I am glad he has done it without me; I can't think where the devil he could pass; I never saw him pass anywhere, but I am glad I am out of it.' They reached Probert's cottage. " John Thurtell stood at the gate; we drove into the yard; Hunt said, ' Thurtell, where could you pass me ?' Thurtell replied, ' It don't matter where I passed you, I've done the trick—I have done it. What the devil did you let Probert stop drinking at his d——d public houses for, when you knew what was to be done ?' Hunt said, ' I made sure you were behind, or else we should not have stopped.' I then took the loin of pork into the kitchen, and gave it to the servant to cook for supper." The three soon after went down the lane. " I carried the lantern; as we went along, Thurtell said, ' I began to think, Hunt, you would not come.' Hunt said, ' we made sure you were behind.' I walked foremost; Thurtell said, ' Probert, he is just beyond the second turning.' When he came to the second turning, he said, ' It's a little farther on.' He at length said, ' This is the place.' We then looked about for a pistol and a knife, but could not find either; we got over the hedge, and there found the body lying; the head was bound up in a shawl, I think a red one (here a shawl that had already been produced, was shown to the witness). I can't say that is the shawl. Thurtell searched the deceased's pockets, and found a pocket-book, containing three five pound notes, a memorandum book, and some silver. John Thurtell said, ' This is all he has got ; I took the watch and the purse when I killed him.' The body was then put into a sack, head foremost; the sack came to the knees, and was tied with a cord; it was the sack John Thurtell had taken out of the gig; we then left the body there and went towards home. Thurtell said, 'When I first shot him, he jumped out of the gig, and ran like the devil, singing out that he would deliver all that he had, if I'd only spare his life.' John Thurtell said, 'I jumped out of the gig and ran after him; I got him down, and began to cut his throat, as I thought, close to the jugular vein, but I could not stop his singing out; I then jammed the pistol into his head; I gave it a turn round, and then I knew I had done him.' He then said to Hunt, 'Joe, you ought to have been with me, for I thought at one time he would have got the better of me. These d——d pistols are like spits, they are of no use.' Hunt said, 'I should have thought one of those pistols would have killed him dead, but you had plenty of shots with you.' We then returned to the house and supped. Hunt sung two or three songs after supper. Some time after this,—the females having retired, "Thurtell said, 'I mean to have Barber Beaumont and Woods;' Barber Beaumont is a director of a fire-office with which John Thurtell had some dispute; Woods is a young man in London who keeps company with Miss Noyes. It was a general conversation, and I cannot recollect the particulars; he might have mentioned other names, but I can't recollect them."

The circumstance of putting the dead body of Weare first into one pond and then into another have already been mentioned, as also other things to which we need not a second time refer. But as the cold-blooded atrocity with which the murder was gone about by Thurtell, and the hearty countenance lent to it by the accessories became more patent from the precise answers of Probert to some of the questions, we have thought it necessary to cite a few.

At the close of the evidence for the crown, although, in answer to the judge's inquiry, the jury decided on going through the case, they revoked that decision at the desire of Thurtell, who strongly but respectfully pressed on their attention the long and harassing time he had stood at the bar, begging for a night's cessation to recruit his strength previous to making his defence. Hunt said nothing; but Thurtell's manner was too earnest to admit of denial, and the court adjourned. Next morning, Mr. Justice Parke, the judge, having announced to Thurtell that now was the time to hear any observations he had to make, the prisoner, after seeming to retire within himself for half a minute—and then slowly,—the audience being breathlessly silent and anxious,—drawing in his breath, gathering up his frame, and looking very steadfastly at the jury, commenced his defence. He spoke in a deep, measured, and unshaken tone, accompanying it with a rather studied and theatrical action:—

"My lord and gentlemen of the jury,—Under greater difficulties than ever man encountered, I now rise to vindicate my character and defend my life. I have been supported in this hour of trial by the knowledge that my cause is heard before an enlightened tribunal, and that the free institutions of my country have placed my destiny in the hands of twelve men who are uninfluenced by prejudice and unawed by power. I have been represented by the press—which carries its benefits or curses on rapid wings from one extremity of the kingdom to the other,—as a man more depraved, more gratuitously and habitually profligate and cruel, than has ever appeared in modern times. I have been held up to the world as the perpetrator of a murder, under circumstances of greater aggravation, of more cruel and premeditated atrocity, than it ever before fell to the lot of man to have seen or heard of. I have been held forth to the world as a depraved, heartless, remorseless, prayerless villain, who had seduced my friend into a sequestered path, merely in order to despatch him with the greater security—as a snake who had crept into his bosom only to strike a sure blow—as a monster who, after the perpetration of a deed from which the hardest heart recoils with horror, and at which humanity stands aghast, washed away the remembrance of my guilt in the midst of riot and debauchery. You, gentlemen, must have read the details which have been daily, I may say hourly, publishing concerning me. It would be requiring more than the usual virtue of our nature to expect that you should entirely divest your minds of those feelings, I may say those creditable feelings, which such relations must have excited; but I am satisfied that, as far as it is possible for men to enter into a grave investigation with minds unbiassed and judgment unimpaired, after the calumnies with which the public mind has been deluged,—I say, I am satisfied that, with such minds and such judgments, you have this day assumed your sacred office. The horrible guilt which has been attributed to me, is such as could not have resulted from custom, but must have been the innate principle of my infant mind, and ' grown with my growth, and strengthened with my strength.' But I will call before you gentlemen whose characters are unimpeachable, and whose testimony must be above suspicion, who will tell you, that the time was when my bosom overflowed with all the kindly feelings ; and even my failings were those of an improvident generosity and unsuspecting friendship. Beware then, gentlemen, of an anticipated verdict. Do not suffer the reports you have heard to influence your determination. Do not believe that a few short years can have reversed the course of nature, and converted the good feelings I possessed into that spirit of malignant cruelty to which only demons can attain. A kind, affectionate, and religious mother directed the tender steps of my infancy in the paths of piety and virtue. My rising youth was guided in the way that it should go by a father whose piety was universally known and believed—whose kindness and charity extended to all who came within the sphere of his influence. After leaving my parental roof, I entered into the service of our late revered monarch, who was justly entitled the ' father of his people.' You will learn from some of my honourable companions, that, while I served under his colours, I never tarnished their lustre. The country which is dear to me I have served. I have fought for her, I have shed my blood for her. I feared not in the open field to shed the blood of her declared foes. But oh ! to suppose that on that account I was ready to raise the assassin's arm against my friend, and with that view to draw him into secret places for his destruction—it is monstrous, horrible, incredible. I have been represented to you as a man who was given to gambling, and the constant companion of gamblers. To this accusation, in some part, my heart with feeling penitence pleads guilty. I have gambled. I have been a gambler, but not for the last three years, during that time I have not attended or betted upon a horse-race, or a fight, or any possible exhibition of that nature. If I have erred in these things, half of the nobility of the land have been my examples ; some of the most enlightened statesmen of the country have been my companions in them. I have indeed been a gambler—I have been an unfortunate one. But whose fortune have I ruined—whom undone? My own family have I ruined—I have undone myself! At this moment I feel the distress of my situation. But, gentlemen, let not this misfortune entice your verdict against me. Beware of your own feelings, when you are told by the highest authority, that the heart of man is deceitful above all things. Beware gentlemen of an anticipated verdict. It is the remark of a very sage and experienced writer of antiquity, that no man becomes wicked all at once. And with this, which I earnestly request you to bear in mind, I proceed to lay before you the whole career of my life. I will not tire you with tedious repetitions,

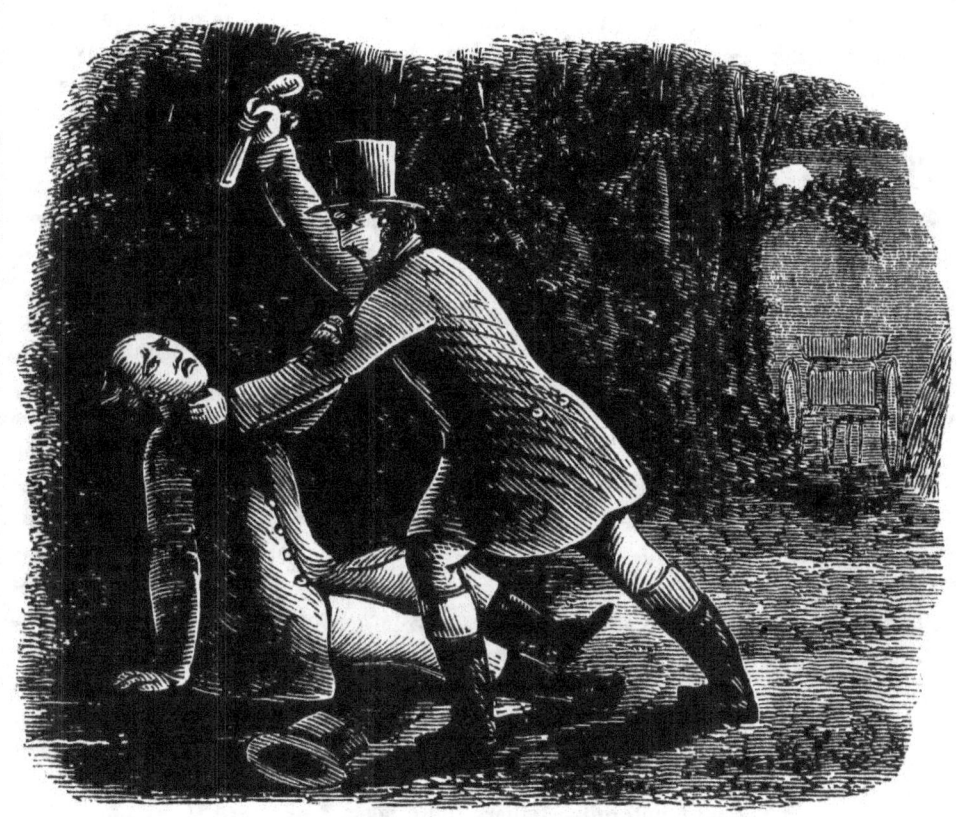

THE SCENE IN GILL'S-HILL LANE.

but I will disclose enough of my past [life to inform your judgments; leaving it to your clemency to supply whatever little defects you may observe. You will consider my misfortunes, and the situation in which I stand—the deep anxiety that I must feel—the object for which I have to strive. You may suppose something of all this; but oh! no pencil, though dipped in the lines of heaven, can pourtray my feelings at this crisis. Recollect, I again entreat you, to consider my situation, and allow something for the workings of a mind little at ease; and pity and forgive the faults of my address.

"The conclusion of the late war, which threw its lustre upon the fortunes of the nation generally, threw a gloomy shade over mine. I entered into a mercantile life with feelings as kind, and with a heart as warm, as I had carried with me in the service. I took the commercial world as if it had been governed by the same regulations as the army. I looked upon the merchants as if they had been my mess-companions. In my transactions with them my purse was as open, my heart as warm, to answer their demands, as they had been to my former associates. I need not say that no fortune, however ample, would have been sufficient to meet such a course of conduct. I, of course, became the subject of a commission of bankruptcy. My solicitor, in whom I had foolishly confided as my most particular friend, I discovered, too late, to have been a traitor—a man who was foremost in the ranks of my bitterest enemies. But for that man I should still have been enabled to regain a station in society, and I should yet have preserved the esteem of my friends, and, above all, my own self-respect. But, how often is it seen that the avarice

No. 6.   G of one creditor destroys the clemency of all the rest, and for ever dissipates the fair prospects of the unfortunate debtor? With the kind assistance of Mr. Thomas Oliver Springfield, I obtained the signature of all my creditors to a petition for superseding my bankruptcy. But just then, that my ill-fortune was about to close—that my blossoms were ripening—there came a frost, a nipping frost. My chief creditor refused to sign unless he was paid a bonus of £300 upon his debt, beyond all the other creditors. This demand was backed by the man who was at the time his and my solicitor. I spurned the offer: I awakened his resentment. I was cast upon the world—my all disposed of—in the deepest distress. My brother afterwards availed himself of my misfortunes, and entered into business. His warehouses were destroyed by the accident of fire, as has been proved by the verdict of a jury on a trial at which the venerable judge now present presided. But that accident, unfortunate as it was, has been taken advantage of in order to insinuate that he was guilty of crime, because his property was destroyed by it, as will be proved by the verdict of an honest and upright jury in an action for conspiracy, which will be tried ere long before the Chief Justice of the King's Bench. A conspiracy there was—but where? Why, in the acts of the prosecutor himself, Mr. Barber Beaumont, who was guilty of suborning refugees, and who will be proved to have paid for false testimony. Yes; this professed friend of the aggrieved—this prostituted prosecutor of public abuses —this self-appointed supporter of the laws, who panders to rebellion, and has had the audacity to raise its standard in front of the royal palace—this man, who has just head enough to contrive crime, but not heart enough to feel its consequences—this is the real author of the conspiracy which will shortly undergo legal investigation. To these particulars I have thought it necessary to call your attention, in language which you may think, perhaps, too warm—in terms not so measured but that they may incur your reproof. But

' The flesh will quiver where the pincers tear,
The blood will follow where the knife is driven.'

" You have been told that I intended to decoy Woods to his destruction, and he has said that he saw me in the passage of the house. I can prove by honest witnesses, fellow-citizens of my native town of Norwich, that I was there at that time; but for the sake of an amiable and innocent female, who might be injured, I grant to Mr. Woods the mercy of my silence. When, before this, did it ever fall to the lot of any subject to be borne down by the weight of calumny and obloquy which now oppresses me? The press, which ought to be the shield of public liberty,—the avenger of public wrongs,—which, above all, should have exerted itself to preserve the purity of its favourite institution, the trial by jury,—has directed its whole force to my injury and prejudice; it has heaped slander upon slander, and whetted the public appetite for slanders more atrocious; nay, more, what in other men would serve to refute and repel the shaft of calumny, is made to stain with a deeper dye the villanies ascribed to me. One would have thought, that some time spent in the service of my country would have entitled me to a little favour from the public, under a charge of this nature. But no; in my case the order of things is changed,— nature is reversed. The acts of times long since past have been made to cast a deeper shadow over the acts attributed to me within the last few days; and the pursuit of a profession, hitherto held honourable among honourable men, has been turned to the advantage of the accusation against me. You have been told that, after the battle, I boasted of my inhumanity to a vanquished, yielding, wounded enemy,—that I made a wanton sacrifice of my bleeding and supplicating foe, by striking him to the earth with my cowardly steel;—and that, after this deed of blood, I coldly sat down to plunder my unhappy victim. Nay, more,—that, with folly indescribable and incredible, I boasted of my barbarity as of a victory. Is there an English officer, is there an English soldier, or an English man, whose heart would not have revolted with hatred against such baseness and folly? Far better, gentlemen, would it have been for me, rather than have seen this day, to have fallen with the tide of battle upon the field of my country's glory. Then my father and my family, though they would have mourned my loss, would have blessed my name, and shame would not have rolled its burning fires over my memory! Before I recur to the evidence brought against my life, I wish to return my most sincere thanks to the high sheriff and the magistrates for their kindness shown to me. I cannot but express my unfeigned regret at a slight misunderstanding which has occurred between the Rev. Mr. Lloyd, the visiting magistrate, and my solicitor. As it was nothing more than a misunderstanding, I trust the bonds of friendship are again ratified between us all. My most particular gratitude is due to the Rev. Mr. Franklin, whose kind visits and pious consolations have inspired me with a deeper sense of the awful truths of religion, and have trebly armed my breast with fortitude to serve me on this day. Though last, not least,—let me not forget Mr. Wilson, the governor of the prison, and the fatherly treatment which he has shown me throughout. My memory must perish ere I can forget his kindness. My heart must be cold ere it can cease to beat with gratitude to him, and wishes for the prosperity of his family."

After this introduction, which was for the most part quite irrelevant and declamatory, Thurtell read a long written argument on the weaker parts of the evidence which had been adduced against him; leaving, however, the stronger portions untouched. He also cited a variety of cases, with the view of impressing the jury with the feeling of the extreme danger there was in relying upon circumstantial evidence,—cases in which verdicts of Guilty had been returned, although afterwards it was discovered that the condemned persons were innocent of the crimes laid to their charge. But the paper which Thurtell read was either so ill-written, or he was so imperfect a reader, that the effect was slight, and different from that of the previous flowery appeal to the jury. He stammered, blundered, and seemed confused throughout. When he finished reading, and laid aside the paper, he appeared to return with gladness and vigour to his memory, and to muster his might for the peroration.

"And now, gentlemen," cried he, "having read those cases to you, am not I justified in saying, that unless you are thoroughly convinced that the circumstances before you are absolutely inconsistent with my innocence, I have a claim to your verdict of acquittal? Am I not justified in saying, that you might come to the conclusion that all the circumstances stated might be true, and yet I be innocent? I am sure, gentlemen, you will banish from your minds any prejudice which may have been excited against me, and act upon the principle that every man is to be deemed innocent until he is proved guilty. Judge of my case, gentlemen, with mature deliberation, and remember that my existence depends upon your breath. If you bring in a verdict of guilty, the law afterwards allows no mercy. If, upon a due consideration of all the circumstances, you shall have a doubt, the law orders, and your own consciences will teach you, to give me the benefit of it. Cut me not off in the summer of my life! I implore you, gentlemen, to give my case your utmost attention. I ask not this so much for myself as for those respectable parents whose name I bear, and who must suffer in my fate; I ask it for the sake of that home which will be rendered cheerless and desolate by my death.   Gentlemen, those who know me best know that I am utterly incapable of an unjust and dishonourable action, much more of the horrid crime with which I am now charged.   There is not, I think, one in this court who does not think me innocent of the charge.   If there be, to him or to them I say, in the language of the apostle, 'Would to God ye were altogether such as I am, save these bonds.'   Gentlemen, I have now done, I look with confidence to your decision.   I repose in your hands all that is dear to the gentleman and to the man! I have poured out my heart to you as to my God! I hope your verdict this day will be such as you may ever after be able to think upon with a composed conscience; and that you will also reflect upon the solemn declaration which I now make—I—am—innocent!—So-help-me—God!"

The solid, slow, and appalling tone in which he wrung out these last words can never be imagined—says one who was present—by those who were not auditors of it.   He had worked himself up into a great actor—and his eye for the first time during the trial became alive and eloquent, while his attitude was impressive in the extreme.   He clung to every separate word with an earnestness which cannot be described, as though every syllable had had the power to buoy up his sinking life, and that these were the latest sounds that were ever to be sent into the ears of those who were to decree his doom!   The final word, God! was thrown up with an almost gigantic energy; and he stood after its utterance with his arms extended, his face protruded, and his chest dilated, as if the spell of the sound had been yet upon him, and as though he dared not move lest he should disturb the still echoing appeal; as if he had the Eternal Judge sustaining him and on his side!   He then drew his arms slowly back, pressed them firmly to his breast, and sat down, half exhausted, in the dock.

When he first commenced his defence, he spoke in a steady, artificial manner, after the style of forum orators; but as he warmed in the subject, and felt his ground with the jury, he became more unaffectedly earnest and naturally solemn; and his mention of his mother's love and his father's piety, drew the tear up to his eyes almost to falling.   He paused; and though pressed by the judge to rest, to sit down, to desist, he stood up resolute against his feelings, and, finally, with one vast gulp, swallowed down his tears!   He wrestled with grief, and threw it!   When speaking of Barber Beaumont, the *tiger* indeed came over him, and his very voice seemed to escape out of his keeping.   There was such a savage vehemence in his whole look and manner, as quite to awe his hearers.   With an unfortunate quotation from a play, in which he long had acted too bitterly—"The Revenge!"—he smoothed his maddened heart to quietness, and again resumed his defence, and for a few minutes in a doubly artificial serenity.   The tone in which he wished he had died in battle, resembled Othello's farewell to the pomp of war; and the following consequences of such a death, was as grandly delivered by Thurtell as it was possible to be!—"Then my father and my family, though they would have mourned my loss, would have blessed my name; and shame would not have rolled its burning fires over my memory!"   Such a performance, for a studied performance it assuredly was, has seldom been seen *on* the stage, and perhaps never *off*.   Thus to act in the very teeth of death, demands a nerve which not one man in a million can be supposed to possess.

When Hunt was called upon for his defence, his feeble voice and shrinking manner were doubly apparent, from the iron-wrought energy which his companion had manifested.   He complained of his agitation and fatigue, and requested that a paper which he had in his hand might be read for him, which was done by the clerk of the arraigns in a very feeling manner.   It had been prudently and advisedly composed by his attorney.   Reliance was placed on the magistrate's promise.   When the paper was concluded, Hunt read a few words on a part of Probert's evidence, in a poor, dejected voice, and then leant his head upon his hand.   He was evidently wasting away minute by minute: his neckcloth had got quite loose, and his throat looked gaunt and wretched.

The judge summed up at great length, Thurtell, with an untired spirit, superintending the whole explanation of the evidence; interrupting his lordship respectfully but firmly, when he apprehended any omission, or conceived any amendment capable of being made. The charge to the jury occupied several hours; and the jury then requested leave to with-draw.   Hunt at this period became much agitated, and as he saw them about to quit the box, he entreated leave to address them; but on his counsel leaning forward and com-municating to the judge what the prisoner had to say, the jury were directed to proceed to the consideration of their verdict.

During their absence, Thurtell conversed, apparently unalarmed, with persons around him.   Hunt stood up in the deepest misery, and manifesting utter exhaustion.   Twenty minutes elapsed, and the return of the twelve was announced.

Whilst way was making through the throng, Hunt leant over the dock, and searched with an eye of anguish for the faces of his doomsmen!   As they, one by one, passed be-neath him, he looked at their countenances with the most hungry agony; he would have devoured their verdict from their very eyes!   Thurtell maintained his steadiness.

The foreman delivered the verdict of *Guilty* against both in tears, and in a tone which seemed to say, " We have felt Thurtell's defence—we have tried to find him innocent—but the evidence is too true!"   The utterance *guilty*, respecting Thurtell, was met with a subdued sigh.

But the murderer shook not to the last: Hunt was broken down—gone!   When asked why sentence of death should not be passed, the latter said nothing, so much was he in wretchedness; but Thurtell stood respectfully up, inclining over the dock towards the judge, and requested his merciful postponement of his death from the Friday to Monday. " It is," said he, " for the sake of some friends that are dear to me, that I ask this indul-gence, not for myself, for I am ready at this moment."   Having urged this on the judge in a calm yet impressive tone, he stood silently waiting his doom.

The judge had put on his black hat—the hat of death—before this appeal; he heard it, and then gave the signal to the crier, who spoke out to the breathless audience those final yet woful words; " Be silent in the court while sentence of death is passed upon the pri-soners!" his own voice being the only sound that broke the silence.

The sentence was passed.   The prisoners were doomed: the world was declared to be no longer for them !

Hunt sobbed aloud in the wildness of his misery; his feelings seemed to crush him to the earth; but Thurtell, whose strength never failed him, though his fate forbade even the most distant glimmering of hope, bore it with an unbroken spirit.   While the very directions for his body's dissection were being uttered, he consumed the pinch of snuff which had to that moment been pausing in his fingers!   He then shook hands with a friend under the dock, and desired to be remembered to others!   Almost immediately, Wilson handcuffed both prisoners; and a few seconds more, saw them led away.

" I confess," says an eye-witness, " I myself was shaken.   I was cold and sick.   I looked with tumultuous feelings at that desperate man, thus meeting death as though it were an ordinary circumstance of his life; and when he went through the dark door, he seemed to me gone to his last account.   It struck me that death then took him !   I never saw him more."

Thurtell never made any direct acknowledgment of his guilt, although after his condemnation, what he circuitously insinuated and allowed to be inferred, amounted to a full confession. Whenever pointed allusion was made to the subject, his manner and answer uniformly conveyed the idea that he was satisfied with what had been done. Still, it was a theme he strove to avoid, for he found that it preyed upon his spirit, and broke in upon that resolution which he thought it becoming in him to maintain throughout. He sometimes spoke with unfeigned distress of his family, and appeared to be very anxious not to say or to do anything that might add to the bitterness of the draught which he had already prepared for their lips. He joined with composure and decency of manner in religious exercises. Very near to the closing scene, Mr. Wilson took an opportunity to say to the convict, "Now, Thurtell, we are alone, with not an eye to see or an ear to hear what passes between us; and if it is your purpose to make a confession, you cannot choose a better opportunity than the present, particularly as it appears to be your firm intention not to make any address at the place of execution." Thurtell, after a little hesitation, with great fervour in his manner, said, "Mr. Wilson, I am satisfied that everything done is just. I forgive everybody, and die in peace and charity with all mankind. That is all I wish to go out to the world." In the course of the morning of the execution, he repeated several times, "Yes, justice has been done me." The name of Probert was mentioned to him, and he was asked did he forgive that man? To this he answered, "I fully and freely forgive Probert all that he has done against me; but as I am a dying man, I would rather encounter such an exit from life as this every day, were it possible, than be Probert as he is with one hundred years to live, and twenty thousand pounds at my command."

Thurtell on the drop met his death, as he had met his trial, without a tremour. His life had been for years one long scene of vice, but he had iron nerves and a sullen low love of fame, which stimulated him to be a hero though on the gallows. He had learned his speech by heart, and often boasted of the effect it would have. A gentleman having complimented him on the firmness and talent he had displayed in his defence, saying, whatever was the result, no one could dispute his title to these qualities, Thurtell answered, "I think I have taken a little of the sting out of the poisoned shafts levelled against me, and I know that the lads of the village will be pleased with my conduct."

It is a fact, to my knowledge, says the eye witness already quoted, that Thurtell said, about seven hours before his execution, "It is perhaps wrong in my situation, but I own I should like to read Pierce Egan's account of the great fight yesterday" (meaning that between Spring and Langan), having just inquired how it terminated.

Thurtell was executed at Hertford, January 9th; but Hunt was sent to the hulks at Woolwich, and afterwards to New South Wales for life. The infamous and despicable wretch had to some extent spoken out when examined at the first before the magistrate, upon a sort of implied promise that his life should be saved if he told the truth; and no doubt his escape from the gallows was mainly owing to this understanding, and the light which he really threw upon the murder.

It was a statement at the time when the murder of Weare was exciting the greatest public interest, that an association had been formed by several desperate characters, comprising amongst others, Thurtell and Hunt, and that they had taken houses in Manchester-buildings and Canon-row, situations which, from their contiguity to the Thames, were every way calculated for their atrocious intentions. Their avowed object, said the report, was to inveigle persons under simulated pretences, who were known to be bearers of sums worthy of plunder, to these abodes of murder, and there first to assassinate, and then despoil them of whatever property they had about them! The names of several persons were mentioned as intended victims to the villanous projects of this society of desperadoes; and indeed some allusion to certain of the parties was made by Probert on his examination at Hertford. Only one instance, however, had occurred it was understood, where any inveigled person was obtained. Thurtell and Woods, the latter already named on the murderer's trial, both paid their addresses to Miss Noyes, sister to Mrs. Probert : the demoniacal jealousy of Thurtell carried him to the resolution of putting his rival effectually out of the way; and to further his ends, a feigned letter was written, purporting to come from the young lady, fixing an assignation with Woods at the very place alluded to above in Manchester-buildings. It had been decided that Woods was to be murdered by Thurtell, and, as a silent and bloodless way of putting an end to him, a pair of dumb-bells were the weapons to be employed. But Woods, almost from instinct, became alarmed on first entering the house, and by a precipitate retreat saved himself from the fate that had been intended for him.

A fact, however, which came to be witnessed at no very distant date after the condemnation of Thurtell and Hunt, and which admits of no doubt, must not be left unnoticed ; being not only connected with the history and case of these heinous culprits in a most striking manner, but as holding out to the contemplation of the reader an impressive lesson upon the hardness of the way which great transgressors have to tread. The fact alluded to was this, that William Probert was brought to the bar of the Old Bailey, London, in April, 1825, charged with the capital offence of horse-stealing, when he was convicted of the same, and received sentence of death. The moral and social lessons contemplated by our recurrence to this felon's case will be supplied by a repetition of the defence which the wretched man set forth, in the course of his trial.

"My lord, and gentlemen of the jury," said he, speaking from a written paper, "if I have this day pleaded Not Guilty to the indictment which has been preferred against me, it is not that I wish, by subtleties, to screen myself from the verdict and sentence which my country may award against one convicted of a capital offence, but that I might have an opportunity to say something in this court, to evince to the public that, whatever may have been the unhappy circumstances of the latter days of my life, I was not driven into my present crime from depravity of disposition, but by a species of fatal necessity, which had placed me beyond the reach of human assistance and charity. The appeal I now make is not with a view to lessen the past error that I fell into, as there is a God on whom I alone rely for mercy; but I beg of the jury to banish from their minds all recollection of former unfortunate circumstances. It cannot have escaped your notice, my lord, and gentlemen of the jury, that immediately after, and ever since my discharge from Hertford Gaol, the public animosity was, and has been kept alive against me by the public press, which has reached every part of England. Wherever I went, even to the smallest village in the kingdom, I was spurned by every one as an outcast of society ; and the chief instrument which prevented my obtaining employment to support myself and family, or to effect a reformation in my conduct, was the public press. I have been the victim of unrelenting prejudice ; I was pursued and pourtrayed as a wretch and a monster ; I could scarcely move from one place to another without my route being marked by the daily papers. Those of my former friends, who might have otherwise rendered me assistance by countenance of their services towards me, shrunk back from the connection, from an apprehension of public reprobation, for being connected in any way with such a one as I have been represented. Every door was shut against me; every hope of future support blasted. My country had spared my life; but individuals had rendered that life of no value, but a curse. I was hunted down like a wild beast of the forest, with desolation around me, and with the most cheerless and dreary prospects before me; I felt my fortitude forsaking me, and I knew not what course to pursue. Heaven and myself only know what I have suffered. Gentlemen of the jury, should you observe any favourable features in my case deserving of commiseration, then I trust you will express a sense of it to his lordship, and recommend me to mercy. And should you, my lord, concur in the same sentiments, I humbly pray your lordship will recommend me to the mercy of my gracious Sovereign, as no former conviction is recorded against me. On my way from the police office to Newgate, my ears were stunned by the horrid yells of the populace, and even my life was threatened. Indeed, my lord and gentlemen of the jury, since the calamitous event which took place at Hertford, I have been a lost man, and, at times, on the brink of self-destruction." Probert then went on to state that his wife and children were involved in his misfortunes, being in want of the common necessaries of life. He appeared much affected, and was at times almost inaudible. He died on the scaffold. He had grown quite grey in a short time, and appeared much older than when, at the memorable trial of Thurtell and Hunt, he stood forward as an approver. Truly, there had not been much in his career of crime to recommend it for imitation. "One hundred years to live, and twenty thousand pounds at his command!" Ah, no! His fleeting and short life was to him "of no value, but a curse;" starvation stared him in the face; and his "ears were stunned by the execrating yells of the populace."

VII.—CAPTAIN GOW.

JOHN GOW, whose assumed name was Captain Smith, was a native of one of the Orkney islands, in the north of Scotland; and, having been instructed in maritime affairs, became so expert, that he was soon appointed mate of a ship, in which he sailed on a voyage to Santa Cruz. When the vessel, being a large one, was ready to weigh anchor from this place, the merchants who had shipped goods on board of her came to pay a parting visit to the captain of the ship, and to give him their final instructions. On this occasion the captain, agreeably to custom, entertained his company under an awning on the quarter deck; and, while they were regaling themselves, some of the sailors preferred a complaint of ill-treatment they said they had sustained, particularly with regard to short allowance. The captain was irritated at the charge, which, it seems, was altogether undeserved, but which was calculated to prejudice him in the opinion of his employers. Conscious of the uprightness of his conduct as well as intentions, he did not reply in anger, only saying that "there was a steward on board who had care of the provisions, and that all reasonable complaints would be attended to;" on which the seamen retired with apparent satisfaction.

The wind being fair, the captain soon after this incident gave orders to his men to weigh anchor, this taking place as soon as the merchants had quitted the vessel. It was observed that Paterson, one of the complainants, was very dilatory in executing his orders, on which the captain demanded, "why he did not exert himself to unfurl the sails," to which the man made no direct answer, but was heard to mutter, " as we eat so shall we work." The captain heard the words but took no notice of them, as he was unwilling to resort to severe measures. The ship had no sooner got fairly under sail, than the captain considered his situation to be dangerous, on reflecting that his conduct had been groundlessly complained of; and on perceiving that his orders were reluctantly attended to, and even positively disobeyed as they at length were. In these trying and perilous circumstances he consulted his mate, and they agreed to deposit a number of small arms in the cabin, with the view of being prepared to defend themselves in case of an attack. This precaution might have been very salutary, but that they spoke so loud as to be over-heard by two of the conspirators, who happened to be on the quarter-deck at the moment. The captain had also directed the mate to order Gow, who was second mate and gunner, to clean the arms, a circumstance that plainly indicated to the latter that the mutiny was at least suspected. Those who had overheard the conversation between the captain and mate, communicated the substance of it to Gow and the other conspirators, who thereupon resolved to carry out their horrible and heinous design without further loss of time and opportunity.

Gow, who had previously made up his mind to turn pirate, thought the present an ad-mirable opportunity to start under new colours, especially as there were several chests of money on board the ship. Accordingly he proposed to his companions, that they should immediately embark in the enterprise, and carry out its first scene with all possible expe-dition and decision, beginning with the murder of the captain and some others, and there-upon instantly seizing the ship. Half the vessel's company were shortly after called to prayers in the great cabin, as was regularly done, that being at eight o'clock in the even-ing, while the other half were doing duty on deck; and, after service, those who had been in the cabin went to rest in their hammocks.

The plan was that the plot should be executed shortly after this juncture. Two of the conspirators only remained on duty, the rest being among those who retired to their ham-mocks. Between nine and ten o'clock at night, a kind of watchword was given, which was, " Who fires first?" On this some of the conspirators left their hammocks, and going to the berths of the surgeon, chief mate, and supercargo, they cut their throats while they were sleeping. The surgeon, finding himself violently assaulted, and being shock-ingly mutilated, managed to spring from his bed; but in a few seconds dropped down dead on the floor of his cabin. The mate and supercargo, holding their hands to their throats, were able to reach the deck, where they solicited a moment's respite, to recom-mend their souls to heaven; but even this was denied them, for the villains, on finding that their knives had failed to slay them, resorted to their pistols, and thus in a moment despatched the unhappy men. The captain, hearing the extraordinary commotion, had demanded an account of its occasion. The boatswain replied that he did not know, but he was apprehensive that some of the men had fallen overboard. The captain hastened to look over the ship's side, on which two of the murderers followed, and endeavoured to toss him into the sea. He, however, disengaged himself, and turned round to take a view of them, when one of the miscreants cut his throat, yet not so effectually as instantly to bereave him of life. The captain implored them to have mercy, but instead of granting it, the other stabbed him in the back with a dagger, and would have repeated the blow, had he not struck with such force, that he could not at once wrench out the weapon. At this instant Gow, who had been assisting in the massacre between the decks, came on the quarter-deck, and fired a brace of balls into the captain's body, which put an end to his mortal existence.

As soon as the dead bodies had been disposed of, by throwing them overboard, Gow was unanimously appointed to the command of the ship. Those of the sailors who had not been in the conspiracy, secreted themselves the best way they could ; some in the shrouds, others under the stores, in dreadful apprehension of sharing the fate of the captain and the other murdered people. Gow, having assembled his associates on the quarter-deck, appointed them their different stations on board, and it was agreed to commence cruising. The new captain next directed that the men who had concealed themselves should be informed that no evil should happen to them if they did not interfere to oppose the new government of the ship, but kept such stations as might be assigned to them. The men, whose terrors had taught them to expect immediate death, were glad to comply with these terms ; but the pirates, to enforce obedience to their orders, appointed two of their number to attend with drawn cutlasses, to terrify the others into submission.

Gow and his companions now divided the most valuable effects in the cabin among themselves ; and then ordering liquor to be brought on the quarter-deck, they consumed the first night after their horrible work in carousing, care being taken, however, that meanwhile those who, unconnected with the conspiracy, had the working of the vessel assigned to them, should do their business in a proper manner as sailors. The crew originally consisted of twenty-four men, of whom four had been murdered, eight were conspirators, and before morning, four of the other men had approved of the proceedings of the mutineers, so that there were only eight remaining in opposition to the new and usurped authority. On the following day, the new captain summoned these eight men to attend him, and telling them he was determined to go on a cruising, that is a piratical voyage, said " that they should be well treated if they were disposed to act in harmony with the rest and majority of the crew." He said that " every man should fare in the same manner ; that good order and discipline were all that should be required." He said further, "that the late captain's inhumanity had been the cause of all the untoward consequences which had so recently taken place ; that those who had not been concerned in the conspiracy need not dread any evil results from it ; that they had only to discharge their duty as seamen, and every man should be rewarded according to his merit." To this address the unfortunate and honest men made no kind of reply ; Gow interpreting their silence into an assent to measures which it was not in their power to counteract or thwart at the time.

After this declaration of the will of the new captain, the eight men were permitted to range the ship at their pleasure ; but, as some of them appeared to work very reluctantly, a strict eye was kept on their conduct. Williams, who acted as lieutenant of the vessel, was distinguished on account of his cruelty towards these poor men, whom he was constantly beating in a savage manner, assuming it as his privilege to rule over them as his caprice dictated.

The ship thus seized had been named the George galley, but the pirates changed the designation into that of the Revenge ; and having mounted several guns, they steered towards Spain and Portugal, in expectation of making a capture of wine, of which article they were greatly in want. They soon made a prize of an English vessel, laden with fish, bound from Newfoundland to Cadiz ; but having no use for the cargo, they took out the captain, and four men who navigated the ship, which they sunk. One of the seamen whom they took out of the captured vessel, named John Belvin, proposed to Gow to enter into all his schemes. The next vessel taken by the pirates was a Scotch ship, bound to Italy, with pickled herrings ; but this cargo, like the former, being of no use to them, they sunk the vessel, having first taken out the men, arms, ammunition, and stores.

After having cruised hither and thither for several days, they found themselves in such distress as to render it absolutely necessary to seek immediate relief; on which they sailed to Porta Santa, a Portuguese settlement, at the distance of about ten leagues. On their arrival at this place, they sent their boat on shore, with a present of salmon and herrings for the Governor, and the name of a port to which they pretended to be bound. The men sent on shore were civilly treated by the Governor, who accompanied some of his friends on board the ship. Gow and his associates received the visitors with great apparent politeness, entertaining him and his companions in the most handsome manner; but the boats belonging to the pirates not returning with provisions, as it was pretended had been expected, and the Governor and his attendants proposing to depart, Gow with his people now threatened to take away their lives, unless they instantly sent written orders for what was required for the ship. The entrapped Portuguese now finding themselves wholly in the power of pirates and murderers, dreading instant death too, solicited that their lives might be spared, and were forward to do whatever was thus masterfully exacted of them; so that before they were liberated, Gow and his associates had got all that they wanted from shore.—After cruising a few days off Cape St. Vincent they fell in with an English vessel, bound from the coast of Guinea to America, with slaves, but which had been obliged to put into the port of Lisbon; and though it was no use to them to capture such a vessel, yet, through the very wantonness of wickedness, they took it, and putting on board of her the captain and men they had first seized, and taking out all the provisions and some of the slaves, they left the ship to proceed on her voyage the best way she could.—Falling in next with a French ship, laden with wine, oil, and fruit, they took out the lading, then gave the vessel to the Scotch captain, in return for the ship they had sunk. The Scotchman was likewise presented with some valuable articles, and permitted to take his men with him; all of whom went, except one, who continued with the pirates through choice.

The day previous to this last-mentioned transaction, the pirates had observed a French ship bearing down towards them; on which Gow ordered his people to lay to; but, on discovering that the Frenchman mounted twenty-two guns, and seemed proportionably full of men, he assembled his people, and said to them that it would be madness to think of their capturing so superior a force. The crew were mostly of Gow's opinion; but Williams, the lieutenant, charged their commander with cowardice, and as a fellow unworthy to be entrusted with any control over those that were better and braver. In short, the behaviour of Williams was so wild, impetuous, and savage, as to threaten a new mutiny,—conducting himself not only in the most abusive manner to Gow, but giving orders for fighting the vessel. The acknowledged captain, however, was firm, and maintained his ground, even although the other presented a pistol to shoot him, which flashed in the pan. This being observed by two of the most active of the pirates, named Winter and Paterson, they both fired at Williams, one wounding him in the arm and the other in the belly. The wretch dropped, when some of the other seamen, thinking he was dead, made to throw him overboard. Upon this he, to their amazement, sprang to his feet, jumped into the hold, and swore he would set fire to the powder-room; and, as his pistol was still loaded, there was every reason to think he would have accomplished his desperate purpose, had he not been instantly seized, and his hands manacled behind him. In this condition he was put among the French prisoners that had been taken from the ship which was laden with wine, oil, and fruit,—the helpless captain being completely terrified at the sight of such a ferocious monster, it having been a common practice with him to flog the poor fellows merely for his entertainment. At length it was determined to put him on board a captured ship, and to request of the commander of such to turn him over to the first English man-of-war that should be met with, in order that he might be punished in that way for his insubordination and crimes; so that, in this manner, the other pirates got rid of the savage.

Gow and his crew at length began to reflect on their peculiar and perilous position; being especially apprehensive that as soon as intelligence of their proceedings reached Portugal, vessels would be sent out in pursuit of them. They were not ignorant that piracy was held to be one of the very highest crimes,—as robbery and depredation on the high seas; that it was an offence against the universal law of society; that with such as they there could be no state of peace; that they were the enemies of every country, and at all times; and, therefore, that they would be everywhere subject to the extreme rights of war.

After much deliberation they steered northward, and, entering a bay of one of the Orkney Islands, Gow assembled his crew in order to instruct them to say that they were bound from Cadiz to Stockholm, but contrary winds driving them past the Sound, till it was filled with ice, they were under the necessity of putting in to clean their ship, and that they would pay ready money for all such articles as they stood in need of. It happened that a smuggling vessel was at this time in the bay, which belonged to the Isle of Man, and being laden with brandy and wine from France, had come north about, to steer clear of the Custom-house cutters. In their present situation, Gow thought it prudent to exchange goods with the master of the smuggler, and thus received opportune assistance, though in other circumstances he would hardly have thought of being so ceremonious.

One evening, when Gow sent a boat on shore, a young seaman, who had been compelled to take part with the pirates, got away from the rest of the boat's crew, and after lying concealed some time at a farm-house, hired a person to show him the way to Kirkwall, the principal place on the islands, and about twelve miles distant from the bay where the Revenge lay at anchor. Here he applied to a magistrate; said he had been forced into the service, and begged that he might be entitled to the protection of the law, as the fear of death alone had induced him to be connected with the corsair crew. Having given a particular narrative of the enormities they had perpetrated, and of their other proceedings, the magistrate issued his precepts to the constables and other peace officers, requiring of them to call in the aid of the people, and to use all possible efforts in assisting to bring to justice such a piratical combination.

About the same period, others of Gow's sailors, who had likewise taken an involuntary part with the pirates, seized the long boat, and having made the mainland of Scotland, coasted the country till they arrived at Edinburgh, where they were imprisoned on suspicion of being of the class of robbers on the high seas. Notwithstanding these alarming circumstances, however, Gow continued to be so regardless and foolhardy, that he did not immediately put to sea, resolving to plunder the houses of the gentlemen on the coast, in order to furnish himself with what he deemed necessary.

In pursuance of this plan, he sent his boatswain and ten armed men to the house of Mr. Honeyman, sheriff of the county, and the gentleman being from home, the servants opened the door without suspicion, when nine of the gang entered in search of treasure, while the tenth was left to guard the outside. Mrs. Honeyman, running to the door, saw the man who stood guard there, of whom she asked the meaning of the outrage; to which he candidly replied that they were pirates, and had come only to ransack the house. Recollecting that she had a considerable sum of gold in a bag, she returned within the house, and contriving unseen to put it into her lap, she hurried out again, passing the man at the door, who, having no idea that she did other but fly for her life, strove not to stop her. The boatswain, not finding money, declared he would destroy the family writings, if their treasure was not made forthcoming; but the threat being overheard by Miss Honeyman, she threw the parchments and papers out of the window, and jumped after them, thus effecting her escape unhurt, and the preservation of the writings. Meanwhile the ruffians seized the linen, plate, and other valuables; after this exploit walking away in triumph to their boat, and compelling one of the servants to play before them a marching air on the bagpipes.

On the following day Gow weighed anchor; but in the evening came and anchored near another of the islands. Here the boatswain and several men were sent on shore in order to plunder the inhabitants, and in search of spoil, but had little success. They next sailed to an island called Calf Sound, with the particular intention of robbing the residence of Mr. Fea, who had been the schoolfellow of Gow. His house stood near the shore, and was of easy access; and though he had servants at the place, they were by no means equal to maintain a contest with the band of robbers. But Gow, having incautiously cast his anchor too near the land, so that the wind could not bring it off, sent first of all, instead of a plundering party, a boat with a letter to Mr. Fea, requesting him to lend him another boat, to assist him in heaving off the ship, by carrying out an anchor; and assuring him he would not do the least injury to any individual. As Gow's messenger did not happen to see Mr. Fea's boat, the gentleman gave him an evasive answer; and, on the approach of night, ordered his boat to be sunk, and the sails and rigging to be concealed. While they were obeying this order of precaution, five of the pirates came on shore in their boat, doubly armed, and proceeded towards Fea's house.

Mr. Fea represented how dangerous it would be for him to assist them in lending them a boat, on account of the reports which had been circulated to their discredit; but he offered to entertain them at an adjoining ale-house, an invitation which they accepted, as they observed he had no company. While they were drinking, Mr. Fea ordered his servants to destroy their boat, and that when they had done so, to call him hastily out of the company, and inform him of it. These orders were promptly and to the letter complied with. Having been called out from the ale-house, he next directed six men, well armed, to station themselves behind a hedge, at a certain spot, and that if, in a short time afterwards, they observed him come along alone with the boatswain, instantly to seize the fellow; but that if he came with all the five desperadoes, he would himself walk forward so as to give them an opportunity of firing upon them without endangering himself.

Having issued these deliberate orders, and with remarkable presence of mind, Mr. Fea returned to the company, whom he now invited to his house, on the promise of their behaving themselves peaceably, assuring them they should receive a warm and welcome reception. The fellows all expressed a readiness to attend him, in the hope of getting the boat; but he told them he would rather have the boatswain's company at first only, and that he would shortly after send for the rest. This being also agreed to, the boatswain set forward, armed, however, with two braces of pistols; and walking along with

Mr. Fea, they at length came to the spot where his men were concealed, and when at this point, the resolute gentleman, quick as lightning, sprang upon the sailor, whom he seized by the collar with all his might, while the others took him into still surer keeping, the whole being accomplished so unsuspectedly by the fellow, and so nimbly, that he was unable to make any defence, or in any way help himself. The villain called aloud for his men; but Mr. Fea, having forced a handkerchief into his mouth, stopped his bawling, while the servants were binding him hand and foot. This done, and one of his people being left to guard the captive, the rest went back to the public-house, which had two doors. Some of them entering by each, Mr. Fea and his men all rushed in at once, making prisoners of the other four pirates ere they had time to handle their weapons. The five ruffians being thus subdued and in custody, they were sent to an adjacent village and separately confined. Mr. Fea now sent messengers round the island to acquaint the inhabitants with what had been done, desiring them to haul their boats on the beach, that the pirates should not swim towards them and steal them, and also giving warning that no person should venture to row within reach of the pirates' guns. The cloud of night was propitious for these exploits and precautions.

By one scheme or another, and by means of an equal display of courage and artifice, Mr. Fea at length captured the whole of the dangerous crew, twenty-eight in number at this time, without a single man being killed or even wounded on either side; and only with the aid of a few countrymen. As soon as they were all properly secured, this active gentleman sent an express to Edinburgh, requesting that proper persons might be provided for conducting the prisoners to that city. As soon as his express arrived, another was forwarded to London to learn the royal pleasure relative to the disposal of the pirates. The answer was that they should be immediately transported to London, in order to their being tried by a court of admiralty, to be held for that special purpose.

The trials came on at the Old Bailey. Gow at first refused to plead; in consequence of which he was sentenced to be pressed in the usual manner, and as the law at that period dictated. The reason which he assigned for his refusal was, that he had an estate which he wished might descend to a relation, and which would have been the case had he died under pressure, but not if convicted after a judicial trial and sentenced to die on the finding of a jury. However, when the proper officers were about to put him to the kind of death which he at first resolved to undergo, he begged again to be taken to the bar to plead. This was allowed. He was convicted along with five others. The rest were acquitted, as it appeared they had acted by compulsion.

They suffered at Execution-dock, August 11th, 1729. Gow's friends, anxious to put him quickly out of pain, pulled his legs so forcibly that the rope broke, so that he fell and had to be taken up again to the gibbet. The body was hung in chains on the banks of the Thames.

THE TWO PERREAUS and MRS. RUDD.

IT was towards the close of the 17th century, soon after the revocation of the edict of Nantz, that an individual of the name of Perreau, one of the French Protestants who sought this country, in order to enjoy the liberty of worshipping God according to the dictates of his conscience, began to lay the foundation for a name and race which promised to become honourably distinguished in the land. Ere long, after his arrival on our free soil, this individual found favour in the eyes of royalty, obtaining employment in several of the public offices during a portion of the reigns both of William the Third and Queen Anne; retiring, however, into private life with a competency in 1710, when a total change of measures took place at court.

Perreau had married a native of England, and had by her a much beloved son, who in due time also took to himself a wife, that brought him a considerable fortune, the first fruits of their union being twins, the parties with whose history we are now to be engaged at considerable length. And assuredly, when taken in connexion with the life, character, and fortunes of Mrs. Rudd, this history abounds with a far greater number of affecting and extraordinary circumstances and incidents, than are to be met with in one of a hundred of such fictitious and romantic narratives as form the staple of our circulating libraries.

The father of the brothers, whose names were Daniel and Robert, was not only affluent, so as to be in a condition to set his offspring well up in the world, but he seems to have taken great delight in superintending their education, and preparing them for maintaining a most respectable position in society. Especially did he regard with parental pride the twin boys, who, in fact, failed not to attract universal attention and regard, being not only remarkable for their comeliness, but so wonderfully alike that strangers to them found it difficult to distinguish the one from the other,—a similitude which extended to their tempers and tastes as well as personal features.

The ancestors of the Perreaus had been connected with the silk trade in France, a branch of manufacture that, as is well known, was brought into this country by the French refugees, who, by the tyranny of Louis XIV., were driven from their native land; and as, notwithstanding the affluence of their father, it was deemed prudent that the youths should be bred to some suitable occupation,—there being at length several other children,—Daniel was articled to an eminent silk manufacturer in London, while the study of medicine was the line chosen for, or by, Robert. Most probably the two youths were in a great measure passive in regard to the choice of professions, for theirs were yielding and facile natures, especially apt, as we shall see, to be taken with attractive and showy appearances.

Daniel, who was destined for the silk business, gave satisfaction to his master in respect of fidelity and honesty, and also of agreeable manners; yet it could not be disguised that he soon discovered a great liking for gaudy trifles, and a readiness to waste time in frivolous amusements, when he ought to have been making progress in the study of his business, if he wished to become eminent in a department which at the period offered excellent opportunities for advancement. Dress, theatrical amusements, and fashionable pastimes had great allurements for him; and as the indulgent father died about the period when the young man's apprenticeship came to a close,—and when each of the twins received their share of fortune bequeathed them, a most critical period thus occurred for the trial of the youthful merchant, who had just entered into partnership with another person of the same trade.

Unhappily, as soon as Daniel Perreau became his own master, his former tastess instead of being checked by a sense of the weight and multitude of cares which were now imposed upon him, took the chief direction of his conduct; while, joined to dissipated tendencies, there was this other propensity indulged, that of building gorgeous castles in the air. While practicably neglecting his affairs, leaving them to the management of others, and squandering money for what could yield him no substantial good, and even in vicious gaieties, he was still dreaming of the great fortune he was rapidly to attain to and the splendid figure which he was destined to make. As was to be expected, embarrassment and failure in business soon overtook him, upon which the young man first tried his fortune in the West Indies, and next in Canada, but with no better success, nor, as it would seem, with a whit more of prudence in his habits. He returned to England, taking apartments at the west-end of the metropolis, where he lived as gaily as ever, having, among those who made claims upon him, always some kept mistress or another, and still cherishing the most extravagant visions of wealth and greatness. In short, he had become a buyer and seller of stock,—a gambler in Exchange-alley, where, for a time, he experienced considerable success:—but we must attend to the other of the twin-brothers.

Robert Perreau was brought up at the same school with Daniel, and during his most early youth discovered such sweetness of temper and such amiable principles, that he was the favourite of all. He attached himself to his brother with a remarkable warmth of fraternity; and he was also noted as a constant peace-maker among his school-fellows; being ever ready to lend them assistance and perform acts of kindness. As it had been determined he should attach himself to the medical department, Robert received a considerably greater amount of academical education than was thought necessary for Daniel; after which he was bound for the usual time to an apothecary, whose business lay chiefly among the nobility and gentry of the west end; thus enjoying an enviable opportunity of making himself well known in that sphere, and to a superior class of customers. Nor were his friends disappointed in their hopes; his master's customers forming a most favourable opinion of him, and predicting very flatteringly concerning his future fortunes. It is true that the young apothecary was not without the tastes of his twin-brother, nor altogether exempt from his practices; but never to the injury of his master. His apprenticeship was honourably served; he afterwards attended the hospitals and advanced his medical knowledge in various ways; and at length, his old master having died, the young gentleman set up for himself in Golden-square—the same neighbourhood where he had served his time, at once commanding a flourishing business,—having for customers and patrons Lord Lyttleton, the Bishop of Carlisle, Lord Wentworth, Lord Sandys, the Messrs. Drummond the bankers, Sir Thomas Frankland, with many others of established name and rank. He was very fortunate too in soon allying himself to a young lady of a respectable London family, so that altogether his prospects were exceedingly fair and promising. In fact, before he had been married more than five years, he was in a position to start a carriage, and maintain a corresponding establishment in every way. All a'ong he kept up a fraternal correspondence with his brother, often assisting him with money. So far did he carry his friendship that he even lent Daniel sums in order to purchase stock in Exchange-alley; nay, more imprudently still, he was the habitual visitor of the other, even when he well knew that the female who came permanently to live with his brother was not his wife, nor could be,—her own lawful husband being alive at the time. As this female henceforward figures most prominently in the history of the Perreaus, and as she was one of the most extraordinary of her sex, it becomes necessary to introduce her formally to our readers.

Margaret Caroline Goodson was born in the north of Ireland, where her father was an apothecary. Much was said, at the time when she became notorious, concerning her descent being from the noble family of Galloway, in Scotland, which traces itself up to Walter Stewart, the Great Steward of Scotland, who married Marjory, the daughter of King Robert Bruce. The fact is, that sometime in the beginning of the reign of George I., a

DANIEL PERREAU BECOMES ACQUAINTED WITH MRS. RUDD AT VAUXHALL.

Major Stewart, who was a near relation of the Earl of Galloway, when in Ireland with his regiment, became the father of an illegitimate child, the mother of our heroine. To the credit of the major be it spoken, he never forgot the duties of humanity, appropriating a part of his income towards the support and education of his natural child; so that although its mother was of lowly rank, the girl was reared in a genteel manner. In due course of time the young lady was wooed and won by Mr. Goodson, the apothecary just referred to; and the only fruit of the marriage was Margaret Caroline, who having been brought up carefully and suitably to her mother's tastes, in her turn, at an early age, became the wife of an ensign of a regiment which was quartered in the place where Mr. Goodson carried on his business in the apothecary line. Miss Goodson, or rather Mrs. Rudd now—the name by which we shall chiefly distinguish her—was eighteen years of age at the time of her union to the poor subaltern, who had nothing to look to for the support of a family but his paltry pay and the kindness of a father, a grocer and tallow-chandler in the town of St. Albans, a man in respectable circumstances, according to his sphere. The young lady, who was handsome and lovely, having also made great progress in education and the accomplishments of her sex, might have formed a far more promising alliance, her charms and superior acquirements having captivated several young gentlemen of rank and wealth. Like other young and inexperienced persons, however, she seems to have been smitten with an elegant exterior and military show, and therefore became bound for better and for worse to the thoughtless ensign. Soon after this, Rudd's regiment was ordered for Scotland, and ere long again had to march for England—a fortunate circumstance for the young couple, had prudence and discretion been their guides. On the contrary, however, they lived, as far as possible, in a style befitting the visions which Mrs. Rudd from the very first made it her study to conjure up, viz., that not only was she nearly allied to nobility, but that she had the assurance of wealth and advancement from the Galloway family. The tallow-chandler was delighted with the prospect set before him, and the preferment which awaited his son. Elated with such hopes, he took his daughter-in-law into his own house, advancing money at her call, and being for the time amply satisfied in return with the glory which she pictured as awaiting them, and the certainty that her young and giddy husband should, before many years elapsed, be promoted to the command of a regiment. Let it not be said that the tallow-chandler's credulity must have been so great, that he deserved to be roundly fleeced of his hard-won gold, otherwise he would have seen into the dazzling picture that was set before him by the young wife. No, it was not with an ordinary woman or a common deceiver that he had to deal, but one of the most skilful as well as fascinating of her sex; one who was as fertile in resources as she was artful in the management of them; one as daring and unscrupulous as to the employment of means, as she was dexterous and high-handed in the invention of them. At length, Mrs. Rudd grew weary of St. Albans, and determined on making London the scene and centre of her future career, resolved to be prepared for whatever issue should occur, and to overleap every barrier that might cross the path of her ambition. Nor was it long before she felt occasion for setting a stout heart against difficulties. Her foolish husband had, at an unguarded hour, or from necessity heedlessly induced by himself, sold his commission, the price of which was speedily spent, to the dismay of his kind father, and the threatening of beggary to Margaret Caroline. True, the blow which the tallow-chandler received by these mad doings, sent him to the grave in the course of a few months, when the money and the goods that remained at St. Albans were claimed by the son. But this windfall furnished but a short-lived stay for the young couple to lean upon. Swiftly was the whole squandered away, as if the day of affluence would never have an end; so that by the time that twelve months of wedded life had been spent, the heedless husband of a dashing beauty, who seems no longer to have cared much for him, found for an abode the Fleet Prison.

Once within the walls of the Fleet, the reckless young man was held by Mrs. Rudd to be the same as dead to her for ever. She scarcely deigned to inquire after him; in fact, during the two years that he was there confined, she took good care to be as one wholly lost to him; having in the interval formed intimacies, not only with gay and licentious persons of her own sex, who contrived to live in splendour, but attracted the attention of persons of quality, and such as lavished their gold upon the fair and the frail. Yet Mrs. Rudd was no indiscriminate barterer of virtue, neither was it without ulterior views that she lived in a style of elegance and grandeur. She had such tales of patrician birth and noble alliance to communicate, such visions of coming greatness to picture, such intellectual powers to command admiration, that even her personal charms and her acquired polish held not half the potency with which she wielded those other weapons of distinction. Besides, she was one of those gifted beings, to whom nothing seems too great or difficult for them to attempt and to grasp, nothing too small or so minute as to be overlooked by them,—her activity and her address keeping pace with the calls that were continually, with renewed tension and closeness, made upon her resources. Accordingly, although she was living in splendour at the time when her unhappy husband was liberated from prison, so utterly ignorant was he of what she had been doing, and of the quarter to which she had betaken herself, that he hurried off to Ireland, in the hopes of finding her where he had at first met with her. Distress of mind, disappointment, and privation, filling and enveloping him soon after his arrival in the sister island, his mind, such as it was, gave way; the cell of a madhouse, so shortly after his release from that of a gaol, receiving him, where he remained for about three years, viz., from 1767 to 1770.

We must pass over many incidents and particulars which have been recorded concerning Mrs. Rudd, as having occurred during the confinement of her husband in a prison and next in a madhouse; and state in general terms that, among those who lavished money and gifts upon this loose and ensnaring woman, a Jew of vast wealth for a considerable period seems to have been the most liberal of any. It was but to coax and to charm the Israelite, and gold as from the treasure of Ophir was laid at her feet, in turn to be squandered by her in expensive entertainments, to which she failed not to attract profligate men, who otherwise made some figure in the world, and also sundry ladies of easy virtue like herself. Towards the latter end of 1769, the amorous Jew left England for a time; so that, had our heroine been less widely celebrated amongst the profligate and spendthrift classes of the British Babylon than she was, poverty might very soon have forced her into meaner lodgings than those where she had been wont to reign over her midnight parties. Amongst others at that day, the handsome Daniel Perreau was figuring,—buying and selling stock at a great rate,—a bold speculator, and never deeming it necessary, in the uncertainty of his gambling transactions, to refrain from those gaieties and vices which would seem most incompatible with strictest calculation in monetary affairs. It was just at the period when Mrs. Rudd was about to feel the loss of the Jew's liberality in a very stern shape, that she ensnared Mr. Daniel Perreau, who, with portions of the gold which was passing through his hands, and also from the assistance of his brother Robert, whose income now averaged a thousand a year, came to the lady's relief, and rushed to the rescuing her from the clutches of the bailiffs. At one start he set her free by the sacrifice of about *four hundred pounds*,—the infatuated man at the same time entering into that criminal intercourse with the wanton which paved the way to the gallows.

Our heroine and the stock-jobber now lived as man and wife together; but whether or not from the first it was known by Daniel Perreau that she was a married woman does not appear. The truth, however, could not long remain a secret to him; seeing that poor Rudd, having in 1770 been released from the madhouse in Ireland, hastened to London in search of his spouse, for he had been informed that she was living in affluence there. What was to be done, the moment it was known that the abandoned husband had discovered the place where his unprincipled wife lived? What but that, although Daniel Perreau affected to be extremely uneasy at the discovery that she was an adulteress, they should clandestinely change their lodgings, removing from Soho-square to Parliament-street, where the lady kept herself in a measure concealed, until the perplexed and baffled Rudd went back to Ireland again, there to drag out a miserable existence.

Our heroine had much to tell Perreau concerning her noble descent and brilliant prospects, and also with regard to her husband's ill-usage, declaring that all her misfortunes were attributable to him,—to his cruelty and his folly. She also professed an unbounded gratitude towards her new companion, and a passionate love, assuring him that he should not only be repaid for his generosity in so far as her most ardent affection could go, but that she should be able to return him substantial favours even beyond those he had so liberally bestowed upon her. In short, the opulent Jew had come back, who seemed to be chained to her chariot-wheels; and from this son of Jacob, not seldom, nor in small supplies, did she obtain assistance for her now reputed husband. And did Daniel Perreau believe all that Margaret Caroline told him? did the adventurer put implicit faith in whatever the impostor alleged? It cannot be credited that a man so conversant with commercial affairs as was the stock-jobber, could place confidence in everything she asserted. Whence came the money with which she repeatedly upheld his credit? He could not but suspect the source; the truth is he did know it, and the considerations too for which the sums were given. But then, as likewise regarded far larger amounts, of which in due course we shall hear, it was his game and interest to affect an entire ignorance of her profligate conduct,—an utter unsuspiciousness of her flagitious life. In a word, though he was strongly allured by the artful woman, she in her turn professing a profound regard for him,—and he was a fine and noble fellow to look upon, —yet, adventurer and impostor-like, they were all along striving to deceive one another. To make matters far worse, the facile, and, in some respects, very faulty apothecary, viz., Mr. Robert Perreau, became inveigled with the pair; not only being dazzled with Mrs. Rudd's brilliant picturings of her origin and prospects, but having also gone to considerable depths along with his brother in Exchange-alley, in order that he might at a bound become enormously rich, and relinquish a business which he deemed too mean and servile for him. To render Robert Perreau's conduct the more censurable, it is only necessary to add that he carefully withheld from his own virtuous wife his knowledge of the fact that Mrs. Rudd's husband was alive, and that she neither was, nor could be, the lawful spouse of his gambling brother. But we must hasten forward to still darker and more desperate transactions, in which our heroine and the two brothers became still more fatally and wofully involved and intertwined.

It was not to be expected that either the rich Jew, or any other wealthy profligate, would long continue to supply Mrs. Rudd with such sums as her expensive housekeeping, and, much less, the Stock Exchange losses called for,—the gambling speculations of Daniel Perreau being upon the whole unfortunate and disastrous. The thousand a year income of Robert had been also sadly encroached upon, in consequence of his partnership in some of these monetary concerns, to his disgrace, be it said, and to the deep wrong of his growing family. What was to be done, especially as our heroine was at length a mother, and with ever-growing tastes, like Daniel Perreau, her companion, for grandeur and parade? What to be done! say you? Ah! the question need not twice be asked, when Mrs. Rudd is in being and has an object to serve. "There are the Adairs, the great house of Adair, the army agent; I am on intimate terms with the family,—with one of them very particularly so. They can't refuse me nothing; in fact, they are bound in honour and justice to let me have money in abundance; and, besides, a relative of my own, a Mr. Stewart, has settled a fortune on me, and it is about to be paid up; so lose not heart, but strike out afresh." In some such terms must Mrs. Rudd often have addressed the Perreaus, especially her companion Daniel, for her conduct was in entire accordance with a speech of this kind.

Could it be that Daniel believed a word that she said? It is not to be thought that he did; but as he wanted money to sport with in the alley, he pretended to be satisfied, caring little how it was come by. It was soon after the first suggestion of her new resource, that she gave him five hundred pounds, which, although borrowed on a forged bond, she told the delighted man had been made her a present by one of the Adairs. This sum being ere long spent, for the pair lived in style,—Daniel Perreau riding out daily with his livery servant behind him—four hundred more was in due time obtained, and by similar means, Perreau all **the** while professing to be satisfied that the money came to the lady in the way of presents, and that the transactions needed not his inquiry. The truth is, he wanted means wherewith to gamble and parade, no matter how or whence they were derived. By two or three turns at the wheel of fortune in Exchange-alley, he imagined he should be able to make all square; and in the meantime he lived as if he had been worth four thousand a-year.

But hundreds at a time could not long suffice. Besides, the gaps that were about to open and yawn till they swallowed up the criminals, had to be filled and satisfied in due time, and all this required new and larger supplies. It would be tedious to follow the writer of the volume entitled a "History of the Life, Character and Conduct of Mr. Robert and Mr. Daniel Perreau, and Mrs. Rudd," wherein, apparently from authentic sources, he narrates a multitude of particular transactions by which not only the parties named robbed their neighbours or members of the public, but strove to deceive one another. In fact, their conduct was such a barefaced farce, with for a season to them of successful issues, as perhaps never has been conceived by the most fertile brain, or at least never met with representation on the boards of a theatre.

A great deal is said in the volume above referred to, with regard to the *professed* belief of the Perreaus concerning the assistance of the Adairs, which Mrs. Rudd declared was at length, with a most lavish spirit, to be extended to them for *her sake*, even to the ob- taining of a baronetcy for Daniel, the procuring him a seat in Parliament, and also about setting up the brothers in a banking establishment; there are also many things told con- cerning the pains the three were at to make their acquaintances repose belief in their ridiculous fabrications. To add to the farce which was to end so tragically, Daniel Perreau and Mrs. Rudd (Mrs. Perreau as she now passed) had taken up their residence in Harley-street, in that aristocratic quarter maintaining the due splendour of the position, although, from what is recorded, their society there, as elsewhere, consisted mostly of adventurers, sharpers, and females of no reputation. But nothing could be done without money; thousands had to be got instead of hundreds; and as one obligation became due, a deeper and heavier one must needs be incurred to cancel the last and to carry out the game still further.

The facts and circumstances now to be described are of such an extraordinary character that they require to be most distinctly set before the reader, the more especially because very considerable difference of opinion has existed with regard, particularly, to Robert Perreau's imputed guilt. One thing is certain that he knew himself to have still a very fair, even high reputation in the world's eye, and that with several capitalists with whom he had already transacted large money matters, he stood in the best esteem. By the Drummonds, the well known bankers, he was much respected. They had readily accommodated him with money for drafts in which his name appeared, having strong re- liance upon that single circumstance; and now that he and his brother, along with Mrs. Rudd, were once more becoming pressed for money, he bethought him of having again recourse to the banking firm just mentioned, a very large sum being now required.   No one, of course, can tell what occurred between the two brothers and the heroine of our strange story, on the eve when the application was to be made to the Drummonds.   The Perreaus had afterwards one story to narrate and Mrs. Rudd another.   Mr. Robert Perreau's conduct, too, at the banking-house and elsewhere at this crisis, was of such a nature as to afford on the one hand presumptive evidence not only of guilty knowledge and forethought, but also on the other points which seemed to be capable of explanation, solely by thinking him innocent, and to have been merely unguarded in his behaviour and mode of doing business.   The facts are these :—

In the month of January, 1775, Mr. Robert Perreau had gone to the Drummonds, desiring to have the loan of £1,400, as he had lately made a purchase, as he said, in the country, to the amount of £12,000,—a statement which does not seem to have been true, in so far as the country purchase was concerned.   He told the bankers that he had a house in Harley-street, Cavendish-square (the same in which his brother and Mrs. Rudd at the time lived so stylishly as man and wife), which, he said, cost £4,000, and that he would leave the title-deeds of that house as a security.   Accordingly he did leave the deeds of the house, and received the £1,400 upon his promising to return it again in ten days.   He did not, however, present himself at the bank till Tuesday, the 7th of March, when he made an apology for not having kept his word, and said he came then to borrow £7,500 on a bond, but that they were to pay themselves out of this sum the £1,400 which he had got in January.   Mr. Robert Drummond, who was the partner in the bank to whom this second application was at first made, said he would have to consult his brother concerning the business, even although the bond bore the signature of wealthy William Adair.   The brother bankers having so consulted together, they both expressed their doubts about the authenticity of the bond; upon which the highly respected apothecary stated that Mr. Adair was his particular friend; that there were family connexions between them; that Mr. Adair had money of his in his hands; and that he allowed him interest for it.   The bankers, however, had still their doubts, and desired Perreau to call next day.   He then took the bond with him, and went away, but in about two hours returned, saying that their suspicions had alarmed him very much; that he could not be easy in his own mind till he had called upon Mr. Adair, whom he luckily met before he went to take his ride; that he produced the bond to Mr. Adair; that Mr. Adair said it was his signature, and that he would pay the bond in May, though in fact it was not payable till July.   The Drummonds still entertained their doubts of such a man as Mr. William Adair having his name upon such a deed, but desired Perreau to leave it with them, which he did, and to call next morning.

In the meanwhile one of the Drummonds showed the bond to Mr. Stephens, of the Admiralty, a friend of Mr. Adair's, who strengthened their doubts.   To obviate any objection, and thoroughly to satisfy themselves, it was agreed that they should call upon Mr. Adair, and show him the bond.   This they did, when the moment the gentleman looked at the document, he told them that, so far from the signature on it being his hand-writing, he did not so much as know Robert Perreau, and that his name had been used in order to impose upon them.   Little did either the Drummonds or Adair imagine what would transpire; the affair was a mystery to them.   The bankers had long considered Robert Perreau as a gentleman of the first integrity, and had employed him in their families. Indeed, they did not believe that he had forged the bond himself; and yet how were they to account for what he told them about seeing Mr. Adair, and being familiar with him ?

About eleven next morning, Mr. Robert Perreau made his appearance at the bank, as he had been desired on the preceding day, and seemingly without the least embarrassment. The Drummonds asked if he still wanted the money? He answered in the affirmative. They expressed to him their doubts in still stronger terms than before. The apothecary, not suspecting, strange to say, that they had taken care to institute proper inquiries respecting a document which dealt with such a large sum, not only repeated his former statement but showed a letter purporting to be from Mr. Adair, signed with the initials " W. A.," containing a statement that his representation was correct. But the Drummonds were not to be thus convinced after what they had learnt, and proposed to Mr. Perreau that he should accompany them to Mr. Adair. Upon this the apothecary talked of that gentleman's having told him there need be no apprehension about the bond; that he was just going out of town, and that he would call upon them as soon as he returned. However, the bankers repeated and urged their proposition, with which Perreau now with apparently the utmost alacrity and cheerfulness acquiesced, viz., immediately to drive to Mr. Adair's,—Mr. Henry Drummond being the party who accompanied Perreau. They found the gentleman at home, Mr. Adair taking the hand of the banker, but only making a bow to the apothecary, as a person he had never seen before. The bond was produced, and the signature firmly repudiated as before. Upon this, Mr. Robert Perreau said to Mr. Adair, " Surely, sir, you are jocular." The banker observed that he should think it was no time to be jocular, when human life was at stake. Perreau said he had the bond from his sister, Mrs. Daniel Perreau, who he desired might be sent for, which was accordingly done. Mr. Drummond asked the apothecary how it was possible for him to say he had received a letter from Mr. Adair, as he pretended, in a most familiar style, adding other stunning and home-driven questions, when the gentleman did not so much as know him by appearance; but in reply nothing could be got from Perreau, other than that he was an innocent man, that he did not mean to impose upon them, and that his sister could explain all.

Mr. Daniel Perreau and Mrs, Rudd having been sent for, the former declared he was quite a stranger to the whole transaction, while the lady confessed herself to be the person who had forged the bond, adding, on this occasion, that she made this disclosure, rather than permit an innocent man with a large family to suffer. After the parties had gone back to the bank, she repeated that she had forged the bond, and also written the letter mentioned and shown by the apothecary, purporting to be signed by Mr. Adair. The Drummonds expressing their doubts of this her statement, the writing being so different from a woman's, she took up a pen, and upon a piece of paper proved to them that she could write the sort of hand which had made them stumble. She at the same time requested most earnestly that the Messrs. Drummond and Mr. Adair would admit her to a private interview; and was answered, that she could have no conversation with them that might not pass before the Perreaus. At length they acceded to her wish, when she told them that Daniel Perreau, her pretended husband, had drawn a knife, which he held to her throat, threatening to kill her unless she would sign the deed in the name of William Adair.

This private consultation being over, the Drummonds told Robert Perreau that they were extremely sorry for what had happened; but that if he would return them the £1,400 which they had lent him some time before, they would drop all proceedings against him, having pity for one whom they had so much respected. In fact, their indulgence was remarkable, for they suffered the three offenders to depart to their respective homes.

The mine had now been sprung, and no doubt these three wretched beings had most trying if not stormy scenes to go through the moment they found they were by themselves. In the account given at much length in the volume to which reference has already been made, written at the period in question, it is narrated that Mrs. Rudd, on her return home, told the Perreaus that she would call on Mr. James Adair, William Adair's son, who would clear up the whole of the difficulty and remove their perils; that she professed to repair to the residence of the said James Adair, and told them that he would take a deep interest in their behalf,—all which story was false; although, from what is several times indicated in this bad woman's history, that gentleman seems to have been on a *questionable* footing of intimacy with her.

The day of the explosion was a Wednesday, and yet the Thursday and Friday sped without the Perreaus and Mrs. Rudd finding themselves under any personal restraint further than what has already been described. Still, matters had reached such a crisis, that there was nothing left but to be exposed to sudden apprehension and arrestment, or to fly the country. This latter course seems to have been that which Mrs. Rudd would at first have eagerly adopted, as well as Daniel Perreau, although Robert contemplated secretly in his own bosom a different scheme, by which he expected and confidently believed that he would extricate himself, though at the expense of the others. However, it had come to be arranged that they should all three pack up and proceed to France, Daniel and the lady being urgent for this escape; and so far had they gone in carrying out their plan, that the carriage was on its way among the streets of London for Dover, when Robert contrived to have the other pair, as well as himself, brought before Mr. Addington, the sitting justice at Bow-street. This must be held to have been a most villanous as well as dexterous stroke of his, by those who believe him to have been guilty, for not only was he thus turning round upon Mrs. Rudd, but upon his brother, in order that he might himself be admitted as King's evidence, so as to escape. When brought before the magistrate, he stated that he came forward, in self-defence, to deliver up Mrs. Rudd, who had given him a bond for £7,500, which was nothing more or less than a forgery. The lady now denied the charge, and mutual upbraidings ensuing, Mr. Addington thought it proper, as both parties seemed to be implicated, to send them to Tothill Fields Bridewell, in order that they should be subjected to further examination, Daniel being at the time discharged. Very soon afterwards, however, the stock-jobber was found to be concerned in the game of forgery which had been carried on; and as he recklessly lost little time in going to visit the apothecary in his place of confinement, he was also detained and made a prisoner, all three remaining in custody till the following Wednesday, when they were brought before Sir John Fielding, at Bow-street. This magistrate, finding from the crowds that beset the office, and other incommoding circumstances, that he could not act satisfactorily for the ends of justice at that place, adjourned the proceedings to Guildhall, before the bench of magistrates, where Mrs. Rudd, instead of Robert Perreau, was admitted witness for the crown. For this turn in her fortunes, she was, of course, not a little beholden to her artful address and extraordinary resources on examination: and yet, as we shall see, she had but little knowledge of the laws of the land in regard to approvers, and the protection which an accomplice is to reckon upon when becoming King's evidence.

On the first of June, Robert Perreau's trial came on at the Old Bailey, for uttering a forged bond for £7,500. There were four counts in the indictment: the first charged him with an attempt to defraud William Adair, Esq.; the second to defraud Henry and Robert Drummond, Esqrs.; and the other two for uttering and publishing the bond, knowing it to be forged. The two bankers and Mr. Adair were the principal witnesses against the prisoner, whose testimonies amounted to what has already been laid before the reader. Mrs. Rudd also appeared to give evidence against Robert Perreau, having been admitted for that purpose by the magistrates, and also before the grand jury. The judges on the trial, however, did not deem it proper to examine her.

When Perreau was called upon for his defence, he read it from a paper, the judge having previously pointed out to him the points which bore against him. The prisoner occupied an hour and twenty minutes in reading his statement, which consisted chiefly of a minute detail of the elaborate artifices which he alleged that Mrs. Rudd had resorted to, in order to engage him in her scheme of getting the forged bonds negotiated,—such bonds, it may here be observed, having been numerous, Mr. Adair's name not seldom having been used as the stalking horse of the party or parties. Some of the matters dwelt upon by the unhappy apothecary were the following :—That a frequent topic of her conversation was the interest she possessed with Mr. Adair. These matters, amongst others, he had been assured of by her: that Mr. Adair had, by his interest with his Majesty, obtained a promise of a baronetcy for Mr. Daniel Perreau, and was about procuring him a seat in parliament; that she had given him to understand that Mr. Adair had promised to open a bank, and to take himself and his brother into partnership; that he himself had received many letters signed "William Adair," which he had never for one moment doubted to have come from Mr. Adair, the army agent, in Pall Mall; that through Mrs. Rudd, Mr. Adair had promised to give them a very considerable portion of his fortune during his life; and was to allow Daniel Perreau £2,500 per annum for his household expenses, and to her, Mrs. Rudd, £600 a year, for pin-money; that Daniel Perreau purchased a house in Harley-street for £4,000, which money Mr. Adair was to give them. Further, that when Daniel Perreau was pressed by the vendor for the purchase money, the prisoner understood that he and Mrs. Rudd applied to William Adair, and that his answer was, he had " lent the King £70,000, and had purchased a house in Pall-mall for £7,000, in which to carry on the banking business; therefore could not spare the £4,000 at that time ;" that Mrs. Rudd told him (the prisoner) that Mr. Adair desired he would get a bond for £5,300 filled up, as he had done once before, and that Mr. Adair would execute it; that after Mr. Wilson, the law-stationer, had filled up the bond, he, Robert Perreau, delivered it to Mrs. Rudd, who gave it back to him a day or two afterwards, executed ; that he borrowed the £4,000 upon this bond, which was dated the 20th December, from Sir Thomas Frankland, and delivered Sir Thomas's draft for the amount to Mrs. Rudd ; that about the 10th of March he told Mrs. Rudd that Mr. Adair's bond, which he had given to Sir Thomas Frankland, was nearly due; and that Mrs. Rudd told him, the following day, Mr. Adair desired he would once more borrow for him £5,000; that he made many objections to being employed in so disagreeable a business; but, at last, supposing he should oblige Mr. Adair, consented, and, accordingly, got a bond filled up by the law-stationer for £7,500, payable to himself. That he delivered this bond to Mrs. Rudd, on Saturday, the 4th of March, in the presence of his wife, his brother, and a Mr. Cassiday ; that Mrs. Rudd returned it to him, executed, on the Tuesday following ; and that throughout he had never entertained the slightest suspicion but that the bonds, one and all, were really executed by Mr. Adair. That when he took the bond to Mr. Drummond's he did *not* say that he " himself had seen it executed by Mr. Adair," but that he knew it was Mr. Adair's handwriting, as he had often seen the letters from Mr. Adair to Daniel Perreau and his wife, or Mrs. Rudd. That when he informed Mrs. Rudd of the observation which Mr. Drummond had made upon the signature to the bond, she went out, and upon her return she told him that she had seen Mr. Adair just as he was leaving home for his morning's ride; and that Mr. Adair told her that the alteration in the signature was merely the difference between age and youth, and that it was his handwriting; and that so instructed he said as much to Mr. Drummond, and that he knew nothing of its being a forgery till the interview with Mr. Adair. The defence was wound up in the following way :—

"My lord, and gentlemen of the jury, I have now faithfully laid before you such circumstances which have occurred to my memory, as necessary for your information, in the order as they happened during my acquaintance with Mrs, Rudd, under the character of my brother's wife. Many have been the sufferers by artifices and impostors, but never man appeared, I believe, at this or any other tribunal, upon whom so many engines were set to work to interest his credulity. It will not escape the notice of the court, that my compassion was first engaged by the story of Mrs. Rudd's sufferings, before my belief was invited to her representations. Let me have credit with you for yielding up by pity in the first instance, and you cannot wonder I did not withhold my credulity afterwards. It is in this natural, this necessary consequence, I rest my defence. I was led from error to error, by such insensible degrees, that every step I took strengthened my infatuation. When Mr. Drummond first hesitated at the handwriting at the foot of the bond, if it did not so far alarm me as to shake my belief in this artful woman, let it be considered that I had been prevailed upon to negotiate other bonds of hers, depositing them in the hands of bankers, who had never spied any defect, or raised the least objection. These bonds have been punctually and regularly paid in due time. The letters sent to me, as if from Mr. William Adair, critically agreed with the handwriting of the bond. Mr. Adair did not keep money at Mr. Drummond's. Opportunities of comparing his handwriting for many years had not occurred, and the hesitation upon his part appeared to me no more than the exceptions and minute precautions of a banker, which could not so suddenly overturn the explicit belief that I had annexed to all that was told me in Harley-street. Can any greater proof be given, than my own proposal to Mr. Drummond, of leaving the bond in his hands till he had satisfied his credulity ? Can your lordship or the gentlemen of the jury for a moment suspect that any man could be guilty of such a crime, whose proceedings were so fair and open ? That single circumstance, I am satisfied, will afford my total exculpation. The resort to Mr. Adair was as easy to Mr. Drummond, as to the books in his counting-house. It does not come within the bounds of common sense, much less does it fall within the possibility of guilt, that any man living should voluntarily, with his eyes open, take a step so directly and absolutely centering in his certain conviction. But this circumstance, strong as it is, is not all the case. I bless God, the protector of innocence, that, in my defence, proofs arise upon proofs,—the least of them, I trust, will be thought incompatible with guilt. It should seem impossible that a guilty person would propose to Mr. Drummond to retain the bond for the satisfaction of his scruples; but that the same person should, after so long a time for consideration had passed after my leaving the bond, which was full twenty-four hours, openly, and in the face of day, enter the office of Mr. Drummond, and demand if he had satisfied all his scruples, unless a man from mere desperation had been weary of his life, and sought a dissolution,—this, I apprehend, would be an absolute impossibility. But I had neither in my breast the principle of guilt, nor had I that desperate loathing of existence as should bring a shameful condemnation upon my head.   It is true I have invited this trial, but it is equally true, I have borne it in the consciousness of my integrity, because I could not otherwise go through the remainder of my days with comfort and satisfaction, unless I had the verdict of my countrymen for my acquittal, and rested my innocence upon the purest testimony I could have on this side the grave.   It is plain I had an opportunity of withdrawing myself; how many men are there, with the clearest intentions, yet from the apprehension of being made the talk of the public, and, above all, the dread of imprisonment and the terror of a trial, would have thought themselves happy to have caught at any opportunity of saving themselves from such a series of distress.   Greater confidence can no man be in of the integrity of his case, and the justice of his country.   When it was found necessary to the designs of Mrs. Rudd, that I and my family should be made the dupes of her connexions with the house of Adair, it may be well believed that nothing but the strongest interdictions could prevent my endeavours to obtain an interview.   In fact, this point was laboured with consummate artifice, and nothing less than ruin to my brother and his affairs was denounced by my breaking this injunction.   It was part of the same error to believe her in this also.   A respectable witness has told you, and I do not controvert his evidence, that my confidence in her assertions, and in the testimonials which she exhibited under the hand, as I believed, of Mr. Adair, were such, in my mistaken judgment, as to be equal to the evidence of my own senses, pressed by the forms of business to say to Mr. Drummond that I had seen Mr. Adair myself; but I neither went to Mr. Adair, nor disclosed those pressing motives which prevented me.   No less free to confess my faults, than I am confident to assert my innocence, I seek no palliation for this circumstance, except my temptation and my failings ; and I trust it will be rather a matter of surprise that, in the course of a negotiation, through the whole of which I was acted upon by the most artful of impostors, that this only deviation was to be found ; and yet this very circumstance carries with it a clearer conviction of my being the dupe of Mrs. Rudd's intrigues than any I have to offer in my defence ; and if my subsequent proceedings, and the alacrity I showed in going with Mr. Drummond to Mr. Adair, together with my conduct before this gentleman is, as I apprehend it is, absolutely irreconcileable with a consciousness of guilt, the circumstances above mentioned will serve to show with what a degree of credulity the artifices of Mrs. Rudd had furnished me. Upon the whole, if, in the above detail, no circumstances are discovered in which an innocent man, under the like delusion with myself, might not have acted, and, at the same time, if there be very many particulars in which no guilty man would have conducted himself as I conducted myself, I should be wanting in respect to your lordship and the jury, if I doubted the justice of their verdict, and, which is inseparable from it, my honourable acquittal.''

A number of witnesses, at the conclusion of this address, were then called, who spoke to the prisoner's excellent character,—persons both eminent in respect of rank and influence being of the list.   Two of the servants of Mr. Daniel Perreau were also examined, who deposed that Mrs. Rudd used to write letters herself, addressed to Daniel Perreau, and desire them to say that they were left by Mr. Adair for him.   The jury, however, after the judge's summing up, and after they had been absent from the hall of trial for about twenty minutes, returned with a verdict of Guilty.

No doubt, the jury never lost sight of the facts that the prisoner had pretended an intimacy with Mr. Adair, of whom he knew nothing, and of his declaration to the Drummonds, that he had seen Mr. Adair about the bond, when, in truth, he had not been near him. One cannot but suppose at this distant day, from the transactions described, that the jury must have said to themselves of the prisoner that, unless he was little better than a fool of the most facile belief, or a mere child in experience, he could never have been imposed upon by the tales and representations he attributed to Mrs. Rudd, even although he had been in possession of grounds for thinking her a respectable woman. On the other hand he was no stranger to her character; he was often in her company; and that he should, time after time, have been an agent in negotiating for her bonds for vast sums of money, out of pity for her, through her impositions, or even to do *Mr. Adair a service*, looks to be so incredible a story as few would patiently listen to. Robert Perreau was perfectly acquainted with the fact that she who lived with his brother as a wife was the spouse of another; very often was he in her society, and could not be, as a man of the world, and in an extensive way of business, entirely ignorant of her ways. Besides, he well knew that his brother was penniless, and obliged to live upon his wits, and had not, as a stockjobber, been at all fortunate in speculation. In short, the defence set up, with all its appeals to the feelings and stress laid upon certain parts of the prisoner's conduct, as being incompatible with a consciousness of guilt, could not well be believed by men of common sense ; and therefore the unhappy apothecary was delivered up to the judgment of the court and the doom which the law awarded.

Next day Daniel Perreau was arraigned, charged with forging a bond on William Adair, Esq., for £3,100, with intent to defraud Dr. Thomas Brooke; other counts accusing him of uttering and publishing the same, knowing it to be forged.

Dr. Brooke, in his examination, deposed that he had long been on terms of intimacy with the prisoner, whom he believed to be a gentleman of the highest integrity; that on the first of November, in the year preceding, he, Daniel Perreau, applied to him to borrow a sum of money for a short period; that he, the doctor, told him he had not at that time any money at his bankers, save what would be barely sufficient for his own private use. Upon this the prisoner replied, "Have you not got some Ayr Bonds? (bonds belonging to a bank in Ayr.) Let me have them, and I will give you as security a bond of Mr. Adair's, the late agent in Pall-mall." To this arrangement Brooke assented, giving him fifteen Ayr bonds, each of the value of £100, which £1,500 was to have been paid back in eight days' time. The witness, who held Mr. Adair's bond in security, was not only not paid back in eight days' time the £1,500, but he did not apply for the sum for a long time after. At length, however, he made application for it to the prisoner, who, in reply, begged him to have a little further patience, as he had lodged the bonds in Drummond's bank, and would take them out in a few days. Upon this Dr. Brooke was satisfied, and heard no further on the subject till he was apprised of Robert Perreau's being taken up for forgery, which led him to suspect that the bond which he had received from Daniel Perreau might be of the same counterfeit character, and which, upon inquiry of Mr. William Adair, he found, most unhappily, to be the fact.

This prisoner's defence was extremely brief, amounting only to a few emphatically uttered sentences, in which he declared that he was unfortunately the dupe of an artful woman, Mrs. Rudd, and had implicitly believed the bond, which he deposited with Dr. Brooke, to be genuine, and really and truly signed, as it purported to be, by Mr. Adair. This he asseverated, in the most solemn manner, to be "the real state of the case; otherwise he would not for the world have been mixed up with such a transaction."

Besides witnesses called to character, there were his two servants, who had been adduced in the brother's case, and who repeated the evidence which they had previously given, viz., touching the tricks, the notes, double raps at the door, and other manœuvres resorted to by Mrs. Rudd, in order to make their master, Mr. Daniel Perreau, believe that Mr. Adair had called upon him. Nevertheless, after a few minutes' consultation amongst themselves, the jury found the prisoner Guilty of "uttering and publishing the bond, knowing it to be forged."

But although both brothers had been found guilty, and were soon after sentenced to die, they were not mentioned in any report to his Majesty till the month of December following, the dismal cells of Newgate being their habitation until it should be known what was to be done with the abandoned Mrs. Rudd, the accomplice, the manifold writer and approver. Having stated that the unhappy twin-brothers were long kept in a state of painful suspense after having been sentenced to die, it may be added as a very extra-ordinary circumstance, that they had once more to appear in a court of justice. In July they were removed from Newgate by a writ of Habeas Corpus to the Court of King's Bench, in order to be examined as witnesses, in a trial upon an action of *trover*, brought by a jeweller against Sir Thomas Frankland. It appeared that the jeweller had lent Daniel Perreau a diamond ring of £500 value, till he, the lender, should be able to make for the borrower one of the same value of a different fashion; that on the detection of the forgeries, Sir Thomas, as a creditor, seized the ring in question as part of Daniel Per-reau's real property. This trial ended in a finding for the jeweller, who recovered the ring, the Perreaus being conveyed back to Newgate.

And now more particularly as concerned Mrs. Rudd, who, although she had not been called upon as King's evidence, either on the trial of Robert or that of Daniel Perreau, yet employed every possible means of obtaining all the advantages of a person that had been so called; contending, through the assistance of able advocates, that the examination she had undergone before the magistrates towards throwing light upon the conduct and transactions of the Perreaus, entitled her to the deliverance and protection accorded to ac-complices who have become approvers. For the maintenance of this doctrine and plea, she brought herself from Newgate by Habeas Corpus into the Court of King's Bench. On this occasion the fluent, resourceful, and dauntless woman addressed the court herself in her own behalf, even while she had her hired counsel. The plea was debated for two days, the decision of the judges being that the magistrates were not empowered to offer her protection, consequently she was remanded to Newgate. The main ground for re-jecting her plea was the fact of her not having disclosed the whole of what she knew, in her examination before the magistrates, respecting the forgeries. These significant and emphatic words of Lord Mansfield, in delivering the opinion of the court, on this occa-sion, mark his feelings relative to the audacious prisoner:—"In some cases," said he, "there arose circumstances which rendered accomplices, even though illegally admitted evidences, objects deserving mercy; and these chiefly were a regular, decent behaviour, and invariable relation of the whole truth, which did not appear to be the case in the present instance."

Some time later, viz., on the 16th September, she was again brought to the bar, in order, if possible, to obtain her discharge from imprisonment, and the liability to be tried in connexion with the enormous forgeries of which we have been hearing so much, her counsel strenuously insisting that, as she had already been admitted an evidence for the King, it would be wholly unprecedented to detain her for trial. On this point of law, the judges differing in opinion, she was again remanded back to prison, until the opinion of all the judges could be had on so important a question. At length, they were prepared with a judgment, a large majority being clear upon the point that the manner of her being admitted as an evidence could not bar her from trial. For the last time she was called upon, and brought to the bar of the Old Bailey, which took place on the 7th of December; and such was the avidity of the public to hear her trial, that the galleries of the court-room were crowded soon after daylight.

A little before nine o'clock, the Lord Mayor, judges, and aldermen being assembled, the prisoner was placed in the dock, the business of the day being opened by Mr. Justice Ashton's acquainting her with the opinion of the judges in her case, explaining the grounds at the same time on which their judgment rested. She was now to be put upon her trial without any further delay or obstacle, being indicted for forging a bond of £5,300, as from William Adair, to Robert Perreau, with an intent to defraud Sir Thomas Frankland, Messrs. Drummond, and Mr. Adair. She said "that as the judges' opinion was in her disfavour, she cheerfully submitted to her trial, and pleaded *Not Guilty*." She was a second time indicted for a forgery for £6,000; a third for £3,100; and a fourth for £7,500. A chair was provided for her accommodation, that she might sit when she thought proper.

The prosecuting counsel having risen, he proceeded to expatiate upon the friendship pretended to have existed between her and Mr. William Adair, and her skill in imitating different handwritings. He next began to call witnesses for the crown, Mrs. Robert Perreau being the first. On her entering the witness-box, one of the counsel in behalf of the accused, asked Mrs. Perreau, "if Mrs. Rudd should be convicted, whether she did not think it would lead to an acquittal of her husband?" She replied, that she "hoped her husband's innocence would fully appear." The counsel insisted upon a positive and explicit answer to his question, when she said, "She hoped it would tend to acquit him." He then objected to her being admitted as a witness, as she was deeply interested in the result. Another counsel for Mrs. Rudd also insisted against the admissibility of Mrs. Perreau, upon the ground that a witness should "not be subjected to any temptation to falsify." The prosecuting counsel, however, argued that it would be impossible to convict any offender, if persons who had an advantage in such conviction were denied to give evidence, and mentioned the cases of accomplices who saved themselves, and persons robbed who had recovered their property by the conviction of the offender. Judge Ashton said Robert Perreau was not convicted of publishing the bond in question, but for uttering another; and he saw no objection to the competency of Mrs. Perreau's evidence. Mr. Baron Burland concurred in this opinion, observing that her interest in the conviction of the prisoner, though it could not destroy the competency of the witness, yet might possibly lessen the credit of her testimony with the jury.

Mrs. Perreau swore that, on the 24th of December, 1774, she saw Mrs. Rudd deliver a bond for £6,300, payable to Robert Perreau, and signed Wm. Adair, and that Mrs. Rudd said she would be obliged to him to procure £4,000 on it from Sir Thomas Frankland. In the evening Robert Perreau brought her something less than £4,000, and paid her in drafts. The next day the parties, and some friends from Wales, dined at Mr. Robert Perreau's, when the above bond was the subject of conversation between the brothers Perreau and the prisoner.

Sir Thomas Frankland deposed, that Robert Perreau came to his house, and borrowed £4,000 upon that bond, paying out of it near ten pounds for interest due for a bond of £5,000; and that he lent the money on the credit of the said Perreau.

John Moody, late servant to Mrs. Rudd, said that he knew her feigned, but not her proper or common hand-writing: that she used to give him letters of her own writing, for him to deliver as coming from Mr. Adair; that she wrote with crow-quill and other pens; that he had seen her direct these letters, which he had delivered five or six times.

Christian Hart, formerly servant to the prisoner, swore that she went to Mrs. Rudd in Newgate, who wrote down a set of instructions for her to swear to, to save her life; and promised her £100 or £200, or even ten times that sum, for her trouble; that Mrs. Rudd told her what a bond was, that she might acquaint the jury. These instructions being read, tended to criminate the Perreaus, and urged a connexion and scheme between Mrs. Perreau and Sir Thomas Frankland, in order to take away Mrs. Rudd's life. Mrs. Hart had written her name on the paper of instructions, and writing it again in court, the hands appeared to agree. She was asked if she knew Counsellor Bailey; she said " No."

The forged bond having next been read, and some other evidence adduced, tending to criminate the prisoner, she was told that now was the time for her to enter upon her defence, if she had any to deliver or make.

" My lords, and gentlemen of the jury," said she, " not knowing what evidence would be brought against me, and as I did not come here this day expecting that my trial would take place, I am ignorant in what manner to proceed on my defence. I should not now be a prisoner, if I had not attended in the first instance as a witness, in the full and perfect confidence of protection; it was in a direct and cheerful compliance with the law, that I have experienced the rigours of a long and severe confinement; and I have no doubt you will make every allowance for a person so circumstanced. As to Mrs. Perreau, she evidently acts under a bias; her intention is manifest; she swears to take away my life, to save the lives of her husband and brother. As for Sir Thomas Frankland, his evidence is sufficient to disgrace itself. Moody is the only person who has attempted to make any proofs of the actual forgery, and he has given such loose, improbable, and contradictory evidence, that I do not fear any disagreeable consequence from any confidence you can place in so base and treacherous a man. That Christian Hart has been employed in this business to swear away my life, in order to save the Perreaus, I trust I shall make plain to you, by the evidence I shall produce. Can you, gentlemen, believe it probable, that I, who had lost all my property, could promise £200, when I might as well talk of raising ten millions as half that sum? No one can seriously think that I could be so mad as to trust my life in the hands of so ignorant, so loose, and so infamous a character. Gentlemen of the jury, you are honest men, and I trust I am safe in your hands."

Witnesses were now called on the part of the prisoner; some of whom spoke to character, and flatteringly of her. Among these was Mr. Bailey—her former counsel—whose testimony, if correct, went wholly to contradict everything that Christian Hart had said and alleged relative to what occurred in Newgate between her and Mrs. Rudd. The presiding judge next summed up, and the jury, after half an hour's absence, brought in a verdict of Not Guilty, a finding which was hailed with the most boisterous applaudings by the multitude outside the court-room! The prisoner appeared almost stupefied with joy at her escape, for the other indictments were withdrawn. The trial lasted nearly eleven hours, during which she not only displayed the most imperturbable composure, but wrote about fifty notes to her counsel.

Mrs. Rudd, at her trial, appeared neatly attired in half-mourning. The moment she was acquitted she went out of court, and finding a hackney coach which was waiting for her, she was driven along the Old Bailey, Fleet-street, and the Strand, to St. Martin's-lane, to the house of a Worcestershire Lord,—a noted peer who had discarded his own lady. This nobleman furnished a house forthwith for the heroine of this eventful story, in Welbeck-street, near Cavendish-square, where she continued for a time to reside, making it part of her business, immediately after her narrow escape, to put forth in writing such statements as were intended to tell against the Perreaus. Indeed, whatever tendency the condemnation of Mrs. Rudd might have had in sparing the lives of the Perreaus, or Robert alone, her acquittal put an end to the respite which had been extended to them ever since Midsummer. They were included in the next report to his Majesty, and ordered for execution along with five other convicts, on Wednesday, the 17th of January, 1776. Meanwhile a most touching petition was presented to the King in favour of Robert, by his disconsolate wife and their three young children, each and all attired in deep mourning. Another petition, with a similar prayer, was submitted to the Sovereign, subscribed to by no fewer than seventy-eight of the leading bankers and merchants of the city of London, — a very remarkable circumstance, proving the deep impression which had been made in his behalf, and respecting his share in the forgeries. In fact, to this hour considerable mystery hangs over the motives and misdeeds of the Perreaus. Every effort proved unavailing for the saving even of Robert's life : the law was to take its course. The following are the principal passages of the account which the Ordinary of Newgate, who officiated in that character at the period, has left us relative to the last hours of the unhappy twin-brothers :—

" When the warrant came down for their execution, the prudence and humanity of the under-keepers (whose office it is to announce the melancholy news to convicts in general), prompted them to decline the painful task, and lay it upon me, to inform them upon what day they were to fall victims to the violated laws of their country. When I addressed them in their cell, upon the awful subject, they received it with apparent resignation, expressing at the same time their grateful sense of their keepers' kindness in their leaving that duty to me. Robert was greatly apprehensive that the final parting with his wife and children would be a conflict too severe and trying to bear with that manly fortitude, which was the peculiar characteristic of him, who entirely acquiesces in the will of Divine Providence. * * * After Mrs. Perreau had taken leave on the Saturday preceding the execution, his two sons were admitted next day, for the same purpose; the one, a youth of fifteen, the other, a child of eight years of age, whom, he told me, with tears in his eyes, he could hardly disengage himself from, owing to their tender affection and feeling for their poor father's miserable situation and impending catastrophe. The disconsolate wife could not refrain from repeating her visit once more on the Monday to take her last and solemn farewell. Towards the evening, when I saw him, he appeared as well composed as could be expected, after the shock he must have undergone. He and his brother being now together, on my informing them that the Jews, at the place of execution, were to be separated from them and the other convicts, and that a mourning coach was to be provided by the sheriffs, without any expense to their family, they jointly showed unusual satisfaction, and told me that I could not sufficiently express for them their gratitude to Mr. Reynolds, the under-sheriff, the kind proposer of that act of benevolence. Accordingly, an additional gallows was erected, in order to prevent any disturbance their minds might have been subjected to, from their opposite principles of religion, in their dying moments. On Tuesday night, after I left them, they were both locked up

ROBERT PERREAU BORROWING MONEY ON THE FORGED BONDS.

together in the same cell; and in the morning, upon my going into the gaol, they sent their servant to inform me that they would be glad to speak with me. When I entered their cell, they showed me their declarations, which they intended to deliver at the fatal tree, and which Daniel particularly protested were strictly true. Before they went up to chapel, with their three Christian fellow-sufferers, they requested to have a little nourishment, as they had not gone to rest all night. * * * The service being ended, they came down into the watch-room, where they sent for the executioner, and presented him with a guinea each. They underwent the preparation of haltering and binding, with a degree of firmness and resolution beyond what might have been expected. Soon after began the mournful procession, as follows :—

"First, the cart, in which went the two Jews, with George Lee, the highwayman, a fine, genteel youth, about 19 years of age, endowed with a deal of natural good sense, improved by a tolerable education, who assured me he was seduced into the paths of vice by associating with bad company. Next went the sledge, with Baker and Ratcliffe, the coiners, two very decent and well-behaved men; and last of all, the coach with the unfortunate brothers, with a sheriff's officer, and, by particular desire, myself. Almost immediately after the coach moved they applied themselves to prayer; and, at proper intervals, conversed with me, and sometimes took notice of the spectators, among whom they recognised several of their acquaintances. Robert said he hoped that wicked woman Mrs. Rudd was not a spectator ; and, when we drew near the place of execution, he added he should not wonder if she was; but Daniel appeared confident she was not. They both professed their forgiveness, and likewise prayed for her, especially Daniel, that she might return to a virtuous course of life. They likewise expressed themselves free from the least indignation against those in power, whom they supposed to be chiefly instrumental in excluding them from the royal mercy. * * * The people in general, as they passed along, demonstrated their pity by their tears and prayers ; and the only reflection thrown out against them was from a miscreant, who exclaimed, ' D———n them, hang them both together;' which being overheard by Robert, he meekly returned the opprobrious execration with a blessing."

The gloomy procession left Newgate a few minutes after nine o'clock, and arrived at the place of execution about half-past ten o'clock. The cart with the two Jews was immediately driven under one part of the gallows (for, as already mentioned, there were two divisions, distinct and separate from each other, a circumstance never before attended to at Tyburn). As soon as the descendants of Jacob were tied to the tree, a rabbi joined them in the cart, and prayed with them nearly up to the very moment that it was driven away. The others—the highwayman and the coiners—were then severally called for by the executioner, driven to their allotted stations, and placed where they were to undergo the last struggle. During this period, which might occupy about fifteen minutes, the two Perreaus remained in the coach with the clergyman. Daniel first entered the cart, and Robert immediately followed him, both ascending the vehicle with great firmness and resolution. They were attired in deep mourning. After the usual formalities of taking away the rope from the arms and waist, the executioner loosened Daniel's neckcloth, put the rope round his neck, and immediately tied it to the tree. He then proceeded in a similar manner with Robert.

These dread preliminaries over, the clergyman prayed with them. His devotions ended, he addressed himself to the two brothers, with whom he conversed for some time. He then asked them to acknowledge the justice of their sentence ; upon which they each put a paper into his hand.

Then, after praying a short time apart by themselves, each holding a prayer-book, the executioner put on their caps. The clergyman now took his leave, which Robert and Daniel acknowledged by bowing, and immediately embraced and saluted each other most tenderly and affectionately. They then took hold of each other's hands, the caps having been drawn over their eyes, and in this manner, the cart drawing away, they were launched into eternity,—their hands remaining firmly clenched together for a brief space. They were of twin-birth ; and, oh horrible fatality ! in their deaths were not separated.

They were both handsome men about five feet nine inches in height, very much alike in person, and about forty years of age. The number of spectators was extraordinary ; many estimated them at not less than 30,000.

The declarations which they handed to the chaplain contained the most solemn asseverations in each document of the unhappy writer's innocence. Their remains were privately interred on the Sunday evening following, in the family vault at St. Martin's-in-the-Fields; the most guilty of the three—holding the brothers to have been guilty—surviving to boast of her cunning and adroitness, as she frequently did afterwards, in that she " carried her point, and hanged the Perreaus," one of whom had idolized her, lavishing every indulgence and luxury upon the worthless and profligate wretch.

IX.—JONATHAN BRADFORD.

JONATHAN BRADFORD kept an inn in Oxfordshire, on the London road to Oxford, in the year 1736. He bore an unexceptionable character. Mr. Hayes, a gentleman of fortune, being on his way to Oxford, on a visit to a relation, put up at Bradford's; he there joined company with two gentlemen, with whom he supped, and in conversation unguardedly mentioned that he had then a large sum of money about him. In due time they retired to their respective chambers; the two gentlemen to a double-bedded room, leaving, as is customary with many, a candle burning in the chimney-corner. Some hours after they were in bed, one of the gentlemen being awake, thought he heard a deep groan in the adjoining chamber, and this being repeated, he softly awaked his friend. They listened together, and the groans increasing as of one dying, they both instantly arose, and proceeded silently to the door of the apartment from whence the distressing sounds issued; and the door being ajar, saw a light in the room. They entered, but it is impossible to paint their consternation, on perceiving a person weltering in his blood in the bed, and a man standing over him, with a dark lanthorn in one hand and a knife in the other. The person thus discovered seemed as petrified as themselves, but his terror carried with it all the significance of guilt! The gentlemen soon discovered that the individual whose life's-blood had been shed was the stranger with whom they had supped some hours before, and that he who was standing over him was their host. They instantly seized Bradford, disarmed him of his knife, and charged him with being the murderer. By this time the accused assumed the air of innocence, positively denied having perpetrated the crime, and asserted that he came there with the same humane intentions as they had done themselves; for that, hearing a noise, which was succeeded by a groaning, he got out of bed, struck a light, armed himself with a knife for his defence, and had but that minute entered the room before them.

These assertions were of little avail; he was kept in close custody till the morning, and then taken before a neighbouring justice of the peace. Bradford still denied the murder, but nevertheless with such an apparent indication of guilt, that the justice hesitated not to make use of this extraordinary expression, " Mr. Bradford, either you or myself committed this murder."

This extraordinary and tragical occurrence was the conversation of the whole country. Bradford was tried and condemned over and over again, in every company. In the midst of all this predetermination, came on the assizes at Oxford; the inn-keeper was brought to trial, and he pleaded not guilty. Nothing, apparently, could be stronger or clearer than the testimony of the two gentlemen,—nothing, it was universally thought, in regard to circumstantial evidence could be more complete or decisive than that which was brought to bear against the accused. The gentlemen testified to the finding Mr. Hayes murdered in his bed; to Bradford's being at the side of the body with a light and knife; to that knife and the hand which held it being bloody; and to the circumstance of the accused, on their entering the room, having betrayed all the signs of a guilty man, whose proceedings had been most stealthy; and to the fact that they had been stirred to the steps which they had at first taken by the groans which had reached them.

Bradford's defence on his trial was the same as before the gentlemen. He had heard a noise; he suspected some villany transacting; he struck a light; he snatched a knife, the only weapon near him, to defend himself; and the terrors he discovered were merely the terrors of humanity, the natural effects of innocence as well as guilt, on beholding such a horrid spectacle.

This defence, however, could be considered but as weak and highly improbable, when contrasted with the powerful circumstances against him. Never, surely, could stronger circumstantial evidence be produced,—never a clearer and more complete combination of facts and links required. There was hardly any need left for the summing up or comment of the judge. The thing was simple, plain, and obvious. Neither was there the slightest ground for extenuation! It was an unprovoked atrocity,—a case of unmitigated and tremendous criminality; and if ever a human being deserved to suffer death for robbing a fellow creature of his precious life, it was assuredly the murderer of Mr. Hayes. What! the host of the inn,—the head of the very establishment whose duty it was in a most special degree to afford security and comfort to all who favoured him with their custom, and entrusted themselves to him without reserve, to be butchered as Mr. Hayes had been, was revolting and frightful to the last degree,—an enormity that would be memorable for ages. How could the jury but instantly bring in the prisoner guilty who had been so clearly convicted of such a murder? Why stir from the place where they had sat to listen to the appalling disclosures, in order to consider of their verdict? Nor did they quit the box before pronouncing those fatal words which bereft the accused of even the slightest hope of escape. In short, Jonathan Bradford was executed very shortly after for the murder of Mr. Hayes, although, as many guilty men have done, he persisted to the last moment that he breathed in declaring that he neither was the murderer of the ill-fated gentleman, nor in the remotest degree privy to the murder: but he died disbelieved by all.

Yet were his asseverations quite true! The murder was actually perpetrated by Mr. Hayes's own footman, without the most distant participation of Bradford in the crime; the fellow, immediately on stabbing his master, having rifled his breeches of his money, gold watch, and snuff-box, and escaped to his own room; things which could have been accomplished, from what afterwards appeared, scarcely two seconds before Bradford's entering the unfortunate gentleman's apartment. The world owes this knowledge to a remorse of conscience in the footman (eighteen months after the execution of Bradford) on a bed of sickness. It was a death-bed repentance or confession, and by that death the law lost its victim.

It is much to be wished that this account could close here; but it cannot. Bradford, though innocent of the actual murder, and not in the slightest degree or manner privy to the footman's crime, was, nevertheless, a murderer of Mr. Hayes in design. He had heard, as well as the actual perpetrator of the crime, what the gentleman had said at supper as to his having a large sum of money about him, and he went to the chamber with the same diabolical intentions—although without concert—as the servant had done. Neither of them wished for, or had an accomplice. On stealthily entering the chamber, and beholding the dreadful spectacle before him in the bed, the landlord was struck with amazement!—he could not believe his senses! and, on turning back the bed-clothes, to assure himself of the fact, in his agitation he dropped his knife on the bleeding body, by which both his hands, and the instrument he brought with him, became smeared. These circumstances Bradford acknowledged to the clergyman who attended him after his condemnation.

We shall have frequent occasion to record instances of capital execution having been inflicted when the persons so suffering were innocent of the crime laid to their charge,—the real truth transpiring when it was too late to rescue innocence. It is not an unusual thing besides, to hear people,—when the amelioration of our criminal law, or of the abolition of death punishment is spoken of,—declare their approval of all such amendments, with the exception of the case of murder, as if this were the fittest or only dreadful offence where the gibbet should be brought into requisition. And yet it would be worth the while of all such sticklers to consider whether or not the crime of murder is that to which the punishment of death is the least properly applicable of all those delinquences and perpetrated offences which enter into the list of our code.

The punishment of death is irrevocable and irremediable, whereas others are not. Now, it might well be maintained that, all human judgment being liable to error, all human punishment should be of a sort capable of being repaired. But it is in the nature of judicial evidence that the proofs of murder should, all other things being equal, be less complete, generally, than those of any other crime. The party injured cannot bear witness, or, where he has survived the violence long enough to make a dying statement, it is not often that his statement can be very distinctly given. He who generally may be supposed best able to identify, not by feature or figure only, but by a multitude of circumstances also, is gone, and a mistake in identity,—that cardinal error, the liability to which has made many a sound lawyer maintain that a well connected chain of circumstances often affords better proof than positive evidence,—may fatally mislead justice throughout a whole case.

With regard to positive evidence, and the possibility of its being contrary to the truth, there are not a few illustrations, even in the history of our criminal procedure. In the autumn of 1838, for example, a seaman, named Horrebow, was sworn to at the Lambeth police-office, by several witnesses, as having been guilty of murder. On the next examination, another seaman, named Robertson was produced, who confessed having himself done the act. Horrebow had been by all the witnesses mistaken for the real criminal, and while the two seamen stood together in the magistrate's presence, they were so marvellously alike as to be hardly distinguishable from each other; the honesty of the witnesses was thus left entirely unimpeached who had sworn to that which was not true.

But most fatal errors, as was exemplified in the case of Jonathan Bradford, which have led to irreparable punishments, have arisen frequently out of circumstantial evidence in respect of murder. And yet this is the crime for which people would specially reserve the punishment which cannot be repaired. Till within the last few years, a law which our ancestors had provided specially for cases of murder was unrepealed and always carried into effect, by which the condemned had to be executed within, at most, forty-eight hours from the time of sentence being pronounced. As if, in the solemnest of all its acts, an act which can never be recalled or repaired, and in cases generally the most subject to erroneous judgments, a humane tribunal dreaded giving itself time to correct its judgment upon farther proof. Can it be a matter of wonder that, under such a system, —as was stated by Mr. Fitzroy Kelly, in his speech on capital punishment in the House of Commons, in 1840, from the returns he held in his hand,—it should have appeared that there were no less than fourteen instances known (and who knows how many more there were, where the truth has not come to light), since the beginning of this century, in which persons have been put to death by law, and their innocence afterwards clearly established? Fourteen instances! more than one in every three years! This is a very awful consideration. Well might one exclaim and demand on listening to such a statement,—What right has man, with this proneness or liability to error, to usurp to himself credit for one of the sublimest distinctive attributes of the Most High, *Infallibility*,—or, if not usurping credit for infallibility,—to proceed, upon his narrow, giddy judgment, to a penalty irrevocable and irreparable, and, therefore, properly belonging only to Omniscience itself?

X.—ELIZABETH CANNING.

THE credulity of the many has been, from the beginning, most readily imposed upon by the clever and designing few. We are, in spite of ourselves, very much the creatures of imagination and the victims of prejudice, which has been justly called the wrong bias of the soul, that effectually keeps it from coming near the path of truth; a task the more difficult to accomplish, since error often bears so near a resemblance to it. Error, indeed, always borrows something of truth, to make her more acceptable to the world, seldom appearing in her native deformity; and the subtlety of grand deceivers has always been shown ingrafting their greatest errors on some material truths, and with such dexterity, that Ithuriel's spear alone, whose touch
"No falsehood can endure,"
would have power to reveal them.

In the history of imposture, deception, and credulity, there has, perhaps, never been such an embarrassing case in England as that of Elizabeth Canning, for more than fifteen months the strange and mysterious affair between her and Mary Squires, a gypsy, as well as other persons, engrossing very much of the attention, conversation, and inquiry of the public. There was such a mixture of contradictions and probabilities, or at least possibilities, belonging to the affair, that it puzzled the acutest judgments to make an absolute determination concerning it. Some of the ablest and most experienced lawyers of the kingdom considered the case patiently without being able to come to a clear and decided opinion, or to penetrate to the bottom of it. The difficulties were laid before the King in Council, but even there it seemed not to have been cleared up. From the beginning to the end it was full of wonders and apparently unaccountable incidents. If Elizabeth Canning's story was true, and the facts alleged on her behalf at the trials were correctly stated, hardly any instance can be given of the like barbarity to which she was subjected, nor have her sufferings been often paralleled; so that she well deserved the pity and charity which were extended to her so generally. On the other hand, to all those who came to the conclusion that she had concocted a false tale and given lying information,— that she had forged a vile story merely to conceal her own evil deeds and shameful proceedings, what punishment was there which could appear too harsh for such a delinquent? What recompense could be adequate for the poor creature, who was condemned to death upon the testimony of the young woman whose name must figure chiefly in the present article? Meanwhile, in so nice a case, where the proof seemed so strong on both sides of the question, it will be the more satisfactory way to give the substance of the evidence that was adduced for each party.

On the 6th of January, 1753, this advertisement appeared in the Daily Advertiser:— "Whereas Elizabeth Canning went from her friends between Houndsditch and Bishopsgate, on Monday evening last, the 1st instant, between 9 and 10 o'clock, whoever can give any account where she is, shall have two guineas reward ; to be paid by Mr. Canning, a sawyer, in Aldermanbury Postern, which will be a great satisfaction to her mother. She is fresh coloured, pitted with the small pox, has a high forehead, light eye-brows, about five feet high, eighteen years of age, well set, had on a masquerade purple stuff gown, a black petticoat, a white chip hat bound round with green, a white apron and handkerchief, blue stockings and leather shoes.—*Note.* It is supposed she was forcibly taken away by some evil disposed person, as she was heard to shriek out in a hackney coach in Bishopsgate-street. If the coachman remembers anything of the affair, by giving an account as above, he shall be handsomely rewarded for his trouble."

Meanwhile the mother of Elizabeth Canning having a very good character, and being well esteemed in her vicinity, where she had dwelt for many years, and the girl having also always borne a good reputation, the neighbours interested themselves greatly in the poor woman's misfortunes, and promised to contribute a larger reward for the discovery of the damsel, which was accordingly advertised, every other method having also been resorted to, in order to gain some intelligence of what had become of her. No spot or place was left unsearched ; even gaols and hospitals were not omitted. But all in vain, and weeks rolled on in this miserable state of suspense, without the slightest tidings being obtained of the girl, till the 29th of January, when she returned to her mother's house about 10 o'clock at night, in a frightful and miserable condition. The account she now gave of what had happened to her, was as follows :—

She stated, that on the 1st of January she went to see her uncle and aunt, who were people of very good character, and lived at Saltpetre Bank, near Rosemary-lane; that having continued with them till towards 9 in the evening, her uncle and aunt—it being late—walked a great part of the way home with her ; that soon after parting with them, she came opposite to Bethlehem-gate in Moorfields, when she was seized by two men who, after robbing her of half a guinea in gold, and three shillings in silver, of her hat, gown, and apron, violently dragged her into a gravel walk that leads down to the gate of Bethlehem Hospital ; about the middle of which one of the men, after threatening to do for her, gave her a violent blow with his fist on the right temple, that threw her into a fit, entirely depriving her of her senses. These fits, she said, she had been subject to ; that they were occasioned by the falling of a ceiling on her head, that they were apt to return upon her whenever she was frightened, and that they sometimes continued for six or seven hours at a time ; that when she came to herself, she perceived that two men were hurrying her along in a large road way, and that in a little while after she had recovered she was able to walk alone ; that, however, they still continued to pull and draw her along ; that she was so intimidated by their usage, that she durst not call out, nor even speak to them. ; that in about half an hour after the recovery of her senses, they carried her into a house, where she saw in the kitchen an old gypsy woman and two young women ; that the old gypsy took hold of her by the hand, and promised to give her fine clothes if she would go their way ; and understanding the proposal to mean the becoming of a prostitute, she utterly refused to comply with it. Upon this the old gypsy woman took a knife out of a drawer and cut her stays off, taking them away from her, at which time one of the men also took off her cap, and then both the men went away ; that soon after they were gone, and about half an hour after she had been in the house, the gypsy forced her up an old pair of stairs, and pushed her into a back room like a hay-loft, without any furniture whatever in the same, there locking her in, and threatening that if she made the least noise or disturbance, she, the gypsy woman, would come up and cut her throat ; and th having so spoken she went away.—She declared, that wnen it was daylight, upon her looking around to see in what dismal place she was, she discovered a large black jug, with the neck much broken, filled with water, and several pieces of bread, amounting to about the quantity of a quartern loaf, scattered on the floor, where was likewise a small parcel of hay. In this loft, she declared, she continued fromt at: me ill out half an hour after 4 o'clock in the afternoon of Monday the 29th January,—being in all twenty-seven days and upwards,—without any other substance than the aforesaid bread and water, except one small minced pie which she happened to have in her pocket for a present to her little brother. She also declared, that she had some part of the provisions remaining on the Friday before she made her escape, this having been effected by breaking out at a window of the loft in which she had been confined, and that having got clear away, she went back to her friends in London in about six hours, in a weak and miserable condition, having been almost starved to death, and without even once stopping at any house or place on the way. She also said, that during the whole time of her confinement, no person ever came near to her to ask her any question whatever, nor did she see any belonging to the house more than once, when one of the women peeped through a hole in the door, and that she herself was afraid to call or speak to any one.

Such was Elizabeth Canning's mode of accounting for her absence from home; even those who favoured her side of the story admitting that it was a very extraordinary narrative, resembling rather a wild dream than a real event.

We must now proceed to the testimonies of witnesses and the array of circumstances which were brought out, with the view to support the damsel's story on the one hand and to demolish it on the other. After attending to such evidence, and some of the arguments by which the whole was sought to be unravelled, our readers may, perhaps, be enabled to see the whole affair in its true light.

The absence of Elizabeth Canning had made so much noise, and appeared so strange, that as soon as news of her return became spread, many people repaired to her mother's house to talk with her; her weak condition, however, not permitting her to answer many questions at a time. In answer to the general question as to where she had been, she said that it was somewhere upon the Hertford Road, because she had seen the coachman, who used to carry her mistress to Hertford, go by, and that she had once heard the name of *Wills* or *Wells* mentioned in the house. Upon this some of those who came to see her observed it most probably was *Mother Wells's*, as it was called, at Enfield Wash, a house of very bad fame; and it came to be determined that the girl, though in a very weak condition, should go before the sitting alderman, and make affidavit of the alleged outrage, in order to obtain a warrant for the apprehension of the infamous female named. Accordingly, on the 31st of January, the young woman was carried before the magistrate, when her deposition was taken; in which deposition she declared, the room in which she had been confined was a darkish, little square loft; that she lay upon the boards; that there was nothing in it except a grate, with a gown in it; that there was a picture over the chimney, also specifying some other slight particulars.

This account differed in some circumstances from what she deposed afterwards, and also from what the room was found to be—discrepancies which were strongly alleged against her story. However, a warrant was granted by the alderman for the apprehension of the accused parties, it being resolved by the damsel's friends that she should be carried down to Wells's house next day, several of those who espoused her cause accompanying her. Among these were Mr. Lyon, the master in whose service she had been at the period of her disappearance; Mr. Wintleburg, with whom she had lived before; and a number of their neighbours and acquaintances. These gentlemen being fired with a just resentment, resolved, if possible, to bring the alleged horrid piece of villany to light. One of them got to Enfield Wash considerably before the others, in order to secure all the persons found in the house, and also to view the room in which Elizabeth Canning said she had been confined. When he had so done, he went to meet the coach which was bringing her to the place, when he asked her some questions about the room, which she described nearly in the manner she had done before, and as he said he had found it. When they arrived at the house, they carried her in their arms—for she was not able to walk—and set her upon a dresser in the kitchen. Then the people, who had been secured, were brought before her, to see if she knew any of them. Upon beholding Mary Squires, the gipsy woman, she declared that this was the person who cut off her stays, and threatened, when she turned her up into the room, to cut her throat if she made any noise. Squires to this made answer, she hoped she would not swear her life away, for she never saw her before. Then Canning, pointing to Virtue Hall, a young woman who was found in the house by the gentlemén, said that she was in the kitchen at the same time, and likewise another girl, who was Squires's daughter.

The gentlemen then carried the complainant up stairs, to examine the rooms above, but none of those first shown was that wherein she said she had been confined. They then asked her if there were any other rooms in the house? She said there was one out of the kitchen; and being carried into it, she declared that that was the apartment in which she had been shut up. They then inquired whether she could remember anything she had seen from the window? She answered that she had seen a hill at a distance, which was Chinkford Hill, and that there were some houses on the other side of the lane; and upon opening the casement everything appeared as she had described it. They next desired her to show them the window by which she had escaped. Upon examining the one she pointed out, they found it large enough for a person to get through, and on the outside some of the plaster was broken away. They likewise found a black jug, a bason, and a tobacco mould, which Canning had spoken of in her examination before the alderman.

When Mary Squires, her daughter, and Virtue Hall were brought before Canning to see if she knew or remembered any of them, John Squires was likewise in the room. She was asked if he was amongst them at the time of the outrage made upon her the first night she was in the house? to which she answered that she could not take it upon her to swear to him, because the man whom he resembled had a great coat on at the time; but that he looked like the person. On their coming before a magistrate afterwards, the man was made to put on his great coat, and now she said he looked more like one of the two men than before, yet that she could not be perfectly positive he was the very person.

On learning what the complainant had said relative to Virtue Hall, a warrant was granted for her apprehension, in order to be brought before a magistrate for examination touching the ill-usage sworn to; and it so happened that she confirmed everything which Canning alleged to have occurred to her in Wells's house. It is true, that when Hall was examined before the justice of peace alluded to, it was a long time ere she could be brought to say anything of an accusing nature. However, as she was taken in the same house, and had lived there some time, the justice was the more urgent to bring her to a confession, since, if such a piece of villany as was alleged had been acted there, she (Hall) must have been cognizant of it. In consequence of threats, persuasions, and arguments, she was at last prevailed upon to declare the particulars sought for, viz., that she had lived at Wells's first as a lodger, but afterwards did as they would have her, and that Mary Squires had also lived there about seven or eight weeks. That on the 2nd of January, Elizabeth Canning was brought in there about 4 o'clock in the morning by two men, one of whom was John Squires, the son of Mary Squires, but the other man was unknown to her; that when Canning was brought in, she had no gown, hat, or apron on; that there was then in the house the said Mary Squires, her daughter, and herself; that when they came in, "Mother," said John Squires, "I have brought a girl—pray take her," upon which the gipsy asked Canning whether she would go their way? that was, be a prostitute and thief. On her answering no, the gipsey took a knife out of a dresser drawer and ripped the lace off her stays, and took them off, and hung them on a chair in the kitchen, then pushed her up into the hay-loft, saying, "D—n you, go up there, if you please;' upon which, the man that came in with John Squires, snatched the cap off her head, and the said Squires took the stays, and both went away together. As to the room in which Canning was put, it was called the work-shop, where was a good deal of hay, pieces of wood, a tobacco mould, and a black jug. That when Canning had been about three hours in the room, the gipsy, Mary Squires, filled the jug with water and carried it to her.

With regard to Susannah Wells, Hall declared she had no husband, and that upon going into the parlour to her, Wells said, "Virtue, the gipsy-man tells me his mother has cut off the stays from the young woman's back, and that he had got them, and that Wells ordered her to take no notice of it for fear it should be known." Hall deposed further, that she (the witness) had been in Wells's house a quarter of a year or more, and the whole time that Elizabeth Canning was there, but never saw her after she was put into the loft; that she (Hall) was the first that missed the girl, upon which she asked the gipsy woman if she had gone? that the answer returned was, "What is that to you? What business have you with it?" That she (Hall) was afraid to go and see whether or not the girl was gone, for fear she should herself be served in the same manner. She further declared that the gipsy woman continued in the house till they were all taken up; and that the gipsies had been in the house from first to last, about six or seven weeks.

In this way the story of Canning seemed to be in the distinctest and strongest manner supported by the testimony of Virtue Hall, so that here was all the appearance of guilt that could be reasonably expected on the part of the accused,—especially the gipsy woman, Mary Squires, and the keeper of the house in which it was alleged the complainant had been confined, viz., Susannah Wells. There was the positive evidence, upon oath, of the alleged sufferer herself, against the woman who was said to have robbed her of a portion of her clothing, and also as related to the ill-usage in the house described,—evidence which was corroborated by the statement upon oath of one who spoke to that of which she said she had been an eye and ear witness. There was also the confirmation furnished by the ocular inspection of the persons that went down to Wells's house, who found not only the individuals there whom Canning accused, and whom she pointed out as soon as they came before her, but the loft nearly in the condition of which they had been told; so that there seemed to be no ground for a suspicion of deceit or delusion,— of credulity or imposture in the case.

It need not be wondered at then, that a vigorous prosecution of the alleged offenders in this instance was urged on by the friends of Elizabeth Canning. Subscriptions were set on foot to assist her in the procuring of that justice which her severe sufferings and the laws of the country were held to entitle her to. Those who more warmly espoused her cause, exerted themselves to the uttermost to procure all the reparation in their power to what they considered to be unjust and oppressed innocence. That nothing might be wanting in the girl's behalf, who was given out to be a creature of great simplicity, altogether harmless, and also to have never lost that character in the course of her services in different families, her supporters published her case in the newspapers; they printed placards in her behalf; and did everything in their power to move the charitable and benevolent of all degrees to contribute something; not barely to assist her in carrying on the prosecution, but to form some recompense for the terrible hardships she had undergone, as well as a reward for so resolutely maintaining her virtue in the face of so much danger.

On this occasion there was manifested the true English spirit of generosity,—a spirit which not only animated the breasts of tradesmen and mechanics, classes that are generally more intimately acquainted with the wants, troubles, and discomforts of the world and the poorer classes, than those of eminence; but persons of the highest rank and most distinguished order took a compassionate share in the movement. Generally speaking, the slightest doubt was not entertained that Canning's case was otherwise than truly represented. Accordingly she was on one occasion sent for to White's Chocolate House, at St. James's; when, after the gentlemen and noblemen there met at the time had asked her a number of questions,—all which she answered to their satisfaction,—they made her up a purse of thirty guineas. In fact, soon after the publication of her story, the money collected for her amounted to not less than £300; the fund having been deposited in trustworthy hands, for the use of the girl, as soon as it should appear, beyond all contradiction, that she had a clear title to it.

Thus far the cause of Elizabeth Canning might be pronounced clear and strong, though it is to be confessed that there were persons from the first who never ceased to suspect gross deceit and villany to have been some how or way connected with her story, which would at length be brought to light.

Nothing of a very particular nature happened after what has been narrated of this affair, until the time of trial of the gipsy woman, Mary Squires, and of Susannah Wells, the housekeeper; the charge against the former being that of an assault on the complainant, and also of robbing her of a pair of stays, value ten shillings,—while the accusation of the other was for feloniously receiving, harbouring, comforting, &c., the said Mary Squires, knowing that she had committed the felony in question.

The accused, whose trials took place at the Old Bailey, on the 21st of February, 1753, were both found guilty; sentence of death having been passed upon Mary Squires, and that of branding and imprisonment in Newgate for six months upon Susannah Wells.

Yet the difficulties and the controversy relative to the strange affair did not stop or find rest here. The good people of the metropolis became more heated and divided than before on the subject, splitting into two zealous parties; pamphlets upon pamphlets being written and circulated relative to the mysterious story of Canning,—some of these *brochures* by men of considerable literary fame; others by eminent professional gentlemen. Most remarkable of all, the author of "Tom Jones" figured on the side of Canning in an especial manner.

Upon the trial of the two women, three witnesses, of good character and credit, appeared in behalf of the gipsy, who, if they spoke truth, clearly made out an *alibi* in her case. One of these swore that she had, on the 1st of January, lodged at his house, the sign of the Old Ship, at Abbotsbury, six miles from Dorchester, in Dorsetshire, along with

George her son, and Lucy her daughter. That she came with lawn, handkerchiefs, and other pedlery wares, to sell about the town, and was there to the 9th of the same month; and that he had known her for three years, and perfectly remembered the time when she last lay at his house.

Another of these witnesses said, that he saw the gipsy woman at Abbotsbury, and on the 10th of January went with her some way together on the road; and that he had seen the landlord's wife at the Ship buy some aprons of her at the time she was there last. The third witness, who kept the sign of the Lamb, at Coom, not far from Salisbury, swore that, on the 14th of January, Mary Squires, the gipsy woman, was at his house, where she lay one night.

These assuredly were staggering contradictions; but what was still more remarkable, and as if there were to be no limits to the mystification connected with Elizabeth Canning's story, the arraigned gipsy, notwithstanding the positive evidence of these three witnesses, and though she had been at the expense to *subpœna* them at so great a dis·tance in the country to attend her trial at the Old Bailey,—when she was called up to say why the doom of death should not be pronounced against her,—notwithstanding such positive and exculpatory testimony, to the amazement of all, she contradicted whatever had been said in her favour, by asserting that on New Year's day she lay at Widow Grevil's house, at Coom; the next day was at Stoptage; that she drank at an ale-house in Basingstoke on the Thursday in the New Year week; that on Friday she lay at a small house on Bagshot Heath; on Saturday at Old Brentford; and that on the Tuesday or Wednesday after she came to Mrs. Wells's house. Thus the testimony of her own witnesses seemed to be overturned! so that it could scarcely be expected that the jury could do otherwise than find her guilty.

In spite of all these things, however, Sir Crisp Gascoigne, the Lord Mayor at the period, had observed in the evidence, and during the course of the trial, certain things and points, which gave him reason to doubt the soundness of the verdict, and especially to suspect the story of Canning herself, as well as the testimony of the girl Hall. It seems to have been a feature in the mayor's character to pursue to its utmost limits whatever matter he took earnestly in hand; certainly he left no stone unturned, no means untried in order to satisfy himself in the present instance. Probably his lordship perceived in the testimony of the three Dorsetshire men such directness and simplicity, as persuaded him not only of their sincerity but of their accuracy, without caring much for the contradictions of the wretched gipsy herself. At any rate, he lost no time in ordering letters to be written to some of the principal inhabitants of Abbotsbury, inquiring whether Mary Squires was known among them, and whether they remembered her being at that place in the beginning of the immediately preceding month of January.

To these letters answers were promptly returned, containing attestations and affidavits of the vicar of the place, the churchwardens and overseers, and other respectable inhabitants, all concurring in their testimony, that Mary Squires, the gipsy woman, had been in that place at the time when the robbery of Elizabeth Canning was sworn to have been committed, and that she had at that period continued for several days there. By one of the answers the Lord Mayor was assured that he might have a hundred more attestations from the people of that town, that Mary Squires and her children were at the place, not only on the day particularly specified, but for several succeeding days,—having been seen and spoken to by a great number of persons. While the mayor was thus assiduous in striving to make a full discovery of the facts, in order that justice might be rightly administered, there were other gentlemen, who were no less suspicious and earnest in endeavouring to sift the matter to the bottom.

On Tuesday, March 6, in the evening, Justice Lediard, a magistrate, and some other gentlemen in company, discoursing upon the case of Elizabeth Canning and the trial of the two women, one present stated that a Mr. Ford had affidavits in his possession from inhabitants of Abbotsbury, testifying that Mary Squires had actually been in that town on the day when the robbery was alleged to have been committed and the other outrage perpetrated. It happened very fortunately that the girl Virtue Hall was then in the *Gate-house*; and upon learning this, the company agreed to send for her, seeing that it was in consequence of her corroborative evidence principally that Squires had been convicted.

The girl being brought before Justice Lediard, he put several questions to her, of a nature calculated to extract the truth from her. He showed her how dreadful her crime would be, how heinous and weighty her offending, if the woman whom she had sworn to be guilty, were wholly innocent after all of the deeds she had accused her of; that she would be chargeable with the blood of an innocent person, whose life she had taken away by means of deep perjuries, and with this farther aggravation that she had done it without any provocation, or the least prospect of advantage to herself. He left it to her consideration, how she would appear before the tremendous tribunal of an all-seeing and Almighty Judge, whose justice could not be evaded, and who only could inflict a punishment adequate to the atrocity, if she had sworn falsely and to the murdering of a fellow creature. He implored her to consider that if she was really guilty of the enormous crime of perjury, the consequences of which were so dreadful, there was yet an opportunity of making some reparation for what was past, by immediately discovering the whole truth, so far as it was known to her, whereby the life, which by her means had been brought into such imminent danger, might be saved.

These and similar representations made a visible impression upon the girl. Her confusion became manifest; tears trickled down her cheeks; she was in the utmost agitation, and as if willing to say something—to drop some word,—showing, as was thought by all who observed her at the moment, that she had some dreadful secret labouring on her mind, which she was almost ready to divulge, yet was fearful of the consequences did she reveal it. What, in fact she did utter on this occasion was some detraction from her former evidence, for she desired that night to consider of what had been stated to her and promised that in the morning she would tell the whole truth.

The gentlemen expressed their willingness to await her own time, exhorting her most earnestly and with all the touching appeals that suggested themselves, to weigh seriously the importance and the urgency of the business; assuring her, for her encouragement, that a recantation of her former evidence should in no way turn to her hurt.

Next day the Lord Mayor, having received the affidavits and attestations which had been transmitted from Abbotsbury, ordered them to be read before him. Hereupon the gentlemen, who the night before had been present at the examination of Virtue Hall by Justice Lediard, acquainted his lordship that the girl was then in the Gate-house, and also in regard to the manner in which she had so recently borne herself to them. Upon this he sent orders to have her brought before him, when she made the following statement :—

She now declared in the most solemn manner that what she had sworn against Mary Squires was false; that this woman was not in the house of Mrs. Wells on the day when the robbery was alleged to have been committed, nor for weeks after; that in fact no such robbery had ever been committed there at all; and that Elizabeth Canning never had been in the house until brought down by those who carried on the prosecution. She further added that she had given the same account to the magistrate by whom she had been first examined, at the same time declaring, that while she lived at Wells's, no person whatever had been confined in that house, nor in any room belonging to it, and that the whole story, so far as related to Canning's being robbed and confined in it, was a pure fiction and gross forgery.

She was then asked what could induce her to swear to such a number of falsehoods as she did at the trial, to take away the life of a person who had never done her any wrong. To this she gave a plain and direct answer, says the account which we follow; but as that account contained reflections on certain parties, including a magistrate and a clerk, who had made themselves active in the case, the particulars of her answer are not stated.

The next day again, being Thursday, the Lord Mayor had Virtue Hall once more brought before him, Elizabeth Canning having been also sent for, in order that the two gilrs might confront one another. Hall had passed a night since her first examination before the Lord Mayor, and therefore had had time sufficient to recollect and duly weigh everything she had already advanced. And that she might not be daunted with the apprehension that any advantage to her hurt would be taken of her confession, the Mayor assured her that she was under his protection, and that nothing she should say on that occasion should be turned to her injury.

Having thus addressed the girl, he demanded of her in the most solemn manner, whether what she had declared when she was last before him was true, or whether what she had deposed at the trial were so? To this she answered that what she had last declared was the truth, and that all she had sworn upon the trial was false.

Finding herself perfectly at liberty to speak her mind freely, without care or reserve, she added that she had always given the same account to every person who had the curiosity to ask her any questions about it; that she ever affirmed that Elizabeth Canning was never at Mrs. Wells's house, before she came down with a power to apprehend the inmates; and that Mary Squires never had been there till about a week before she was taken up, this being three weeks after the pretended robbery was alleged to have been committed. All which, she affirmed upon oath, she had always declared, until she was terrified into swearing falsely.

As soon as the Lord Mayor became convinced that Virtue Hall had made an ingenuous and true confession of the real truth, he ordered Elizabeth Canning to be brought before him and confronted with her. Hall now repeated what she had already declared to the face of the other girl, and this with such firmness and composure, as strengthened the conviction of the Mayor that she spoke the truth, and was not at all afraid of being convicted of falsehood when so doing; adding, that while she kept the secret of the perjury with herself, she had experienced neither peace nor rest of mind, but that now she was in a measure easy, having unburdened her conscience.

Elizabeth Canning was next allowed to speak, and to put any questions to the other she thought fit; but as she asked nothing but what Hall had spoken to already, and by which she now firmly stood, it is unnecessary to go into the repetition.

Soon after this the Lord Mayor, accompanied by some of the aldermen, went to Newgate to examine Wells concerning the robbery of Canning in her house at Enfield Wash; for as this woman already knew the extent of the punishment to be inflicted upon her, it could not serve her any very important end to conceal the truth. Being accordingly closely interrogated, she spoke out, declaring her own innocence, and also that she had never beheld the girl Canning in the whole course of her life, until the time that she (Wells), with others, were taken into custody at Enfield Wash.

Sir Crisp Gascoigne succeeded in his efforts to obtain a respite for Squires, the gipsy woman, but who would certainly have suffered a violent death, had his lordship not strenuously interfered in her behalf. As it was, so great had been the pity excited in the breasts of multitudes for Elizabeth Canning, so violent the public indignation against the condemned woman, and so wedded to the first impressions formed of the still perplexed affair, that the Mayor rendered himself extremely unpopular by his activity and success. Floods of ink were expended in publications by those who continued to espouse Canning's side of the question; nor were her opponents less active. However, the gipsy woman not only obtained a respite, but ere long a free pardon,—the more thoroughly the mysterious affair was looked into, the more improbable the details of the late prosecutrix, the more startling the discrepancies in the evidence of her case being felt to become. And this brings us to the last scenes of the mysterious drama; party feeling and the controversial heat still gathering fervour and vehemence all the while. But as the mass of evidence against Canning was daily gaining weight, and had become enormous, it was resolved to put her upon her trial for perjury—a trial memorable were it only because of its duration, for it lasted five days, more than a hundred and twenty witnesses having been examined in the course of it.

On Monday, the 29th of April, 1754, Elizabeth Canning was brought into the court of the Old Bailey, at 9 o'clock, indicted, for that she, not having the fear of God before her eyes, did wickedly endeavour, by wilful and corrupt perjury, to take away the life of one of his Majesty's subjects, in falsely swearing a robbery against Mary Squires, a gipsy. To this indictment the prisoner, who so recently had acted as prosecutrix, pleaded *Not Guilty*, and put herself upon her trial.

Canning was dressed in a clean linen gown, and had a black bonnet on; for extremely minute are the reports even relative to such points that were printed at the time, although from the one-sided views adopted in most of those publications, it requires care and patience to furnish an impartial account of the numerous facts and circumstances belonging to the subject. Her behaviour was becoming and composed, and altogether calculated to produce an impression favourable to her. And yet not less affecting was the appearance of the lately condemned Mary Squires, with whom the prisoner so strangely had been made to change positions; for the poor creature had to be carried into court in an armchair, being sick and faint, and "her head sinking very much." She was dressed in a stuff gown, having "a white whittle over her shoulders, a white napkin pinned over her head, and a black bonnet on." She was about eighty years of age, and had the features of the gipsy tribe in a very remarkable degree. She had frequently, owing to her faintness and the heat of the crowded court, to be carried out into an adjoining room, to receive the benefit of fresher air, during the time of the examinations, and again to be brought back when her presence was necessary; her son George, and her daughter Lucy, attending her assiduously all the while.

The trial of Canning was in many respects one of the most remarkable that ever occurred in England. No doubt, to a dispassionate and unprejudiced reader of the evidence adduced, and of the improbabilities and inconsistencies of the various statements which she made, together with what, after all, were found to be the discrepancies as respected ascertained facts,—such as the condition of the room in which she said she had been confined,—it must be clear that her tale was false, and that the gipsy had been murderously accused. In her first examination before the sitting magistrate, it was put down that she had been shut up in a little dark, square room,—though she said there were two windows in it, one glazed, the other partly boarded and partly glazed,—whereas the apartment instead of being small, square, and dark, measured about thirty feet in length, by nine in breadth, and the casement of the one window was so large, that a fat man might have got out of it, and therefore the place must have been light. Then it was so low, that a child might have leaped out of it to the ground. In the first information it was said that she lay upon nothing but bare boards, whereas there was half a load of hay in the loft; she deposed also that her water failed her on the Friday before her escape on the Monday, although on the trial of Squires she swore that she drank the last of her water about half an hour before she made her escape. In her first information she said there was only an old stool or two, an iron grate, an old table, and an old picture over the chimney; whereas, instead of a grate, the floor of the chimney was found covered with cobwebs, that seemed the work of generations of spiders; three saddles were found in the apartment, fastened to the walls, with the webs of the same race of insects, which she had never spoken about; and a large nest of drawers were also found there, with a bed made of straw; and there was no picture over the chimney,—nothing but an old casement, which was covered with dirt and cobwebs.

Besides there was a great number of witnesses of unquestioned respectability, from Abbotsbury, in Dorsetshire, who swore positively and harmoniously that the gipsy had been in that place during nearly the whole of the first half of the alleged January, and for days previously,—nor does it seem to have been possible to mistake her identity, seeing that her face and features are described as being such as to strike a sort of horror in the beholder,—there was a couple, man and wife, who also deposed upon oath that they had lain in the very room in which Canning alleged she had been confined, during the whole of the month of January, and that no such person as the prisoner was ever seen at the place whilst they lodged at Wells's. Three countrymen swore, too, that they had been employed in lopping trees close to Wells's house on the 8th of January, when they talked to Virtue Hall and Sarah Howell, who were at the time looking out of the loft where Canning said she had been shut up, but they neither heard of her nor saw her at the time.

Three of the persons who had accompanied Elizabeth Canning when she was carried to Enfield Wash, in order to see whether she could make her story good, were examined on her trial, and each of them deposed that he had dropped her cause from that time, having seen and heard enough at Mrs. Wells's to convince them that the girl was an imposter. And yet strange admissions came from the lips of these same three Londoners on being cross questioned. The conclusion of the evidence of one of them, a Mr. Nash, was to this effect,—that from the very time, viz. his going to Enfield Wash, he thought Canning was a wilful deceiver, or else was greatly deceived, and that he had given up espousing her cause from that very day. He was asked that question three or four different times, and each time replied, that from that very hour he had left off having any thing to do in her favour; that he had often declared what he deposed now, in common conversation. Being interrogated why he did not come forward with this statement upon the trial of the gypsy, he said, he was present at the part of the trial, but being butler to the Goldsmiths' Company, and having a great dinner to get for them that day, he left the Old Bailey by 11

ELIZABETH CANNING RECEIVING VISITS OF CONDOLENCE.

o'clock; and that while he was discontented at the evidence of Canning he also thought that the gypsy would not be convicted; for, if he had thought so, he would have stayed and given the same testimony as he did now; that soon after he heard that the poor creature was respited, he went voluntarily to the Lord Mayor, being dissatisfied in his own mind, and told him he could let him into the whole affair. He was next asked whether he had not heard the gypsy positively sworn against by Canning, before he left the Sessions House, which must needs convict her, if she was believed? He owned he had; upon which it was very properly said, that it was very extraordinary, when the life of a fellow creature was in the balance, that he should not stay and throw in his weight on the side of what he believed was just and true.

A Mr. Hague, and a Mr. Aldrich, gave much the same account with that of Nash; both declaring that they dropped Canning's cause from the time of their going out with her to Wells's house. They both owned, too, having been present at the trial of the gypsy, and gave *their* reasons for not then coming forward to declare what they knew concerning the inconsistencies of the girl's story, when the life of a human being was at stake, one of them answering; he was so shocked at the turn the case took, that he had not power to speak what he felt about it! and the other, that he was engaged to dine with a gentleman in Smithfield, and left the Sessions House before the trial was quite finished!

But the anomalies attaching to the cases of Mary Squires and Elizabeth Canning did not stop here; and amongst these is to be mentioned the fact that a number of witnesses came forward in behalf of Canning on her trial, chiefly from Enfield Wash, who positively swore that the gypsy had frequented that place and neighbourhood during the period when the prisoner alleged she had been confined in Wells's house. In fact, it seemed to some extent to be a contest of swearing against swearing, maintained too by numbers, not a few on each side being considered persons of respectability; so that were it not for the gross improbabilities of Canning's story, taken merely by itself, her discrepancies and several versions, and also its contradictions to clearly ascertained facts, it would be a difficult matter to come to any satisfactory conclusion with regard to the truth, as discoverable from the conflicting stories.

It is not easy to say how far the strong prejudices and heated passions which pervaded the community might go to pervert the testimonies of persons who were otherwise held to be trustworthy. Certain it is, however, that the controversy which had been evoked on the subject, had, by the time Canning's trial took place, arisen to a high pitch of fervour, if not of rancour, not only on the part of those who formed the masses, but of the newspaper and pamphleteering press. The accused girl was the popular favourite, the multitude deeming it proper and magnanimous to lift up their voices against the Lord Mayor, and the authorities that sided with him. In order to show to what extremes the partisanship was carried it is only necessary to take notice of sundry circumstances and incidents which occurred both within the Sessions House and also beyond its walls in relation to Canning's trial.

At the very commencement of the trial, the counsel for the prosecution challenged no less than *sixteen* of the jury, a proceeding which had seldom been paralleled except in cases of treason, and thereby showing how deeply the public mind was infected one way or another relative to her story. Again, after a long sitting on the first day of the trial, when the court proposed an adjournment, this was strongly objected to by the prisoner's counsel, although without carrying their point. The prosecution then moved that Canning should be delivered into the custody of the keeper of Newgate; but this was warmly spoken against by her counsel, and she was admitted to bail till the next morning, her former bail entering into fresh recognizances. The girl was then put into a coach as privately as possible; but the populace being made aware of the measure, hung upon and followed the carriage, shouting and huzzaing madly, so that she was obliged to take to a house in the Old Bailey and there remain till nearly midnight, before the crowd so dispersed as to allow her to repair to her mother's without being accompanied by vociferous and excited partisans. But the mob not content themselves with huzzaing and expressing their determination to see Canning righted, who, it was alleged, after enduring unheard of cruelties and bearing them with heroic virtue, was now sought to be victimized by the chief magistrate of the metropolis and a powerful clique,—for many of the crowd collected near the court-house were audacious enough to insult and attack Sir Crisp the moment he made his appearance at the close of the first day's proceedings in the trial. No doubt the real and respectable friends of the accused girl were innocent of such an outrage, and felt anxious to clear themselves of the imputations cast upon them which followed the assault. That night accordingly they had the following handbill circulated among the multitudes that were assembled in the Sessions House yard, and neighbourhood :—

"Although nothing can be said to have been proved against Elizabeth Canning till her evidence has been heard, which before to-morrow night may establish her innocence beyond a doubt, yet various attempts have been used to prejudice the public against her. Among other charges utterly false and infamous, it has been published that her managers (who have scarcely received enough from the charitably disposed to pay the current charges of this tedious trial) have hired you to obstruct justice. None of you present, none living, can say, that one word prompting you to espouse her side has been uttered by any one concerned for her. If you have any regard for public justice, for this poor injured girl, or for yourselves, by all that is dear to you, be persuaded to peace, and without the least murmur or insult to wait the event of this business. God and her innocence have hitherto supported her, in the opinion of many through unexampled distresses : leave it to God and her innocence to carry her through this, and all will be well."

Notwithstanding this handbill and other strong disavowals, the friends of the girl were accused by the opposite party with being instigators of the riotous and outrageous mob, even while they were apparently doing all in their power to persuade to peace. Great care was taken by them that Canning should go to, and come from, the Sessions House, day after day, during her trial, in such a manner as to avoid all public expression of sympathy for her. She was put in different dresses, going out at private doors and windows, in order to avoid recognition.

When the court met the second day, according to adjournment, it was informed, "in a moving and pathetic manner," as the report we quote has it, of the great danger to which Sir Crisp Gascoigne, the Lord Mayor, had been exposed from the indignant mob,—the court being asked at the same time for a guard to protect his person when he went from the Sessions House at night. The jury also fearing for themselves, should their verdict be contrary to the popular wish, moved that a guard might be allowed to them. The Recorder then set forth, "in a very eloquent speech, the insolence and ill consequences of such popular proceedings; that the magistrates of the city of London were too respectable a body to be thus insulted by a mob; that he himself had met with some insults; but he would have them to know, that the magistrates were not to be terrified; that they would go to the bottom of the inquiry in hand." One of the counsel for Canning then rose and told the court that he would venture to assert that none of the friends of his client had been concerned in the disturbance complained of. But supposing even that their zeal had carried some of them too far, yet it ought not to prejudice the poor girl, who could have no hand in it. He therefore trusted the jury would not allow their minds to be in any way swayed against her by anything which a senseless mob had done or might do during the trial. On the part of his client he had even a serious complaint to prefer, of a gross outrage, in fact, done to her, which might be attended with the worst results. He then read a paragraph from a newspaper wherein Canning was spoken of in bitter and calumniating terms, and this before the investigation into her case, or the trial had been brought to a close; and that the publication of such an article in a newspaper was cruel in the highest degree. The court was of a like mind, and recommended an information to be made against the printer of the paper, who was afterwards severely fined for the indecent and reprehensible interference.

It has appeared proper to take notice of these singular circumstances, with the view not only of showing to what a height the popular fervour had risen in relation to Eliza-

K 2

beth Canning and her story, but in some measure to account for the extreme partizanship into which the community was divided on this occasion, to the infecting, no doubt, of the testimony advanced both for and against her. Before concluding, the reader will find further strange evidences of the length to which people went in the course of the girl's trial, and also after her case had reached the period when the jury gave utterance to their verdict.

In fact that verdict was of itself a curiosity, as at first conceived and phrased. After having been absent for upwards of two hours, the jury returned with a finding of " Guilty of Perjury, *but not wilful or corrupt*." Such a verdict, however, could not be received, for it was self-contradictory and meaningless. The twelve were therefore told that they would have to reconsider their finding, and say whether the accused was *Guilty* or *Not Guilty*. They accordingly again withdrew, and shortly after came back with a verdict of *Guilty*, but recommending the prisoner to the mercy of the court. Upon this Elizabeth Canning was immediately committed to Newgate; her sentence being postponed to next Sessions, which began in the month following. Meanwhile, two of the jury who tried her, made an affidavit that they did not mean by their verdict, to bring her in *Guilty of wilful and corrupt perjury*. When the next Sessions began, the court was moved for an arrest of judgment, or a new trial; this, however, was overruled, and the court proceeded to pass sentence upon the girl; yet, differing in their opinions what this sentence should be, they divided, when *eight* of those whose judgment was to be taken were for only laying a small pecuniary fine on her, and *nine* for a month's imprisonment, and at the expiration thereof, that she should be transported to some of his Majesty's plantations for seven years; so that by a majority of only *one*, the severer sentence was carried.

But the extraordinary passages in Elizabeth Canning's history while in her native country, though only now nineteen years of age, did not terminate with a sentence of condemnation for wilful and corrupt perjury; she was to undergo a month's imprisonment, and during that interval there was room for the enactment of various scenes in which she took a part.

It may be stated that when the jury first returned into court with a finding of "Guilty of perjury, but not wilful and corrupt," there was a great shout of gladness raised by the audience; but that when they came back with their amendment, there was a gloomy silence. With regard to the girl's behaviour under the shock of such a verdict, a gentleman—one of those favourable to her, be it observed—who attended her that night to Newgate, thus wrote to a friend:—

"Sir,—I shall with great alacrity inform you of what I know of the distressed good girl (as I make no scruple still to style Elizabeth Canning) under her present circumstances. I accompanied her to her prison. In her way thither, and during my stay with her, she was not distressed, as one might have imagined any person to be under confinement. Her behaviour was steady, serene, and tranquil; and the greatest of her concern seemed to be for her poor mother, lest she should be too much shocked at hearing the ungrateful news. I have visited her sundry times since, and have in general found her behaviour to be cheerful and resigned to the lot Providence has been pleased to choose for her. She once said, she hoped she should not be there long, but if she was she would endeavour to submit to it. In short, her whole behaviour under her present circumstances, has been (as far as I am a judge of human nature) just such as we might suppose that of conscious innocence to be; not bold and impudent, nor sullen and moody, as if conscious of crimes she had been unwilling to be detected in."

It is to be borne in mind that the girl felt herself in her imprisonment, as indeed she had been from the first, warmly backed by not a few who seemed resolved to cling the closer to her interests the more deeply she got involved, in consequence of her own fabrications—fabrications which she, perhaps, began to put some credence in herself, just as people have frequently been known to come to a belief in their own falsehoods, in consequence of oft repeating the lies. She was attended after her condemnation by friends, sometimes several at a time,—or rather by circles of enthusiasts,—who believed, or pretended to believe, her innocent; and who, instead of admonishing her to declare whatever was the truth, seem to have done all in their power to buttress her up, so as to adhere to her story, telling her that the Almighty was with her and would be on her side, even were she on the pillory. The following extract from the affidavit of one Thomas Butts, which appeared in the "Gazetteer" of June 13, the month immediately after that in which Canning received sentence, he being, observe, one of the girl's stanch partisans, affords some insight into the character of the sort of drama that was performed in the prison chamber of the girl :—

"Thomas Butts, of the parish of St. Luke, in the county of Middlesex, gentleman, maketh oath and saith, that about four o'clock in the afternoon of Saturday, the 11th day of May, 1754, there were present in that room in the prison of Newgate, the said Elizabeth Canning, Thomas Colley, her uncle, James Thorne, a young woman, whose name this deponent knows not, William Kemp, and this deponent, and no other person or persons. During which time, Richard Akerman, the keeper of the said prison, came up to the said room, and introduced three persons therein, two of whom declared their names to be Lediard and Smith, and that they were justices of the peace; the name of the other this deponent doth not remember to have heard. And this deponent further saith, that whilst the said Richard Akerman and the other three persons last named, continued in the room, a conversation was begun and carried on between the persons, and to the following import :—

"Akerman—These are gentlemen in the commission of the peace, that are come to see Mrs. Canning."

"Lediard—I have the honour to bear his Majesty's commission. I have come to see you, Mrs. Canning, believing you may have something upon your mind that you may wish to disclose. I have a great friendship for you, and pity you most heartily in your unhappy condition. I have come, therefore, to examine you, and ask you a few questions."

"Smith—Aye, Justice Lediard has been the girl's good friend, and has it in his power to save her; and, for my part, my heart bleeds for her."

The reader is to understand, that as steps had been taken to procure the recantation of Virtue Hall, as already shown, it had been suggested in open court, after the conviction of Canning, that "a conviction might be likewise obtained from her ;" but that the friends of the convicted girl seem to have taken good care no opportunity should be afforded for working upon her conscience to serve such an end. To proceed with the contents of the affidavit :—

"Butts—Gentlemen, you make large professions to this girl; but we don't know that you are her friends. You may, or you may not; but this we know, that she has enemies who come here endeavouring to trepan her; and she has been advised by her friends to enter into no examination, or answer any questions. I believe, Betty, you don't choose to answer any questions—do you ?"

" E. Canning (rising up)—No, Sir; I don't choose to answer any." (Sits down again.)

" Smith—Pray, Sir, who are you, that take upon you thus to dictate to the girl."

" Butts : My name, Sir, is Thomas Butts; I am one of his Majesty's land-waiters, and I live in Ratcliffe-row, in the parish of St. Luke. (Here Smith, with a pencil, wrote, or pretended to write down what was said.) And now, Sir, pray who are you?"

" Lediard—Sir, he is also a Justice of the Peace, and his name is Smith. By what authority did you ask the justice that question? I think it was very impertinent.'

" Kemp—Pray, Sir, how could my friend read Justice in his face?"

"Lediard (to Butts)—Pray, Sir, how long have you known this girl?"

" Butts—I have known her about three weeks."

' Lediard (to Kemp)—And how long have you known her, Sir?"

" Kemp—I have known her about half an hour."

" Lediard—Then curiosity brought you here."

" Kemp—Sir, I came from two motives, curiosity and pity. I say pity, because I believe her innocent of the crime laid to her charge, and I think she has hard usage."

" Smith—There! you see how this poor wretch is, by pretended friends, spirited up to persist in her story. We are her friends, and would help her; but you deceive her with vain hopes; for what can save her from transportation?"

" Butts—What can save her, Sir! his Majesty's clemency."

"Smith—His Majesty, Sir! What can he do in the case of perjury?"

" Lediard—To be sure his Majesty can pardon, he being the fountain of all mercy."

" Smith—I don't pretend to understand much of the law."

" Butts—His Majesty is a gracious prince. She has many friends since her trial that she had not before. I believe a hundred to one. I therefore hope her case will be properly represented to the King."

And all this took place in the prison and hearing of the condemned girl, the conversation, even as given by Mr. Butts in writing—a number of days after its occurrence, and when he manifestly thinks to show off to no small advantage,—being at least most unseemly before the buoyed-up girl, whose wholly improbable, and sometimes different story, had been overwhelmed by what at this distance of time must be pronounced triumphant proofs. No wonder that shortly before her departure for New England, she, or others for her, published a declaration in which she repeated her charge against Mary Squires and also the rest of her refuted tale. And, having mentioned such a declaration, either as emanating directly from herself, or some of her zealous supporters, it is worthy of notice, that although this "simple, artless, and modest creature," as she was represented to be by her friends, and which she seems to have appeared in manner, looks, and conduct when in the presence of observers,—that although she chose only to append her mark to her informations against the gipsy, she could write better than most persons in her station of life.

The affair of Mary Squires and Elizabeth Canning, though the one was a vagabond gipsy and the other a humble servant girl, was one of importance, and worthily interested the community; for, independently of their individual conditions, it bore directly upon the preservation of British liberty. Accordingly it kept hold for a considerable period of no small share of public attention at home, and was talked of in other countries. No doubt it was at first, and indeed may still be regarded as wrapped in mystery. Plentiful enough, to be sure, were the conjectures with regard to the cause of her absence from home, the character of the place where she had been concealed,—the motives for her conduct and the instigators to her persistance in her story. Into these and other conjectures which were thrown out to clear up the obscurity, we shall not conduct our readers. One thing however, is certain, that but for the prosecution in which Canning became the defendant, a very considerable sum of money would have accrued to her, or to others in her name, collected from the benevolent; and even as the affair ended, she appears at last to have received some large presents, one lady alone sending her £120, to assist in securing for her a *suitable provision* abroad.

It is now only to be added that she was conveyed to New England, where she is said to have married advantageously; and that, blindly or perversely, faithful to her cause, many of the partisans she left behind her persevered to their dying hour in asserting her innocence.

XI.—MONSIEUR D'AUGLADE.

FRANCIS, COUNT DE MONTGOMMERY, and Monsieur D'Auglade, lived in the same mansion in the street Royale, of Paris. The house consisted of four floors, the two lowermost of which were occupied by the Count, his wife, and family; and the two upper by Monsieur and Madame d'Auglade, with their only daughter, and servants. The two families visited each other, and were altogether on good terms, though there existed no peculiarly strong or sincere friendship between them. Count de Montgommery was wealthy, and had an establishment corresponding to his rank and means. He even kept a domestic chaplain or almoner, a person found only in houses of the highest distinction. Monsieur d'Auglade, on the other hand, though he made a decent appearance in society, and was received into the best company, was understood to be rather straitened in his circumstances. Such was the condition, individually and relatively, of the principal parties in the following affair.

Count de Montgommery and his lady having projected a visit to their country-house of Villeboisin, invited Monsieur and Madame d'Auglade to accompany them. The invitation was at first accepted, but afterwards it was declined, upon some slight plea. The count and countess accordingly set out by themselves for their estate, and were attended only by their chaplain, François Gagnard, and other domestics, on Monday, the 22d September, 1687, proposing not to return till the evening of the succeeding Thursday. During their absence, the town house was left under the charge of a female servant, named Formenie, with whom a page, and four girls who worked at embroidery, also remained. Some trifling presentiment of evil having arisen in the mind of Count de Montgommery, who was somewhat superstitious, he returned with his suite to town on the Wednesday, a day earlier than he had at first intended. Nothing unusual was observed about the count's apartments at first, excepting that the door of a chamber on the ground floor, in which some of the servants slept, was found to be unlocked, though the chaplain had locked it, and taken the key with him on his departure. Formenie and her companions had never touched the door, and had believed it always to be locked. This circumstance, however, did not excite much notice at the time. The count and countess took supper after their arrival, and had just finished their repast, when Monsieur d'Auglade entered by the door common to his apartments and those of the count. This was about 11 o'clock. Monsieur d'Auglade had been supping out, and finding the Montgommeries to have returned, he went into the chamber where they were, and chatted with them for some time; after which Madame d'Auglade came down likewise, and joined in the conversation.

On the evening of the following day, Count de Montgommery gave information to the authorities that he had been robbed. The lock, he stated, of his strong box had been forced during his three days' absence, and there had been taken away thirteen bags, containing each a thousand livres in silver coin, eleven thousand five hundred new louis-d'ors, and a pearl necklace, valued at four thousand livres. On the announcement of this enormous loss, Monsieur Deffita, one of the heads of the criminal department, and other officials, went to the count's apartments. The first impression on the mind of every one was that some person about the house had committed the robbery, and therefore a search was resolved upon. Monsieur d'Auglade and his wife came forward at once, and requested that their apartments might be first examined. This was assented to. The lowermost of the floors occupied by the d'Auglades was begun with, the master and the mistress of the house themselves conducting the officers through all parts of it. Coffers, cabinets, beds, and, in short, everything, were turned over and examined, without any vestige being found of what was sought. After the first floor had been minutely investigated, Monsieur d'Auglade led the way to the upper story, his wife declining to go, on account of an attack of faintness. In the upper flat, on examining an old trunk, full of clothes and linen, a twisted rouleau of seventy louis-d'ors was found in it, wrapped up in a paper which contained a printed genealogy. On opening this rouleau to count the money, the hand of Monsieur d'Auglade was seen to tremble, and he himself said "I tremble." Count de Montgommery *declared the paper containing the genealogy to be his*, and said (what he had not said before), that his louis were of the coinage of 1686 and 1687, the same as those in d'Auglade's rouleau were. Suspicion at once thrown, as it now was, upon the unhappy man, other circumstances were not long in occurring to increase it. On descending to the chambers of Count de Montgommery, Madame d'Auglade observed to the officer, Monsieur Deffita, that one room, she had heard, had been found unlocked, and that in it something might be found perhaps, adding unguardedly, that some of the servants might have been guilty of the act. When, on searching that same room, five of the missing bags of livres were discovered, with a sixth, in which the sum of a thousand livres was incomplete; Madame d'Auglade's readiness in pointing out the room, and in suggesting an accusation of others, increasing greatly the suspicion against herself and her husband. Moreover, the count declared that he would answer for the honesty of his servants, and seemed wholly persuaded that the d'Auglades were the actors in the robbery. So strong also was the impression against them in the mind of Monsieur Deffita, that he made the remark to Monsieur d'Auglade, shortly after the discovery of the louis-d'ors in the trunk, "the thing is as clear as a self-evident proposition." The result of the search was, that, at the requisition of the count, with the consent of the public prosecutor, Monsieur and Madame d'Auglade were thrown into prison, confined in separate places, and prevented from seeing any one. Their effects were all sealed up at the same time.

The following are the chief circumstances, in addition to the discovery of the louis-d'ors and the genealogical paper, and other grounds of suspicion mentioned, that came out against the prisoners on further inquiry, and led to their condemnation. The d'Auglades knew that the count had large sums by him; they made a frivolous excuse to break through the engagement to go into the country; on the Tuesday night, which in all probability was the night of the robbery, Monsieur d'Auglade supped in his own house, which was rarely or never the case at other times; he sought and obtained from Count de Montgommery the keys of the street door, before the latter's departure, which keys were necessary for the carrying away the stolen property; and, when interrogated separately about the seventy louis-d'ors, the two prisoners contradicted each other, the husband saying that he did not think his wife knew of him having that money, and that he had not touched it for several weeks; whereas she asserted that she had several times counted it over along with him, and that the last reckoning of it had taken place only three or four days before their rooms were searched. Monsieur d'Auglade's previous character was also inquired into, and the report was that he addicted himself to gambling. A robbery was also proved to have taken place in the same house before Count de Montgommery came to live in it, and while the d'Auglades were inhabitants of it, the authors of which had never been detected.

All these circumstances, slight as each of them was singly, were held in the mass, and were linked together, to justify the application of the torture to Monsieur d'Auglade, in order to extract from him a confession of that guilt which he persisted in denying. He was a man of a weak frame of mind, and of a sensitive spirit. The torture he bore with extraordinary firmness, nevertheless, and not a word or sign, in acknowledgment of the charge, could be elicited or extorted from him. But this did not, according to the laws of that day, establish his innocence. On the contrary, though never regularly convicted in a court of justice, he and his wife were condemned by an arbitrary decree to all the penalties attending conviction. On the 16th of February, 1688, after undergoing the torture and lying five months in confinement, Monsieur d'Auglade was sentenced to the gallies for nine years, and his wife to banishment from Paris and its environs during the same period; besides which, all their property was confiscated, in order to make restitution to the Count de Montgommery of the money he had lost. The sums which the d'Auglades were decreed to pay, amounted in all to about thirty-two thousand livres.

Monsieur d'Auglade went with a chain of convicts to Marseilles, where he died. His health had gradually declined in prison, and the torture gave the crowning blow. He died in a resigned and even cheerful frame of mind, with his eyes fixed on another world, praying for forgiveness to all who had injured him and his. Madame d'Auglade's health also broke up on confinement, and prevented her from being ever removed from Paris, in pursuance of her sentence. But her cares were greatly soothed by the presence of her daughter, a child of five years old, and of a sweet and affectionate disposition. After the mother recovered in some degree, the child fell ill, chiefly owing to the wretched nature of the lodgings to which they were doomed. The mother sought and obtained the favour of being removed to a cell of a somewhat better description; and here she was occupied in attending upon her child, when a great change took place in the condition of the unhappy and interesting pair.

Within a short period of the decease of Monsieur d'Auglade, certain anonymous letters came into the hands of the criminal authorities, announcing that the writer had retired into a cloister, and that he felt it necessary to unburden his conscience by revealing the true authors of the robbery of the Count de Montgommery's property. These were, the writer said, a man named Vincent Belestre and the chaplain Gagnard, the latter of whom had been in the count's service at the time, but had since left it. A woman named Comble was also mentioned as one who knew all the particulars. Though the Count de Montgommery's partisans averred these letters to be an invention of Madame d'Auglade, yet inquiries were made into the characters of Belestre and Gagnard, which were found to be of the very worst order. They were discovered also to have exhibited about the time in question a sudden influx of wealth. These circumstances induced a search for them, which was unsuccessful, until, as if providentially, both men came into custody upon other charges. A short time afterwards the writer of the anonymous letter, who was a needy priest of the name of Fontpère, and the woman Comble, were brought forward, when a strong body of testimony came out respecting the robbery. It was now brought home beyond all possibility of doubt to Belestre and Gagnard. The latter had given his accomplice impressions of all the necessary keys, and Belestre had fabricated false ones, by the aid of which he had committed the robbery. We do not go into all the particulars which came out one by one with an avenging and resistless force against the accused; suffice it to say, that in the end Gagnard confessed the whole. He and his associate in guilt paid the penalty of it with their lives. It is remarkable that the chaplain said shortly before his execution, that, had he been questioned at the time the house was searched, he was in such a state of agitation as must have made him confess all. A considerable amount of property, purchased with the stolen money by Belestre, and the valuable pearl necklace, were recovered by the Count de Montgommery.

These discoveries could not restore the innocent d'Auglade to life, but his name, at least, might be cleared from reproach. Madame d'Auglade properly demanded that the justification of her husband's fair memory and of her own innocence should be pronounced, and she also justly claimed the restitution of their property, as well as damages from the Count de Montgommery for his calumnious accusation. This produced a trial of some importance, as the count justified the proceedings which had taken place, and insisted, among other pleas, that damages might as well be sought from the ministers of the law as from him. The answers made by Madame d'Auglade to his recapitulation of the evidence against her husband and herself, showed clearly that if men could at the time have rid their minds of the unhappy prepossession against the accused, the issue of the case would not have been what it was. She showed that a slight given by the count's sisters to her husband had caused his refusal to go to the country with the count, and proved from what parties the rouleau of seventy louis-d'ors had been got by her husband. The printed genealogy, she also proved, had been sold to her by a broker. Many other points were satisfactorily, as concerned her and her husband, cleared up by this unfortunate lady, some of which, indeed, had been manifest enough from the very first, had not the eyes of justice been dimmed or perverted. Apparently, the court now felt the count's rash confidence in stating that *he would be responsible for the honesty of his servants*, had prevented the guilty parties from being examined and detected. His assertion, also, that the printed genealogy belonged to him, had materially influenced the case, although it was utterly devoid of foundation. Upon these and other grounds, the court decided that the count should restore all the property of the d'Auglades, and should pay all the expenses, from first to last, which the cause had occasioned; which last heavy imposition was regarded by the court as a sufficient assignment of damages against the count.

Thus ended this remarkable case, in which an unfortunate and innocent man lost his life, after dreadful sufferings, almost on mere suspicion and an array of slight circumstances that had been united where they were, of themselves much apart, by insinuations, conjectures, and some degree of misrepresentation. We may congratulate ourselves that such things could not occur in our day, where the accused have equal facilities with the accuser. Though the loss of a husband and a father was too severe a bereavement to be ever forgot, Madame d'Auglade and her daughter had the consolation of entering society with honour and an unblemished name. The sympathy of the world was so much excited in their favour, that a portion of one hundred livres was collected and presented to the child of the ill-fated d'Auglade. In course of years, the young lady became the wife of Monsieur des Essarts, counsellor-at-law.

XII.—DICK TURPIN.

ONE of the most remarkable exemplifications of the changes in society within the memory of some who are still amongst us, is found in the character of the crimes which are now committed in comparison with those prevalent some seventy years ago. The lapse of that time has, in this one respect alone, wrought a great alteration, especially in London and its vicinity. The metropolis and its boundaries may not be more virtuous, but assuredly they are more safe. Turn over the pages of some London newspaper, say of the middle of the last century, or for a number of years after that period, and you will feel yourself transported into a city whose customs were as alien to us almost as those in which the squabbling retainers of the Capulets and Montagues could only be kept from fighting by all the clubs of all the citizens. For example :—

"1738, September 11. A gentleman was stopped in Holborn about twelve at night by two footpads, who, on the gentleman's making resistance, shot him dead and then robbed him. *Some of the villains* have since been apprehended."—"1760, February 24. An apothecary in Devonshire-street, near Queen's-square, was one night last month attacked by two ruffians in Red Lion-street, who, presenting fire-arms, and menacing him with death if he resisted or cried out, carried him to Black Mary's Hole, when by the light of a lantern perceiving he was not the intended person, they left him there without robbing him. This mysterious action has not yet been cleared up, though they are suspected to be the same fellows who lately sent threatening letters to Mr. Nelson, an apothecary in Holborn, and another tradesman."—"1763, July 23. One Richard Watson, tollman of Marybone turnpike, was found barbarously murdered in his toll-house; upon which, and some attempts made in other toll-houses, the trustees of turnpikes have come to a resolution to increase the number of toll-gatherers, to furnish them with arms, strictly enjoining them at the same time not to keep any money at the toll-bars after eight o'clock at night."—"1763, October 17. A man was lately robbed and barbarously murdered on the road to Ratcliff Cross. Finding but twopence in his pocket, they first broke one of his arms, then tied a great stone about his neck and threw him into a ditch, having first shot at and mangled his face in a shocking manner. The unhappy man had, notwithstanding, scrambled out of the ditch into the road, but expired soon after he was found; and two days after, another man was found murdered in the Mile End-road." To go a little farther back, an ordinary of Newgate thus writes, in reference to one of his impenitents, in 1726 :—"He stopped the Earl of Harborough during broad daylight in Piccadilly; one of the chairmen pulling out a pole of the chair knocked down one of the villains, while the earl came out, drew his sword, and put the rest to flight, but not before they had raised their wounded companion, whom they took off with them." There seems from the account given of some other rascals by the same grave chronicler, to have been quite as little security within the *liberties* of the city, as in Westminster or the suburbs :—"Their next robbery was at the house of a grocer in Thames-street. The watchman passing by as they were packing up their booty, Bellany seized him, and obliged him to put out his candle to prevent any alarm being given. Having kept him till they were ready to go off with the plunder, they took him to the side of the Thames, and threatened to throw him in if he would not throw in his lantern and staff. *It need not be said the poor man was obliged to comply with their injunctions.*"—"1761, December 31. Murders, robberies, many of them attended with acts of cruelty, and threatening letters, were never, perhaps, more frequent about this city than during this last month. One highwayman in particular, by the name of the Flying Highwayman, engrosses the conversation of most of the towns within twenty miles of London, as he has occasionally visited all the public roads round the metropolis, and has collected several sums. He rides upon three different horses, a grey, a sorrel, and a black one; the last of which has a bald face, to hide which he generally hangs on a black cat's skin. He has leaped over Colnbrook turnpike a dozen times within this fortnight, and is now well known by most of the turnpike-men on the different roads about town."

The insecurity was particularly great of all who were obliged to walk abroad at night. The police system was in a most inefficient state. Besides, the streets, lanes, and courts of many parts of the metropolis were narrow and irregular, such as may still be seen in the neighbourhood of Clare Market, Chancery and Fetter lanes, and encumbered with buildings, offering facilities for unforeseen attacks, and for the escape of malefactors. The straggling character of the suburban villages, and the numerous fields that intervened between the inhabited spots within the bills of mortality, also afforded many lurking places.

Accordingly, it may be truly said, there was a time, and not very long since, when no man might securely travel in the vicinity of London nor indeed in certain other parts of England, singly or in company, without fire arms. Every horseman who appeared on the horizon was suspected to be *a Golden Farmer* or a *Sixteen-string Jack*; and every pedestrian, especially if the unfortunate wight carried a stick, which was, of course, considered to be a bludgeon, was looked upon as a footpad, and the wayfarer prepared either to resist, or "stand and deliver," as suited his *pluck*. Now all this is changed; paper money, stage-coaches, or, still surer, railway-carriages, and the police-officer, have outwitted these heroes of the road, and you may travel any thoroughfare in Britain without having your journey signalized with an adventure of the least moment.

In fact highway robbery, according to the usual acceptation of the term, is now an unknown crime, Haynes, of Hounslow-heath memory, being the last of those termed highwaymen. The not uncelebrated John Townsend, Bow-street officer, before a committee of the House of Commons on the police of the metropolis, in 1816, with his usual homely, shrewd, and unceremonious philosophy, spoke in the following terms relative to the point mentioned :—"There is one thing which appears to me most extraordinary, when I remember in very likely a week there would be from ten to fifteen highway robberies. We have not a man convicted for highway robbery lately; I speak of persons on horseback. Formerly there were two, three, or four highwaymen, some on Hounslow-heath, some on Wimbledon-common, some on Finchly-common, some on the Romford-road. I have actually come to Bow-street in the morning, and, while I have been leaning over the desk, had three or four people come in and say, ' I was robbed by two highwaymen in such a place ;—I was robbed by a single highwayman in such a place.' People travel safely now by the means of the horse patrol that Sir Richard Ford planned.

Where are these highway robberies now ? as I was observing to the Chancellor at the time I was up at his house on the Corn Bill. He said, 'Townsend, I knew you very well so many years ago.' I said, 'Yes, my lord, I remember you first coming to the bar, first in your plain gown, and then as king's counsel, and now Chancellor. Now your lordship sits as Chancellor, and directs the executions on the recorder's report;—but where are the highway robberies now?' And his lordship said, 'Yes, I am astonished. There are no footpad robberies or road robberies now, but merely jostling you on the street. They used to be ready to pop at a man as soon as he let down his glass;—that was by bandittis.' "

Further, the cruelty with which highway robberies used to be accompanied had decreased nearly as much, according to Townsend, as their frequency. In his early days the plan followed was the attempt to put down the ferocity of the highwayman by an application of the penalties of the law, still more unsparing and merciless. Townsend relates that Lord Chief Justice Eyre once went the Home Circuit, beginning at Hertford and finishing at Kingston, when crimes were so desperate, that in his charge to the grand jury at the former of these places he told them to be careful what bills they found, for he had made up his mind, whatever persons were convicted throughout the circuit for capital offences, to hang them all. And he kept his word; he saved neither man nor woman. In one case seven people, four men and three women, were convicted of robbing a pedlar in a house in Kent-street. "They were all convicted," says Townsend, "and all hanged in Kent-street, opposite the door; and, I think, at Kennington-common eight more, making fifteen; all that were convicted were hung." And, generally, he observes in another part of the evidence, " With respect to the present time and the early period of my time, such. as 1781—2, 3, 4, 5, 6, and 7, where there is one person convicted now, I may say I am positively convinced their were five then : we never had an execution wherein we did not grace that unfortunate gibbet with ten, twelve, to thirteen, sixteen, and twenty, and forty, I once saw at twice—I have them all down at home." The wholesale slaughter, however, seems to have done no good at all,—to have failed in effecting the end contemplated; the more hanging. there were only the more and the more hardened and desperate criminals to catch and hang : crimes of violence only decreased when the law began to restrain its own violence—as if the law and its administration were scarcely more operative in suppressing or checking crime than in giving to it its peculiar character and temper.

One thing, whatever be the cause, is certain, highway robbery is now only committed by occasional desperate men, and generally in the suburbs of the metropolis, or in a crowd, where a gang of persons sometimes surround the person, robbing him in the face of all the standers by. Nothing but the vigilance of the police can cope with those desperate characters, as the recklessness from want of money, places the offence out of the pale of all precautionary measures. It may be relied on, that the generality of thieves of the present day have an abhorrence, or are on some account reluctant, to violence being committed on the person, at the same time that they find it impossible to pursue the career of the lawless *heroes of the road* of the bygone period.

We repeat that the character and feelings of the public thief as of all other classes of society, have undergone a visible and decided change within the memory of the living. Whether it has been for the better is another question. Formerly the heroes of their party were fellows conspicuous and famed for open and daring acts of plunder, in whom the whole fraternity had a pride, and whom they all felt ambitious to imitate, failing only to do so from lack of the same quantum of courage.   The more desperate and numerous the instances of robbery, the more were the parties lauded and admired.   It was then also the fashion of these men to boast of their conduct under punishment.   In those days there must be no snivelling, no peaching, no contrition; and the malefactor must die bravely to entitle him to fame.   The Turpins and Jerry Abershaws of the day were the objects of their boasting and imitation; such men as, on the road to execution, would stop and drink gin, offering libations to the success of all highwaymen, and, when on the gallows, kick off their shoes, swearing with an oath they "always said they never would die with them on;" or, like Despard, who, when brought out for execution, remarked to the executioner that it was a fine morning, and wondered what sort of weather it might be in the other country, adding, "but never mind, I shall soon know all about it."   All this kind of monstrous heroism has subsided, and their leaders now are men rendered famous for scheming, subtlety, and acuteness.   Formerly, the passport to enrolment under their banners was a name for boldness and terrible acts of outrage; now a certificate must be brought of the man never having committed an indiscreet act in his calling; that he has never done any atrocious or outrageous thing that will lend it notoriety for the world to talk of; but who, on the contrary, can say that he "is up to all the moves on the board, that he knows a trick or two, and how to make his wits keep him."

But it is with the noted highwayman, Richard Turpin, that the present article has mainly to be engaged, whose name cannot but at once occur to the general reader as standing in the foremost rank of the heroes of the road; although we cannot promise, consistently with the real facts of his career, or the truth to which we are bound to adhere, to give any hopes, at the starting with his story, of presenting that brave, generous, and engaging character which certain romancers have pictured; or set forth robbery and villany as perpetrated by him in any other guise than as the deeds of a cruel, plundering, and wholly unprincipled ruffian, who ran a career of dastardly crime, of cowardly violence, or at best of reckless desperation; who lived in terror, peril, constant insecurity, and brutalising vice; and who died with the disgusting bravado of a senseless fool, or as the beasts that perish.

Richard Turpin was the son of John Turpin, of Hampstead, in Essex.   Having received some school education, he was apprenticed to a butcher in Whitechapel, where he served his time, but chargeable with sundry irregularities and misdemeanours during the period.   When still but young, he married the daughter of one Palmer, and set up for himself at Suson, in Essex; where, not having any credit in the markets, and people being in general distrustful of him, he was tempted to maintain himself by dishonest and indirect courses, not even scrupling to help himself to the cattle and sheep of neighbouring gentlemen and farmers.   On one occasion he stole a pair of oxen of Mr. Giles, of Plaistow, which he conveyed to his own premises, and there killed them.   However, some of the servants of Mr. Giles had in a measure detected him in the theft; and having learned that Turpin usually sold the hides of his beasts at Waltham Abbey, they went thither, and were convinced on seeing two skins, which had been purchased from the suspected party, that they were the hides of the identical animals stolen.   The men immediately returned to Suson; but, on perceiving them, Turpin, shrewdly concluding what was the purpose of their visit, contrived to elude their grasp, after they had obtained access to him in his house, by leaving them in a front apartment of his dwelling, while he made his escape through a window in another direction. Having thus effected his escape, but with a blown character, the thief did not choose to run the risk of any more such home visits.   Being now thrown loose upon the world, unprincipled at the very best, and ready to strike out into any wild or wicked adventure which should offer, is it to be thought strange that he in a very short period was found figuring in a gang of smugglers, that lurked about the hundreds of Essex ; and next, on the failure of this lawless enterprise, that he joined himself to a band of deer-stealers.

Almost immediately on Turpin's uniting himself with this last vile association, they made Epping Forest and adjoining parks the scenes of their depredations, having in a brief space got a considerable amount of money.   Here it was that Turpin got acquainted with Gregory, Fielder, Rose, and Wheeler, who were designated the Essex Gang.   But even their system of deer-stealing did not prove profitable enough, or so rapidly as was considered necessary, they being besides narrowly watched by the park keepers, and liable to sudden arrest.   Something new, and of a more summary nature as regarded the enriching their pockets, was to be discovered ; and what more promising or more natural in the onward march of such scoundrels, as a career of plunder, burglary, and highway robbery ?   It was at Turpin's suggestion that the gang commenced their course of outrage and depredation upon the dwellings and persons of the unoffending, the insecure, and those who had aught to lose.   Abroad and round the country the villains went, under the cloak of night,—their system being, whenever they found a house in which anything worthy of their seizing was known to be there kept, and felt assured that they were the stronger party, for one of them to knock at the door, and the moment it was opened, for the rest to rush in and plunder it of whatever suited them,—the inmates, by threatenings, bonds, and other modes of barbarous usage, having been in the meanwhile cowed and mastered.   We will not weary the reader with a recital of anything like the whole of such outrages of the kind indicated, as were perpetrated in the course of a short time by these miscreants.   A few instances must suffice.

Turpin having informed his associates in crime that he knew an old woman at Laughton, who, he was certain, had several hundred pounds by her, away the band went, obtaining an entrance into the hapless creature's mansion in the manner mentioned above. The first thing they did, on getting access into the house, was to bind the old lady and her maid.   They next demanded the whole of her money, and on being told by her that she had none in the house at the time—being very loth to part with her gold,—they threw out such horrid threats, and were proceeding to such acts of monstrous cruelty,— even going so far as to be about to place her on her own fire,—as forced her to discover where the cash was kept that she had by her at the moment, all which they fleeced her of, the sum amounting to upwards of £400.   The next person they robbed was a farmer, whose dwelling they entered, and whose people they subdued in like manner as had been done at the old woman's premises, £700 being the booty which they carried away at this adventure,—their villanies and ruffianism taking this additional complexion, from this time forward, viz., to wreak out their vengeance against whatever persons should at any time attempt to baulk their schemes and efforts.   Accordingly they not only committed robberies upon a large scale, but often maltreated the helpless ones who had the misfortune to fall into their hands, savagely beating and otherwise cruelly dealing with their victims.   Frequently would the villains continue in the house for a time to eat and drink at their will, while the inmates were forced to remain in quietness and silence ; and on other occasions not only was murderous flagellation inflicted, but women were made to submit to worse than the loss of life.   One of their most frightful and monstrous exploits took place at the house of Mr. Lawrence, near Stanmore, in

Middlesex. Here they seized several persons and treated them in the most ruffian-like manner. They tied a boy's hands, whom they found putting up sheep after nightfall, with his own garters; and with a pistol held at his head, made him do their bidding. They seized Mr. Lawrence, threw a cloth over his face, and after Turpin had ripped up his small clothes with a knife,—taking from the pockets all the money found upon the gentleman, they forced him to go through with them several parts of the house, in order to name to them what was to be found in the same that was worthy of their notice; and when they fancied that their victim gave not all the information wanted,—they barbarously struck him on the head with his pistols, and dragged him from one place to another by the hair of the head. After other pieces of barbarous usage towards this gentleman and several of his household, the burglars retired laden with spoil, including plate and linen; warning the terribly abused people, who were locked up in the parlour by this time, that they, the robbers, would return in a short while to see if any of the family had dared to stir from their place of confinement, when the punishment for so doing before ample time had been allowed for a safe bestowal of the stolen property, would subject every one of the inmates to a sudden and terrible death. In short, the gang had become the terror of the districts in which they prowled, these being hitherto such as had London for a central station. The public press had begun to complain of the success of Turpin and his confederates, declaring, day after day, that their robberies exceeded both in number and audacity almost all that had ever been practised in England; and concluding with charges against the authorities of the land for allowing such daring, insolent, and wide-spread villany to rear its head, much more to persevere in its bare-faced atrocities. The multitude and magnitude of the robberies, together with the loud complaints uttered relative to their permitted existence, at length aroused the government of the country, so that a proclamation was issued in the king's name, promising a pardon to whomsoever of the criminals who had been concerned in entering the house of Mr. Lawrence, &c., that would come forward as king's evidence, and also a reward of fifty pounds for the apprehension of any one of them, the money to be paid on the conviction of the offender.

This advertisement in the *Gazette* made no apparent impression on the hearts of the bandit crew, of whom Turpin had become the acknowledged leader. While flushed with success, they had no notion of being taken, and, if possible, to still more barbarous extremes they pushed their villanies. On the 7th of February, 1736, Turpin, Fielder, Rose, Walker, Bush and Gregory, meeting at the White Bear Inn, Drury-lane, resolved on robbing one Mr. Francis, a farmer, near Marylebone, that same evening; and accordingly they went to his house, where, finding a servant in the cow-house, they there tied him fast, and threatened to shoot him if he made the least noise. They then led him into the stable, where another of Mr. Francis's men was quickly served in the same way; and just as they had finished with him, Mr. Francis himself, who had been abroad, came in. In a moment pistols were presented to his breast, and the direst threatenings uttered, backed by the most horrible and profane oaths, that if he stirred or spoke he was a dead man. He, too, was bound, and left, with the other two mastered persons, under the charge of Turpin and Bush, who stood over them with loaded pistols, whilst the other five robbed the house. But even this the scoundrels did not perpetrate without first tying Mrs. Francis, her daughter, and the maid-servant, each of whom they cruelly beat; after which one of the gang stood over them, while the others plundered their dwelling. An hour and a half was spent in the performance of these various cruelties and in the rifling; and having packed up, they, as usual, on their departure, threatened to return and murder the whole if the least noise were made, before they got clear off.

The whole country in the vicinity of London was upon this in a sense armed, for no man's property was considered for a single night to be safe. A reward of a hundred pounds was advertised to any person who should apprehend any one of the gang; and Turpin's person was particularly described in the King's proclamations. "He is about thirty," said the description of him; "by trade a butcher, about five feet nine inches high, brown complexion, very much marked with the small pox, his cheek bones broad, his face thinner towards the bottom, his visage short, pretty upright, and broad about the shoulders."

These proclamations and the rewards offered made the bandit crew somewhat shy; but what broke up the fraternity was the fact of Turpin, Fielder, Rose, and Wheeler, with two women, being traced to an alehouse at Westminster, and there pounced upon. The ringleader, however, managed to make his escape out of a window; but the other three villains were captured. Wheeler was admitted an evidence, and Fielder and Rose were executed and hung in chains; Turpin resolving henceforward to have no accomplice, but to rely solely on his own resources.

Nor were these resources few or slight as a highwayman. He had several steeds at his command,—one here and another there,—and each of them animals of rare mettle. He was almost unequalled as a horseman, not seldom achieving extraordinary feats in clearing turnpike gates, outstripping pursuers, and in the performance of similar exploits where his jockeyship and the capacity of his charger had to be put to the stretch. So perfect were his skill and manner in the saddle, so clever his management of whatever animal he might happen to mount, so intimately acquainted was he with every cross-road in the neighbourhood of the metropolis,—a book of which he constructed, and carried constantly about his person,—as well as with many other parts of England, particularly the counties of Chester, Lancaster, York, &c., that he baffled all attempts at capture. His ride to York in a marvellously short time from the suburbs of London has been much celebrated, although it was not performed so much in the course of outstripping a persevering and formidable pursuit, as for the sake of establishing an *alibi*, a trick he was much accustomed to, so that he was in a sense an ubiquitous personage, and, if not in various places at exactly the same time, yet so rapid were his journeys, so numerous were his almost simultaneous visitations at different parts of a district, levying his contributions at each with a high hand, that it was difficult to believe that any one mortal could have perpetrated the several deeds ascribed to him. In fact the only way in which the descriptions given of the horse and the rider could be reconciled on certain occasions, was by supposing that the attacks were performed by confederates similarly mounted and similarly accoutred.

Dick Turpin having got rid of several of his accomplices and staunchest of his band, in the manner stated above; finding himself, too, blazoned abroad as the prince of highwaymen, and possessed of the belief that his hour was not yet come, at the same time aware that the secret of his ubiquity was becoming blown about the metropolis, that every turnpike keeper in those quarters knew him and his courses, that the vigilance of the police was aroused, and that he was tracked to his haunts; reflecting on all these things,— after a number of hair breadth escapes,—he reluctantly quitted the heathy hills of Bagshot, the plains of Hounslow, the gorsy commons of Highgate, Hampstead and Finchley, the marshy fields of Battersea, almost all of which he had been known to visit in a single night, and, leaving these beaten tracks to the occupation of young and less practised hands, he bequeathed to them at the same time his own reversionary interest in the gibbets thereupon erected, and betook himself to the country, to some of the more promising provinces, although by no means without the design or the result of frequently paying a flying visit to the metropolis,—the rallying point of all his desperate adventures of this description. Meanwhile, it was towards Cambridge that he set his face, as he was not known in that county.

Now, it was on his way thither, that meeting a horseman genteely dressed, and well mounted, Dick, without a reluctant sigh, and in the habitual style of his profession, called out the wonted words, " Stand and deliver !"   But who should this be but the noted Tom King, " the Gentleman Highwayman," who, it was said, made it a point to rob nobody but gentlemen.   Turpin not liking so much talk as the other seemed inclined for, swore he would blow his brains out if he did not deliver his money immediately ; on which King burst into a loud laugh, crying, " What ! dog eat dog ! come, come, brother Turpin, if you don't know me, I know you, and should be glad of your company."   Mutual explanations, assurances, and promises of fidelity were interchanged upon this ; they swore that nothing but death should ever part them ; they entered into partnership, and robbed together for near three years.

But the names and persons of the two partners could not long continue unknown in any country side they frequented ; and as no house would at length entertain them, they formed a design of resorting to a cave for their more settled home, making choice of such a spot between King's Oak-road and Loughton-road.   Here they found, or made, a retreat large enough to receive them and their horses, the spot being screened and surrounded in a manner that admirably served their purposes, as it was sequestered, sheltered, and secret, yet so contrived, or rendered by their care, that while they were hid from the eye of the world, they could behold and reconnoitre every person that travelled the adjacent road.

In the near neighbourhood was a noble wood which numbered many patriarchal trees. Ancient oaks, whose broad gnarled limbs the storms of centuries had vainly striven to uproot, some of them now sternly decaying ; gigantic beech trees, whose silvery stems shot smoothly upwards, sustaining branches, of such size, that each, dissevered, would in itself have formed a tree ; the sprightly sycamore ; the dark chesnut, the majestic elm, festooned with ivy ;—every variety of wood, dark, dense, and closely interwoven, save where labyrinthine paths could be traced by such as were familiar with the imposing mysteries of the scene.   Even across or over these paths not unfrequently projecting boughs stretched, compelling a rider to incline his head, and apparently barring to the stranger all advance in such a direction.

It was in such a spot, locality, and neighbourhood, that the partner-highwaymen took up their head-quarters—men whose pursuits and thoughts were ill in keeping with the beautiful romance of the scene beside them, however propitious might be its shades and intricacies to their lawless habits.   While the cave was their retreat, Turpin's wife supplied them with victuals, and often stayed all night ; whilst one or other, if not both of the villains, were abroad upon their dangerous and criminal pursuits, the report of which could not be stifled or forgotten.   Neither could the offer of reward,—£100 for the apprehension of Turpin, which from time to time was advertised, continue to be lost to the minds of the needy, and the daring.   In fact, many persons were induced by the offered sum to undertake his capture.   Amongst the rest one Thompson, a park-keeper to the

King, had a servant who was eager to earn the promised tempting sum; and this man set out with a guide to the *rendezvous* of the highwaymen. Nor did Turpin, who was alone at the time, and sauntering in the neighbourhood of their rustic and curious retreat, shun the approach of the two men. Indeed, he had not the slightest suspicion of the intention of Thompson's servant, but took the pair for poachers. Accordingly as they approached the hero of our sketch, he shouted to them that there were no hares near to the thicket, and that they might save themselves the trouble and the loss of time of looking for game in that part.

"Hares and game, indeed!" cried Thompson's servant; "here is just the sort of game we have come after. It is a Turpin and not what a greyhound would chase that we are looking for, and now that I have got him, I'll take care to keep him. Best to surrender at once," added the man, "if you have regard to your own welfare."

The person who thus spoke was an intrepid and powerful fellow; yet he seems not to have calculated wisely concerning the danger and difficulty of an enterprise by which a man who knew that capture and conviction, that deliverance to justice and certain death, were synonimous to him. Somehow Turpin contrived to retreat with apparent good nature and acquiescence to the mouth of his cave; keeping the reward-seeker in easy conversation and at arm's length the while. But no sooner had the wily outlaw reached the exact spot upon which he had fixed his eye than, suddenly stooping, he seized a loaded carbine that lay there, pouring its contents into the body of the rash intruder, and bereaving him of life in an instant: nor did the other volunteer trouble our hero, taking to his heels, and spreading the report of what had been done.

Turpin's own account of this affair, given shortly before his execution, was, that having been out one whole day from his hiding-place, without obtaining any booty, and being very much tired, he lay down in a thicket, turning his horse out loose, but without its saddle. When he awoke, he went in search of the animal, and meeting with Thompson's servant, enquired of him if he had seen a stray horse? To this the man returned, "I know nothing of Turpin's horse, but have found Turpin himself;" and thereupon presented his blunderbuss at the inquirer, who instantly jumping behind a broad oak, avoided the shot which was fired at him, and in return discharged his own carbine at the assailant, whom he killed; one slug going through his breast, and others penetrating vital parts. This done, Turpin repaired to a large yew-tree, in which he concealed himself so closely, that though the reports of the blunderbuss and carbine, and especially the discovery of the dead man, soon drew thither a number of persons, yet he continued undiscovered nearly two whole days and one night in the tree, after which he effected his escape. Such was the criminal's own version of the transaction.

Turpin and his partner in business now found it high time to decamp and bid farewell to the friendly cave; £200 instead of £100 being forthwith offered as a reward for Dick's apprehension. Their course was towards London, Epping Forest and its vicinity being the scene of numerous depredations by these hardened and lawless fellows, who not only had become unfitted for the habits of peaceful society, but who knew not, even supposing them to have had the mind to pursue regular courses, where for a single day they could feel themselves safe from arrest, conviction, and capital punishment. As if instinctively, they directed their faces towards the great centre of rogueries, Turpin, in particular, turning to some of his old haunts with a sort of infatuated attachment.

According to Dick's own account, given after his condemnation, he no sooner quitted the yew-tree, amid the dark foliage of which he had so long concealed himself after slaying Thompson's servant, than he stole a black horse out of a close near the highway that was at no great distance; but finding he was observed by some people working in a field not very far off, he threw some loose money towards them, which stayed pursuit. Still, the possession of the black horse might have proved most perilous to him, he therefore turned it loose, and forthwith betook himself to a chesnut mare, which happened to present itself, and with her made the best of his way to his earlier haunts in the vicinity of London; Epping Forest again obtaining a particular share of his attention and practice. Here, according to his own tale, among many other exploits, he one day stopped a country gentleman, who clapping spurs to his horse was hotly pursued, and would have escaped, but for the highwayman's dexterity in sending two bullets into the horse's buttocks, which suddenly led to a surrender. Fifty shillings was the first fruit of this outrage; but, on stripping the victim, the robber found two guineas more, out of which he returned five shillings, telling the gentleman it was more than he deserved, "because of his intentions to have cheated him."

Another time, meeting a gentleman and a lady each on horseback, in a lane near the forest, Turpin stopped them, by merely presenting a pistol; for, thereupon, the lady swooned, and then he had little difficulty in mastering and rifling the gentleman, whose pockets yielded seven guineas and some silver; while, as for the swooning party, he took from her a watch, a diamond ring, one guinea, and fifteen shillings.

On attending to any account which a ruffian, hardened in outrage, gives of his enormities, it will be generally found that he not only attempts to exaggerate them or lend them a peculiar gloss, but that in spite of himself he renders his crimes more revolting than they seemed before; and this because he is not skilled in the art that is requisite in lending enchantment to vice, or in robbing crime of its deformity. It has, in fact, in most instances, been left to the practised writers of fiction to make our Turpins and Sheppards other than terrific examples of infatuation and unalleviated wretchedness; unless, indeed, when all sense to mental pain has been smothered by them in the sinks of worse than bestial indulgence, or when like to fiends their violent passions have been let loose during the perpetration of deeds of blood and rapine. Deny them the transient fury of the one occasion and the idiotic loathsomeness of the other, and they can be viewed but as of the basest of cravens and the most miserable of outcasts with whom society has been cursed.

What then is to be said of those writers who by their high colourings, their distortions, and absolute falsities in point of fact, have rendered for the greedy appetite of youth, and the uncultured, if not depraved tastes of the multitude, some of the most notoriously wicked of our race the subjects of a romantic and attractive interest?—What but this, that just in proportion to the skill with which they deck such flagitious characters and plagues, and recommend the story of their lives to ignorant admiration and vitiated fancy, they are pestilent in their doings, and most ill-advised in their aims? In some of that class of productions to which allusion is made, whatever may be the direful fate to which the leading characters are brought at last, vice is made to be held in the ascendant throughout the most interesting scenes of the narrative. What more unwise? or what more pestilent than such representations and issues?

Such, however, is not the design nor the tendency of the present publication; so that the simplest of our readers will in no way be tempted to imitate the career of the wretched criminals whose cases are immediately before us. But we must proceed with our story.

TURPIN DEFYING THE OFFICERS TO CATCH HIM.

Passing over many of their outrages, seeing that a great sameness of manner, incident, and result belonged to a majority of their ruffian deeds, we have to mention that not above two miles distant from Waltham, or Waltham Holy Cross, as it is sometimes called, a large irregular town of Essex, which is situated near the river Lea, they attacked in broad-daylight a Mr. Bradele, of London, who was taking an airing with his children in his chariot. It was King who made the first onset, for he was the bravest and most chivalrous, as well as the most generous of the pair of robbers; but Mr. Bradele, being a gentleman of spirit, in a moment betook himself to measures of resistance, perceiving only one of the highwaymen at the instant. Upon this King shouted for Turpin by the name of Jack, crying, "Here is courage as much as strength to cope with; hold the horses (meaning those of the chariot,) and let's see who'll have the best of it, the charioteer, or I, the footpad, for the time being." Mr. Bradele now discovering that there were two to one, his children too in their terror hampering as well as most deeply concerning him, and being also not blind to the sort of reckless bravery of his assailant, exclaimed that he would come to terms with them. "I will readily part with my money," said he, "and trust that that is all you want." "And the watch to boot," interjected Turpin; "quick, there is no time to lose, and the finger ring likewise." "I prize both ring and watch far beyond their value," answered Mr. Bradele; "you will not surely rob me of things I set so much store by." "Let the ring remain where it is then," replied King; "and as for the watch, what say you, Jack? Time presses; here seems to be a good honest fellow; we are more of gentlemen than to deprive him of anything he values so much." "Do as thou wilt, comrade," cried Turpin, "only no more palaver." "Why then," said King, "you must pay us, Mr. Charioteer, six guineas in place of the ticker; we never sell for more, though the trinket be worth six times as much." Mr. Bradele promised not only not to inform against them, but also to leave the money named at the *Dial* in Birchin-lane for them. "And you swear no questions will be then and there asked when payment is called for," said Turpin suggestively. But before the gentleman had time to make a response, the same villain exclaimed, "Ha! horsemen are in sight; best to take security in hand; and as we are in need of nags, we'll borrow the gentleman's pair of trotters, instead of his watch, and be off."

The thing was hardly said before it was done, when away, in diverging directions, the robbers scampered, Turpin being hotly pursued by the two riders who had so suddenly made their appearance. Away he sped, putting a degree of mettle into, or rather extracting it out of, the animal he strode, which Mr. Bradele had never dreamt that his horse possessed, who stood gazing from his stationary carriage with eagerness at the chase. Away went Turpin, now hidden by bushes and trees, and again emerging into sight, to gratify Mr. Bradele with a view of his steed's capacity and the horsemanship of the rider,— now to stretch along a dead level, with a shower of mud thrown behind by the hoofs of the started animal, and anon to descend a slope so as merely allowed the upper portion of the highwayman to be discernable. And yet the fugitive had need of all the mettle that was under him, and all the resources of his art as a jockey on this, as on many other occasions; for those who had so unexpectedly taken up the chase were still better mounted and hardly less acquainted with the business of maintaining a keen gallop. A bridge too, over one of the tributaries of the Lea, was directly a head of the runaway, and a little further on a turnpike, the gate of which might be found closed, so as to bar all further means of escape in that direction. Mr. Bradele's anxiety to know how it would fare with the parties at that critical part of the road had become extreme, and when he beheld the highwayman enter upon the spanning arch, the other horsemen being by this time not many yards in the rear, he cried out, "The scoundrel will be taken to a certainty, and we'll have our horse again." Nor did his predictions wholly fail in point of accuracy; for in less than half an hour the animal, greatly blown, was brought back to him; but not the skilled jockey who had put it to its speed. In short, Turpin had flung himself from the animal's back as soon as he reached the other side of the stream that was bridged over, then diving into the thickets and plantations that opportunely offered him means of escape, he instantly disappeared. Before the darkness of the night set in, Mr. Bradele's other horse was found quietly cropping the grass, at a spot not greatly distant from that in which it had been mounted by King; not a trace of the robbers was discovered on that occasion, beyond the points already mentioned; every covert, nook, and lane of the entire district being as familiar to them, especially to Turpin, as those to which a fox has been habituated from the moment it first may have been forced to provide for itself in any district or locality.

Turpin and his companion kept about Epping forest for some time longer, and till they were harrassed almost to death, resorting thither at night from their places of concealment, and carrying on with more desperate hands than ever their system of plunder and robbery. When nothing else was to be got from a traveller than the steed he rode, Turpin, especially, never scrupled, by means of a most formidable display of fire-arms, to possess himself of such an article; and this even when he himself might be mounted, provided the person who was made to stand and deliver had a better animal.

One night, when Dick was alone and coming over the forest, he found his courser to be unequal to a certain affair upon which he had set his mind. Almost immediately after he had made this discovery, most luckily, as he considered the occurrence, one Mr. Major, the owner of the famous race-horse, Whitestockings, riding by on that same animal, the villain resolved not only to take from him whatever money he was possessed of, but his steed also; and although they were not more than three hundred yards from the Green Man at the time, the fellow accomplished the outrage, exchanging horses with the other in a twinkling. The command to "stop and deliver," together with the sight of a pair of pistols, completed the transaction, as well as deprived the aggrieved party of a will to shout for assistance. As soon, however, as Mr. Major got to the Green Man, he acquainted the landlord, Mr. Boyes, with what had happened him almost at the threshold of the inn. "I dare swear it is Turpin that has done it, or one of his crew," said Mr. Boyes; "I'll endeavour to get intelligence of Whitestockings. This that has been left you is no doubt a stolen article also, and I would have you advertise it." Mr. Major did so, the animal proving to have been stolen from Plaistow-marshes, while the very saddle upon it had been taken from one Arrowsmith.

Mr. Major had been robbed on Saturday night, and Mr. Boyes received intelligence on the Monday morning that such a horse as the former had lost was left at the Red Lion, Whitechapel, London. Boyes went there and found that the information was correct; he therefore resolved to wait till some one came to claim the animal or to take it away. Nor was he disappointed, for about eleven o'clock that very night, Tom King's brother made his appearance, claiming the horse, on which he was instantly seized. The fellow swore that he bought it honestly, and could bring proof of the transaction; but the very whip with which Mr. Major rode, and which had been taken from him by Turpin, being found upon the impudent rascal, and the name of the proper owner appearing on the bottom of the whip, served to strengthen the accusation. A constable having been sent for, and the fellow betraying fear, he was told if he would divulge the truth so far as he knew it concerning the real stealer of the horse, he should be released. "If you will go to the corner of Red Lion-street, close by." he now said, "you will see the parties you wish to come at." Mr. Boyes made no more ado than proceed thither, instantly getting his eye upon Tom King; and having cleverly gone a little way round, he fell upon him boldly. King drew a pistol, and clapping it to Mr. Boyes's breast pulled the trigger. But the powder flashed in the pan and did no more. King struggled to get out his other pistol, but it had got so twisted in his pocket as not to be readily forthcoming. However, Turpin was near at hand, on horseback, and now rode up, when King with a profane oath called out, "Shoot him, Dick, or we are taken." Turpin instantly fired, aiming, as he thought, with most deadly certainty at Boyes. But the bullet had another office to perform, for it missed Boyes and entered the body of the highwayman. "Dick, you have killed me outright," was the exclamation which escaped from King; when away from the scene of danger the other sped as fast as his horse's legs could serve him.

King lived a week afterwards; many times during this period, so awful to him, charging Turpin with cowardice and most disgraceful acts, even in the creed of such a reasoner. He also gave information where Dick might in all probability be found, in order to be brought to justice; naming a notorious house by Hackney Marsh, at the same time advising those to whom he spoke to be cautious how they went to work against the Essex highwayman; telling them that Turpin uniformly carried three brace of pistols about his person besides a loaded carbine slung beneath his outer garment. On inquiry it was found that Dick had gone directly from Red Lion-street to the house mentioned by King, and that on entering it he had not only spoken despairingly in consequence of the disaster which had overtaken his companion in crime, but had vowed vengeance against the landlord of the Green Man. "What shall I do?" he cried, "Where shall I go? I will be the death of Boyes; for I have lost through him the best fellow I ever had in all my life."

We shall not much longer concern ourselves with the notorious Turpin; for although his depredations were by no means at an end on the death of the criminal associate he so much prized, yet it would be little more than to repeat ourselves were the account to be extended to any considerably additional length. Besides, the villain's career henceforward was rather that of a stealer of horses and a dealer in the same than a formidable highwayman. Having found his old haunts to become too hot for him, he withdrew to Long-Sutton in Lincolnshire, where he resided for some time. Having stolen many horses in that neighbourhood, he was at length apprehended for that crime and sheep-stealing; but as a constable was conducting him to a justice of the peace, he made his escape, after which he got to Brough, near Machet Cave, in Yorkshire; from thence he went to North Cave, and from thence again to Welton.

He frequently went into Lincolnshire, however, under a pretence of seeing his friends, always bringing back with him three or four stolen horses, which he sold or exchanged for others in Yorkshire. The name he now took unto himself was that of Palmer, his wife's maiden name. Meanwhile at Welton he lived in some show of respectability, frequently going out a-hunting or shooting. It was after a little adventure of the latter kind that he not only acted with a silly and ostentatious insolence, but so as to bring himself into inextricable trouble; forming a poor and pitiful conclusion to his more notorious exploits. On an evening in the month of October, 1738, returning after a fowling excursion, he wantonly shot one of his landlord's cocks in the open street. Upon this a neighbour of the name of Hall remonstrated with him, saying, "You have done wrong in killing thus needlessly your landlord's cock." To this reasonable speech Turpin in a bullying manner replied, "If you will only stay until I charge my piece I will shoot you with as little regard as I have done the dunghill bird." Such was the occasion of our *heroic* highwayman being carried before a magistrate, and next day again before the bench of justices who were then sitting in their quarter sessions at Beverley. These justices thinking it necessary to make some inquiries into the character and pursuits of the prisoner beyond what concerned the shooting of his landlord's cock, and receiving anything but satisfactory answers from him, nay, false ones, as was soon discovered upon inquiries made far and near, they ordered him to be kept in custody meanwhile. Almost immediately he was accused by several parties with horse-stealing, and having been tried at York upon two separate charges of the kind, he was found guilty and thereon condemned to die. It now came out also that his real and proper name was not Palmer, but Turpin, —in short the notorious highwayman Dick Turpin,—a fact which precluded the slightest glimmer of hope that the sentence of the law would be relaxed in his case.

In York Castle this hardened fellow lived in as much pleasure as the liberties of the prison would permit; eating, drinking, and carousing with any one who would spend their time with him. Nor did he change his behaviour after his condemnation. An amazing number of people came to see him, of which circumstance he felt proud instead of ashamed. One of them, who pretended to have known him in times past, happened to declare in his hearing that he would lay half a guinea " that this is not Turpin." Upon which the condemned felon whispered to the keeper, "Lay him the wager, and I'll go you halves."

He continued this unseemly manner to the last, spending his time in joking and telling stories, without any symptom of contrition or fears for the future. A few days before his execution, he bought himself a new fustian frock and a pair of pumps, in order to take his leave of the world in them. The morning of the day on which he suffered, he gave three pounds five shillings amongst five men, who were to follow the cart as mourners, also hatbands and gloves to several persons. He also left a gold ring and other articles to a married woman at Brough, with whom he had some acquaintance, although he acknowledged that his own wife was alive. On the way to the place of execution he conducted himself with a dreadful, a disgusting assurance, bowing and chattering to the spectators as he passed. It was remarked that, as he mounted the ladder, his right leg trembled, on which he stamped it down with a vaunting air, looking around as if for applause. He talked to the executioner for some time, in anything but a fitting strain, and at last threw himself off the ladder with a flourish, and in an instant passed into eternity.

Although the body was buried very deeply in the grave, it was taken up by resurrection men, with the view of having it anatomized. The mob got notice where the corpse had been carried to, went to the place, brought it away through the streets in triumph, and buried it in the same grave, where it had first been deposited, having first filled the coffin with quick lime. Altogether, the life as well as the death of the notorious Turpin conveys a woful lesson. We seek in vain in them for anything that can tempt even the most thoughtless to a similar career with that which he ran; the teaching is of quite an opposite character, and on this account his case has been presented in this collection. There is in the simple fact of his stating to the hangman at the place of execution that he was "thirty-three years old," only an awakening announcement, accompanied with saddest suggestions. Nor can we but experience horror with regard to the number, manner, and circumstances of the executions of criminals in England, not only at the period at which this villain's name was in the mouth of so many people, but for many years afterwards, ay, even down to the present period. A writer in the year 1737, describing a scene which he says he witnessed at Tyburn, when several men were executed together, observes that three of them "were nicely decked out," although "they had ropes about their necks, and were to be instantly hanged;" nay, that one of them having coughed, hemmed, and wiped his nose, and put on a new pair of white gloves, made, with seeming indifference and levity, a ludicrous speech which was meant to amuse the mob and to imbue people with a notion that he was a heroic fellow, whilst others of the wretches dealt in grimaces and comical gestures during the shocking harangue. The writer adds :—" While I was examining the intrepidity of these rogues, who affected to die like heroes, the hangman began to whip the horses, which abruptly drew away the *theatre*, and the *comedians* remained swinging in the air. To shorten their pains, some lugged them by the heels, others struck them on the stomach; in short, by the easy manner wherewith this ceremony was performed, I readily perceived that the English are very far from having any share of that prudent delicacy of other nations, among whom people generally conceive a just horror for men whose crimes bring them to their *exit*. There are criminals amongst us (he continues), who would have the glory of dying like gentlemen ; whereas they leave the world either as brutes or as idiots, having nothing so much in their thoughts as how to obtain a few idle praises. And what is not less strange, people laugh at the scene, as if striving to efface the whole ignominy of the shameful execution ; so that I am at a great loss to say which of the two is most out of his senses and the greater disgrace to our kind,—he who can bestow commendation, or at least countenance, on the horrid follies of hardened scoundrels, or the rascal himself, who believes he can blot out his villanies by expressing levity or effrontery at the dying hour for the same. Truly there is much to answer for connected with these executions, apart from the criminals."

XI.—THE DUCHESS OF KINGSTON.

THE trial of the Duchess of Kingston for bigamy was one of the most extraordinary episodes in Patrician history that occurred in this country during the reign of George III. The event accordingly created a most unwonted sensation at the time of its occurrence, even greater than the trial of the rebel lords had done thirty years before. The singular life and character of the defendant, her high station, as well as the eminent rank of the other parties concerned, lent such attraction to the Duchess's case that scarcely any other subject was thought or talked of in London while it lasted. With talents of no mean order, with personal attractions which charmed every eye, and with accomplishments captivating, even after the influence of beauty and youth had ceased, the celebrated lady lived] a memorable example of the inefficacy of wealth or grandeur to secure happiness. Indeed very few women have ever made themselves more notorious than this Duchess of Kingston. The history of her life has all the interest of a romance. Prints of her are still to be found in the costume in which she appeared at a fancy dress ball given by the Venetian Ambassador in London, when she was the beautiful Miss Chudleigh, her indiscretions being at least equal to the graces of her person and accomplishments.

Elizabeth Chudleigh was the only daughter of Colonel Thomas Chudleigh, the younger son of Sir George Chudleigh, of Ashton, in the county of Devon, a family which had long been held in great respect in the West of England. She was born in the year 1720. Her father, early in life, entered the army ; and though it does not appear that he was ever engaged in any service that could give him an opportunity of distinguishing himself, for either courage or conduct, yet he died with the rank mentioned, being also at the period lieutenant-governor of Chelsea Hospital. This event took place when his daughter was very young, and, of course, the tutelage of her mind and care of her education devolved on the mother, who, having nothing to depend on but the pension she derived as a widow from the rank her husband had held in the army, and a small salary as house-keeper of Windsor Castle, however solicitous she might be to cultivate the manners of her infant charge, it is obvious she must have been precluded from bestowing on the girl those liberal attentions she would otherwise have shown to her offspring. Still the widow manifested enterprise and a desire to maintain her past position in society. On the death of her husband, finding it necessary to lay down a plan of domestic economy, being resolved at the same time to keep up such an appearance as would entitle her to retain those respectable connexions she had formed, she bethought her of having a small neat house, in a fashionable part of the metropolis, where she might take in a lady as boarder and lodger. She succeeded in her scheme, and so as to enable herself to furnish a table in a style of plenty, and sometimes elegance, to which the scantiness of her regular finances would not otherwise have permitted her to aspire.

Elizabeth, without the instruction of masters, soon became distinguished in the circles of her mother's acquaintances. Nature had endowed her with boldness of disposition, fluency of speech, a vivid fancy, and smartness of repartee. Her manner was admired; her clever sayings were retailed; and her company solicited. Among those in high life who visited at her mother's, was the celebrated Mr. Pulteney, afterwards created Earl of Bath for betraying his party, and recanting those political principles he maintained while a commoner. At this time he was confidential friend to the Prince of Wales, a principal leader of the Opposition in parliament, and greatly countenanced by his royal highness. Of course his interest was very great at the court of the prince, then kept at Leicester House.

Mr. Pulteney being dazzled with the brilliant sallies of Miss Chudleigh's conversation, and her personal charms, resolved on drawing her from obscurity, and placing her in a situation where her qualities might be seen to the greatest advantage. He applied to the Princess of Wales in favour of the young lady, and at the age of eighteen she was appointed maid of honour to her royal highness. Mr. Pulteney knowing the narrowness of Miss Chudleigh's education, recommended to her the sedulous cultivation of her understanding, and undertook himself some share of the pleasing office of preceptor. Under this tuition she improved considerably; their literary exercises were frequent. She read to him, he read to her; and when separate they repeatedly corresponded by letters. Their ages were very different, and yet scandal made busy about their intimacy, although able only to whisper suspicions. But to the suppression of the tittle tattle of the day the Princess of Wales lent all her aid, showing the young lady such particular notice and attention as assured people of her favourable convictions concerning the maid of honour. It must be confessed at the same time that Mr. Pulteney's endeavours to attach his pupil to any thing like severe study or to the solid improvement of her mental powers, proved but very partially successful; so that her learning, like her judgment, was only of a superficial order. But though deficient in regard to sound sense, cultered understanding, and wholesome literature, she delighted every company in which she mingled, with the excursions of her imagination and her vivacity.

No man understood better than Mr. Pulteney the value of money, or the uses to which it might be put; and finding that avarice was among the tastes of his scholar, he carefully instructed her in that direction. She was now mounting in the hemisphere of fashionable life, and why should she not turn to the most profitable account such powers as she wielded; among which the flashes of her wit and the charms of her face and figure were the most obvious and commanding. In fact, so potent and attractive were these that the Duke of Hamilton, amongst others, was smitten by her; and such grew the ardour with which he loved her, and the perseverance of his suit, that Miss Chudleigh, whose interest and vanity were equally concerned, was not backward to making a promise that she would become his wife, on his grace's return from the grand tour which he was then about to make. The engagement was even reduced to writing, a mutual promise of a constant correspondence by letters having been also passed between them.

The year after Miss Chudleigh had been appointed maid of honour, being on a visit with her aunt, Mrs. Hanmer, at Mr. Merrill's, who had married her cousin, and then resided in Hampshire, they went to Winchester races.   The young lady's beauty had some time before made an impression on the Hon. Augustus John Harvey, of the Bristol noble family, then a lieutenant in the navy, who followed her to Mr. Merrill's. The lieutenant had been made acquainted by Mrs. Hanmer with Miss Chudleigh's position in respect of the Duke of Hamilton, and had not ventured to stand forward as an avowed rival till his grace was on his continental tour.   But now, being favoured by Mrs. Hanmer, a woman familiar with intrigue in high life, an adept in subtlety, and a proficient in the knowledge of the female heart, he felt himself doubly armed, and at once laid siege to the beauty, even although she had an aversion to him.   In fact, Mrs. Hanmer told him not to despair since he had herself on his side.

What is it a woman will not attempt in revenge for injured pride? Her resentment on such occasion is boundless, it will stop at no barrier,—nor deem any sacrifice too precious.· Virtue has been abandoned—husbands dishonoured—assassinations perpetrated, when the female heart found itself stung by neglect and comtempt.—To rouse the pride, to awaken the resentment of Miss Chudleigh against her lover, the absent duke, were the means by which Mrs. Hanmer worked, in order to forward the suit of Lieutenant Harvey; and for this purpose she intercepted the letters of his grace, excited the jealousy of her niece by means of misrepresentation, and in short evoked the deepest indignation towards the distant lover.   On the other hand, Harvey was continually in view.   His assiduities were unremitting, and his professions breathed with all the warmth of a sincere affection. Maddened by the forgetfulness and the apparent despite of the duke, teased by the tender assiduities of the gallant sailor, and the incessant solicitations on his behalf by her subtle and artful aunt, the young lady at length consented to break the contract which she had made with Hamilton, and by marrying executed an irrevocable bond, which precluded her from any legal or honourable connexion with another than her wedded lord.

The marriage ceremony, however, was performed privately, in a chapel adjoining the house of Mr. Merrill; but strange to relate, notwithstanding the ardour of the young husband, the first night was the last in which he was permitted, by the consent of his wife, to live with her, and this for reasons, such at least as were generally given out, —with which we shall not occupy our pages.   The young wife was not open in her accusations against her lord, confining them to her confidential aunt, but being at the same time resolute in her determination of never cohabiting with Mr. Harvey more; nay, nor, if possible, appearing in the character of his wife.

Having consulted her aunt, this convenient relation undertook to prevail on the lieutenant to keep the marriage secret; and this she did not find a difficult task.   There were strong reasons on both sides which made the arrangement necessary.   Harvey feared the displeasure of his family and friends on account of so early and imprudent a match as that which he had formed; while the young lady well knew that her position and employment as a maid of honour to the Princess of Wales must necessarily cease the moment it became known that she was a married woman.

Notwithstanding the acquiesence of the young husband to conceal the marriage, he continued to visit his wife; but soon after the solemnization of the bond, to her great satisfaction, he was ordered on an expedition to the West Indies; whence he did not return till the autumn of 1746, an event which greatly mortified her. After remaining at home for about a month, he was ordered to the Mediterranean, but again returned in the following January.   When at home, however, he experienced from his wife, whose marriage was still a secret to the world, every kind and mode of rejection which in their peculiar circumstances could be manifested towards him. He was received, when he called upon her, with frowns and gloom; his appearance distressed, his departure cheered her spirits. And yet this unhappiness, which obtruded at times daily upon her private hours, was not observed in public, where she continued to be the centre of the fashionable circle, her vivacity and beauty being held to have gained additional charms rather than to have become diminished; neither sigh nor tear betraying uneasiness of mind, so that a crowd of titled and untitled beaux constantly surrounded or followed her.

No wonder that Harvey manifested to his wife jealousy and resentment; nay, he now determined upon asserting those rights of a husband from which the young lady had taken every means in her power to exclude him, whatever might be the consequences, that did not lead to a public disclosure of their union. He beheld her an object of general admiration, and though the treatment he received at her hands might well have alienated his affections and his esteem, he was resolved that she should be made to succumb to his will, however brief might be the existence of his rule, or limited its character. He insisted upon a private interview, while she strove to conduct every negotiation by letter. She entreated his forbearance, but he swore that if she did not comply with his demand, an immediate disclosure of their marriage should take place. This threat had the desired effect, and a meeting occurred at his lodgings, there being at the time no person in the house but a negro man-servant.

Mr. Harvey, on the instant his wife was introduced to the apartment, where he received her, cut off every possibility of retreat by securing the door. A warm expostulation took place, but this proving unavailing, the lady assumed an apparent docility; and the interview, somewhat protracted, was conducted thereafter with a show of complacency. In due time a boy made his appearance in the world, and the maid of honour became a mother.

The celebrated Cæsar Hawkins was the confidential *accoucheur* on this occasion; but as the lady had taken every precaution to conceal from the prying eyes of the courtiers, who daily surrounded her, the growing appearance of pregnancy, the wretched infant at its birth was in such a sadly debilitated state, that it could not long survive,—its death being not to the regret, but to the great joy of the maternal parent. These events took place at Chelsea, to which village Mrs. Harvey had retired, under pretence that a change of air had been advised as necessary to her health. On her return to Leicester House, however, in spite of all her precautions, she found that a buzzing report had prevailed not very favourable to the reputation of a supposed maiden.

The Duke of Hamilton having finished his tour, returned to England, and immediately made the lady a tender of his hand. It being impossible, however, for Mrs. Harvey now to accept the generous offer, and not wishing to make him acquainted with her marriage, he naturally gave credit to the reports concerning her, and ere long wedded one of the beautiful Misses Gunning. Still the fascinations of the *maid of honour* did not suffer even by the mortification of discovering the imposition which had been practised on her by her aunt and husband. His Grace of Ancaster being smitten, made an offer of his heart, which also was rejected. Others in high station experienced a similar answer, to the astonishment of her friends and acquaintances, the mystification of many a coterie, and the distress of her mother,—for the secret of the marriage remained undivulged.

To free herself from importunity, Mrs. Harvey determined on travelling, and chose the circle of Germany for her tour. For some time she resided at Berlin, from which she removed to Dresden, and being perfect mistress of the French tongue, her vivacity and adroitness gained her admission even to crowned heads. The King of Prussia and the Electoress of Saxony conferred many favours on her, made her several rich presents, and on her departure from the continent became her correspondents ; honours which were ever after continual subjects of her boastful vanity. As she found herself so much respected and admired abroad, it is rather extraordinary she should have revisited England, during the life of her husband at least. But she panted for the pleasures of her native land ; nor, on her return, was she without repeated proofs that her charms had suffered no diminution during her absence. She continued to be the favourite toast of *bon ton,* the idol of the men, the envy of the women. Her suitors were numerous as ever,—she breathed in an atmosphere of sighs,—every butterfly of fashion hovered round her. Lord Howe was the only person, however, whom she did not repel with indifference. He had even the reputation of being favoured in a way that did not well accord with the fact of Elizabeth Chudleigh being a *maid of honour.* Her intimacy, besides, with Lady Harrington and Miss Asher, who rioted in dissipation, gave a stamp to her character. She was constant at the midnight orgies of their pleasures, and may be supposed with too much probability to have participated in their several indulgencies.

Harvey, irritated by her contumely, and provoked by her licentiousness, thought it a duty he owed himself to repel the one and restrain the other, and informed her he would disclose his marriage to the Princess of Wales. The fulfilment of this resolution his wife rendered unnecessary, for she had either previously acquainted her royal highness with her situation, or, on the spur of the occasion, had anticipated her husband's information. At any rate his end was frustrated ; Mrs. Harvey was a confidential favourite, being honoured with the patronage of the Princess to the hour of her royal highness's death.

The quarrel between the secretly-married pair having now taken place, and the lady following her own inclinations uncontrolled, she became the subject of much scandal. Her personal charms, as well as the situation she held in public and polite life, rendered her conspicuous ; while a conduct which was not marked with a strict attention to decorum, gave birth to a host of stories which were industriously propagated by the busy and exaggerating tongue of calumny ; some of which might well be flatly contradicted, whilst others deserved such a degree of credit as belongs to probability. Among the former may be reckoned the tale of the Somerset House masquerade, at which, as was roundly and oft asserted, she appeared in a shape of flesh coloured silk so nicely and closely fitted to her body as to produce a perfect review of the unadorned and unclad mother of mankind ; it being added that this fair representation of frailty, conscious of her condition, like Eve after the first act of disobedience, had contrived a method of giving as evident tokens of modesty, by binding her loins with a partial covering, or zone of fig-leaves. The truth, however, is, that at this masquerade, given by the Venetian Ambassador, Mrs. Harvey appeared in the dress of Iphigenia, and covered such parts of her skin as a strict conformity to the character she had assumed required, with flesh-coloured silk, and which had at least an indelicate appearance ; so much so indeed as to induce the Princess of Wales to give her favourite a tacit reproof, by throwing a veil over her.

Another circumstance which happened a considerable time after her marriage made a deal of noise among the courtiers at the period ; a female infant was found on the stairs, leading to the apartments of Mrs. Chudleigh, in Windsor Castle, and after being taken care of by that lady, went to live with her daughter, the *maid of honour,* as an attendant on her person, having been called Elizabeth, by which she was distinguished without a surname. This young woman continued with Mrs. Harvey till her death, which occurred when she was about twenty. The circumstances now mentioned and others gave rise to a belief that the mistress and maid were mother and daughter.

Mrs. Harvey's dress, equipage, and expences, while maid of honour, also suggested numerous speculations. For a number of years after her marriage, she not only displayed a style of living greatly superior to her known income, which was only six hundred pounds a year, but built elegant houses and furnished them magnificently. Many supposed she was supplied by royal bounty, in return for licentious favours, although of this conjecture no proofs ever were made public.

At length her morning meditations, her nightly thoughts, came to be engrossed with the contrivance of schemes to procure a dissolution of the marriage bond. Lawyers were consulted, but no means could be devised except proofs of adultery against their fair client. So dangerous an experiment as to adduce these would never do, although not so much for the sin as the risk. The wife could not take the benefit of her own wrong doing. Time, however, brought about an opportunity, on which female ingenuity instantly seized. The parson who performed the marriage ceremony having rested with his fathers, it appeared upon inquiry that the parish register was not in cautious hands. An inspection was requested, for which a handsome bribe having been given, the clerk suffered himself to be amused on one side of the vestry, while Mrs. Harvey dexterously tore from the book the leaf which contained the record of her marriage, and, depositing it in her bosom, she conveyed it home, where it was committed to the flames, never more to rise in evidence for or against her.

By this exploit Mrs. Harvey considered herself absolved from those sacred vows she had made at the altar to her husband, and at liberty to receive the addresses and the hand of the first lover she should approve of. It so turned out, however, that Mr. Harvey, not long after the said exploit had been achieved, succeeded to the Earldom of Bristol, so that his rank and fortune now became objects of serious consideration and envy on the part of his lady. In short, on reflecting with regard to the succession to the family honours and revenues of her husband, she deeply repented of her rashness in destroying the written evidence of her marriage. Still she resolved even now not to be denied the gratification of her ambition and avarice. To re-establish her claims, she took a step analogous to the bold and dishonest one just mentioned. She made another journey to Mr. Merrill's, under the pretence of paying that gentleman a friendly visit, but in reality to procure the re-insertion of her marriage with Mr. Harvey in the register book; and for this purpose took with her an attorney in whom she had long confided. The officiating clerk was easily worked upon; money was given as before, and promotion promised. The book was managed by the lady to her perfect satisfaction, and her spirits were so elevated on the occasion, that she opened her heart to the clergyman's wife, informed her of the birth and death of her child by Mr. Harvey, and told her that the proof she had now obtained might be a hundred thousand pounds in her way.

The Earldom of Bristol having descended to Mr. Harvey, and he being taken ill soon after, viz., in 1759, his lady set about assuming her title and rank; but an event occurred about the very same period, which again led her to change her mind. It was this; the Duke of Kingston became so ardent a lover, that she began to look up to a still loftier position among the nobility than that of a countess, and to the acquisition of an amount of wealth superior to any that had engaged her attention since being circumvented out of the title of the Duchess of Hamilton. She might still rank in the ducal list. How to obtain this honour and fortune became, accordingly, the subject of her most earnest meditation;

again she was lacerated with the lashes of repentance on account of the rashness with which she had forged new fetters for her own binding. Application was made to the bar, to the civilians, but no remedy could be devised.—Several years passed over, Mrs. Harvey cohabiting with the duke under the name of Miss Chudleigh, but with such circumspection and decorum, that though there could be no doubt of a guilty connexion, yet no certain evidence of it ever came to public light.

The Earl of Bristol having recovered from his illness, in 1760, and having intimated a wish for a dissolution of his marriage, was sounded by a friend of his wife, on the subject of a divorce. His lordship, however, resented strongly the motive of the application; and though he declared his hearty sorrow and regret for having ever united himself by the ties of wedlock to such a woman, yet he roughly swore that he would see her at the devil before he gratified her vanity, by assisting her to become a duchess. Still, after all, the earl was so far a match for his wife, that he soon after having thus peremptorily expressed himself, changed his mind; the cause of this resolution being the fact of his having formed an intimacy with a lady whom he wished to marry. No sooner had his lordship undergone the revolution of mind, than he bluntly sent to his wife to say that he " wanted a divorce," but she must supply the grounds and the evidence for their legal separation !!!

Now, however desirable it might be for Mrs. Harvey, or rather, the Countess of Bristol, to become Duchess of Kingston by dissolving the marriage bond with her lord, this was not the way that met her approbation; nor could it have been propitious to her designs on her ducal paramour, for her to be the means of recording her own infamy in a court of law, by supplying proofs of her adultery. The common lawyers and the civilians were therefore again consulted; and now these ingenious gentlemen advised a cause to be instituted on the part of the lady, to set aside the Earl of Bristol's marriage claims; and these being most weakly supported by his defence,—the witnesses who could prove the marriage having been kept back,—a formal sentence of *jactitation* was pronounced in Doctors' Commons by which she was declared free of all matrimonial contracts, and of course left at liberty to marry again.—By a jactitation of marriage is meant a process sometimes resorted to in the Ecclesiastical Courts, as, when one of the parties gives out that he or she is married to the other; yet unless the party so declaring makes out a proof of the actual marriage, he or she is enjoined perpetual silence upon that head; which, however, is the only remedy those courts can give in such a case, and by no means amounts to a divorce.

In the way mentioned, were the wishes of the noble lord and his countess completely gratified, but still not without being attended with reports prejudicial to the characters of each of them. Among others, the Earl was accused with having received a very considerable pecuniary consideration for his collusion. However, the definitive sentence having been pronounced in Doctors' Commons, on the 10th of February, 1769, on the 8th of March following, Lady Bristol obtained the fulfilment of her ambition, by being married to his grace the Duke of Kingston, the ceremony having been solemnized with the utmost magnificence. What must appear remarkable was the fact that favours were worn on the occasion not only by the principal nobility, but by most of the illustrious personages in the kingdom, the new duchess having even been received at court. It is equally true that during the life of the Duke, a space of five years, not a doubt was promulgated, or a legal step taken to impeach the marriage. The civilians, tenacious of their jurisdiction, had held that the decree of their judges was not liable to be disturbed by an extrinsic court, and the duchess rested perfectly contented under their opinions, which, though certainly sanctioned by an acquiescence of ages, will presently appear to have been founded in presumption, and contrary to the wise superintending power of the common law of the land.

The duke died, having not only proved a fond husband, but to have been so fascinated by his ambitious wife, or so worked upon, that she was enabled to turn his understanding to every measure her inclination, caprice, or passion dictated. No wonder then that she procured from him a *will* bequeathing the income of his vast estates to her for life; so that no sooner had his Grace paid the debt of nature than his relict found herself not only immensely rich, but of a mind to cut a figure in a characteristic manner with her wealth. She visited Rome shortly after becoming a widow, with the intention of residing there for a considerable period. The celebrated Ganginelli at that time filled the Papal chair, and as his holiness was an ecclesiastic of moderate principles, and a tolerant spirit, he received her Grace's visit to him with great cordiality, conferring on her various privileges which had hitherto been only enjoyed by princes, lodging her also in the palace of one of the cardinals. And in gratitude for those favours, so flattering to the pride and vanity of the lady, notwithstanding her avarice, she treated the Romans with certain public spectacles, which took wonderfully with the degenerated Italians of the Eternal City. But yet, while festivity and papal countenance were elating her heart in Rome, a storm was gathering in the dominions of her proper sovereign, which threatened to level her and her honours in the dust.

A woman named Craddock, who, in the capacity of a servant, had been present at the marriage of Mr. Harvey with Miss Chudleigh, being reduced to indigence, applied to the attorney of the duchess for relief. But it was in vain she urged her distress, in vain she menaced a discovery of all she knew, to the relations of the Duke of Kingston. She was set at defiance by the lawyer, as directed by the duchess, so that, stimulated by rude rebuffs as well as by indigence, she at last made good her threatenings.

For private reasons, well known to the confidential friends of the Duke of Kingston, and among which was disrespect towards the duchess, his Grace harboured an inveterate dislike against Mr. Evelyn Meadows, his eldest nephew, and son to his sister Lady Frances Pierrepont. On that account he cut him off from the inheritance; and by his will made his younger nephew his heir. To the elder nephew it was that Mrs. Craddock communicated what she had to say, and the information was most joyfully received, promising to him a restitution of what he considered his right. In short, a bill of indictment was very speedily preferred against the duchess on a charge of bigamy. The bill having been found by the grand jury, it was advised, if her Grace did not appear in proper time to plead to the indictment, that process of outlawry should be commenced against her; it was thus the cloud thickened, being very artfully conjured up by her enemies. In fact, the intelligence of the gathering storm and its early bursting, was like the shock of a paralytic stroke to the duchess. It for a time threatened the overthrow of her reason. But she recovered, and finding that not a moment was to be wasted idly before appearing in England, unless she made up her mind to be beggared, she ordered her carriage and drove to her banker.

The name of this person was Jenkins, who, although he had at one time only been a broker of curiosities in Rome, was now banker to almost every British subject that visited the metropolis of the holy see. In this house the duchess had placed money and securities to a large amount, for the purpose of answering such sums as she should think fit to draw for. Mr. Jenkins, however, had been made aware, cleverly enough on the part of the lady's enemies, of her predicament, and knowing that she would require and demand her money before quitting Rome, ordered himself to be denied to her, the intent being to delay her reaching England till judgment of outlawry could be obtained, the execution of which would have operated upon her property at home; and although not to the advantage of the Duke of Kingston's relations, for the confiscations would of course have gone to the crown, yet the thing would have been to her great inconvenience. Time after time Mr. Jenkins was denied, until the duchess became alarmed and began to suspect his motives. To her honour be it said, she not only suspected the banker, but she mustered her spirits, resolved not only on enforcing an interview with him, but on obtaining a restitution of the money and security she had deposited in his hands. Accordingly she armed herself with a brace of pistols, and forthwith made for his house. The answer was as before, that Mr. Jenkins was not at home; but the resolute creditor now placed herself at his door, declaring she would there remain sentinel, and not once quit her post, until the man she desired should confront her by his appearance, ay, even though a month should elapse before she obtained satisfaction. This resolute procedure had the desired effect. The unworthy fellow was astonished and ashamed, being also alarmed not only for what the incensed lady might do to him, but for the credit of his bank. He came forth; she obtained what she demanded; and instantly departed from Rome, commencing her journey to England.

Unhappily for the duchess, before she reached the Alps in her rapid and homeward journey, a violent fever overtook her, brought on, no doubt, by the perturbations, anxieties, and exertions which she underwent; this severe illness terminating in an abscess which quickly gathered in her side. Thus tormented in mind and body, her condition was pitiable; and being now unable to travel in a carriage, she slowly pursued her melancholy route in a litter contrived for the purpose; and thus it was she reached Calais.—The abscess having broken, she found considerable relief from corporeal pain; but her mental wretchedness was extreme, till at length her reason again seemed to be in a measure dethroned; one of her great alarms being that her case precluded bail, and that on her arrival in England she should be consigned to the cell of a prison. In fact, she imagined that a charge of bigamy was nothing less than that of a felony without the benefit of clergy. Happily for her and opportunely, however, Lord Mansfield, who had just made a trip to France at the period, paid a visit to her grace, and explained to her the nature of the offence with which she was charged, and the consequences not only of the indictment, but of conviction if this took place; and being greatly eased of her fears from the great lawyer's information, her health rapidly improved, and she embarked for Dover.— On her arrival at Kingston-house, she discovered that neither absence nor the prosecution had frightened away her acquaintances; and amongst the most zealous of whom in her behalf, she found the Dukes of Newcastle, Ancastar, and Portland, besides a number of other distinguished personages. The first step was to put in bail to the indictment, which was done before Lord Mansfield, his Grace of Newcastle and Lord Mountstuart becoming her sureties, whilst many persons of rank and fortune offered to join them. These voluntary acts of friendship could not but considerably alleviate her distress; and coming from such parties her vanity was flattered and her mind strengthened to meet with considerable intrepidity the trial which was in preparation; one of the most severe that a woman of her rank had been subjected to for many years. Nor is it to be lost sight of, that it was to her ownself that she had principally to impute her wretched situation, and all its consequences. Avarice had superseded prudence; ambition, virtue. She had depended on cunning and chicanery, and she now also found that, instead of purchasing off the evidence against her, she had applied to lawyers, whose interest it was to promote litigation. Mrs. Craddock had in her old age solicited a decent maintenance for the remnant of her life; and had offered, in case of acquiescence, to retire to her native village and never more to obtrude herself upon the peace of the duchess. The offer had been rejected; she who was now to be brought before an august tribunal on a criminal charge, though wallowing in wealth, would not consent to allow the poor woman more than twenty pounds a year, and on the hard condition that she should live sequestered in an obscure spot, near the Peak of Derby. It was now too late to be liberal, as the duchess sorrowfully felt, regretting that she did not rather part with thousands, than allow herself to be brought to the pass in which she was at length inextricably fixed.

Before coming to the actual trial, the duchess, as if she had not by this time furnished sufficient matter of conversation for the town, contrived to engage herself in a paper war with no other an antagonist than Samuel Foote, the dramatist. This unprincipled wit had come to the knowledge of certain private incidents of her life, through the medium of a woman who had formerly been her confidante, and these he introduced into a play called the "Trip to Calais," in which the duchess was to be brought forward under the name of Lady Kitty Crocodile. When he had finished this notable performance, so that it was ready for the stage, he gave her an intimation of what he had done, and had the base effrontery to ask two thousand pounds for the suppression of the piece. It is said he actually refused sixteen hundred pounds. Fortunately he was, in as far as gain to himself was concerned, wholly foiled in his infamous plot, for the Lord Chamberlain refused to license the play, and though he threatened to publish it, a counter-threat of an action of law made him abandon his project. Thereupon he wrote to the duchess that the affair was at an end, and she very foolishly published his letter with her own answer to it. This drew forth a reply from Foote, and in the encounter of their wits in the correspondence her grace had certainly not the best of it. While her grace was thus ill-advisedly indulging her caprice and malice; while she was thus amusing the public with a farce in which she made a conspicuous and ridiculous figure, as the principal character, her folly retorted upon herself. In wit, humour, and satire, Foote had every advantage over her and her literary assistants, who crowded the prints with anonymous squibs and paragraphs reflecting on his character, but which, instead of serving their patroness, betrayed their own insufficiency, the weakness besides of her head, and the malevolence of her heart. Every anecdote of her life, in return, was brought forward, and many, even innocent actions, were aggravated into grave indiscretions or offences. She sought calumny and found it; she felt the stings she had provoked, and this at a time when she should have studiously avoided every step that could disturb the past, and leant upon the sympathy which popularly attaches to the object of prosecution, whatever the grounds of accusation, so long as that object is passive and humble. With those in power it was certainly the wish that the duchess should behave discreetly; they even appear to have hoped that she would come to some accommodation with the prosecutor. However, this was not done, the duchess meanwhile losing no opportunity or means untried in order to strengthen the chances of an acquittal.

The indictment having been removed from the King's Bench into the High Court of Parliament, the trial commenced on the 15th of April, 1776, before the Peers in Westminster Hall, which was thronged with a regal and aristocratic audience. Queen Charlotte was present with the young Prince of Wales, and four other of her children; the crowd of peeresses, foreign ambassadors, and people of consequence was immense. When the prisoner, after the usual formalities, had been placed at the bar, Earl Bathurst, who was then Lord Chancellor, acting for the occasion as Lord High Steward, addressed her in a short speech to the following effect :—

He pointed out the nature of the crime whereof she stood indicted; the fatal consequences thereof in respect to domestic peace, morality, and public society; how detestable in the eye of the Omnipotent; and how far it behoved her to prove her innocence. He also acquainted her with the odiousness of the felony charged in the estimation of the law, and that at one time it was punished with death, though it had come to be within the benefit of clergy. The rigour of the sentence was relaxed in favour of all offenders; and what must be hailed by her as a great privilege, that part of the doom which remained in force on ordinary occasions was remitted by express statute to persons of her rank. He also acquainted her that innocence alone could protect her, as no plea to the jurisdiction of the court could avail her. The Lord High Steward having addressed the duchess, she spoke thus :—

"My Lords, I, the unfortunate widow of your late brother, the most noble Evelyn Pierrepont, Duke of Kingston, am brought to the bar of this right honourable house without a shadow of fear, but infinitely awed by the respect that is due to you, my most honourable judges. My Lords, after having, at the hazard of my life, returned from Rome in a dangerous sickness, to submit myself to the laws of my country, I plead some little merit in my willing obedience; and I entreat your Lordships' indulgence, if I should be deficient in any ceremonial part of my conduct towards you, my most honoured and respectable judges; for, the infirmities of my body and the oppression of spirit under which I labour, leave your unhappy prisoner sometimes without recollection; but it must be only with the loss of life, that I can be deprived of the knowledge of the respect that is due to this high and awful tribunal."

The Attorney-General Thurlow, afterwards Lord Chancellor, stated the case against the prisoner, not only giving an able narrative of the facts, which we have already sketched, but dwelling upon the malignant and pernicious example which it set. He also commented strongly on the collusion which had been practised in order to obtain a *jactitation* of the marriage with Harvey, so as to pave a way to an adulterous union with the Duke of Kingston, and laid down the law broadly, plainly, and truly, that no sentence in an ecclesiastical court against a marriage, in a suit for *jactitation*, can preclude the proof of the marriage in an indictment on the statute which makes bigamy to be felony; nay, that admitting such sentence to be conclusive as to the fact of marriage, the effect of the sentence might be avoided by evidence of fraud and collusion in obtaining it—these gross practices having occurred in the case under discussion.

The evidence for the crown having been adduced, which fully bore out the allegations of the Attorney-General, the prisoner in her defence addressed the lords in a read speech; her counsel thereafter calling several witnesses in her behalf, who, however, in no way invalidated a single circumstance charged against her in the indictment. The investigation lasted five days. The Lords found the duchess Guilty,—one peer, the Duke of Newcastle, having alone qualified his verdict by saying she was guilty "erroneously, but not intentionally." Some pains were taken, but unsuccessfully, to prevent her receiving the benefit of the peerage; but it was at last allowed her, for to all intents and purposes she was the Countess of Bristol; so that she was discharged, after having prayed the benefit of the peerage, according to the statutes, on paying the fees. She appeared perfectly composed during the long and harrassing investigation, as well as tiresome formalities of the tribunal; but when informed by the Lord High Steward that she was discharged, she swooned away, and had to be carried from the Hall.

Thus ended a prosecution of great magnitude, not merely on account of the parties immediately concerned in its issue, but the Ecclesiastical Court, which, by the judgment of the House of Peers, so solemnly pronounced in this cause, was taught to feel and acknowledge the superior jurisdiction and controlling power of the common law of the land. But though shame and ignominy were brought home upon the duchess, and public justice vindicated, her private enemies received no benefit, his Grace of Kingston's will having been drawn up with such legal caution, that notwithstanding the law had declared her second marriage void, she contrived to enjoy for her life the great revenues left her by the duke; while Mr. Evelyn Meadows found himself ruined by the immense expense of the prosecution.

Yes, her fortune still remained; her first husband, too, was still alive; and the prosecutors, stimulated by disappointment, took fresh measures against her. To restrain her from leaving the kingdom, was now a material object; her personal property was great, and the effect was to wrest it from her. For this purpose it was first of all deemed necessary to prevent her from quitting the country, and application was therefore made for a writ *ne exeat regno;* but happily for her ladyship she received information of the proceeding; and being advised instantly to leave the kingdom, she ordered her carriage to be driven about the streets with a confidential servant in it; and having sent cards of invitation to a party to dine at Kingston-house, her design of flight was so well covered, that by means of a hired post-chaise, which waited for her in the suburbs, she reached Dover unmolested. Here she took to an open boat, engaged suddenly for the purpose, and soon got to Calais in safety.

The efforts of her enemies were now directed to set aside, if possible, the will of the Duke of Kingston. This kept the apprehension of danger for some time longer alive in the breast of the countess, as we shall hereafter style her; and so long as that apprehension lasted, it was necessary, in policy, to affect a particular regard for certain persons in England, who had the power of rendering her a service. Among these was the well-known Dr. Schomberg, who, in characteristic return for the zeal he manifested in her cause, was presented in her name with a ring, brilliantly encircled, the stone a deep blue, and upon it the words " Pour l'Amitie." The intrinsic value was never once considered by Schomberg—it was the presumable tribute of gratitude which affected the mind. He wore the trinket, and almost in every company he proclaimed the donor. But a short time elapsed before one of the encircling brilliants fell out, and to have it repaired a jeweller was applied to. Having looked at it, the tradesman lifted his eyes to the doctor, and then re-examined the ring; and having two or three times with a smile conducted this alternating mode of scrutinising the distinct objects, he at length said, " I hope you will not be offended, sir; but it is not really worth your while to have anything done for your ring; the middle stone is a composition, and the whole did not cost in Paris more than a few shillings." " Is that the case? " cried the recipient of the lady's deep acknowledgments; " then I will soon dispose of it." Saying this, he trampled the article under foot, and then tossed it away.

The will of the Duke of Kingston being found irrefragable, it now appeared to become the leading purpose of the Countess of Bristol to dissipate rather than expend her great annual income. A house which she had purchased at Calais was not sufficient for the purpose; a mansion at Montmartre, near Paris, was fixed on, and its purchase speedily made. There were here not a few obstacles to enjoyment, which were not considered until the bargain was concluded. The mansion was in so ruinous a condition as to be uninhabitable. The surrounding grounds were like the field of the slothful rather than the vineyard of the industrious. A lawsuit with the party with whom she had dealt was the consequence. She went to St. Petersburgh.

The arrival of an English woman of distinction at the Russian capital was at that period a novelty, and she met with attentions even from the empress which could not but flatter the visitor's egregious vanity. But then the English ambassador at the Muscovite court refused her the respect she claimed, denying her the title of duchess, and showing that he regarded her as the reprobated character she was held at home. Other mortifications ensuing, she returned to France even before her lawsuit was adjusted. She purchased another mansion, the scale of which was truly magnificent. The brother of the French monarch was the owner of a domain, according in every respect with his dignity. This was the territory of St. Assize, at a pleasant distance from Paris, abounding in game of various much prized species, and rich in all the embellishments of nature. The mansion contained three hundred beds. The value of such a property was too considerable to be expended in one payment; the countess therefore agreed to discharge the whole of the price demanded, which was fifty-five thousand pounds, by instalments. The purchase was a good one.

Such was her situation, when one day, while she was at dinner, her servants received intelligence that judgment in the lawsuit had gone against her. The sudden communication of the news produced an agitation of her whole frame. She flew into a violent passion, and burst an internal blood-vessel. Even, this, however, she appeared to have surmounted, until a few days afterwards, when preparing to rise from her bed, a servant who had long been with her endeavoured to dissuade her from it. The countess said, " I am not very well, but I will rise." On a remonstrance being attempted, the lady peremptorily declared, " I will get up, and walk about the room ; ring for the secretary to assist me." The servant obeyed, the countess was dressed, and the secretary entered the chamber. She then walked about, complained of thirst, and said, " I could drink a glass of my fine Madeira wine, and eat a slice of toasted bread. I shall be quite well afterwards. Let it be a large glass of wine." The servant reluctantly obeyed, and her mistress drank the wine. She then said, " I am perfectly recovered,—I knew the Madeira would do me good. My heart feels oddly,—I will have another glass." The servant here observed that such a quantity of wine in the morning might intoxicate rather than benefit. The countess persisted in her order, and the second glass being produced, she drank that also, and pronounced herself to be charmingly indeed. She then walked a little about the room, and afterwards said, " I will lie down on the couch ; I can sleep, and after that I shall be entirely recovered." She seated herself on the couch, a female having hold of each hand. In this situation she soon appeared to have fallen into a profound sleep, until the women felt her hands grow gradually colder than usual. It was the last and mortal sleep ; the countess was found to have expired as the wearied labourer sinks into the arms of rest. Thus, on the 28th of August, 1788, at the age of sixty-eight, the celebrated Elizabeth Chudleigh, generally designated the Duchess of Kingston, departed this life.

XII.—RICHARD PATCH.

THE hope of eluding detection, the belief that no punishment or even exposure will follow the perpetration of crime, prompt to many, perhaps to most, enormities of the kind. And yet it is no less true that " Evil shall hunt the wicked person, to overthrow him." No human eye beholds the murder; it is done upon the unwarned, the unprotected, in solitary places, and at the silent, darkest hour of night ; and the Great Ruler of Events, at times, appears to have permitted an impenetrable veil of obscurity to be thrown around the heinously base and monstrously cruel deed. And yet, however carefully the crime has been contrived, to a certainty, the triumph of the perpetrator will be brief and most unsatisfactory. The result even at best will fearfully disappoint; for there is One, whose unwinking eye hath witnessed the deed, and who,—it may be by the most unlikely means, the most insignificant circumstance, even by agencies that are wholly invisible in respect of human cognizance, and subtle as the thin air we breathe,—can make the hidden guilt apparent as the sun at noon-day, who can unravel the most complex villany, and whose language to the transgressor of every grade and hue is this, " Be sure thy sin will find thee out." Innumerable are the instances which might be adduced in demonstrative illustration of the fact, that the All-Seeing and All-Just Being will eventually unmask crime, laying bare the designs and the acts of the transgressor, often by instruments the most unlooked for, and circumstances the slenderest and most artless, at the very moment, too, when the criminal deems himself safest, and built up in stoutest security. We present some cases in point.

Many years ago a criminal, for some deed of violence, was convicted of the same at Chelmsford, and condemned to be executed. There had been an accomplice, the greater villain of the two, who eluded the pursuit instituted after him, and was thought to have wholly escaped all likelihood of being found. That which to the condemned man proved most grievous, after the fact of his detection and condemnation, was the circumstance of his accomplice having obtained and carried off by far the greatest share of the plunder, which, for aught that appeared, he would enjoy in peace and security. Many and most earnestly anxious were the inquiries of the wretched criminal relative to his partner in crime,—whether he had been discovered, and whether any clue had been obtained concerning the quarter to which he had betaken himself. To all such eager questionings, however, the condemned man received answers which were the most unsatisfactory to him, being not only to the effect that his guilty partner had not been apprehended, and also that no trace of him had been discovered, but that it was confidently believed he had made his escape to some foreign land, where he might live without dread, and spend his ill-got treasure in any way he pleased. At length, and after an unusually protracted interval, the condemned one is brought out for execution, this world and all its interests being about to close upon him for ever, and the vast concerns of an immortal state about to open. He stands on the very verge of an everlasting existence of weal or of woe. The last offices of the chaplain and also of the executioner are nearly finished. The minister of religion has uttered the concluding prayer ; the fatal noose is already round the neck; the cap that is to hide the convulsions of the visage from the greedy gaze of the surrounding multitude is about to be drawn over the face ; the last strained and agonised look of

M 2

the doomed is taking its final survey of mortal beings and earthly things,—a survey, however, which is observed to be intensely keen and searching,—when all of a sudden he exclaims, "Yonder he is! seize him!—him, my partner in crime, and the guiltier of the pair! There! There! You have him, and I die happy!" The fool-hardy accomplice, little dreaming that any one could recognise him in his carefully contrived disguise, in that dense crowd of strangers, had,—moved by some horrid impulse—resolved to see his associate in iniquity and pupil in crime pay the forfeit of his life to the outraged laws of the country; and having with an infatuated effrontery fulfilled his resolve, he is captured, tried, condemned, and executed,—struck down by the very last man and unlikeliest witness in the world that could have been supposed to appear against him.

A lady and her husband were stopped by a highwayman one evening when travelling, and not only robbed by the villain, but savagely treated, the gentleman receiving such bodily injuries as bereft him of sight. The robber escaped; nor were there any circumstances or vestiges of the terrible outrage which seemed at all calculated to lead to his identification or place of resort. A number of years elapse, and the flight of each one of them serves more completely to obliterate the recollections of the event, and the lines, at first but faint, by which the highwayman might have been tracked, have wholly vanished, according to human impressions. Worse and worse, the gentleman from loss of his vision becomes not only helpless but almost penniless, and is thrown into prison, where his wife tends him with a womanish tenderness and wedded fidelity. The room where the prisoner is allowed to spend the daytime overlooks the racket-ground; and one fine noon, when his beloved spouse and assiduous daily visitant is by his side, the accents of a voice which will never be forgotten by her, till death or disease take away her senses, smite her ear; for they are the utterances of him that robbed them of their purses, and blinded the eye-balls of him who was her stay and shield. She listens, and by each added expression and word grows the more fully persuaded that the immediate cause of their disasters is within a few yards distance of them, a prisoner for debt, as was her husband. She is thoroughly convinced; she gives information in accordance with her convictions. The retributive hour has arrived. The robber is committed for trial and is condemned, after which he confesses all, and perishes from amongst men, acknowledging that justice has overtaken him after years of impunity, ay, and of hugged assurance of safety while time endured.

Mr. Bonar was a wealthy merchant, who lived in Broad-street, close to Astley Cooper, the celebrated surgeon. They were on the most intimate terms, not only on account of the medical services of the one to the other, but as visiting friends and near neighbours. It was, therefore, with no less horror than astonishment, that early one morning his servant Charles, suddenly informed Mr. Cooper that Mr. Bonar had been murdered in the course of the previous night, and that Mrs. Bonar was in a most dangerous state from wounds which she had also received from the assassin. The person who brought this message was one of Mr. Bonar's servants, of the name of Nicholson, a man who had previously lived in the family of Mr. Tyrrell, one of Mr. Cooper's particular acquaintances. He had ridden on horseback from Chiselhurst, where Mr. Bonar had a country house, to which he usually retired after his day's business was finished in London, and where the catastrophe had occurred. Mr. Cooper was at work in his private dissecting-room when the news was related to him, and immediately on hearing what had happened, desired Charles to go and inform a friend of the deceased, who lived opposite, of the dreadful event, and to inquire if he would at once accompany him to Chiselhurst. This was assented to, and they set off in a post-chaise; but although they arrived there before life was extinct in Mrs. Bonar, Mr. Cooper's services were of no avail towards averting the fatal event. After making certain observations in reference to the medico-legal inquiry, which would in all probability be instituted, they returned to town.

The conduct and manner of the servant when he brought the message in the morning, was singularly strange and confused. When Charles was relating Nicholson's account of the affair to his master, he mentioned that the man waited in the hall; but on turning round, in obedience to Mr. Cooper's desire that he might be brought up, to his surprise, he found the very individual standing at his elbow. Charles then went to deliver his master's message to Mr. Bonar's friend, as already mentioned, and on reaching his house, was informed that he was dressing. The importance of his errand induced Charles at once to ascend to this gentleman's dressing-room; and having hurriedly informed him of the fact of the lamentable occurrence, he was doubly struck with surprise by again finding Nicholson by his side, for he had no idea that he had even entered the house. Charles supposed that his strange behaviour was caused by the fright which he had experienced at the sight of his murdered master and mistress. Mr. Cooper, however, had drawn from it, and from other circumstances of the man's appearance, the conclusion that he was the perpetrator of the crime of which he himself had brought the account.

The particulars which we are here giving are taken from the " Life of Sir Astley Cooper," (at the period spoken of, Mr. Cooper,) by Mr. Bransby B. Cooper, the nephew of the distinguished surgeon; and we go on further to cite from the work, as under :—
" Mr. Frederick Tyrrell was, at the time that this occurrence took place, an apprentice to Mr. Cooper, and I being aware that Nicholson had lived for some years in his father's family, begged him to give me an account of the affair, so far as he was acquainted with it, thinking that he might be able to explain particularly the circumstances which had induced my uncle to conclude this servant to be the murderer. The following is his statement:—

" ' Nicholson came up to town on one of the coach-horses of Mr. Bonar, between six and seven o'clock, a.m., and rode up the paved passage called Church passage, where I then lived, close to my father's at Guildhall. I was just up, and went down to the door, in consequence of a violent ringing of the bell, and there I found Nicholson on horseback, who said that his master and mistress had been murdered in the night. He said he had discovered what had taken place when he went to call his master in the morning, according to previous orders. He said further, that he hoped his mistress might yet be saved, and appeared most anxious that Mr. Cooper and myself should immediately proceed to Chiselhurst. I directed him to ride on to Broad-street, to inform Mr. Cooper of the circumstance, that he might make any preparations which would be necessary for his visit, and said that I would follow him as soon as possible.—When I arrived in Broad-street, I found Mr. Cooper already prepared to start for Chiselhurst; but he said he could not take me, because I must look after Nicholson, whom he declared to be the murderer. —Nicholson had disappeared, and I immediately commenced a search after him, and sent information respecting him to the principal police offices in London. I was, however. at the time perfectly satisfied in my own mind that this man was not the murderer; for he had only quitted my father's service ten or twelve days before this event, after having lived at Guildhall between three and four years. He had been a most excellent servant, and on some occasions, when illness had occurred in the family, had evinced unusual kindness and attention.—He was apprehended in the afternoon, and taken to the Counter

Prison in Giltspur-street. I went there to see him, and was accompanied by the governor to the cell in which he was confined. Whilst speaking to him, a little black and dun terrier dog placed his fore paws on his knees, and began to lick his breeches, which were made of some dark-coloured velveteen. Observing this, the governor directed him to remove them. On afterwards holding them up to the light, the front part of each thigh was evidently stained, and a little moisture proved it to be with blood. The governor remarked that my dog was a sagacious little fellow, but I could not own him, for I had never before seen him; and all the inquiries which were made subsequently could not discover a master for him. It was the more extraordinary because a public notice was posted at the gates of the prison forbidding the entrance of dogs. In the evening I went to the prison, to beg to have the dog, as I heard he had not been owned; when, remarkable to say, he had disappeared as strangely as he had entered, and was never afterwards found.—Your uncle told me that he could not explain why he suspected Nicholson to be the murderer; he only saw him for a few moments, and had hardly time, I should have thought, to have noticed him sufficiently to have ever known him again. He was drunk at the time when I first saw him in the morning.' "

Perhaps the part sustained by the little terrier dog in this instance was as remarkable as in any case of murder where a dumb animal has figured. But to cite a little more from the " Life of Sir Astley Cooper : "—

When Nicholson was examined, notwithstanding the strongly suspicious circumstances of the spots of blood found upon the breeches, there was not brought against him evidence sufficient to warrant his being detained in prison, and he was accordingly set at liberty, but at the same time was desired to remain at the house at Chiselhurst. A day or two after his former visit, Mr. Cooper was sent for, late in the evening, to this place. The man had attempted to destroy himself by cutting his throat. On his arrival, he found him still alive, and after some difficulty, on account of the resistance of the man himself, succeeded in arresting the flow of blood and closing the wound. As soon as the fellow, who declared his intention of taking every means in his power to resist all attempts at cure, was placed under proper restraint, Mr. Cooper returned to town.

The next day he had to repeat his visit, the man having contrived to tear away the dressings from his throat. He found him perfectly quiet, having been brought to this condition partly by weakness from loss of blood, and partly by the influences of a priest who was with him; for this servant, as had been both his master and mistress, was a Roman Catholic. The priest had been endeavouring to elicit from him a confession of the murder, of which his attempt at self-destruction had partly indicated him to be guilty; but had not succeeded in his endeavours. However, on Mr. Cooper's informing him that in all probability he had but a few hours more to live, he expressed a willingness to make a confession. A magistrate was sent for, and in his presence, as well as that of the priest, of Mr. Cooper, who wrote down the facts as the two former elicited them, and of Mr. Cooper's servant, the wretched murderer relieved his mind of the dreadful secret, and explained all the circumstances of the transaction.

From this time, strange to say, Nicholson became perfectly passive, offering no opposition whatever to the treatment to which he was subjected for the cure of his wound; so that in a short time he was able to appear in court, and receive the sentence of the law for his crimes. This was carried into effect at Pennington Heath, near to the scene of the murder.

One of the chief circumstances which had in the first instance rendered the perpetration of the deed by Nicholson a matter of doubt in the minds of many, was the utter absence of any motive which could have induced him to commit so horrible an act towards his master. The account in his confession was remarkable. He said that for some time after the family had gone to bed, he sat before the fire in the hall, drinking ale, until he fell asleep. The next thing, according to his account, that he remembered, was ascending the stairs towards his master's bed-room with the hall poker in his hand,—his afterwards stopping on the way, and addressing himself by name, saying, "Nicholson, what are you going to do?" and a reply, which he strenuously maintained he heard made to him by a voice at his side, "To murder your master and mistress." Whether he spoke truth in this,—narrating what he firmly believed,—or not, certain it is that the promptings of his own wicked heart and of the Evil One drove him to the commission of the terrible deed, giving real shape and actual interpretation to the infernal language, so that the tempter for a brief season had the triumph. We proceed to another case, and with still more particularity of detail and greater fullness, beginning with a scene in which the same celebrated surgeon of whom the reader has been just hearing, bore his characteristic part.

"Mr. Cooper," says his nephew, in the *Life*, "was one day in 1805 suddenly sent for, by a general practitioner of the name of Jones, to see a Mr. Isaac Blight, a ship broker, at Deptford, who had received a severe injury from a pistol-ball which had been fired at him. When that eminent surgeon arrived at the house, he was told by his patient that, whilst sitting in his parlour, his attention had been first aroused by the door of the room being suddenly opened. On turning round, he perceived an arm extended towards him, and at the same instant the report of a pistol, and the sensation of a severe blow, convinced him that he had been intentionally shot at. He said he had not the least idea by whose hand the act had been committed; but related the fact that his partner, Mr. Patch, whilst sitting in the same room, a few days before, had been alarmed by the report of a gun, apparently discharged on the wharf, and by a ball, which at the same time passed through the shutter into the room, and he expressed his firm belief that the same hand had been employed on both occasions. Upon examining the seat of injury, it was at once evident that the case was hopeless,—the ball had passed deeply into the body, and the discharge from the wound proved that there was injury to a vital and very important organ."

Mr. Blight's house closely adjoined the Dock, and fronted the Thames; the back part of the premises being surrounded with a strong paling. It was on the night of the 19th September,—at which time Mr. Blight and his wife were at Margate,—that the gun or pistol, loaded with ball, had been fired, on the previous occasion, through the window. Every search at that time had been immediately made; but the offender escaped detection. The next day, Mr. Patch wrote Mr. Blight, to inform him of the circumstance, when the latter instantly came to town; but neither he nor Mr. Patch were able to fix on any party whom they deemed liable to suspicion. It was about the same hour on the night of the 23d of September that the second shot was fired with the fatal effect already hinted at, the ball having entered Mr. Blight's body a little below his ribs, passing through his back, and lodging in the wainscoating behind him. The only person in the house, when the murder was committed, was a female servant, who also heard the report of fire-arms, but was in a kitchen at some distance. The unfortunate gentleman was instantly put to bed, and the surgeons with all possible expedition procured. Mr. Blight, during the night and the following morning, was sufficiently collected to be able to answer any question relative to the horrid transaction, although all that he could communicate relative to it was extremely scanty, amounting only to this, that after Mr. Patch, who had been sitting with him, went away, "he sat alone, and neither heard nor suspected any one; that at last he saw the door of the room open slowly, and almost at the same moment he was shot. He neither saw nor heard the person who fired at him. He was not conscious of having an enemy in the world."

"Mr. Cooper's observing mind," says the *Life*, "led him closely to investigate every circumstance connected with the case, and even to examine minutely the spot on which the act was perpetrated. He placed himself in the position in which Mr. Blight had been when he received the wound, and, with his natural acuteness, at once perceived that no one but a left-handed person could have so stood with respect to the door as to have concealed his body, and at the same time to have discharged the pistol at his victim with effect. This at once made a strong impression on his mind, and having already been prepossessed with the idea that Patch was the culprit, he became convinced of the correctness of his suspicion, directly he ascertained that he was a left-handed man. So certain did Mr. Cooper feel that he had detected the perpetrator of the deed that, on reaching home, he immediately said to his servant, Charles, in secresy, 'You will see, Charles, that Mr. Patch, the partner of Mr. Blight, has been his murderer.'"

The murdered gentleman expired in the afternoon of the 24th, but no suspicion seems to have attached to Mr. Patch by other persons than Mr. Cooper, until a coroner's jury sat upon the body, who after long and patient deliberation, returned a verdict of " Wilful Murder by some person or persons unknown." Patch was still fully at liberty. Mr. Graham, of Bow-street, however, anxious to penetrate the mystery, personally inspected the premises where the foul deed had been committed, examining on the spot Mr. Patch and the maid-servant,—both at his instance being taken into custody. Indeed, while the inquest was held on the body, a variety of facts came to light which tended to criminate the partner of the deceased, who was without much delay committed to stand his trial—the servant girl having been discharged on condition of appearing to give evidence.

But we must proceed to the main business of this article, viz., to present in a connected and regularly progressive story the entire facts of the case, as these were brought out on the trial, some of which have been anticipated in connexion with the name and character of Sir Astley Cooper.

The trial, which excited an unusual degree of public interest, took place on the 5th of April, 1806. The prisoner was attended by a few of his friends, and displayed an unruffled composure. Lord Chief Baron M'Donald was the presiding judge. The Clerk of the Arraigns having read the impeachment, the prisoner in a firm and distinct voice pleaded to it, "Not Guilty." Mr. Garrow was counsel for the prosecution,—Mr. Serjeant Best for the prisoner; and as the case was one which required more attention from the jury who tried it, according to the learned judge's opinion, than any that ever came before him, it will be necessary in our narrative to go closely and minutely into its entire history. In fact, the reader will, in the course of that narrative, be made to feel, from the body of circumstances which belong to the case,—many of them, taken singly and separately, most slight and trivial,—that there is such an irrefragable and necessary concatenation, as cannot but be held as plainly showing the finger of Providence in the detection of the murder,—the very hand of Heaven itself, leading one through many bye-paths and secret ways, till he has at length mastered the labyrinth, and burst upon the guilty man with a conviction, staring one as broadly in the face as the light of day.

We begin with a detail of the relative situations in the world of Mr. Blight and Richard Patch. The former, as already stated, was a ship broker at Greenland Dock, in the parish of St. Mary's, Rotherhithe. The sister of the accused, Sarah Patch, was a maid of all work in his house. In the spring of 1803, Patch, then in circumstances of much distress, with rags on his back and penury in his face, first appeared at Mr. Blight's, on a visit to his sister. His story was, that he had left the West of England from circumstances which it is needless to detail; that he was without employment, and was willing to engage in the service of Mr. Blight on any terms. He was upon this benevolently engaged, being to receive his victuals and drink, and a salary of £40 per annum. Shortly afterwards the terms of the engagement were commuted into a fixed salary of £100 per annum, which Patch was to receive, and to board himself.

Such was the introduction of Patch into the house of Mr. Blight. Some time after, the latter became embarrassed, and called a meeting of his creditors, when a composition was offered, the accused being a chief instrument in the affair. One creditor, however, did not consent to accept the proffered terms; so that the whole transaction with the other creditors was invalid. His property, therefore, was in danger; and in order to secure it, he did what in truth could not be called honest,—he made over to Patch, for a sum of £2,000, all his property without reserve. This conveyance was in the ordinary way, by a bill of parcels, receipts, &c., to which was added a letter in the name of Blight, to the solicitor of certain lands, holden in the city of London, requesting to have the lease renewed in Patch's name. The intention of Blight by this transaction was to protect his property; certainly not to convey it to Mr. Patch. He argued in this way :—" Relying on the integrity of Mr. Patch, I know if my creditors step forward to seize my property, that he will act as my faithful friend, and secure it for me; again, should they not proceed harshly against me, those papers are in the possession of my wife, and are so much waste paper."

Patch, as may be imagined, never paid one penny of the two thousand pounds; most probably he was not worth half so many shillings. Still, the transaction shows how he had grown in the confidence of Mr. Blight. In July, 1805, Blight and his family paid a visit to Margate, previous to which trip he thought it necessary to enter into new engagements with Patch. For himself, he stipulated that he should retire,—the accused to conduct the business, and to have one third of its profits; but for this share he was to pay the sum of £1,250. But how was the fellow to pay such an amount? Where was he to obtain it? The fact is, he never intended to fulfil the bargain according to its terms, although he somehow contrived to get together £250, and to hand this sum over to the other, leaving one thousand pounds unpaid. Whence was this to come? Blight required security for it; and Mr. Patch gave him a draft for the money on a man of the name of Goom. This draft was to be paid on the 16th of September following. Who was this Mr. Goom? Why, a friend of Mr. Patch, as he, the accused, represented; telling Blight that he had lent to Goom a sum exceeding £1,000 upon the sale of an estate, and that Goom had given him a draft for the money, which would be due at the time stipulated by Patch, to conclude his bargain with Mr. Blight. The time elapsed, and Goom's note became due. What shift had Patch at this juncture? He went to his bankers, and told them that the draft which he paid in upon Goom would not be honoured; that Goom, though a substantial man, was somewhat irregular, and would not face his draft; he withdrew, therefore, the check upon Goom, and gave his banker a check of the 20th of the same month, upon himself.

On Thursday, the 19th of September, Blight prepared to visit his wife at Margate, where he proposed to make a stay, expecting that Goom's draft would be honoured. The prisoner accompanied Blight as far as Deptford, and took an affectionate leave of him. From Deptford he proceeded to the bankers, telling them what has been related above, about Goom not being able to *face* the draft, and at the same time desiring them not to present it. The reader now begins to get some insight into this tragical case, and to approach by distinct degrees to the woful scene of the catastrophe. The apparatus is now preparing; and the first act of the eventful drama is about to be performed.

"And if Patch was indeed the guilty party," the reader may here be supposed to observe, "he was one of the worst men that the history of our race presents; for we find him deliberately placing his benefactor and friend in a situation where he could secretly murder him. His case, in truth, ought to be considered as extending to a degree beyond murder. It is a case of the darkest ingratitude—a charge from which all mankind recoil with a peculiar dislike and offence. To extravagance, avarice, sensuality, censoriousness, and cruelty, people will, without exciting much display of virtuous indignation, plead guilty. But hint, however gently and tenderly, *ingratitude*, and a most indignant disclaimer follows. Ah! if Patch was indeed guilty of the charge brought against him, his name must for ever stand forth in the foremost rank of the most deeply-dyed miscreants."

Mr. Blight and family are at Margate; Mr. Patch has a thousand pounds to pay on the next day after the departure of his friend. For this thousand pounds he had given a draft, which he had withdrawn and substituted one on himself; upon his faithful payment of this money he well knew that his connexion with Blight subsisted. If he paid it, one-third of the business was his; if he failed to pay it, the artifice of delay and more of his other lying expedients would not avail him long even with the easy and kind-hearted Mr. Blight; and the partnership would be for ever at an end. Patch had started with deceit and falsehood; he had gone on and ever into new and greater depths with his lies and evil designs; and now he had come to such a crisis as would admit of no retreat, save by confessing himself a villain, unless, indeed, he found heart to deal the final stroke and jump to the last extremity.

As to Goom, who was he? Why, Mr. Goom owed Patch no money—Mr. Patch was never in a condition to lend him gold or silver; Mr. Goom knew the person of Patch, but that was all, and never had been a sharer with the fellow in any money transaction whatever. He had not even seen the accused for many years.—The trick of Mr. Goom's draft could not last long. Something of a more graduated and a bolder villany was required, or the ends of Mr. Patch could not be answered. The act to be performed, it is true, was not only a bold one, but it demanded cunning, subtlety, and to be enveloped in mystery; all which qualities and features will be found to have accompanied the transactions to be detailed, in such a way that, but for what we must characterise, without being superstitious, the directing hand of Providence in tracing the villany, the murder of Mr. Blight might to the present hour have remained a question of perplexity.

On Thursday, September 19th, as we have already stated, Mr. Blight left his house, Mr. Patch, with a single maid-servant, being left alone in it. The family were wont to spend their evenings in a front parlour facing the Thames. Mr. Patch was sitting in this parlour about 8 o'clock in the evening, when he desired Esther Kitchener, the maid-servant, to get him sixpennyworth of oysters for his supper. During her absence, a gun or pistol was fired through the shutter of the front parlour, in which Mr. Patch had been just sitting. On Kitchener's return, she found Patch in conversation with some persons at the gate of Mr. Blight's house, relating the circumstance, viz., that he had been shot at. Patch asked them whether they had heard the pistol? They had. Had they seen anybody? No. And yet had any one escaped by the way meant by Patch in his questions, they must have seen him, situated as they had been. But no; the invisible assassin had perhaps escaped by water. And yet, according to the situation of Mr. Blight's premises, it became clear, on further examination, that if an assassin had fired the pistol (supposing it anybody but Patch himself), he could not possibly have escaped by water. It was at the time ebb-tide and low; and had such a fugitive leaped from the wharf, he must either have broken his neck by the fall, or been smothered in the mud. Again, had he rushed out of the gate, the persons already alluded to, who were in that direction, must have seen him. And again, had he attempted to get off by scrambling over certain pallisades, these, owing to their slight nature, must have given way, and betrayed by the crash the party. Besides, three witnesses deposed, that they saw the flash of the pistol, and heard the report, but, to their great astonishment, saw nobody issue from the premises. A correct and minutely constructed model and plan of Mr. Blight's premises were produced during the trial, which served much to elucidate the parole evidence. In short, on listening to the testimony of the witnesses, and beholding the tangible plan of the house and its adjuncts, it was seen to be impossible for any man who had fired the pistol or gun to have escaped without observation, or at least, without some index of his having been there. Besides, there were little touches in the depositions of the persons with whom Patch conversed regarding the supposed assassin immediately after the alarm occasioned by the report of fire-arms, that could not but seem to implicate him. When one asked Patch if he should fetch a person to sleep with him in the house, as the circumstance of the shot was very alarming, the fellow gave for answer, "I think not, I'm obliged; the party will not again trouble me this night." On being questioned as to his means of self-defence, Patch said he had a pair of pistols which cost nine guineas, but he had no ammunition, and yet, when offered powder and ball, he said, "Never mind; the villains will be here no more this night." In short, with all his apparent perturbation, he took none of those means which one would suppose natural and necessary in his alleged circumstances, in order to protect himself, or to arrest or punish the party that might meditate murder.

Providence, in truth, seems to have ordained in this instance, that whatever might have been the contrivance of Mr. Patch, there should yet be a more subtle complication of circumstances which should entirely defeat him; his cunning was to find an overmatch in simple coincidences,—his artfulness was to be exposed by means of the most commonplace facts, but directed by the All-seeing Judge. Nor have we yet noticed the whole of these distinct and obvious witnesses which marshalled themselves to his confusion. It soon became manifest, from the position in which the ball entered, that it must have been fired by a person who stood close to the shutter, for had it been fired from below the wharf, the ball must have sprung upwards; it could not have entered in the way in which it did. Again, had the pistol been fired from that *only* situation in the yard in which an assassin could have lurked, it would not have struck the shutter at all, there being a crane between the shutter and this corner of the yard, which must have received and kept the ball. If then, from neither of the positions alluded to, the ball could have been fired, so as to take effect in the way it did, where and by whom could it have been fired?

The model of the premises, combined with other circumstances, plainly enough returned the true answer:—The pistol was fired by no man but by Patch; and it was fired by him to serve some other purpose than merely to make a hole in the shutter with wanton levity.

Besides, we have seen how coolly Patch acts, whatever his pretended alarm, when his means of defence for the night were suggested. It is to be added, that when some conversation passed between him and the persons to whom he at first related the circumstances of the fired firearms, relative to steps to be taken for the discovery of the author of the mischief, and also to prevent its renewal, he acted in a self-betraying manner. One proposed that Mr. Patch should offer a reward of £50. He said he would. Another that the police should be alarmed, and inquiry made. The fellow assented ; but did he make inquiry ? did he alarm the police, or put curiosity in motion ? No, for this was not his object.

On the next day, the 20th of September, the day of the fatal draft becoming due, he wrote to Blight, then at Margate, recounting the adventure of the pistol, saying he knew not whether the shot was intended for himself or Mr. Blight. The letter concluded remarkably, showing deliberate, cool-blooded, and deeply-plotted murder to have been in the contemplation of the writer. "I sha'l be glad to have a line from you," said he, "*but much better pleased to see you*, as you are my only friend." Would it not have occurred to a pure mind, that an application to the police in such a case was advisable ? This even was pressed upon him by the neighbours. Why call Blight to town ? and what is most material of all, why not mention Goom, and the money due that very day ? The letter was far from being a short one ; and yet upon the important subject of the thousand pounds draft, it was absolutely silent.

On Monday, the 23d, Mr. Blight comes home from Margate. The first object which engaged his attention was no doubt the firing of a shot into his parlour. The next, as a matter of course, was about the payment of the draft, about which he had become uneasy. To all his inquiries on that head, Patch never communicated that he had been to the bankers and told them that he had a substitution to satisfy them instead of it ; but he not only replied to Mr. Blight, that the money was forthcoming, but even went to London, with an inhibition for him not to return until he had got it. Patch returned from London in the evening. Whether he satisfied Mr. Blight or not about the money is unknown, as the unfortunate gentleman was murdered that very night. They drank tea together apparently on friendly terms till 8 o'clock that night. For the *first* time, they took their refreshment in the back parlour, in which Mr. Blight was shot ; for the *first* time, be it borne in mind, for it becomes a very remarkable circumstance.

Suppose that an assassin, be he whom he would, had fired off the pistol on Thursday evening when Patch represented himself as being shot at, where would this assassin have gone on the Monday night ? Why, if any where, that is, if he meant to shoot Mr. Blight in his own house, to the front parlour,—to that parlour into which he had fired the shot on the previous occasion, and which he must have supposed Mr. Blight to have inhabited. Surely he would not have gone to the back parlour, a room in which the murdered man seldom or never sat. This circumstance formed a very strong presumption that the assassin, whoever he was, knew what no one who was not intimately acquainted with Mr. Blight's family could know, and which, perhaps, three hours before, Mr. Blight did not know himself—namely, that he should pass the evening in the back parlour, a room that he seldom or never inhabited.

But it is now 8 o'clock ; Mr. Blight, after the fatigues of the day, has fallen asleep, and Mr. Patch, quitting the parlour, goes into the kitchen. He asks the maid for the key of the privy and the counting-house, as he had a pain in his bowels. He goes out of the kitchen, passes the door of the back parlour, which had been left open, and in which Mr. Blight was still dozing; opens the street door, then the counting-house door and the privy door, as was distinctly announced to the servant by a slam, the report of a pistol almost immediately after being heard by her. A few moments more and her master staggers into the kitchen, with his hand upon his head and with these words in his mouth, "Esther, I am a dead man!" Screaming, she runs to shut the front door, which she finds wide open; gets about half-way back along the passage, when she hears violent knocking at the door. It is Patch, demanding admittance. She opens the door, and his dress much disordered, he rushes in, with the words in his mouth, "Oh, my dear Blight!" running affectionately to the poor man, catching him in his arms, and hugging him with a great display of anxiety and fondness.

Blight had received a mortal injury, and the inquiry comes, who dealt it? An assassin whom nobody knew; nobody had seen; one who had perpetrated the horrid act, and had escaped! "How escaped?" exclaimed the prosecuting counsel in his opening address to the jury at the trial; "here, gentlemen, we must pause, and confess with grateful praise our acknowledgements to Heaven, which has manifestly interfered to throw a light upon this dark transaction, and, by a wise ordination of circumstances and accidents, which some may call chance, but which I call Providence, had so disposed every matter incidental to this story, upon that memorable night, that it was not merely a moral, but an almost physical impossibility, that any murderer of Mr. Blight, but Richard Patch, could have escaped an instant detection."

In the front of the house was a paved court, a wharf, and the river rolling at the bottom; and just under the windows, and indeed spread all over the place, was a quantity of dirt, occasioned by the breaking up of ships on that spot,—this dirt being accordingly of a peculiar nature and composition, a circumstance to be kept in mind. At the back of the house, at one side, was a railing, or slight palisade; and upon the other, a very strong paling, with a gate, which opened into the road, while the main door opened into the yard.

Scarcely a minute elapsed between the report of the pistol and Mr. Blight's staggering into the kitchen, the maid instantly from fear clapping to the front door, but at which Patch instantly thereafter knocked violently. If the assassin escaped at that door,—and through that door, whoever he was, he must have passed,—Patch could not but have bolted against him. Why did he not?—But to proceed: Suppose that the assassin had escaped by the front door then into the yard, and next into the road, without meeting with Patch, —why, even then he must have been encountered by some body else; for, extraordinary enough, it so occurred that at every avenue by which an assassin or fugitive could escape at the time, there were persons who must unavoidably have observed him, one of these people having had in his hand a lighted link or flambeau, while another was a parish watchman. It was not pretended that a fugitive could have at the time escaped by water, not only because there was no boat near, but because any one who might have attempted to escape by the wharf, would have run the risk of breaking his neck by the depth he must necessarily have descended at a jump, or of being suffocated in the mass of mud below. Upon some of the points just alluded to, as well as other significant particulars, the testimony of Christopher Morgan had no small weight. The deposition of this witness was to the following effect :—

He was passing Mr. Blight's yard about eight or nine o'clock, when he learnt that

that gentleman had been shot. He immediately went to the house door, and inquired if he could be of any assistance. Mr. Patch came out of the front door, and witness asked should they search the premises. Patch answered he would be extremely obliged to them, and pointing to the hulk of the " Carnatic, East Indiaman," told them to examine that first, because a rumbling noise had been heard in it when the former pistol was discharged. They immediately proceeded to the edge of the wharf, but found it impossible to board the vessel; there being a space of sixteen feet between the land and the hulk on the river. If a person had endeavoured to escape that way, he must have sunk up to the middle in mud. Having looked attentively through the premises, without discovering any body, or finding the least trace of any person having entered, they adjourned to the house. After some conversation, witness begged Patch to commission him to go to Bow-street for assistance. Patch replied, " He did'nt see the necessity." Witness remonstrated, saying, an early inquiry would be of the utmost importance. The other repeated, three or four times, " He saw no necessity for it. He was in as much danger as Mr. Blight, for he had been shot at only on Thursday last." Patch then conducted witness into the front parlour, and explained to him the position he occupied when the ball penetrated the Venetian blind, and drove a splinter against his head. When he returned to the parlour where Mr. Blight lay, witness commented on the carelessness of Patch in leaving the door open, and several times repeated his request for a commission to the police office, adding that human nature was not so depraved as to kill a fellow-creature without some inducement. Patch upon this turned round and remarked that " he had as much reason to suspect him as any man." Finding his services were not acceptable, he went away.

It is to be remarked that although Patch knew perfectly well the situation of the "Carnatic," in relation to the breast of the wharf, yet he directed the witness and others first to that quarter and object; they at the same time, finding the mud below as smooth as ice, and not in any part in the slightest degree broken or disturbed. Mr. Garrow, the prosecuting counsel, when he arrived at the point in the history of the horrid transaction to which we have brought the reader, upon ample and sufficient grounds spoke to the following effect, conveying a most distinct and able view of the facts and arguments belonging to the portion of the case embraced by the extract :—

" Having shown," said he, " the impossibility of any one else being the perpetrator of this deed, let us examine, independent of every other motive, the peculiar facility which was afforded to Patch, if his mind were bent upon it, to perpetrate this act. Mr. Blight, harassed by fatigue, was reposing in his easy chair. Patch goes out to the privy; leaves open the back parlour door and the street door, a thing unaccountable in itself, and which could not have been left open by accident, because the door was so managed by means of a spring, that, unless there were a design to keep it open, it must inevitably have shut itself. Well, he not only, contrary to all custom, and most assuredly with a design, leaves the street door open, but he opens the gate of the yard. I will next state why he did both, and will show such a necessary chain of corresponding circumstances in the transactions of only a few minutes, as must explain, beyond a doubt, the reasonableness of every artifice employed, and every method of proceeding, as far as was effective, to perpetrate the murder of Mr. Blight, to direct suspicion upon others, and exculpate himself.

" When he asked the maid for a candle to go to the privy, he pretended he had a pain in the bowels—this I will prove, by evidence that will fully meet the case, delicate we cannot expect it to be, but this cannot be avoided—I say, gentlemen of the jury, I will prove to you, that this pain in the bowels was a pretence. When he took the candle from the maid, why did he want the key of the counting-house? I will tell you. In the counting house he had doubtless lodged his instrument of murder; in the privy I do not doubt he loaded it; and then, having left open the street door, and the door of the back parlour, he stole softly round, fired at Blight, and was out of the street door in one moment, and knocking at it almost the next. Thus the street door and the parlour door were left open for evident purposes, and the yard-gate was thrown open, because there is no doubt that having discharged his pistol, he flew to the side of the wharf, and threw it into the Thames. Thus, the interval of time between the firing of the pistol, the staggering of Blight into the kitchen, the clapping to of the front door by the maid, and the violent knocking at the same door by Patch, was occupied by the prisoner's casting into the Thames, or otherwise making away with, the instrument of murder.

"But it will he asked, could a man have stolen to the door of the back parlour, and fired off a pistol, without his footsteps being heard? Most probably not in ordinary circumstances, when it is considered how near the kitchen was, with the maid-servant within it, to this parlour. A common step would have alarmed the girl, and a loud step might have awakened Blight. The murderer of the poor gentleman took a peculiar precaution,—he was without shoes; he paced silently in his stockings; and these stockings I will have produced to you; they will be proved to be splashed with that very composition of dirt which was in the front of Mr. Blight's house, and which doubtless adhered to the feet of the prisoner, when he went to the bank of the Thames to throw away his pistol. I will prove to you likewise that, contrary to his usual custom, in variance with his common dress, Mr. Patch, on that particular day, wore shoes and stockings,—his perpetual dress was boots. On that memorable day, however, he wore stockings—broadribbed white stockings—the stockings which were besmeared and plashed over with marl,—which were found by a most intelligent clerk of Bow-street, Mr. Stafford, in the prisoner's room, concealed, and folded up in a manner indicating that they were clean, and as they had been returned from the wash. I will prove to you, likewise, that he denied these stockings; and that a circumstance of a particular nature occurred respecting them. When he gave out his foul linen to the wash, these stockings *only* were kept back. Why were they kept back? Because they furnished a strong circumstance of suspicion in themselves, and, as connected with other circumstances, an indubitable proof of guilt. These stockings were most positively denied by Mr. Patch, when he was taxed with them; but they will be proved to be his by his washerwoman, who is one of the witnesses for the Crown in this prosecution.

"Further, in the search that was made about the premises of Mr. Blight, the officers found, in the tunnel of the privy, a ramrod, which from every circumstance of its position and appearance, had but recently found a station there. I will bring a *nightman* as evidence on this point, and likewise as to the circumstance, which may reasonably be inferred, that the prisoner's pain in his bowels was also a pretence."

The witnesses for the crown amply substantiated the opening address of the prosecuting counsel; nay, bringing out apparently slight but telling circumstances which were not touched upon by Mr. Garrow in his speech,—as for instance, after the mortal shot had been fired, and some of the neighbours had arrived, Patch declared that Mr. Blight and he had been on the alert all day; that all the evening they expected a visitor of the (assassin) kind, and that they had been on the wharf a few minutes before. Now, these were falsehoods; for Mr. Blight came home tired, having travelled all night; and there had been no examination of the wharf, or any part of the premises in the evening,—nor any particular signs that a dangerous visitor was expected that night. Again, the moment that Patch heard that a ramrod was found in the privy, he exclaimed, "I have nothing to do with that; I did not place it there." Now, nobody had as yet told him he had placed the ramrod in such a place. No one had even as yet whispered to him that there was any suspicion that he was the murderer. No person had given him any reason to believe that the uncharitable world had pointed at the bosom friend, the companion, the individual raised from misery and distress to a state of affluence and comfort, as the assassin. In fact, at the moment, no such suspicion had been entertained. Why then was he startled—why think of uttering an exculpatory cry? It was that silent monitor within, which, though in general by its still small voice it admonishes in secret, now and then betrays the guilty into self-condemning utterances and exclamations.

Next, let us attend to the demeanour of Patch by the bedside, and on the death of Mr. Blight. Mr. Cooper, the surgeon, on being called in to attend the dying man, enquired of him, in the presence of Patch, whom he suspected; to which Blight answered, "Mr. Patch tells me there is reason to suspect one *Webster*." Mr. Cooper then inquired of Patch who this Webster was, and upon what grounds he was suspected? "He is a man who has stolen Mr. Blight's planks, and whose son has absconded," was the answer: the manner of Patch at the moment, together with other suspicious circumstances, convincing the observant surgeon, as told already, that he (Patch) was the culprit himself. At another time the villain said that he suspected a man of the name of *Clark*; stating that this Clark had once quarrelled with Mr. Blight upon some trivial cause. Now, it can very readily be conceived why Patch thus endeavoured to throw the idea of guilt upon the heads of the men mentioned: it was to keep it from his own. However, both the individuals, whom he so wickedly specified, were in a condition to prove the clearest *alibi* for themselves, so there was speedily an end put to any insinuation against them.

After the death of her husband, Mrs. Blight returned to her home; for, knowing the anxiety which her husband had felt relative to Goom's alleged money affair, she was eager to know from Mr. Patch if the thousand pounds had been paid. To this the villain answered boldly, "that the money had been paid;" that Goom had breakfasted with Mr. Blight on the Monday of his murder, and had given him the sum promised and agreed upon. Need the reader be informed that Goom had never seen Mr. Blight in his life? However, Mr. Patch had an end to gain,—he had a momentous object in his eye, viz., that the deceased had received the money, though no account should appear upon his books, or anywhere else, of Mr. Blight's disposal of so large a sum. What then? Why, nothing less than this, that Patch was prepared to asseverate that he had often advanced the deceased large sums of money, which his wife never knew anything about; for that he, Mr. Blight, was so infatuated as to be in the habit of dissipating large sums in affairs of gallantry and other extravagances; thus, not only manifesting the extreme of villany, but showing how one enormous crime required others to buttress it.

Having accomplished the destruction of Mr. Blight and got him out of the way, it next remained for Patch,—hushed, as he supposed, the story of the thousand pounds to be,—to go a step farther. The reader has already heard something of a conveyance on the part of the deceased, which was intended to elude his creditors,—also of the bills of parcels, a letter, and the receipt for £2,000. Mrs. Blight, it will be remembered, had the custody of these papers. But a coroner's inquest is holden, Mr. Patch attends to give evidence, and upon his return, he asks the widow for the documents, saying, "I have been examined before the Coroner, and it was necessary to prove the property to be mine; so you must hand me the papers." Unsuspectingly Mrs. Blight at once delivered them up; and he to whom they are given, fancying that he is at length running fairly before the wind, calls himself proprietor of the whole stock, house, goods and chattels, that belonged to the murdered one. This he maintained on his first examination before the magistrate, and no doubt would have stuck to the story, had no new obstacle come in the way, though he had only paid £250. He even had made application for the renewal of the leases before alluded to; so that hitherto Mr. Patch may seem to have been going smoothly with the tide. But the current was about to run in a different direction; it suddenly set in against him with a fearful thickening; the entire villany began to be disclosed. Nature concatenated circumstances without number and of unmistakable significance, to his undoing; an infinitude of incidents,—the whole world seemed to rise up to his confounding and conviction. For example, previous to the servant-maid Kitchener's examination before the Coroner, as she deposed, Patch held this conversation with her; "Esther, you will be asked many questions; some suspect me. You know you heard me shut the privy door, and open the counting-house door, after you saw the flash." "I shall speak nothing but the truth," replied the girl. "You will be asked many questions," he continued; "take care what you say; keep to one story."—Now was not this the anxiety of guilt, the fearful, suspicious tampering, to rebut accusation?

But there was more of such incautions ebullitions and the self-detection of the compunctious mind. Upon his return from one of his examinations he made use of these words:—"I have been as near hanging as ever man was, and if I had I should have been as happy as I am now."

Such were the facts which came out in evidence upon the trial of Richard Patch for one of the darkest cases on record of deliberate ingratitude and treacherous murder. When the prisoner was called upon for his defence, he addressed the court in a firm tone of voice, and said, "I beg, my lord, that this paper (producing a roll of M.S.) may be read by one of the officers of the court." This was done. The defence, evidently the production of some law-man, was lengthy, elaborate, and full of special pleading, but grappled with no facts, and refuted no criminating evidence; yet it concluded with expressing a hope that he had fully satisfied the jury on the leading features of the case, as well as with an appeal in consideration of his four children, praying, if they, the jury, "had any doubt of his criminality, that they would let them have the advantage of that doubt, by giving them back their father and protector."

The *twelve*, however, after a brief deliberation, found him Guilty. Few minutes elapsed ere the judge put on the black and dooming head gear, and thus addressed the culprit:—"Richard Patch, you have been tried by a most humane, upright, and considerate jury, who have pronounced you guilty of the most atrocious crime known in the laws of this or any other country. It commenced in ingratitude, continued in fraud, and terminated in the foul assassination of your friend and benefactor. From what has already passed on this subject, little remains for me to do but to pronounce the awful sentence of the law. You are to be taken back from whence you came, and thence to the place of execution, there to hang by the neck until dead, and then to be delivered to the surgeons to be dissected and anatomised; and may the Lord have mercy on your soul."

Patch suffered the awful sentence of the law, with two other persons convicted of coining, on Tuesday morning, April 8th, in front of Horsemonger-lane Gaol. At the place of execution, when the chaplain endeavoured to draw from him a confession, his answer was to the effect that he had acknowledged his sins before God, but did not feel disposed to satisfy the curiosity of men. Such was the termination of this extraordinary case of purely circumstantial evidence.

XIII.—HONORE MIRABEL.

HONORE MIRABEL, a young peasant of Pertuys, a small country district in the neighbourhood of Marseilles, came, in the year 1726, before the judicial authorities of the city mentioned, and demanded justice for an injury which he declared had been done to him. On being asked to narrate the particular grounds of his complaint, he did so, to the following effect:—He stated that he chanced one night, in the month of May, about eleven o'clock, to be lying under an almond-tree, near the farm-house where he was resident as a servant. From the spot where he lay, he beheld, by the light of the moon, the figure of a man at the upper windows of a neighbouring cottage, which was only a few paces' distance from him. This cottage was inhabited by a woman, and the sight of a man in such a place surprised Mirabel. He thought himself called upon to ask the man what he did there; but to all questions of this kind the figure gave no reply. The obstinate silence of the person piqued the peasant, and with an impulse to redress wrong-doing, he resolved to penetrate the mystery. The door leading to the cottage was open; he entered, and mounted some steps leading to the spot where the figure had been standing, but it had departed, and was not to be seen. Mirabel then began to think he must have beheld a spectre or some unearthly visitant. When the idea once struck him, it took a firm hold of him, so that he became greatly afraid, descending the steps as rapidly as he could, after which he made for a well in the vicinity, in order to draw up some water, being thirsty from very fear. While he was drinking, he heard behind him a broken voice— such a voice as he thought must be that of some apparition or supernatural being,—saying, "Mirabel, there is a treasure buried here; thou hast but to dig for it, and it will be thine; all that thou hast to do in return, is to cause some masses to be said for my soul." The language discovered to the peasant, as he interpreted the same, that the apparation was a poor suffering Catholic soul in want of prayers. He also beheld a stone drop close by him, and concluded that it was intended to mark the spot where he was to dig.

The mind of Mirabel could not sustain alone the weight of so much good fortune. Before doing anything further, he went to a neighbouring farm, and communicated the whole affair to a servant named Bernard, and to the mistress of the house, Madeleine Caillot, whom Bernard served. These three, at five o'clock in the ensuing morning, went to the spot to dig for the treasure. Scarcely had they broken the earth, when they found a packet of dirty linen, on striking which with the pickaxe they heard something tinkle. They were greatly overjoyed at this, but did not dare to touch the packet with their hands, for fear of catching from it some infectious disease, of which the late owner might have died. By breaking an almond-branch, however, they managed to lift the parcel, and to swing it, without what they did being discovered by any other passer-by; and having thus suspended it by means of the branch, and keeping it all the while at a due distance from their persons, they carried the packet to Mirabel's place of abode.

Here they fumigated it, and then took courage to open it. What a glorious sight met their eyes! More than a thousand large gold pieces, of Portuguese coinage! Mirabel's vision was enraptured; he thought to himself that for the rest of his life he had nothing to do but to eat, drink, and be merry. How he got rid of Bernard and the dame who had been present at the discovery, does not appear. He did get rid of them, however, in some way, appearing to have had the whole or the great bulk of the treasure to himself. And now his only thought was, how to keep it secure; how to preserve it from robbers, and all intromittents of whatever order.

In prosecution of this object, Mirabel went,—to continue his own statement—to a storekeeper of Marseilles, named Auquier, and asked his counsel as to the disposal of the treasure. Auquier immediately formed the design of tricking the young peasant out of the gold. To effect this, the storekeeper frightened Mirabel by telling him that all the gold would be confiscated by the king's officers, if they could get a sight and a hold of it. The young man, therefore, did not dare to use his treasure, but Auquier lent him money, went with him every where, in order to gain more deeply into his confidence, at the same time taking other means to effect the desired and selfish object. Auquier also showed to Mirabel his own money, consisting of gold and silver pieces, kept in an *osier basket*, with the view to induce a reciprocal act on the peasant's part; and at last he was induced to give over the found treasure to the custody of the storekeeper; it was put, on the 6th of September, into Auquier's hands in two bags, one of which was tied with *a gold-coloured ribbon*. The store-keeper, Mirabel averred, gave a receipt for the gold in these terms :— " I acknowledge myself to owe to Honore Mirabel the sum of twenty thousand livres, due at his option, deducting the sum of forty livres due by him to me. At Marseilles, 27th September, 1726. Signed, Auquier." Some few days after this transaction, Mirabel, in passing along the highway, was attacked by a man of great strength and bulk, who struck the peasant a blow with a sword, and pierced his vest and shirt. Mirabel became suspicious that Auquier was the author or instigator of this assault, and demanded back the treasure, or the payment of the obligation. Auquier denied the receipt of the gold— in short, he denied all knowledge of the affair..

Such is the substance of the deposition made by Honore Mirabel before the criminal authority, or lieutenant-criminal, as the public prosecutor is called, of Marseilles. The peasant demanded justice against Auquier, who, he declared, had cheated him out of his property or money. Will it be credited that, so late as 1726, this ridiculous story of an apparition and of a found treasure was listened to by the judge before whom the case came with the greatest gravity, and that steps were immediately taken for an inquiry into the matter, with as much seriousness and stern strictness, as if Mirabel had been suing for the recovery of openly possessed property, which had descended to him regularly from his ancestors. This part of the story seems, however, to have been at once set down as possible and probable, so that the first point into which an investigation was made, was the existence or not of the gold in Auquier's hands, not as to whether the peasant possessed such a sum, or had come by it in the way alleged. The house and premises of the storekeeper were examined, No gold, either in coins or otherwise, was found there; but two things were found, which were thought to be evidences of Mirabel's veracity; one of these articles was an *osier basket*, such as the young man deposed Auquier to have kept his own gold in; and the other article was a *gold-coloured ribbon*, such as Mirabel asserted to have been about the mouth of one of his bags of gold. When Auquier himself was interrogated, he stated that he had known Mirabel since the previous month of May;

that he had twice, once in his own house, and once at an inn, eaten with the peasant, and lent him two crowns; and that Mirabel had declared himself the finder of a treasure, which he proposed to put into his—Auquier's—hands for safety, upon the security of a regular obligation before a notary. But all the peasant had asseverated regarding the actual delivery of the treasure and other circumstances, Auquier declared to be utterly false.

Such were the results of the first investigation. The osier basket and the gold-coloured ribbon, as well as the admission of a proposal, at least, to lodge a treasure with him, were held, by the judge in the matter, as strong testimonies against the storekeeper, who was taken into custody. Witnesses were then examined relative to the story of the treasure-finding. Madeleine Caillot, the woman whom Mirabel asserted to have been present with the man Bernard and himself at the time, was brought forward, and corroborated the peasant's story. She said she had seen Mirabel dig, and find the linen packet; that she had *seen one*, at least of the gold pieces in it; and she identified the gold-coloured ribbon that had been found at Auquier's as one which Mirabel had shown her. This woman also said that Mirabel had shown her a cut in his vest and shirt, and told her that he had been attacked. Several other points in the young fellow's story were confirmed by Madeleine Caillot, but they were all got on hear-say from himself, with the exception of those particularised. Another witness on Mirabel's part, named Gaspard Deleuil, deposed, that on the 6th of September he had met Mirabel, and from a little distance, being desired by the peasant to wait, he had seen the latter deliver a packet to a man, who handed him a bit of paper in return. Deleuil also stated, that being joined again by Mirabel, the latter told him that the person who had received the packet was Auquier, and that it contained a treasure which he—Mirabel—had lately found. A third witness deposed to having heard the treasure and apparition story at the time from Mirabel, and also to having seen one of the pieces of gold contained in a bag which was full of them. The same witness further deposed to having reproached Auquier for his treachery to Mirabel, on which the store keeper grew *pale as death*, and desired the witness not "to speak so loud." Mirabel further presented in evidence the obligation already mentioned. It appeared either to be an imitation or a disguisal of Auquier's handwriting. Mirabel affirmed it to have been purposely disguised by the accused.

These were the principal depositions made before the chief judge at Marseilles, and they appeared to that functionary so strongly to prove the guilt of Auquier, that that unfortunate person, who unflinchingly maintained his entire innocence, was sentenced to the torture, in order that confession might be extorted from him. Happily, before this decree could be executed, an appeal was made by Auquier to the local court, called the Parliament of Aix, a town at no great distance from Marseilles. Here the cause was again heard, counsel appearing for both parties. The Parliament of Aix, after listening to serious and lengthened arguments, directed that Bernard, one of the original treasure-finders, should be summoned to appear, and give evidence. It seems unintelligible why this man was not called at the very outset; but, indeed, the wise judge of Marseilles seems to have taken that part of the story almost for granted.

By the summoning of the man Bernard, the first clue was given to the unravelling of the strange affair, and the life and honour of an innocent man were saved. Bernard deposed before the Parliament of Aix " that Mirabel, on a certain day, came and told him of an apparition having pointed out a treasure in the earth; that they went out to dig for it, but saw nothing; that Mirabel, however, persuaded him to go a second time, along with Madeleine Caillot, and assist in digging for the treasure, which digging proved a foolery again, neither linen nor anything else being seen." Bernard, moreover, stated that Mirabel had shown him a paper which had cost a crown in drawing up. On the billet purporting to be an obligation from Auquier to Mirabel for twenty thousand livres being shown to Bernard, the latter declared it to be the same, to the best of his belief, as that which the young peasant had shown to him as having cost a crown.

Here was a new light thrown on the treasure-finding and the treasure-finder, and in a short time other circumstances were discovered, which showed the deception to have been cunningly planned, rendered the more wonderful, besides, from the apparent simplicity of its author, who was but a plain, unlettered peasant. After Bernard had made his deposition, Madeleine Caillot came forward, and confessed that she had never seen any treasure or gold found by Mirabel, and that she had affirmed the contrary solely at his pressing entreaties. Auquier also, having had time to consider, said that on the day when the peasant affirmed him to have received the bags of money, he was eight leagues distant from the spot. The billet also, or obligation, seemingly from the store keeper to Mirabel, was distinctly shown to have been forged. Other evidence, which it is unnecessary to recapitulate, finally brought it plainly to view that corruption of witnesses, forgery of handwriting, skilful selection of time and place, and, in short, every possible means of deception, had been provided and prepared by Mirabel for the success of his scheme. On becoming satisfied of this, the Parliament fully acquitted Auquier, sentenced Madeleine Caillot to pay a fine, and doomed Mirabel to the galleys for life. As he still persisted, however, in asserting the truth of his whole story, he was sentenced to undergo the torture before going to the galleys; and now it was that he changed his tone. In short, he confessed the whole to be a deception and a lie, declaring the idea to have occurred to him as a means of exciting notice, and relieving him from the hard labour to which his situation in life subjected him. But the conversion of his deception to the purpose of injuring Auquier, the young villain asserted had been the suggestion of another person, a man named Barthelemy, who had suborned the witness Deleuil and others to carry out the plot.

Barthelemy, a person known to be the bitter enemy of Auquier, was immediately arrested, and the charge brought clearly home to him. He was sentenced, like Mirabel, to the galleys for life, while Deleuil and another of the most perjured witnesses were doomed to be hung by the armpits for a time in the public streets—a severe mode of pillorying people long practised in the country where these scenes took place. Thus ended the treasure-finding of Honoré Mirabel, a fellow who showed talents in conducting it worthy of a better cause. Auquier regained his place in society, but it is lamentable to think what might have been his fate, had the Parliament of Aix been guided in their decisions by the same superstitious prejudices which actuated the supreme criminal judge of Marseilles. We may really congratulate ourselves on knowing that the lapse of a century and a quarter has made a beneficial change in the world in this respect; for certainly any man who should come forward now-a-days to claim restoration of property got after the fashion of Mirabel, would find some difficulty, in the first place, in persuading a French or English court that he ever possessed it. Many have been the melancholy consequences of yielding credence to superstitious stories and tales of supernatural interference; but the foregoing seems to have novelty in it; at the same time that it illustrates how widely and grossly justice might be perverted, in discussions relative to affairs of every kind, were its ministers to allow themselves to be biassed by credulity in regard to the spiritual world, or supposed announcements by the departed.

XIV.—LORD AND LADY SOMERSET.

THE account of the fearful Overbury tragedy, with which Lord and Lady Somerset were so deeply connected, necessarily introduces a number of persons, and great variety of character, extending to different conditions of life; the narrative at the same time presenting vivid glimpses of James the First of England's court. Very voluminous, and sometimes contradictory, are the details which exist relative to the poisoning of Sir Thomas Overbury,—an enormity, in certain of its features and associations, no less mysterious than unexampled; interposing considerable difficulty in the way of him who is desirous of giving a clear and compact view of the entire transaction, and its more immediate bearings. Still, there remains no doubt with regard to the main facts of the memorable events; so that by furnishing a plain, direct, and faithful report of these, rather than striving to unravel every intricacy belonging to the case, and, while avoiding all merely disquisitional and argumentative matter, by giving rapidity and animation to the whole, it is believed a momentous and instructive story will be produced, as well as one of most enchaining interest.

Surely there have seldom been two delinquents moving in the higher walks of life, whose criminal history is so pregnant with terrible teachings, and also so fitted to arrest the mind, absorbing its attention, as that of Lord and Lady Somerset. Quite independently, too, of the immediate and flagrant offences for which they were arraigned before their peers, and also of the list of wretches whom they swept within the vortex of their criminality, there is such a glance obtained, through the titled felons, of royal doings, and courtly manners,—ay, and even of legal obliquities, together with sacerdotal servility, as cannot but astound the many. The reader, for instance, is led to behold the "Second Solomon,"—the monarch of this mighty realm,—shuddering under tremours, —not from a sense of heinous guilt, of which his conduct furnishes too sure an evidence, —but lest his deeds might be made patent; tremours which are only to be accounted for, and in any tolerable way explained, by a supposition that blasts his character as a man for ever; while the picture presented of his court is one of such gross immorality, of such venal adulation, and of such detestable, unmitigated vileness, as to convince one that at the period mentioned the palace of the British monarch was steeped deeper in the filth of iniquity and abomination than has ever been recorded of the most degraded of the inferior orders in this country. The appalling history upon which we now enter requires to be introduced by notices of certain historical characters and events, although not directly belonging to the criminal case indicated at the head of this paper.

Robert Cecil, Earl of Salisbury, was a mortal enemy to the famous Robert Devereux, Earl of Essex, the favourite of Queen Elizabeth, and one of the chief instruments of his ruin. Essex left a son, who being but nine years old, did not give Cecil much uneasiness, though James, at his coming to England, restored him to the family estate and honours. Meanwhile, as this minister could not be ignorant of the King's affection for the father, he was apprehensive that, one time or other, he should be made to pay for all his artifice to ruin that ill-fated earl. It was chiefly on this account, that in order to preserve the King's favour, he judged it proper to unite closely with the Howard family, by his own son's marriage with the Earl of Suffolk's eldest daughter. The young Earl of Essex, however, was advancing to the age of manhood, and the minister, dreading that he might one day prove a thorn in his side, had deemed it to be his interest to become reconciled to him, and accordingly set about this process of healing with compassing the marriage of the young lord to the Earl of Suffolk's second daughter, younger sister of the powerful minister's daughter-in-law. Besides his own advantage by this alliance, the wily politician afforded James the pleasure to see in strict union three families for which he evinced great affection, viz., those of Howard, Devereux, and Cecil. This last mentioned marriage was celebrated in 1606, the Earl of Essex being then in his fifteenth year, and Frances Howard, his bride, in her thirteenth year. As the married pair was yet very young, it was thought proper that the earl should betake himself to foreign parts, till they were both considerably more advanced in years. During his absence, the juvenile countess became a perfect beauty, and soon eclipsed all the court ladies.

Essex returned to England in the year 1610, when he found his countess in the prime of virgin age and beauty, but also extremely proud of her own charms, which had become the theme of fulsome admiration. He was himself fascinated with the beauty and symmetry of her features, which were heightened—if we may trust the painters—by that mixture of the sprightly and the soft in expression which lends to female beauty its greatest power of enchantment. Her dress, when she was in her full blazonry, was so adorned with jewels, that her path looked like a milky way. When excited by the homage paid to her, it might be said of her as had been declared of another, that "corruscations and lightnings of joy appeared in her countenance, that expressed more than an ordinary smile, being almost elated to a laughter, which could not clear the sky of her fate, but was rather a forerunner of more sad and dire events; which shows how slippery nature is to toll us along to those things that bring danger, yea, sometimes destruction, with them." But although the young earl was charmed by his lovely countess, he met not with that return which he expected. She daily coined fresh excuses to delay the consummation of the marriage, showing as much reluctance as he did eagerness. He bore her freaks for some time patiently, lest he should excite in his beautiful bride an aversion to him. Shortly after, he fell so dangerously ill of the small-pox, that his life was despaired of; but the strength of his constitution overcoming the distemper, he at length recovered; the countess having from the first hailed the illness as a God-send, had prayed incessantly that death might take him. Meanwhile, and during the interval, the King was disgracing himself by a new and despicable minion, whom we shall observe gradually thrust forward to the dictatorship of the court and almost of the kingdom.

This creature of the royal caprice and bounty, who so soon acquired the government of the King himself, and through him of his three kingdoms, was the infamous Robert Carr, or Ker, born of a gentleman's family in the neighbourhood of Edinburgh, whose introduction to the especial notice of James is thus related:—Carr had made some abode in France, in what capacity does not appear, and had just returned from that country with the acquisition of the courtly garb and distinguished air by which a fine and comely person is set off to the greatest advantage, when one of the King's Scottish courtiers, Lord Hay, selected him as his page or equerry, at a tilting match, probably that which celebrated the anniversary of the coronation, on July 25th, 1606. The office assigned the youth was to present to the sovereign, according to established usage, the shield and device of his master. In the performance of this duty, Carr was thrown from his horse, and broke his leg in the fall. James ordered him to be carried into a neighbouring apartment, sent a surgeon to attend him, and frequently visited him in person. It was from his opportune fracture that the prosperity of the young man took its date. The

King almost from the first looked upon his patient as an adopted son, if not something more and far other. He took the pains to instruct him in Latin grammar; and, what was better to the purpose, in "the craft of a courtier." After his recovery he was daily distinguished with marks of the royal favour; riches and honours poured upon him; the lands which escheated to the crown, and the presents offered by those who solicited his mediation with the sovereign, gave him a princely fortune. On Christmas-eve, 1607, he was knighted and sworn gentleman of the bed-chamber. In the ensuing February, Sir George Chaworth writes to the Earl of Shrewsbury, that "Sir Robert Carr is now the especially graced man;" and the following passages from a letter, written most probably in 1608, will further show the progress of the royal phrenzy, and also the abominable sycophancy of the courtiers. It is addressed to Sir John Harrington:—

"If you have good will and good health to perform what I shall commend, you may set forward for court whenever it suiteth your convenience. . . . I will now premise certain things to be observed by you toward well gaining our prince's good affection. . . . Robert Carr is now most likely to win the prince's affection, and doth it wondrously in a little time. The prince leaneth on his arm, pinches his cheek, smooths his ruffled garment, and, when he looketh at Carr, directeth his discourse to divers others. The young man doth much study all art and device; he hath changed his tailors' and tiremen many times, and all to please the prince, who laugheth at the long-grown fashion of our young courtiers, and wisheth for change every day. You must see Sir Robert Carr before you go to the King. . . . Carr hath all the favours; the King teacheth him Latin every morning, and I think some one should teach him English too; for as he is a Scotch lad, he hath much need of better language. The King doth much covet his presence; the ladies too are not behind-hand in their admiration; for I tell you, good knight, this fellow is straight-limbed, well-favoured, strong-shouldered, and smooth-faced, with some sort of cunning and show of modesty; though, G— wot, he well knoweth when to show his impudence. . . . Will you come to court and think to be well-favoured? . . . Will you say that the stars are bright jewels fit for Carr's ears? . . . Your lady is virtuous, and somewhat of a good housewife; has lived in a court in her time, and I believe you may venture her forth again; but I know those who would not so quietly rest, were Carr to leer on their wives, as some do perceive, yea, and like it well too they should be so noticed. If any mischance is to be weighed, 'tis breaking a leg in the king's presence, for this fellow owes all his favour to that bout; I think he hath better reason to speak well of his own horse than the king's roan jennet. We are almost worn out in our endeavours to keep pace with this fellow in his duty and labour to gain favour, but all in vain; where it endeth I cannot guess, but honours are talked of speedily for him."

And honours did come speedily. Mention has already been made of his princely income; ere long he was successfully and rapidly created Baron Branspeth, Viscount Rochester, Knight of the Garter, and at length Earl of Somerset. Still, he affected to take no part in the conduct of affairs, till the death of Cecil, Earl of Salisbury, when several important offices became vacant, and when the court became agitated with intrigue to obtain place. Most fortunate were they who professed themselves the dependents of the favourite, who meanwhile transacted business as prime minister and principal secretary. Unequal, however, to the task himself, he employed the aid of Sir Thomas Overbury, who, from Carr's first introduction to the King, had been his guide and assistant.

This guide was the son of Nicholas Overbury, Esq., of Burton, in Gloucestershire. He gave early indications of genius; and, in his fourteenth year, became a gentleman com-moner at Oxford, from which he removed to the Temple; but not continuing there long, he travelled in France, where he so improved himself, that on his return he was looked upon as one of the most finished gentlemen of the period. In the service of Carr he proved himself an able and artful counsellor, but violent, capricious and presuming. Though he had been banished from the court for an insult offered to the Queen, he was soon recalled at the solicitations of Rochester; but he could never obtain the good-will of James, who continued to look on him as a rival in the affections of his favourite, so that the King of England was jealous of his paltry minion. By the public he was courted on account of his influence with his patron. Valuable presents were given to secure his favour; and on the very morning of the 21st of April, 1613, he boasted to Sir Henry Wotton of his good fortune, and of the flattering prospects which lay before him Yet that very day, before sunset, he was committed a close prisoner to the Tower, one of those instances of the flagrant exercise of arbitrary power which were so monstrously put forth by the silly pedant and abominable tyrant who occupied the throne of the British empire at this date.

It was in the interval during which the young Earl of Essex was on his travels, that Robert Carr became the King's favourite. When he gained his master's heart, he made a conquest almost at the same time of the beautiful Countess of Essex, whose father was Lord Chamberlain at the time; suffering herself to be taken with the charms of the young Scot, and entirely giving herself over to this new passion, without daring, however, for a time to reveal it to the person that caused it. One would say that the adventurer must have been strangely obtuse, or wholly satiated with the beauties of the court, when he could remain blind to the blandishments of the lovely and gloating countess; she who had become the boast of the aristocracy, her wit, graces, and acquirements raising her above all competition. Among her many admirers and suitors, was Prince Henry; but she preferred the King's favourite, the upstart Rochester. Meanwhile Essex had returned from his travels, he had even recovered from his severe illness, and he now pressed his spouse to consent to the consummation of the marriage; she, on the contrary, feeling assured that if she could avoid this alternative for a time, it would not be impossible to obtain a divorce, through the great influence of Rochester, who was beginning to dis-cover her passion for him, and through the added sway of her father Suffolk, and the Earl of Northampton, her uncle. Still, she wanted some time to lay her measures; but was so constrained by means of Overbury, who not only came to perceive how the intrigue was tending, but to feel assured, that unless it was crushed in the bud, he himself, who had hitherto been the pander to the licentious pleasures of his patron and others of the courtiers, would have all his hopes blasted. Sir Thomas therefore objected to the " baseness of the woman," and the infamy of such a marriage as she and Rochester contemplated; de-claring that he both could and would throw an insuperable obstacle in the way of their union. The adulterous countess was thus driven to an extremity. But as Rochester had betrayed to her his adviser, she resolved that not even the astute Overbury should stand in the way of her sensual gratifications; and what will a vindictive and lewd woman not devise and perpetrate rather than have the fury of her passions thwarted?

But first, how was she to obtain a divorce from her husband Essex? Her scheme was this :—she proceeded to a Mrs. Turner, a physician's widow, that professed to cure cruels, who prepared philters and love potions, managed intrigues, and even professed to practise sorcery,—a woman of dissolute life, and capable of the vilest and most criminal deeds.

"Sweet Turner," said the countess, "I am out of all patience with the importunities of my husband, so that all comfort is gone, as I told you in my last letter. As you have already taken pains in my behalf, although of no avail, pray do continue your efforts. Essex is still as well as ever he was; and that which is not less disheartening, Rochester is as cool as before. Sweet Mrs. Turner, do all that your skill can command, for never so unhappy a creature as I ever sought your help. My miseries I cannot longer endure. Serve me, and you shall have as much money as you demand."

"Lovely countess, you know that you shall have my best services," answered the widow; "and that you may understand with what anxiety I have gone about your case, learn that I have consulted Dr. Foreman, of Lambeth, the conjuror, telling him your wishes and distress, and he declares himself both able and willing to lend me effectual assistance in your behalf through this piteous affair. What is more, he hath desired me to bring your ladyship with me to his laboratory, in secret and in disguise, and assures me that you need not despair."

"Thanks! a world of thanks to my sweet Turner," cried the countess; "there is gold for you—my entire purse; plenty more is forthcoming; only accomplish my will. After sunset I will drop in upon you, in a garb so cunningly contrived and draped, that even Rochester himself would not recognise me; and then for Lambeth."

The countess was as good as her word. Under the cloud of night, she wended her way from Essex-house, where she persisted in living apart from the young earl, towards the residence of Mrs. Turner, and thence they coached it to Foreman's; where a conversation took place, which, like several other portions of the proceedings in this extraordinary history, must not be transferred to these columns, being totally unfit for the public eye in our day, however much they might delight and occupy the bench of bishops, as well as the King himself, at the time, as shall be seen in the sequel. Suffice it to say that the conjuror, together with the dealer in love potions, undertook, by means of powders and other strange appliances, which were stealthily to be administered both to Rochester and Essex, not only to inflame and stimulate the one, but to incapacitate and emasculate the other—the result, as it was to affect the countess's young husband, being intended to form the ground of a divorce, or rather of a judgment declaring the nullity of the marriage from the first. Such was the arrangement in substance, the young lady undertaking not merely to keep wholly aloof from her lord, but to furnish the necessary funds for the practitioners. She soon found that in so far as concerned Rochester, there was little occasion for magic or other artificial excitements, beyond herself. The flame of his bosom for her began to burn nearly as fiercely as her own. Frequent were their assignations; and although at first these were kept as private as possible, in time they used so little caution, that not a courtier, male or female, was a stranger to their guilty amours. The King himself was fully aware of the abomination as practised in his own palace; but nothing pleased him more than to know of such intrigues being carried on under his immediate eye.

It was yet but the slightest of the difficulties which had been got over; for Essex still insisted and grew more peremptory in his demands for his marital rights. The countess shut herself up in a room for some time, refusing not only to see him, but to suffer the light of the sun to enter, pretending to have given herself over to an excessive melancholy; corresponding, however, all the while with Mrs. Turner and Dr. Foreman,—every letter complaining more bitterly than before of the weakness of the powders and other stealthy means which were being used upon her husband. Several of these letters are now before us, as printed from the originals; the burden of them being that her lord was as lusty as ever; that it would be difficult to hold out much longer; and that if she should chance to yield, she should be the most unfortunate woman in the world. In one letter to the conjuror she says, "I think I shall never be happy in this world: the heavens favour me not." Yet, ere long, she was thus far favoured that Essex, having become acquainted with her illicit attachment and intercourse, at once scorned an object so unworthy of his affections, and thenceforward seemed to concern himself very little about her. Still, there were insurmountable obstacles to the full accomplishment and realisation of all the criminal purposes and desires cherished by the countess and her paramour:—first, Sir Thomas Overbury was as obstinate as ever, because of his own interests, in his opposition to the contemplated union of the guilty pair; and secondly, the marriage with Essex had not been dissolved or pronounced null. Add to these important considerations the fact, that the countess was resolved to make sure of Rochester before his passion for her should be allowed to cool, amid the galaxy of beauties and the pressure of courtship to which he was exposed in the court of the King of England. Promptitude and decision were felt by the lady, therefore, to be indispensable; and accordingly she set to work in right good earnest, her paramour, who had not half her spirit and talent, going wholly along with her as she dictated. Now it is that the terrible story begins to develop its horrors and monstrosities.

How was Overbury's influence and opposition to be got rid of—the party against whom the countess cherished the most unappeasable malice ever since Rochester had imparted to her the nature and tendency of this knight's counsels?

"Did he not speak in this wise to you, my chosen?" said she to the object of her impure love; "and have you not told it to me, that he called me filthy and base; that you would utterly ruin your honour by wedding me; and that also he would utterly thwart you in the attempt, if you proceeded further in the business?"

"Truly, all this and much more to dissuade me from my love,—also in disparaging and traducing you, my adored, did he say," answered Rochester; "to which I, bewitched by your charms, and moved to wrath by his sleighting of you,—replied, that my own legs were straight and strong enough to bear me up, and that I would be even with him yet; and thus I left him, both of us in great anger. However, next morning, having behaved to him with my usual courtesy and kindness, he seemed to have forgotten, and also to desire that I should forget, all that had passed in wrath between us; and thus it is that we stand. Nevertheless my displeasure doth not sleep."

"It is not anger or displeasure either that will satisfy me," exclaimed the fury; "I shall have revenge, deep and terrible, befitting the insolent wrong that the caitiff would do us."

"Yes, revenge is the proper return," ejaculates Rochester; "you are far more quick-thoughted than I am, my beloved, and to you the thing shall be left; therefore instruct me, and I shall wholly obey."

"The thing is easily accomplished," says the countess. "I have taken counsel with my uncle, Northampton, and his plan is clear and simple,—it may be instantly put into a condition of forwardness."

"To dismiss him—to banish him at once from court, will be dangerous," timidly observed the King's favourite. "You know, my adored, that he is in possession of sundry secrets which must not see the light."

"He and his secrets shall perish together," cried the countess. "He must and shall be sacrificed—yes, sacrificed, my chosen, in the most literal sense of the term." Having uttered these words with a fiendish spite, the lovely demon threw herself into the arms of her guilty paramour, abandoning herself to him; at the same time extorting from him, without the slightest difficulty, not only the most unreserved promise that he would fling from him every kindly remembrance of her intended victim, but allow himself to be guided by her counsels and schemes entirely.

" Do all this, and we shall speedily be made one by the voice of the church, and by the law of the land," exclaimed she, as she hung upon his neck; "refuse or falter, and, Rochester, you slay me. Now judge which of the two you will consent to sacrifice ?"

Embraces fond and prolonged gave the hearty acquiescent answer, in a manner more significant than mere language could express; and the knight's doom was sealed. Such is the nature of the compact which was entered into by the flagitious pair, as gathered from the documents and the testimonies soon after made public, and which any one may examine for himself in their printed and permanent shape.

The scheme of dealing with Overbury was as follows,—the wily, corrupt, and intriguing Northampton, uncle to the countess, together with her father, as there is too much reason to believe, having lent their advice to the enormity :—

Rochester proceeded to extol to the King,—who at this period appears to have been almost entirely under the control of the minion,—the abilities of Overbury, intimating at the same time that he took too much upon him, and was grown intolerably insolent, and therefore that he should be very glad to have him removed, by some honourable employment, praying his Majesty to send him ambassador to Russia. The King liking the proposal, makes the appointment immediately. Rochester having proceeded thus far, acquaints Overbury with the King's intention, and pretending that he could not live without him, entreats him to refuse the employment, promising to procure him a better at court; adding, that indeed it would not be in his power to hinder the King from being angry at first, who probably would resist his refusal, but he did not question his being able to appease him in a few days. Overbury fell into the snare; and when James sent for him to acquaint him with the appointment, he humbly besought his Majesty to make choice of some other person. As soon as he had retired, Rochester aggravated to the King his pride and insolence, in daring thus to refuse his Majesty's gracious offer, adding it was requisite to chastise him; that he was himself affected by it, for he should infallibly be blamed for using his interest for him. In short, by Rochester's double dealing, as prompted by cleverer heads, the King commanded Overbury to be sent to the Tower; the favourite having some few days previously caused a creature of his own, Sir Gervase Elways, to be made lieutenant of the fortress. Overbury was at once put into close confinement in a room, and not suffered to keep one of his servants, or to receive the visit of a single relative or friend,—a rigour not used even towards the greatest offenders.

The victim was now where the Countess of Essex and Viscount Rochester wished him, in order to despatch him more easily; for, as might have been stated a little earlier in the narrative, the lady in her fury had before this offered £1,000 to Sir John Wood to take Overbury's life in a duel, a plan that in some way failed. However, the doomed knight was now completely in the power of his fell enemies; still there were some difficulties. He could not well be got rid of by stabbing, because the lieutenant of the Tower, who had to answer for the prisoners, would not have allowed [it; and besides, a murder openly committed in one of the King's prisons, would have made too much noise in the world. It was resolved, therefore, to make use of poison.

For this terrible end Mrs. Turner was again applied to, who provided a trusty person, one Weston, that had been a servant to her husband; Sir Thomas Monson recommending the same to the lieutenant, to wait on the prisoner as footman. But even this was not sufficient; whatever was brought to Overbury to eat, being dressed in the lieutenant's kitchen, it was necessary to engage him in the plot.—Some accounts say that the Earl of Northampton sounded him on it, hinting that everything was done with the King's knowledge.—For the latter allegation, at least, there is no proof to sustain it.—Others affirm that the lieutenant refusing to be concerned in the crime, yet not daring to discover what was intended and going on, on account of the quality of the parties who were at the head of the murderous company, took care to seize the victuals sent from time to time by Rochester and the countess to the prisoner, and to throw them away, a supposition by no means improbable, since otherwise Overbury would have been soon killed. The lieutenant, however, did not succeed in hindering a certain jelly, sent by Sir Thomas Monson, to be given to the prisoner, which almost did the fatal business; whereupon the lieutenant was more careful that Overbury should be seen but by Weston alone; this being a check upon the villain, since he perceived that none could be accused but himself, and therefore he durst not make such haste as Overbury's enemies desired. Now, an inconvenience arose from this delay, for every one was growing surprised to find the King using such grievous rigour upon a friend of Viscount Rochester, for so slight an offence as he was charged with, if the refusing to go as ambassador to Russia was an offence at all. It could not be conceived, and it was vainly attempted to discover the cause of the extreme severity.—But the scene must for a little while be shifted, in order that we may get a view of another portion of the drama which was enacting.

Whilst the ill-starred Overbury was languishing in his confinement, the guilty parties had the second momentous object for them to look after—the annulling of the Countess of Essex's marriage, that she might be in a condition to espouse Rochester. To effect this, without the King's favourite appearing to be concerned, Northampton undertook to speak to the King, acquainting him with the countess's complaint against Essex, her wedded lord, and presenting her petition to the same effect. It is not easy to deal with this part of the case, owing to the nature of its leading features, its indelicate details, and the arguments raised. Suffice it to say that the countess not only alleged that her marriage with Essex had not been consummated—a statement which he did not contradict,—but that it never could be by him, owing to incapacity—an allegation which he indignantly denied—and upon these grounds she besought his Majesty to let her complaint be examined; and, if well founded, to have liberty to wed another. Upon this petition the King commissioned the Archbishop of Canterbury, and several others of the prelates, together with some laymen, to hear and determine the affair. This court proceeded very gravely to the trial of the cause, the report of the examinations and the statements elicited being at the moment we indite these words before us, including those of the countess herself and of Essex, her husband. The first thought that rises in the mind, after the surprise that any creature in the shape of woman, though found in the deepest sinks of iniquity, could ever be so degraded as to mouth the words and express the meanings to which the countess gave utterance, is to find that the bishops—apparently with an appetite and a *goût* quite fresh, healthy, and eager, entered upon the inquiry, putting questions, propounding difficulties, and pursuing arguments, with a knowledge, subtlety, and discrimination that would have done them credit on any knotty, polemical point; not even, like true logicians, dispensing with that precision and perspicuity of language essential to a fair and an accurate treatment of metaphysical niceties. Nothing, in the way of allusion, would satisfy them, but the plainest and most explicit language; and when we say that the result was everything which could be calculated to sate polluted minds in the way of gross idea and broad obscenity of expression, we shall fail to communicate an adequate notion of the revolting examination. Examination! say we? Why, it was not half completed until the countess should be *inspected*. But here the bishops manifested some degree of delicacy,—they do not propose to be the ocular inquisitors themselves,—they have the modesty to appoint a midwife or matron-conclave to do the business for them and report. The order is obeyed; the female representatives of the mitred court perform their office with all due particularity—the countess appearing, some said, in a veil before them—and then give in their report, viz., that Frances Howard was still a virgin. With the public a strong persuasion existed that not only the parties in the suit, but the judges who pronounced in their favour, acted in opposition to the dictates of their conscience; and it was a well-grounded reproach to the unprincipled James that, instead of remaining a silent spectator, he had spontaneously come forward, and expressed himself in the progress of the cause with the warmth and partiality of an advocate; a gross interference which was most probably in part prompted by affection to his favourite, or some other vile ground for wishing to gratify him, whose gratitude or policy unexpectedly relieved the immediate wants of the King with a present of £25,000. At any rate, James undertook to brow-beat the bishops; he answered their arguments; he forbade them to take additional examinations; he increased their number; and at last procured a decision in favour of the divorce, by a majority of seven to five. The Archbishop of Canterbury was of the minority; and he even published his reasons against the decision; but the pedant King took the pains to answer the prelate, and to maintain the justice of the sentence, upbraiding him with founding his opinion on Puritan principles. Dr. Bilson, Bishop of Winchelsea, one of the judges, having spoken very strenuously to prove the nullity of the marriage, found his son soon after knighted; but the people were so malicious as to call him *Nullity Bilson*.

If after the divorce, the countess—whose bad character was notorious and well-known to the bishops—had married any other than the Viscount Rochester, her conduct might have met with some justification. But the sentence was hardly pronounced, when the favourite openly made his addresses to the wanton, their marriage taking place in the royal chapel; and that the bride might not lose in title by the exchange, the bridegroom had been previously created Earl of Somerset. At the celebration of the union, the lady had the boldness to appear with her hair hanging in curls to her waist, the appropriate distinction of a virgin bride. The king and the chief of the nobility honoured the nuptials; James, in person,—whose base nature was insensible of guilt or shame in gratifying his desires—giving away the bride. A sumptuous mask was exhibited by the courtiers; a long succession of feastings and rejoicings also taking place, in which the city strove to equal, if not to outshine the court, attesting the servility of the men, who, to ingratiate themselves with the royal favourite, could make public manifestations of glorying in the celebration of a marriage, which in private they stigmatized as adulterous and illegal.

While the Countess of Essex's marriage was being annulled, the unhappy Overbury was languishing in the Tower, without having the comfort of seeing any friend, and as if he had been guilty of the most heinous crimes. He had been extremely sick with the poison that was continually in small doses given him, without knowing the cause of his illness. But when he learnt what was transacting, he no longer doubted who were the authors of his misery. In this lamentable state, he saw no other remedy but to write to the favourite, intreating him to deliver him out of his wretched condition. Rochester answered that the King being still highly incensed, he had not yet been able to speak in his behalf, but hoped to do it in a few days. It indeed appears that he sent a certain powder in his letter as a sure remedy to cure his distemper. But Overbury had the good sense not to take it; so that the two flagitious lovers became exceedingly impatient, because of the knight not dying soon enough. What was to be done? To this question the first practical answer given was suggested by superstition, Mrs. Turner being required by the countess to make use of the black art, with which she professed to hasten the catastrophe. But even sorcery failed to hurry the victim quickly enough to his grave.

"He hath now been six months a prisoner, and still is in the land of the living," said the countess to her paramour, nearly at the same date at which the sentence of divorce was pronounced in her favour. "What will it signify that we should be made man and wife, my chosen, should the wretch get his freedom,—for the thought of him escaping my vengeance would poison my peace for ever. The people, too, are becoming clamorous, and he cannot much longer be shut up alive. What then? He shall die, and that at once, perdition to him!"

"Yes, my beloved, he must not be allowed ever to come from his confinement," observed the favourite; for you know that he can work my ruin if set free. Do as ye would with him, and I shall take my share of the blame."

It was early in September, 1613, that this dreadful determination was taken; and two days afterwards an agonising death, occasioned by the administration of corrosive sublimate, ended Overbury's earthly miseries; one Franklin, an apothecary's apprentice, having assisted Weston in forcing the murderous element upon the prisoner. The report gained ground that these two miscreants, seeing the extraordinary effects of this poison, and fearing if they suffered it to operate any longer, it would leave marks on the body, and rise up in judgment against them, smothered him with the bed-clothes. When he was dead, he was on the very same day hurried to the grave, without waiting the inspection, or even the arrival of any friend or kinsman, and without the holding of a coroner's inquest. The Earl of Northampton's account in his letter to the favourite, and in the report which he basely strove to circulate, declared that Overbury died of a foul disease, and was so rotten that the corpse could not be kept any longer. Thus did the uncle of the countess show his participation in the murder, having the blasphemous hardihood to state, in his letter to Rochester, that the justice of God was to be admired in the death of such a wicked instrument.

Overbury dead, and Frances Howard wedded to Carr, what now was there to mar their happiness, or to stand in the way of the guilty pair's triumphing over every other obstacle? The reply is, that George Villiers had begun to captivate the King, and that every step which this young man made in the royal favour, not only rendered more imminent the apprehensions of Somerset, but his fall proportionate to the other's elevation. Somerset's insolence and rapacity from the first were gross, for he permitted no suit to pass without an enormous bribe, which, together with his want of personal merit and of hereditary consequence, soon made him feel that his decline and descent might become more rapid than even his rise had been. He accordingly felt that above all things, it was his interest to secure himself from the danger to which he might be exposed by the discovery of Overbury's murder. He, therefore, watched a proper opportunity to represent to James, whose favour he at length found would be the sole remaining barrier to his complete disgrace, that in the high offices which he had borne under the crown, and in the secret and important affairs with which it had long been his Majesty's pleasure to intrust him, it was not improbable that he might, through inadvertence, have fallen into errors which, in strictness of law, might expose him to the penalties of a *præmunire*. For his protection against this danger, he humbly besought the King to be pleased to grant him a pardon under the great seal for all his past offences.

"Why, man," cried James, "I will not only grant thee pardon of all manner of treasons, misprision of treasons, murders, felonies, and outrages whatsoever, done and committed by thee, but, man, I'll do much more than this;—I shall hold thee guiltless of all these several sorts of crimes and delinquencies, which thou mayest happen hereafter to commit, down to thy dying day."

The King in fact, without scruple or the slightest hesitation, signed this ample indulgence and boundless license; but as it had to be carried to the Lord Chancellor (Egerton) in order that the great seal might be affixed to the document, that functionary absolutely refused to solemnise the absurd and mischievous deed, alleging truly that to do so would subject himself to a *præmunire*. This obstacle was found insuperable; and, deprived of his meditated defence, Somerset had nothing left him but to await in secret dread the result of the thousand accidents which might betray to some one who desired his destruction the black story of Overbury's fate, known already to certainly not fewer than eight or ten persons, more or less implicated in the horrid conspiracy. And thus poetical justice was beginning to make its sanctions good, the very exterior of the once handsome and elegantly attired favourite evincing such inward wretchedness and unwonted negligence of person as failed not to attract the notice of the court. Dreadful must have been his soul's pangs; and, to render the condition of his guilty partner hardly less woful than his own, they gave themselves up to such a system of recrimination and domestic contention as seems to have bred a reciprocal hatred not less bitter than their love had been unruly before and offensively obtrusive.

Meanwhile the rivalry between Somerset and Villiers was growing daily more keen, creating disturbance to James, who showed some anxiety to compose it. "Go," said he to the younger favourite, "and tell Somerset it is my gracious will that he be friends with thee."

"Friends with thee, thou backbiter!" exclaimed the older favourite; "no, I will have none of thine offered service; and thou shalt have none of my favour. I will, if I can, break thy neck, and of this make thyself sure."

It was not till after this open and ill-timed declaration of hostilities, that any inquiry was instituted into the secrets of the prison-house; nor is it an improbable conjecture of a contemporary writer, that, "had Somerset complied with Villiers, Overbury's death had still been raked up in his own ashes."

The suspicion that Overbury had been carried off by means of poison, had been kept half alive by successive rumours; it was also whispered very generally that the murder might be traced, were an eager and searching inquiry instituted, through inferior agents, to Somerset and his countess. These things reached the ear of James, who sent for Sir Gervase Elways, lieutenant of the Tower, questioning him so ably and closely,—for the pedant prided himself with some reason on his skill on such occasions,—that the terrified man was brought to a confession of such particulars as left little doubt of the guilt of Lady Somerset and also of his favourite.

Weston was next examined by the Chief Justice Coke, and was with some difficulty brought to confirm the whole story of the lieutenant. He owned carrying to Overbury tarts and jellies sent by the countess, which he believed to be poisoned, and which he was enjoined not to taste. It also came out that he had received a sum of money from this lady, through her agent Mrs. Turner, as a reward on the death of their victim. Another part of the wretch's statement, corroborated by a different witness, was, that Somerset sent a letter to Overbury, in the same inclosing a white powder, which he requested him to take, and not to fear, though it made him sick, for out of that circumstance he would draw an argument for his liberation.

Several other accomplices were traced out and strictly examined; after which the King, partly through fear of infamy, and partly through a sense of justice, despatched an order to the chief justice, to make out a warrant for the apprehension of Somerset. Yet still James kept him in ignorance of his approaching fate, admitting him into his company, and apparently into his good graces, as intimately as usual. The remarkable circumstances of the King's final parting with his once-beloved Carr, are amongst the strangest particulars of the extraordinary drama, reflecting the reverse of honour upon the pedant: they are thus recorded by Weldon, the contemporary writer:—

James having taken his farewell for a time of London, " was accompanied by Somerset to Royston ; where no sooner he brought him, but instantly took his leave, little imagining what viper lay amongst the herbs. Nor must I forget to let you know how perfect the King was in the art of dissimulation, or to give it his own words, king craft. The Earl of Somerset never parted from him with more seeming affection than at this time, when he knew Somerset should never see him more; and had you seen that seeming affection, as the author himself did, you would rather have believed he was in his rising than setting; the earl, when he kissed his hand, the King being about his neck, slabbering his cheeks, saying, ' For God's sake when shall I see thee again ? On my soul I shall neither eat nor sleep until you come again.' The earl told him, ' On Monday,' this being on the Friday. ' For God's sake let me,' said the King.—'Shall I, shall I ? ' then lolled about his neck. ' Then for God's sake give thy lady this kiss for me.' In the same manner at the stairs head, at the middle of the stairs, and at the stairs foot. The earl was not in his coach when the King used these very words, in the hearing of four servants, one of whom was Somerset's great creature of the bed-chamber, who reported it instantly to the author of this history,—' I shall never see his face more.' "

There has been another account of the strange scene with certain variations. According to this the warrant of the chief justice was served upon Somerset at Royston, who exclaimed that " Never such an affront was offered to a peer in presence of the King."—" Nay man," said James, ominously, " if Coke sends for me, I must go;" to which was added, as soon as Somerset's back was turned, " The de'il go with thee, for I will never see thy face mair." In a short time Coke himself arrived, to whom the King committed the investigation of the matter, concluding with this imprecation, "God's curse be upon you and yours, if you spare any of them; and God's curse be upon me and mine, if I pardon any of them."

Coke, receiving such strict orders, was very active in the affair; but he had other motives besides the love of justice for his officiousness. He had been indebted for many previous obligations to Somerset; but he now saw that the earl could never more be of use to him. Still, fearful of taking upon himself alone the responsibility of a proceeding in which so great a personage was implicated, he besought James that other commissioners might be joined with him in taking the necessary examinations. This was granted; the King at the same time bitterly complaining that Somerset and his wife had made him a go-between in their adultery and murder. Coke and his brother commissioners took three hundred examinations, and then reported to the King that Frances Howard had employed sorcery to incapacitate her lawful husband, Essex, and to win the affection of Rochester; that to remove Overbury, the great bar to the adulterous marriage of the lovers, a plan was concerted between them and the countess's uncle, the late Earl of Northampton, to have the victim committed to the Tower; and that, in short, she and her second husband were the instigators of all the horrible and murderous cruelties that were perpetrated for the destruction of the unfortunate gentleman. The King also now pretended to believe that the favourite, about whose neck he had had such a loathsome way of lolling, even in the presence of others, was guilty of having received bribes from Spain, engaging to place Prince Charles in the hands of that court.

Weston, the warder, who had continuously administered the poison to Overbury, was first arraigned,—for he, as well as Somerset and his wife, and the other agents employed, were secured without any difficulty—but by the direction of Serjeant Yelverton, who was " an obliged servant of the house of Howard," he remained mute, to the great perplexity of Coke, who well knew that unless the principals in the murder were convicted, the accessaries could not be put upon their trials. He proceeded, nevertheless, to cause all the confessions and examinations which had been obtained by himself and his brother commissioners in private to be publicly read,—a step of more than doubtful legality assuredly; and, having done so, he adjourned the court for a few days, to give the accused leisure to reflect on the horrors of the *peine forte et dure,* for he threatened to make him speak out through the pains of torture. On his reappearance the wrecth was found more tractable, and pleading Not Guilty, the trial proceeded. It was now proved, in addition to what has already been stated, that whilst he had been in Mrs. Turner's service he was employed as a trusty messenger between the Countess of Essex and her paramour, Rochester—that the guilty pair frequently met at Foreman's, the conjuror, who was now dead—and that it was at the countess's request, expressed through Sir Thomas Monson, that Elways, the lieutenant of the Tower, had received him into his service and set him over the prisoner. After a strong charge from the chief justice, in which he could not resist the temptation of remarking that poisoning was " a Popish trick," Weston was found guilty, and underwent the sentence of the law. When he was on the scaffold at Tyburn, Sir John Holles and Sir John Wentworth, with other devoted friends of the fallen Somerset, rode up to the gallows, and endeavoured to make him retract his confession; but the man merely said, " Fact, or no fact, I die worthily !" and so was hanged.

Sir Thomas Monson, chief falconer, was also arraigned, to the extreme uneasiness of the King, having recommended Weston to be warder of Overbury,—Simon Mason, the servant of Monson, who had been employed to carry a poisoned tart to the ill-fated knight, being likewise brought before the court. " Simon," said the chief justice, " thou hadst also a hand in this poisoning business." " I had but one finger in it," cried he, " which cost me both skin and nail." He had, it seems, out of liquorishness, as he was carrying the tart, tasted with his finger a little of the syrup. His ingenious answer caused him to be acquitted, as it was thought he would not have tasted the syrup, had he known it to be poisoned.

With regard to Monson, Coke exhorted him to confess his share in the murder and throw himself on the mercy of the court. But he rejected the advice indignantly; for he was aware that the King feared he would "play an unwelcome card on his trial," if he so willed. To this performance, however, he was not driven, for almost immediately after being placed at the bar, some yeomen of the guard, acting under James's private orders, to the astonishment and indignation of the public, carried him off to the Tower, from which he was in a short time liberated. So much concerning the righteous zeal of the King for the impartial execution of justice, for which, in the course of these trials, both Coke and Bacon fulsomely eulogized the abominable pedant.

The trial of the infamous Mrs. Turner, one of the most beautiful women of the age,—the person who introduced yellow starched ruffs,—was calculated to awaken a more thrilling interest than any of the other accessary criminals. She had in her youth been a dependent in the family of the Earl of Suffolk, and a companion to his beautiful daughter, Frances Howard. When they renewed their intimacy in London, the young lady was the unwilling wife of Essex. Her trial disclosed a hideous medley of profligacy and superstition; and what was hardly less monstrous is the fact that Coke, the other judges, Bacon, and the spectators, believing in witchcraft, considered her trafficking with love potions, and so forth, as the most damnable of her crimes. Some of the magical apparatus used by her as well as by the deceased wizard, Foreman, were produced in court,—such as pictures, puppets, enchanted papers, and magic spells, in order to make her appear more odious. At this moment "there was heard a crack from the scaffolds (or gallery), which caused great fear, tumult and confusion, among the spectators and throughout the hall, every one fearing hurt, as if the devil had been present, and grown angry to have his workmanship showed by such as were not his scholars." There was also produced a list on parchment, written by Foreman, signifying "what ladies loved what lords" in the court. The chief justice clutched at this startling document, glanced his eye over it, and then would not suffer it to be read. People immediately said that the first name on the list was that of Coke's own wife, the Lady Hatton. Many of the fair sex, and of the aristocracy, as well as gentlemen, went in coaches to Tyburn to see Mrs. Turner die. She came to the scaffold rouged and dressed, as if for a ball, with a ruff, stiffened with yellow starch, round her neck, but otherwise professed great penitence. The fashion of yellow starch was not merely introduced by this woman, but it went out with her at Tyburn. Elways, the lieutenant of the Tower, made a strong denial of his guilt at his trial, but confessed all on the scaffold.

But now for the principal criminals in this terrible and great case, in which an unfortunate gentleman, by means of a series of most strange and complicated circumstances, fell a sacrifice to the malice and base designs of a woman, and a member of one of the most celebrated Patrician races in Great Britain. After the unsparing chastisement of so many accomplices,—Weston, Turner, the apothecary Franklin, and Elways,—in this deed of darkness, the public must have naturally anticipated a similar severity on the still more guilty principals; and the emphatic eulogiums of the chief justice, and of Bacon, the attorney-general, on the righteous zeal of the King, were calculated to confirm the expectation. But long delays were interposed, with the view, it was pretended, of finding grounds for the impeachment of Somerset's loyalty, in regard to the Spanish affair with Prince Charles, of which, however, nothing could be made; so that it was not until May, 1616, that the earl and countess were brought to trial. Indeed, amid even the various and contradictory accounts handed down by the memoir writers of the age, it is easy to discover that James had all along a dread of bringing his once " slabbered " favourite to an arraignment; for he unceasingly manifested such a state of painful anxiety, of trick and manœuvre so unparalleled, as must force every one to this conclusion, that Somerset was possessed of some dreadful secret, the disclosure of which would have been fatal to the King.

The two prisoners, who were kept separate in the Tower, during the interval between their incarceration and their trials, were constantly beset by ingenious and importunate messengers from court, who never failed to assure them that if they would only confess, all would go well with them, and that they would not only be secured in their lives, but their estates. Nay, there was held out indirectly to Somerset, "a glimmering of his Majesty's benign intention to re-instate him in all his former favour." Francis Bacon was the main go-between from James to the accused pair, and therefore the reader may rest satisfied that they were "agitated with a powerful hand," as the messenger's own official letters to the King and Villiers state. At length the countess was brought to confess her guilt, but Somerset held out stoutly, indignantly declaring that "Life and fortune are not worth accepting when honour is gone." To escape the disgrace of a trial he earnestly solicited admission to the royal presence, saying that, in a quarter of an hour's private conversation, he could establish his innocence, and set the business at rest for ever. James, however, shrunk from this interview ; nor would he even receive a private letter from the prisoner. When this was refused, the earl assumed a bolder tone, declaring that at the bar he would take ample vengeance on the prince, and reveal such things as his ungrateful sovereign would not like to hear. Further means were suggested by the trembling King to work upon the accused. The confession of the countess, which did not materially bear against the earl, was communicated to him by Bacon, Coke, the Lord Chancellor, and others, who severally pressed him to speak out, alleging that as she who had led him to offend, had confessed her guilt, he ought to feel still less reluctance to make a clear conscience of it, and not to shut the gates of his Majesty's mercy altogether against himself. Still the reasoning was thrown away. James now received a letter from him, but not a private one; the tone of which, though enigmatical, was bold, like the tone of a man writing to another over whom he had power. But the King was inexorable in his demand for a confession, or, if denied this, for having the prisoner brought to the bar of trial, taking care it should be communicated to Somerset, that if he indulged in irreverent language with respect to the sovereign, he would promptly be removed, without any stay of the proceedings on account of his absence; and this menace, together with the understanding that, if he held his tongue, things would not go very hard against him, caused him to refrain from implicating James in any way, on his trial.

It was on the 24th of May that the countess was arraigned, her husband's case having occupied the following day. There was a vast multitude of courtiers and nobles present, besides a suffocating crowd of other spectators. Even the Earl of Essex, the lady's first husband, was an auditor of her trial, although it is said that he was not visible to the mass of people present. Westminster Hall, of course, was the scene of this extraordinary proceeding; Lord Chancellor Ellesmere having officiated as Lord High Steward. He was seated under a "Cloth of Estate," at the upper end of the hall, there being nearest to him an Usher with a White Rod, the insignia of his office. A little farther off, stood Garter King-at-Arms, and the Seal-bearer, who were on the High Steward's right hand, while the bearer of the Black Rod was on his left; eight Sergeants-at-Arms being placed on each side, more behind. On either side of his lordship, on benches somewhat lower than his seat, sat the twenty-one peers who constituted the Steward's court; while the judges in their scarlet robes sat in a row somewhat lower than the peers, the most distinguished of them, both by his position during the trials and his fame, being Sir E. Coke. At the lower end of the hall were the King's Counsel, headed by the Attorney General, the renowned Sir Francis Bacon. The accused stood beyond these again, separated by a bar, where they could be beheld by every one in the hall. An officer holds an axe as he stands before a peer or peeress under trial, the edge of which is turned from the accused; but if sentence of death is pronounced, it is then immediately turned towards them.

To Bacon was intrusted the conduct of the trials, having been directed previously by the King as to the entire management of what should have been regarded as the most solemn of proceedings. Especially was he instructed not to drive Somerset to such a pitch as would give "occasion for despair or flushes." Accordingly, the Attorney General adroitly strove to put people on a wrong scent, for the purpose of preventing the earl from making any dangerous disclosures, and the court from getting any insight with regard to some iniquitous secret which it imported the King to conceal. In any event James was resolved to save the life of the heinous criminal, on which account Bacon advised that all reviling should be forborne, and that although the arraigned should he made "guilty to the peers," yet that he should not be rendered "odious to the people."

The countess, as already stated, was arraigned separately before her peers. The lovely but guilty woman looked pale, and sick, and spiritless; and yet an eye-witness observes, that although she won pity by her sober demeanour, still in his opinion it was more sober and confident than was fit for a lady in such distress, but that "yet she shed, or made show of some tears divers times." She trembled excessively while the clerk read the indictment; she hid her face with her fan at mention of the name of Weston; and she spoke with a voice scarcely audible, when she pleaded guilty. She was now hurried from the bar, that she might not interrupt the attorney-general by saying that her confession did not involve her husband, Bacon, during her absence delivering an artful speech, stating the evidence he had to produce if she had rendered it necessary by pleading not guilty. She was now recalled for a few moments, in order to hear sentence of death pronounced against her. An eye-witness records that she, "after sentence given, in a most humble, yet not base manner, besought the Lord High Steward, to whom she first directed her speech, and then likewise to the rest of the lords, that they would be pleased to mediate his Majesty on her behalf for his gracious favour and mercy, which they promised to do; and then, expressing her inward sorrow by the many tears she shed, departed." Within a few days she received a pardon.

On the day of the arraignment of the countess, Somerset, who ought to have been tried along with her, received a warning from Sir George More, lieutenant of the Tower, that his trial was appointed for the following day. But the earl declared that he would not go unless carried in his bed, adding that the King had assured him he should never be brought to the bar, nay, that James dared not to bring him to trial. This language made the lieutenant quiver and shake; so that away goes he "to Greenwich, late as it was, being twelve at night, and bounces up stairs as if mad." The King, who was in bed, on hearing what the lieutenant had to communicate, fell into a passion of tears, crying, "On my soul, More, I wot not what to do! Thou art a wise man; help me in this great strait, and thou shalt find thou dost it for a thankful master: thou shalt have a suit worth hundreds to thee."

"I have been with the King," said More, the instant he returned to Somerset; "I find him a most affectionate master unto you, and full of grace in his intentions; but he prays that to satisfy the clamour for justice that you appear at Westminster, although you shall return instantly, without any further proceeding; only you shall know your enemies and their malice, though they shall have no power over you."

With this trick of wit, says a memoir-writer of the period, Somerset's fury was allayed, so that he was got quietly, about eight in the morning, to Westminster Hall. Yet, it being feared that his former bold courage might revert again, and that he might fly out into some strange discovery, two servants were placed on each side of him, with a cloak on their arms, who were ordered, if the prisoner did in any way assail the King, to hood-wink him, and carry him instantly from the box.

The prisoner was after all quite composed when he was arraigned, the attorney-general taking good care not to ruffle him in any way, and avoiding such invectives as were usually employed against prisoners. He abstained from such disturbance by the King's orders, as he admitted, declaring also that he was not disposed to blazon the earl's name in blood. Accordingly he handled the case most tenderly, never urging the guilt of the prisoner without bringing forward the assurance of the royal mercy. All along, however, Somerset maintained his innocence, displaying far more ability during the trial than the world had given him credit for, and defending himself so ably and pertinaciously that the trial lasted eleven hours. Still, he never mentioned the King, and rejected every exhortation to confess. The peers at last found him guilty, and sentence of death was pronounced, whereupon he implored the intercession of the Lord High Steward, and the rest of the peers, to his Majesty, for mercy. In like manner, as the countess had been, he was ere long offered a pardon, which, however, he refused, declaring that he was an innocent man, and that he would accept nothing less than a reversal of the judgment. After a few years' imprisonment he sought that which he had before rejected, and with his lady he retired into the country, there to reproach and to hate each other. The King would not permit the earl's arms to be reversed and kicked out of the chapel of Windsor, and upon his account it was ordered " that felony should not be reckoned amongst the disgraces of those who were to be excluded from the Order of St. George." Further, to keep the discarded favourite and depository of royal secrets from desperation, he was allowed for life an income of £4,000 annually,—a splendid income in those days.

Towards the close of James's life, the Earl of Somerset is again heard of, with some degree of publicity. Buckingham, in his turn, was no longer the favourite; and the King had come to entertain a notion such as few other men were capable of—to make his peace with his old minion, and to place that convicted murderer once more at the head of the nation. Perhaps James thought that the man's crimes might be forgotten; and certainly many persons had long been complaining that the government of Buckingham was incomparably worse than that of his predecessor. By means of a third party, Somerset opened a communication with the King, and dwelt at length, and with some ability, on the misconduct of Buckingham. From a letter which has recently come to light, it would appear that Somerset acted in concert with a party that maintained that James was little better than a prisoner, and that his son, Charles, was wholly guided by Buckingham, who, in all things had shown himself a rash, heady young man, a novice in the management of business. Buckingham, though probably ignorant of Somerset's movements, felt that he had lost the good will of his old master; but this only made him cling closer to the son, who would soon be King.

The countess died in 1632, and consequently in the reign of Charles I.; the earl survived her thirteen years. They had an only child, Lady Anne Carr, who was born in the Tower, having been named after the Queen, in the hopes of propitiating her Majesty.

She became the wife of William, fifth earl, and afterwards Duke of Bedford. She was the mother of a large family, one of whom was William Lord Russell, who died on the scaffold in the time of Charles II. It is said that her mother's disgraceful and most criminal history was never communicated to Anne Carr, until a year or two before her death.

It is impossible to peruse the preceding pages and the account of the fearful tragedy of Sir Thomas Overbury's murder, without having the mind continually directed to the loathsome King. What might not be said of the profligacy of his court of nobles, and of the countenance which he lent to its abominations? But instead of indulging in deserved invective, let us conclude with a characteristic eulogy, which may serve our purpose fully as well, although in an inverse way. James died, and his favourite divine and politician, Bishop Williams, after a rhapsody of panegyric that is utterly nauseous, relative to the pedant's outrivalling King Solomon, adds these words with a scandalous effrontery :—" If we look at home in his own dominions, never were the benches so gravely furnished, never the courts so willingly frequented, never rich and poor so equally righted, never the balance so evenly poised as in the reign of our late sovereign."

XV.—DR. DODD.

THERE is much to be gleaned from the life and death of Dr. Dodd. How lamentable his end! And yet, as the law of the land then stood,—however merciless may have been the prosecution of him by Lord Chesterfield, or however unwise and inexpedient the rigour with which the crime of forgery was punished,—we cannot but think that his guilt was far deeper than that of multitudes who have died on the scaffold for a similar offence; and, consequently, that few criminals ever had less claim to such a display of popular feeling and sympathy as accompanied his conviction, condemnation, and death.

Still, the history of this churchman abounds with impressive lessons that can never be unseasonably considered; there being at all times clerical idols and worshipping multitudes who require to be warned, counselled, and taught that popularity is a snare,—that it is an incense which intoxicates as well as exhilarates. Indeed, to whomsoever presented, it is perilous. It is a cup which must not be quaffed; seeing that poison lurks within it to him who serves at the altar; for if he drains it and looks to it for the stay and the stimulant which is to sustain him, he is undone. Much reason especially have those preachers to tremble, who are admired by the great and caressed by the vain. How full of promise was the morning of Dodd's life! How steadily and surely did he in early manhood progress along the path towards professional eminence! For long he had the stimulus everywhere of a crowded auditory; for year after year he was lavishly remunerated by devoted flocks, who poured favours and flatteries upon him. He was gifted by nature; he was eloquent and persuasive; he was adorned with learning, and indefatigable in his labours,—many of them benevolent and humane in a remarkable sense and degree; and yet he was suddenly, through his own misdeeds, hurled from the giddy pinnacle of popularity to the depths of merited contempt, becoming an appalling disgrace to his cloth. If he was greatly noted because of his talents and his success, he became no less memorable on account of his follies than of his tragical fate.

> "If parts allure thee, think how Bacon shined,
> The wisest, greatest, meanest of mankind."

Or, to quote Dr. Dodd's own words, on Sterne's Sermons, in the "Christian Magazine," 1766, p. 504—"We are astonished a man can deliver such sentiments, and act such a life."

Dr. William Dodd was the eldest son of the Rev. Wm. Dodd, M.A., many years a minister in Lincolnshire,—and was born in 1729. After being educated at a private school, he was admitted a sizar of Clair-hall, Cambridge. Handsome, genteel, and elegant in his person, he sacrificed to the Graces no less than to the Muses; and though he was entered of the lowest order, in dress and appearance few of his superiors could surpass him. Yet, attentive as he was to outward accomplishments, and too fond of pleasure and dissipation,—being in particular, as he himself expresses it, "a votary of the god of dancing, and being in return distinguished by the favour of those fair priestesses who presided at his mysteries;"—yet, by the help of a lively imagination, a retentive memory, and close application, he exhibited his talents to advantage in every collegiate and academical exercise for his first degree. Among other noticeable points, he displayed considerable skill in versification at an early period. It was in 1745 that he went to the University, and in 1747 he began to publish little pieces of poetry. He gave to the world, anonymously, "A Pastoral on the Distemper among the Horned Cattle;" "The African Prince, now in England, to Zara at his Father's Court;" and "Zara's Answer." In 1750 appeared "A Day in Vacation at College," a mock-heroic poem in blank verse; abridgments of Grotius, "De jure belli et pacis," and of "Clarke on the Being and Attributes of God," with Sir Jeffrey Gilbert's "Abstract of Locke on the Human Understanding," all inscribed to Dr. Keene, then Vice-Chancellor of the University, and afterwards Bishop of Ely. He published also a new book of the "Dunciad," occasioned by Mr. Warburton's edition of the "Dunciad Complete," in which Warburton, with very little propriety, but much abuse, is made the hero. About the same time the young adventurer published proposals for a translation, by subscription, of the "Hymns of Callimachus, the Fragments of Orpheus, &c.," from the Greek; and wrote a tragedy, with choruses, called "The Syracusan." He continued to make frequent appearances in this light way, in which there were always marks of sprightliness and ingenuity; but at the same time imbibed more and more that taste for expense and dissipation which finally ruined him. In January, 1750, he took the degree of B.A. with reputation; and that of M.A. in 1757. Before he was in orders, he had begun and finished his selection of "The Beauties of Shakspeare," which he published soon after in 2 vols. 12mo.; and, at the conclusion of the preface, notified, as if resigning all pursuits of the profane kind, that "better and more important things henceforth demanded his attention." Nevertheless, in 1755, he published his translation of the "Hymns of Callimachus," &c., in English verse; in the preface to which he was assisted by Mr. Thorne, (afterwards Bishop of Norwich). Happy would it have been, had he remained longer in the friendship of that excellent man, whom, however, he soon disgusted by his vanity and unbecoming conduct.

It was in 1753 that Dodd received orders; and being now settled in London, he soon became a very popular and celebrated preacher. He obtained several lectureships, and was appointed to preach a course of Lady Moyer's lectures. In short, he advanced his theological character greatly and at a rapid rate, by an almost unexampled number of oral discourses as well as an uninterrupted publication of sermons and tracts of piety. Indeed, from the time that he unadvisedly settled in the metropolis, he continued to find the booksellers of service to him; the more especially as, much to the surprise and concern of his friends, who little thought he would have married for love only,—knowing also that he might by such a step have connected himself very advantageously,—he so early as April, 1751, and soon after quitting the University, entered into the wedded state with Miss Mary Perkins, a young lady who then lodged in Frith-street, Soho, and who, whatever were her personal attractions, was certainly deficient in those of birth and fortune. All his views at Cambridge were thus at once defeated. And to complete the measure of his imprudence at the time, destitute as he was of all resources but what his pen afforded, he immediately took and furnished a house in Wardour-street, dancing on the brink of a precipice, and thoughtless of the morrow. However, as already stated, his exertions were most various and most unremitting in order to gain support and to forward his prospects; his lectureships and his published tracts speedily becoming remarkable for their frequency and number. And further, to keep up the profession of sanctity, and to increase his popularity, he was extremely zealous in promoting charitable institutions, distinguishing himself in a special manner with regard to the Magdalen Hospital, which was opened in 1758, becoming preacher at the chapel of the charity, for which he was allowed £100 yearly. But, notwithstanding his apparent attention to spiritual and charitable matters, probably his own temporal interests at the time were uppermost in his mind. And yet all his expedients did not prove successful, his subservient flattery being sometimes seen through. In 1759, he published in two vols., Bishop Hall's "Meditations," and dedicated them to Miss Talbot, who lived in the family of Archbishop Secker; and again, on the honour which the Marquis of Granby acquired in Germany, he addressed an ode to the marchioness which was too fulsome not to miss its aim. The dedication to the other lady was especially resented on account of its extravagant flattery, giving such offence to the Archbishop, that, after a warm epistolary expostulation, his Grace insisted on the sheet being cancelled in which the tumid effusion had found a place.

Dr. Squire, who in 1760 was made Bishop of St. David's, had published the year before a work entitled "Indifference for Religion Inexcusable;" on the appearance of which Dodd wrote a sonnet, addressing it to the author, who was so well pleased with this mark of his attention, that in 1760 he made him his chaplain, and in 1763 procured for him a prebend of Brecon. He also egregiously flattered this prelate in the "Public Ledger," in which he then wrote; and about the same time he was supposed to have defended the measures of administration in certain political pieces. From 1760 to 1767 he superintended and contributed largely to "The Christian's Magazine," for which he received from the proprietors £100 yearly. In a critical notice which appeared in that periodical of three sermons "On the Wisdom and Goodness of God in the Vegetable Creation," occurred the following paragraph :—"Though this discourse contains the finest instruction, though every part of the subject is moralized in the most beautiful manner, yet, from the trifling complexion of the times, we fancy it will be a greater encouragement to the purchasers, when we recommend it as affording the highest entertainment. Besides the pleasure the author gives, he discovers an extensive knowledge of the subject he has chosen; he seems to have previously qualified himself by reading the best authors who have treated upon botany, and even the skilful in that science may receive some hints deserving their notice. His style is at once elegant and nervous, neither careless nor yet affected. Sufficiently open and diffuse for the pulpit, yet neither tedious nor redundant in the closet. In short, such a style as we would recommend to the imitation of those young divines who would desire to instruct without being tedious, and who would acquire popularity without meanness." At the time when this panegyric appeared of the three sermons in question,—these having been published by their author, viz., Dodd, it was not known that the same was his own reviewer. The discovery, however, helped to a knowledge of the man's character, so that one cannot much wonder to find Dr. Kendrick thus picturing him—

————"that mild man of God,
The reverend doodle Doctor Dodd."

Still, "The Christian's Magazine," together with the vain man's other employments and contrivances, brought in for him money enough to support a person of moderate habits. But a very considerable fortune would have been too small for the luxurious style of living in which the hero of the present story delighted to indulge.

After all, however, he preserved theological appearances to the great public, and was indefatigable in his efforts and enterprizes. In order, among many other displays, to enlarge his fame, he at length meditated a design of publishing a large Commentary on the Bible. With the view of giving the greater *éclat* to this undertaking, it was announced that Lord Masham had presented him with MSS. of Mr. Locke, found in his lordship's library at Oates; and that he had helps also from MSS. of Lord Clarendon, Dr. Waterland, Gilbert West, and other celebrated men. He began to publish this Commentary in 1765, in weekly and monthly numbers; and continued to do so regularly till it was complete in 3 vols. folio. It was dedicated to his patron, Bishop Squire, who died in 1766, lamented, it may be believed, very sincerely by Dodd, who in the same year took the degree of LL.D. at Cambridge, having been, through the interest of some of his city friends, appointed one of his Majesty's chaplains. In connexion with this appointment may be mentioned a characteristic anecdote, and one which was long remembered at St. James's. November was the doctor's month of waiting; and this melancholy season, as well as the chaplain's gloomy apartment, he determined to enliven by the society of some of his female friends. At "the rustling of silks and the creaking of shoes," for which he could find no precedent, old Groves, the table-decker, stood aghast, the maids of honour could not repress their smiles, and his more serious brethren were by no means edified; so that there needed not the Lord Chamberlain's interdict to make all succeeding chaplains think the novelty

"More honour'd in the breach than the observance."

About the same period Dr. Dodd moved to a residence in Southampton-row, which he elegantly furnished, and also a villa at Ealing. He exchanged too his chariot for a coach, to accommodate his pupils, one of these being Philip Stanhope, afterwards Earl of Chesterfield—the vain divine regarding the accession of the young gentleman to his establishment as the most fortunate circumstance in his life, whereas it turned out eventually the most unhappy. Near to the same date at which we have arrived, the doctor gained one thousand pounds in the lottery, and forthwith employed the sum in building a new chapel at Pimlico, near the palace of the Queen, from whom it took its name. And again, about the very same time, he translated and published some "Sermons on the Duties of the Great," from the French of M. de Massillon, Bishop of Clermont, preached before Louis XV. during his minority, and inscribed them to the Prince of Wales. Admired as Massillon was as an orator, and instructive as a moralist, many of his tenets, as to church-authority and civil government, were much better suited to the meridian of Versailles than that of St. James's. Our preacher, it seems, when he fitted up his chapel near the palace, had flattered himself with the hopes of having some young royal auditors, and had accordingly assigned a particular pew or gallery for the heir-apparent. But in this, as in many other of his ambitious views, he was doomed to disappointment, not even at the time escaping ridicule and satire. Scott, the moderniser, or rather burlesquer, of Martial, for example, addressed the following Ode to the reverend doctor :—

> " Meek, humble, modest, Parson Dodd ;
> Believe me, it is mighty odd
> 　　That you such hopes should dish up :
> For after all, my good friend Will,
> Whate'er you think, you will be still
> 　　A priest, but not a bishop.
>
> " The parties which you tried to fix
> Of ladies (monstrous thus to mix !)
> 　　To grace the chaplain's table :
> Carnal with spiritual thus to join !
> Flounced petticoats with gowns divine !
> 　　O fie ! ev'n that's not able.
>
> " Another string you've tried to touch,
> Which if it serves your purpose much,
> 　　The world might justly wonder :
> Thus did Salmoneus rattle o'er
> That brazen bridge, to make it roar
> 　　Like Jove's imperial thunder.
>
> " Of French translations we've enough,
> And all such meagre flimsy stuff,
> 　　Both sacred and profane :
> But what will suit proud Louy's court,
> Should not to George's here resort,
> 　　As all such preaching's vain.
>
> " Massillon's pen flows much too fine,
> In polished periods every line,
> 　　To stand the British test :
> The heart of George will never bow
> To French discourses, since we know
> 　　We have by far the best.
>
> " Thus, while you warn a prince's ear
> Of specious flattery to beware,
> 　　You gild the Gallic pill
> In such a manner, as to suit
> Your honest views with George or Bute ;
> 　　And so farewell, dear Will ! "

In a more serious strain there was a singular circumstance in the life of Dr. Dodd, connected with his office of chaplain to the King. On one occasion he had chosen for the subject of his sermon this theme :—" The frequency of Capital Punishments inconsistent with justice, sound policy, and religion." This discourse, which was published by him, had been intended to have been delivered at the Chapel Royal, St. James's, but omitted on account of the absence of the court at the time. The following extract exhibits what were the ill-fated man's sentiments on the deeply important point :—" It would be easy to show the injustice of those laws which demand blood for the slightest offences ; the superior justice and propriety of inflicting perpetual and laborious servitude ; the greater utility to the sufferer as well as to the state, especially wherein we have a variety of ne—

cessary occupations, peculiarly noxious and prejudicial to the lives of the honest and industrious, and in which they might be employed who had forfeited their lives and their liberties to society." How little did the preacher himself think at the time he prepared this discourse for the ears of royalty that he would soon be nearly interested both as a prosecutor and a convict in its subject! As a prosecutor he was unfortunately called upon to appear early in the succeeding winter against one William Griffiths, for robbing him and his wife near Pancras, on their return from his living, and discharging a pistol into the carriage, which, happily, (as it was then thought) only broke the glass. For this outrage, being tried and convicted on their evidence at the Old Bailey, the highwayman was executed at Tyburn, the event occurring in 1773.

In 1772 Dr. Dodd was presented to the living of Hockliffe, in Bedfordshire; but such a preferment was of little avail in supplying his wants. The habits of expense had gained an irresistible ascendancy over him; he was vain; he was pompous; he slavishly courted the society of the great, the titled, and such as were above him in the artificial scale; and hence he became every year more deeply involved in debts, till at length he felt as one about to be utterly overwhelmed. To relieve himself he was tempted in 1774 to a step which ruined him for ever in the estimation of those who had not previously seen through the man; and this was, to procure by indirect and foul means the rectory of St. George's, Hanover-square. On the preferment of Dr. Moss to the see of Bath and Wells in the year named, that rectory fell to the disposal of the Crown; on which event Dr. Dodd was so infatuated as to cause an anonymous letter to be sent to Lady Apsley, offering the sum of £3,000, if by her means he could be presented to the living. The letter was immediately communicated to the Lord Chancellor, her husband; and the document being traced to the sender, it was laid before the King. The immediate result was that Dodd's name was ordered to be struck out of the list of chaplains to his Majesty; and the press getting hold of the particulars, satire and invective were poured out without measure upon the head of the puffed-up preacher. The transaction even became the subject of entertainment, in one of Foote's performances at the Haymarket. All the answer which the misguided man made was a short letter in the newspapers, requesting the public to suspend their opinion, and promising an explanation of the affair, which, however, never appeared, unless, indeed, some attempt which he resorted to, in order to throw all the blame on his wife, in regard to the vile application to Lady Apsley is to be instanced.

Stung with shame, if not remorse, at the thoughts of his deeds and the turn which they had taken in their results, our preacher decamped for a season, going over to his pupil, Lord Chesterfield, now at Geneva, who added to Hockliffe the living of Winge, in Buckinghamshire. At this time the doctor is said to have had about eight hundred pounds a year in preferments. Still, his extravagance continued undiminished, and drove him to other infamous schemes. Even now, had he devoted himself to the diligent discharge of his duties as a country pastor,—leaving the metropolis, and disposing of his chapels,—the remainder of his chequered life might have been honourably distinguished. But undeterred by the warnings of the past, fresh means of advancing his worldly interests and his income, some of them alike foolish and criminal, were resolved upon. He became the editor of a newspaper; and is said to have attempted a disengagement from his debts by a commission of bankruptcy, in which, however, he failed. From this period every step he took led to complete his ruin. In the summer of 1776 he went to France; and, as if he had a mind to wanton in folly, paraded in a phaeton at the races, on the plains of

Sablons, tricked out in all the foppery of French attire. He returned in the beginning of winter, and proceeded to exercise his functions with the same formality and affected earnestness as formerly, particularly at the Magdalen Chapel, where his last sermon was preached, Feb. 2, 1777. It is said that his text was taken from Deut. xxviii., verses 65 and 66 :—" And among these nations shalt thou find no ease, neither shall the sole of thy foot have rest: but the Lord shall give thee there a trembling heart, and failing of eyes, and sorrow of mind: and thy life shall hang in doubt before thee; and thou shalt fear day and night, and shalt have none assurance of thy life." One can hardly help feeling, on reading the life of this infatuated person, that there was a fatality in all his actions, the tendency of which every one who knew him well could see, although he himself was utterly blinded to them. Only two days after preaching the sermon just alluded to, he signed a bond, which he had forged as from his pupil Lord Chesterfield, for the sum of £4,200;—the said nobleman being Philip Stanhope of Mansfield Woodhouse, who succeeded his relative, the great Lord Chesterfield, as fifth earl, on the 24th of March, 1773. By his second wife, Henrietta, daughter of the first Marquis of Bute, he was father of his successor, the present Earl of Chesterfield. But, as to the forgery committed by Dr. Dodd :—

The doctor being in want of cash to pay his tradesmen's bills, and having been preceptor to the Earl of Chesterfield, he pretended that his lordship had an urgent occasion to borrow £4,200, but did not choose to be his own agent, and begged that the matter might be secretly and expeditiously conducted. He employed Mr. Robertson, a broker, to whom he presented a bond not filled up or signed, that he might find a person who would advance the requisite sum to a young nobleman who had lately come of age. After applying to several persons who refused the business, because they were not to be present when the bond was executed, Mr. Robertson, absolutely confiding in the doctor's honour, applied to Messrs. Fletcher and Peach, who agreed to lend the money. Mr. Robertson returned the bond to the doctor in order to its being executed; and on the following day the doctor produced it as executed, and witnessed by himself. Mr. Robertson, knowing Mr. Fletcher to be a particular man, and who would consequently object to one subscribing witness only, put his name under the doctor's. He then went and received the money, which he paid into the hands of Dr. Dodd, £3,000 in notes of Sir Charles Raymond and Co., the remaining £1,200 in bank-notes. The money being thus obtained, the doctor gave Mr. Robertson £100 for his trouble, and paid some of his own debts with a part of the remainder.

It appears that the doctor intended to replace the money and pay off the bond, in a short time, without the knowledge of any person but the broker, and the gentlemen of whom the money had been borrowed. It happened, however, that the bond being left with Mr. Manly (attorney for Messrs. Fletcher and Peach), he observed, in the writing of the condition, a remarkable blot in the first letter e in the word *seven*, which did not seem to be the effect of chance, but done with design. He thought it odd, but did not suspect a forgery; yet he showed to Mr. Fletcher the bond and the blot, and advised him to have a clean bond filled up and carried to Lord Chesterfield for execution. Mr. Fletcher consented; and Mr. Manly went the next day to his lordship, who, having previous notice of the intended business, asked him if he had called about the bond. Mr. Manly said he had; and his lordship answered, " I have burnt the bond." This appeared very extraordinary, but was soon explained by Lord Chesterfield saying he thought the gentleman had called about a bond for £500, which he had given some years before, and had taken up and burnt. Mr. Manly now produced the much more serious document, in regard to which he had waited upon his lordship, and was struck with amazement on finding that Lord Chesterfield utterly disowned it. Mr. Manly went directly to Mr. Fletcher to consult what steps to take. They immediately, along with a Mr. Innes, proceeded to Guildhall, to prefer an information respecting the forgery, against Dr. Dodd and the broker. Mr. Robertson was taken into custody, and with Fletcher, Manly, Innes, and two of the Lord Mayor's officers, hastened to the house of the doctor.

They opened the business, and the doctor was very much struck and affected. Manly told him, if he would return the money, it would be the only means of saving him. He instantly returned six notes of £500 each, he drew on his banker for £800, and a judgment on his goods for the remaining £400,—which judgment was immediately carried into execution. All this was done by the doctor in full reliance on the honour of the parties, that the bond should be returned to him cancelled; but notwithstanding this restitution, he was taken before the Lord Mayor, and charged with the forgery. This took place Feb. 8th, 1777, and the unhappy man thus answered the accusation:—" I cannot tell what to say in such a situation. I had no intention to defraud Lord Chesterfield; I hope his lordship will consider my case; I was pressed extremely for three hundred or four hundred pounds to pay some tradesmen's bills; I meant it as a temporary resource; I should have repaid the money in half a year; I have made satisfaction, and I hope that will be considered. My Lord Chesterfield must have some tenderness towards me; he knows I love him; he knows I regard his honour as dearly as my own. (Here he wept bitterly.) I hope he will, according to that mercy that is in his heart, show clemency to me. There is nobody wishes to prosecute; pray, my Lord Mayor, consider that, and dismiss me. Mr. Robertson is certainly innocent."

Clemency, however, was denied; and the wretched man was committed to prison. His trial soon after followed, the evidence against him being clear and conclusive. No witnesses were brought forward to speak in his favour, or to throw any additional light on the crime he had committed, beyond what has been stated. He had been led into court by his curate and intimate friend, the Rev. Mr. Butler, and to the last passage of the solemn proceedings in public of that day, this gentleman manifested to the accused the deepest sympathy, so as to lend him all possible countenance, in order to the deliverance of his defence, which contained the following passages:—

" Upon the evidence," said he, " which has been produced against me, I find it very difficult to address your lordships; there is no man in the world who has a deeper sense of the heinous nature of the crime for which I stand indicted than myself. I view it in all its extent of malignancy towards a commercial state like ours; but, my lords, I humbly apprehend, though no lawyer, that the moral turpitude and malignancy of the crime always, in the eye of the law, of reason, and of religion, consist in the intention. I am informed, my lords, that the act of parliament on this head runs perpetually in this style, *with an intention to defraud*. Such an intention, my lords and gentlemen of the jury, I believe, has not been attempted to be proved upon me, and the consequences that have happened, which have appeared before you, sufficiently prove that a perfect and ample restitution has been made. I leave it to you to consider that if an unhappy man ever deviates from the law of right, yet, if in the single first moment of recollection he does all he can to make a full and perfect amend, what, my lords and gentlemen of the jury, can God and man desire further? There are a variety of little circumstances too tedious to trouble you with, respecting this matter. I hope you will consider the case in its true state of clemency ; for, indeed, although I have met with all candour this day in this court, yet I have been pursued elsewhere with excessive cruelty. I have been prosecuted after the most solemn assurances, after the most soothing delusive arguments of Mr. Manly, for he had given me the strongest hopes, if ample restitution was made, and which was at once actually done, that no further notice would be taken of my conduct in regard to the bond. . . , My lords and gentlemen of the jury, oppressed as I am with infamy, loaded as I am with distress, sunk under this cruel prosecution, you cannot think life a matter of value to me. No, for I solemnly protest that death, of all blessings, would be the most pleasant to me after this pain. But yet I have ties which call upon me,—ties which render me desirous even to continue this miserable existence. I have a wife—(here tears streamed from his eyes, and, with few exceptions, all in that crowded court shared visibly in his emotion)—a wife with whom I have lived seven and twenty years in the most perfect conjugal felicity,—for her I feel. I have creditors, honest men, who will lose much by my death, and for the sake of justice towards them I hope some mercy will be shown to me. I solemnly declare it would have been in my power to replace the money in three months. Of this I assured Mr. Robertson repeatedly, having his strong assurances that no man should be privy to the transaction but Mr. Fletcher and himself ; and since no injury has been done to any man upon earth, I trust in an acquittal, confiding in the tenderness, justice, and protection of my country."

One of the judges who tried the case, viz., Mr. Baron Perryn, proceeded to sum up the evidence, which he did with minuteness and impartiality. He said that the *gravamen* of the indictment was this :—" That the bond was forged by the prisoner with intent to defraud Lord Chesterfield and Mr. Fletcher. If the jury believed it was done to defraud one or other of the parties, it mattered not which, then they must bring in the prisoner guilty. As to the defence set up, the only point for consideration was, whether the forgery was committed with an intent to defraud, the intention to be interpreted from the nature of the thing done, and the manner in which it was gone about, rather than from any asseveration of the accused after finding that his conduct had been fully discovered. With regard to the other points of the defence, these could have no weight with the jury ; for if such a defence was listened to in the present case, no criminal brought to a bar of justice would fail to make use of it."

The jury retired, and after a short absence returned with a verdict of Guilty ; soon after presenting a strong memorial recommending the unhappy prisoner to his Majesty as a fit object for the exercise of the Royal mercy.

It was in May when Dr. Dodd was brought up for judgment ; and now being asked why sentence of death should not be pronounced against him, he addressed the court in the following terms :—" My lord, I now stand before you a dreadful example of human infirmity. I entered upon public life with the expectations common to young men whose education has been liberal, and whose abilities have been flattered ; and when I became a clergyman I considered myself as not impairing the dignity of the order. I was not an idle, nor I hope, an useless minister ; I taught the truths of Christianity with the zeal of conviction, and the authority of innocence. My labours were approved, my pulpit became popular, and I have reason to believe that of those who heard me some have been preserved from sin, and some have been reclaimed. Condescend, my lord, to think if these considerations aggravate my crime, how much they must embitter my punishment.

" Being distinguished and elevated by the confidence of mankind, I had too much confidence in myself, and thinking my integrity what others thought it, established in sincerity and fortified by religion, I did not consider the danger of vanity, nor suspect the deceitfulness of my own heart. The day of conflict came, in which temptation seized and overwhelmed me! I committed the crime which I entreat your lordships to believe that conscience hourly represents to me in its full bulk of mischief and malignity.

" To an act now waiting the decision of vindictive justice, I will not oppose the counterbalance of nearly thirty years (a great part of the life of man) passed in exciting and exercising charity; in relieving such distresses as I myself now feel; in administering those consolations which I now want. I will not otherwise extenuate my offence tha by declaring, what I hope will appear to many, and what many circumstances might make probable, that I did not intend finally to defraud; nor will it become me to apportion my own punishment, by alleging that my sufferings have been not much less than my guilt. I had fallen from reputation, which ought to have made me cautious; and from a fortune which ought to have given me content. I am sunk at once into poverty and scorn; my name and crime fill the ballads in the streets,—the sport of the thoughtless, and the triumph of the wicked !

" It may seem strange, my lord, that, remembering what I have lately been, I should still wish to continue what I am. But contempt of death, how speciously soever it might mingle with heathen virtues, has nothing in it suitable to Christian penitence.

" Many motives impel me to beg earnestly for life. I feel the natural horror of a violent death, and the universal dread of untimely dissolution. I am desirous to recompense the injury I have done to the clergy, to the world, and to religion; and to efface the scandal of my crime, by the example of my repentance. But above all, I wish to die with thoughts more composed, and calmer preparation!

" The gloom and confusion of a prison, the anxiety of a trial, and the inevitable vicissitudes of passion, leave not the mind in a due disposition for the holy exercises of prayer and self-examination. Let not a little life be denied me, in which I may, by meditatio and contrition, prepare myself to stand at the tribunal of Omnipotence, and support the presence of that Judge, who shall distribute to all according to their works; who will receive to pardon the repenting sinner; and from whom the merciful shall obtain mercy.

" For these reasons, my lord, amidst shame and misery, I yet wish to live; and most humbly implore that I may be recommended by your lordship to the clemency of his Majesty."

The duty of pronouncing sentence upon the doctor devolved to the Recorder, who, amongst other pertinent observations said,—" Your application for mercy must be made elsewhere; it would be cruel in the court to flatter you ; there is a power of dispensing mercy, where you may apply. Your own good sense and the contrition you express will induce you to lessen the influence of the example, by publishing your hearty and sincere detestation of the offence of which you are convicted; and that you will not attempt to palliate or extenuate, which would indeed add to the degree of the influence of a crime of this kind being committed by a person in your position, reputation, and known abilities. I would, therefore, warn you against anything of that nature. Now, having said this much, I am obliged to pronounce the sentence of the law, which is that you, Dr. William Dodd, be carried from hence to the place from whence you came; that from thence you are to be carried to the place of execution, where you are to be hanged by the neck until you are dead."

To this Dr. Dodd replied, " Lord Jesus, receive my soul!"

The exertions to save the convicted and condemned doctor were, perhaps, beyond all example in any country. The newspapers were filled with letters and paragraphs in his favour. Individuals of all ranks and professions exerted themselves in his behalf. The talents of Dr. Johnson were engaged to give a fair colouring to his case ; parish officers went in mourning from house to house to procure signatures to a petition to the King ; and this petition, which, with the names, filled twenty-three sheets of parchment, was actually presented. Even the Lord Mayor and Common Council of London went in a body to St. James's to solicit mercy for the culprit. In vain! As clemency had been denied the Perreaus, it was deemed inadvisable to extend it to Dr. Dodd; it having been observed to his Majesty that if Dr. Dodd was pardoned, the Perreaus were murdered.

We have already named some of the many and diversified works which the doctor gave to the world as an author, but of all his productions that have appeared in print the most curious and striking is that entitled "Thoughts in Prison, in five parts, viz., the Imprisonment, the Retrospect, Public Punishment, the Trial, Futurity," to which are added his last prayer, written the night before his death, the convict's address to his unhappy brethren, and other miscellaneous pieces, some of which were composed for him by Dr. Johnson. Prefixed to the manuscript is this note by Dodd,—for his imprisonment extended over several months,—"I began these Thoughts," says the unhappy man, writing in Newgate, the 23d April, 1777, after his conviction, "merely from the impression of my mind, without plan, purpose, or motive, more than the situation and state of my soul. I continued them on a thoughtful and regular plan; and I have been enabled wonderfully, —in a state which in better days I should have supposed would have destroyed all power of reflection,—to bring them nearly to a close. I dedicate them to God, and the reflecting serious among my fellow-creatures; and I bless the Almighty for the ability to go through them, amidst the terrors of this dire place, and the bitter anguish of my disconsolate mind ! The thinking will easily pardon all inaccuracies, as I am neither able nor willing to read over these lines, with a curious or critical eye. They are imperfect, but in the language of the heart ; and had I time and inclination, might, and should be improved. But——   W. D."

The unhappy man was attended to the place of execution, in a mourning coach, on the 27th of June, by the Rev. Mr. Villette, the ordinary of Newgate, and the Rev. Mr. Dobey, a personal friend. Another criminal, named Joseph Harris, was executed at the same time. It is impossible to give an idea of the immense crowds of people that thronged the streets from Newgate to Tyburn. When the prisoners arrived at the fatal scene, and were placed in the cart, Dr. Dodd exhorted his fellow-sufferer in so generous and devout a manner as testified that he had not forgotten the duty of a clergyman. He was also most fervent in prayer apart by himself; and throughout this last dreadful scene maintained a becoming demeanour, a seemly fortitude.

His life, he confessed after his condemnation, had for a number of years been "fearfully erroneous;" but his death, to all appearance, was that of one who had become truly penitent. Popularity had been at once his snare and his ruin ; and the injury he inflicted on religion will be admitted by all who feel with an exemplary thinker, that, "A minister by preaching twenty years with the tongue of an angel, shall not edify his *hearers* so much as he shall corrupt his *seers* by one material slip in his conduct."

XVI.—THE REV. MR. HACKMAN.

MR. HACKMAN's history assuredly presents one of the most passionate tales of love on record; a passion, in his instance, which not only on a sudden obtained such a mastery over him as to enslave him wholly for a time, but that during a protracted intimacy, in spite of great disparities, and amid some of the most forbidding circumstances, amounted to absolute delusion if not utter madness. Among the unexampled peculiarities of the case, the long correspondence of the parties by means of letters that are extant,—several of which we shall lay before the reader,—is not the least remarkable, heightening indeed very strikingly its singularity,—more especially as in this correspondence there is displayed an unwonted amount of talent, feeling, and romantic interest, furnishing one of the most remarkable (sometimes elegant as well as ardent) series of amatory epistles that reality or imagination ever gave birth to.

James Hackman was born at Gosport, in Hampshire, of parents in genteel life. After giving him a good school education, he was sent to St. John's College, Cambridge, where he remained for some time, for it appears that at the first he had been designed for the ministry. Being, however, very young when sent to the University, and of a sprightly turn, it was at length deemed to be more fitting that he should be apprenticed to a mercer in his native town, his father being in trade; but even this direction was found to be incompatible with his volatile nature; and as he was entitled to a considerable patrimony, he persuaded his parents to purchase for him, when he was about nineteen years of age, an ensigncy in the 68th regiment of foot. Soon after obtaining his commission he was entrusted with the command of a recruiting party at Huntingdon, whence he was invited by Lord Sandwich to Hinchinbroke, to partake not only of the general pleasures of that place with his lordship's other visitors, but at times to partake of the special hospitalities and peculiar favour of that nobleman. It was here where he first saw and became acquainted with Miss Reay, of whose charms of face and figure he was at once a great admirer, and still more so of those of her conversation and other accomplishments; for she was not only beautiful and elegant in her person, but of great sweetness of manners, and also remarkably well skilled, amongst other winning acquisitions, in music, both vocal and instrumental. Frequently being in her company, where she lived under the protection of Lord Sandwich,—to whom indeed she had borne nine children, being at this period near twice the age of the young ensign,—he grew violently enamoured of her.

Miss Reay was the daughter of a staymaker in Covent Garden, and had served her apprenticeship to a mantua-maker, in George's-court, St. John's-lane, Clerkenwell. She had been bound when only thirteen, and yet during the whole period she served at her calling is said to have been particularly noticed by Lord Sandwich. He then took her and treated her with every mark of affection, save making her his wife. At the time of Mr. Hackman's introduction to her, she had lived with his lordship for a period of nineteen years. Reference has been made not merely to the violence of the young officer's love, and other extraordinary features in the history of his passion, but to the correspondence between him and the object of his devotion. To portions of some of these letters we must now draw attention, giving them in the order in which they were written.

" Huntingdon, Dec. 4, 1774.

" Dear M———. Ten thousand thanks for your billet by my Corporal Trim yesterday. The fellow seemed happy to have been the bearer of it, because it made me happy. He will be as good a soldier to Cupid as to Mars, I dare say ; and Mars and Cupid are not now to begin their acquaintance, you know. Whichever he serves you may command him, of course, without a compliment ; for Venus, I need not tell *you*, is the mother of Cupid, and mistress of Mars. At present the drum is beating up under my window for volunteers to Bacchus,—in plain English, the drum tells me that dinner is ready ; for a drum gives us bloody-minded heroes an appetite for eating as well as for fighting ; nay, we get up by the beat of it, and it every night sends, or ought to send us to bed and to sleep. To-night it will be late before I get to one or the other, I fancy ; indeed, the thoughts of you would prevent the latter. But the next disgrace to refusing a challenge is refusing a toast. For my part, no glass of any liquor tastes as it should to me, but when I kiss my M. on the rim. Adieu ! Whatever hard service I may have after dinner, no quantity of wine shall make me drop or forget my appointment with you to-morrow. We certainly were not seen yesterday, for reasons I will give you. Though you should persist in never being mine,—

" Ever, ever yours."

" Huntingdon, Dec. 6, 1775.

"My Dearest M.—No, I will not take advantage of the sweet, reluctant, amorous confession which your candour gave me yesterday. If to make me happy be to make my M. otherwise, then, happiness, I'll none of thee. And yet I *could* argue. Suppose he *has* bred you up—suppose you *do* owe your numerous accomplishments, under genius, to him —are you, therefore, his property ? Is it as if a horse that he has bred up should refuse to carry him ? Suppose you therefore *are* his property, will the fidelity of so many years weigh nothing in the scale of gratitude? Years ! Why, can obligation (suppose they had *not* been repaid an hundred-fold), do away the unnatural disparity of years ? Can they bid five-and-fifty stand still (the least that you could ask), and wait for five-and-twenty? Many women have the same obligation (if, indeed, there be many of the *same* accomplishments,) to their fathers. They have the additional obligation to them (if, indeed, it be an obligation) of existence. The disparity of years is sometimes even less. But, must they therefore take their fathers to their bosoms ? Must the jessamine fling its tender arms around the dying elm ? To my little fortunes you are no stranger. Will you share them with me ? And you shall honestly tell his lordship, that gratitude taught you to pay every duty to him till love taught you there were other duties which you owed to H. Gracious Heaven, that you would pay them ! But did I not say I would not take advantage? I will not. I will even remind you of your children ; to whom, alas ! I could only show at present the affection of a father. M., weigh us in the scales. If gratitude out-balance love—so. If you command it, I swear by love, I'll join my regiment to-morrow. If love prevail, and insist upon his dues, you shall declare the victory and the prize. I *will* take no advantage. Think over this. Neither will I take you by surprise. *Sleep upon* it, before you return your answer. Trim shall make the old excuse to-morrow. And, thank Heaven, to-night you sleep alone ! Why did you sing that sweet song, yesterday, though I so pressed you ! Those words and your voice were too much. No words can say how much I am yours."

To Mr. Hackman.

" H., Dec. 7, 1775.

" My dear H.—Here has been a sad piece of work ever since I received yours yester-day. But don't be alarmed,—we are not discovered to the profane. Our tender tale is only known to—(whom does your fear suggest?)—to love and gratitude, my H. And they ought both, for twenty reasons, to be *your* friends, I am sure. They have been trying your cause, ever since the departure of honest Trim yesterday. Love, though in my opinion not so blind, is as good a justice as Sir John Fielding. [Sir John Fielding, the magistrate at Bow-street, was stone blind]. I argued the matter stoutly—my head on his lordship's side of the question, my heart on yours. At last they seemed to say, as if the oath of allegiance which I had taken to gratitude, at a time, when, Heaven knows, I had never heard of love, should be void, and I should be at full liberty to devote myself, body and soul, to—. But call on me to-morrow before dinner, and I'll tell you their final judgment. This I will tell you now, love sent you the tenderest wishes, and grati-tude and I could never pay you all I owe you for your noble letter of yesterday. But, oh my H., think not meanly even of this! Do not you turn advocate against me. I will not pain you! 'Tis impossible you ever could. Come then to-morrow, and surely Omiah will not murder love. Yet I thought the other day he caught our eyes conversing. Eyes speak a language all can understand. But is a child of nature to nip in the bud that favourite passion which his mother Nature planted, and still tends? What will Oberea and her coterie say to this, Omiah, when you return from making the tour of the globe? They'll blackball you, depend on it. What would Rousseau say to it, my H.? You shall tell me to-morrow. I will not write another word, lest conscience, who is just now looking over my left shoulder, should snatch my pen, and scratch out *to-morrow.*"

[Omiah was an Otaheitan, under Lord Sandwich's care.]

To Miss ——

Huntingdon, Dec. 7, 1775.

" My dearest soul—I hope to Heaven, Trim will be able to get this to you to-night! Not I only, but my whole future life, shall thank you for the dear sheet of paper I have just received. Blessings, blessings! But I could write, and exclaim, and offer up vows and prayers, till the happy hour arrives. Yet hear me, M. If I have thus far deserved your love, I will deserve it still. As a proof, I have not hitherto pressed you for anything conscience disapproves. Our love, the inexorable tyrant of our hearts, claims his sacri-fice, but does not bid us insult his lordship's walls with it. How civilly did he invite me to Hinchinbroke, in October last, though an unknown recruiting officer! How politely himself first introduced me to yourself!"

Here we must pass over part of the correspondence. Folly rushed into guilt. Yet strange to say, Hackman, after unrestrained, unresisted indulgence, grew more and more importunate for marriage with the frail object of his mad, unseemly passion. Omiah, however, in spite of all the arts and concealments of the guilty pair, had frequently taken notice of their familiarities in his lordship's absence ; and, although he could only speak by gestures and signs, he communicated to his protector what he beheld and thought. His lordship was greatly hurt on the discovery, and charged the lady with infidelity. It is said, she confessed to the accusation, and promised reform. However this may have been, she for a time continued to maintain an intercourse with her infatuated lover, although more secretly than before. But to return to the correspondence :—

To Mr. H.

Hinchingbroke, 10 Dec., '75.

"Your two letters of the day before yesterday, and what you said to me yesterday in my dressing-room, have drove me mad. To offer to sell out and take the other step to get money for us both, was not kind. You know how such tenderness distracts me. As to marrying me, that you shall not do upon any account. Shall the man I value be pointed at and hooted at for selling himself to a lord, for a commission or some such thing? My soul is above my situation. Besides, I will not take advantage, Mr. H., of what may be only perhaps (excuse me) a youthful passion. After a more intimate acquaintance with me of a week or ten days, your opinion of me might very much change. And yet you *may* love me as sincerely as I——. But I will transcribe you a verse which I don't believe you ever heard me sing, though it's my favourite. It is said to be part of an old Scots ballad, nor is it generally known that Lady A. L. wrote it. Since we have understood each other, I have never sung it before you, because it is so descriptive of our situation, how much more so since your cruelly kind proposal of yesterday! I wept, like an infant, over it this morning :—

　　'I gang like a ghost, and I do not care to spin,
　　I fain would think on Jamie, but that would be a sin ;
　　I must ee'n do my best a good wife to be,
　　For auld Robin Gray has been kind to me.'

"My poor eyes will only suffer me to add, for God's sake, let me see my *Jamie* to morrow. Your name also is **Jamie**."

To Miss ——.

"*Huntingdon,* 1 Jan. 1766.

"Lest I should not see you this morning, I will scribble this before I mount honest Crop, that I may leave it for you.—This is a new year. May every day of it be happy to my M. May—but don't you know there's not a wish of bliss I do not wish you?—A *new* year—I like not this word. There may be new lovers—I lie—there may not. M. will never change her H. I am sure she will never change him for a truer lover.—A new year ; 76, where shall we be in 77? Where in 78 ? Where in 79 ?—In misery or bliss, in life or death, in heaven or hell—wherever *you* are there may H. be also !"

Most of what this thoughtless pair had hitherto written was sufficiently silly and foolish—sometimes profane. Henceforth a more serious and interesting tone pervades their letters ; especially on the part of Hackman, the passion grows sadly violent and infatuated. The lady communicates to him on the 23d of February, 1776, the following particulars :—

"Where was you this morning, my life ? I should have been frozen to death with the cold, if I had not been waiting for *you.* I am uneasy, very uneasy. What could prevent you ? Your own appointment too ; Why not write if you could not come ? Then I had a dream last night, a sad dream, my H.

　　' For thee I fear, my love ;
　　Such ghostly dreams last night surprised my soul.'

"You may reply, perhaps, with my favourite Iphis,

　　' Heed not these black illusions of the night,
　　The mockings of unquiet slumbers.'

"Alas ! I cannot help it. I am a weak woman, not a soldier. I thought you had a duel with a person whom we have agreed never to mention. I thought you killed each other.

I not only saw his sword, I *heard* it pass through my H.'s body. I saw you both die; and with you, love and gratitude. Who is there, thought I, to mourn for M.? Not one! You may call me foolish; but I am uneasy, miserable, wretched! Indeed, indeed I am. For God's sake let me hear from you."

To Miss ——.

"*Cannon Coffee-house*, 17 *March*, '76.

"Though you can hardly have read my last scrawl, I must pester you with another. I had ordered some dinner; but I can neither eat, nor do anything else. 'Mad!' I may be mad, for what I know, I am sure I'm wretched. For God's sake, for my life and soul's sake, if you love me, write directly hither, or at least to-night to my lodgings, and say what is that *insuperable reason* on which you dwell so much. 'Torture shall not force you to marry me.' Did you not say so? Then you hate me; and what is life worth? Suppose you had not the dear inducement of loving me (*if* you love me! Oh, blot out that *if*), and being adored by me,—still, do you not wish to relieve yourself and me from the parts we act? My soul was not formed for such meannesses. To steal in at the back door, to deceive, to plot, to lie. Perdition! the thought of it makes me despise myself. Your children,—Lord S. (If we have not been ashamed of our conduct, why have we cheated conscience all along by 'He' and 'His,' and 'Old Robin Gray?' Oh! how have we descended, M.!)—Lord S., I say, cannot but provide for your boys. As to your sweet little girl, I will be a father to her, as well as a husband to you. Every farthing I have I will settle on you both. I will—God knows, and you shall find what I will do for you both, when I am able. What would I *not* do! Write, write; I say write. By the living God I will have this *insuperable reason* from you, or I will not believe you love me."

To Mr. H——.

"*A.*, 17 *March*, '76.

"And does my H. think I wanted such a letter as this to finish my affliction? Oh, my dear Jamie, you know not how you distress me. And do you suppose I have *willingly* submitted to the artifices to which I have been obliged, for your sake, to descend? What has been *your* part, from the beginning of the piece, to *mine?* I was obliged to act a part, even to *you*. It was my business not to allow you to see how unhappy the artifices, to which I have submitted, made me. And they did embitter even our happiest moments. But fate stands between us. We are doomed to be wretched. And I, every now and then, think some terrible catastrophe will come of our connexion. 'Some dire event,' as Storgè prophetically says in Jephtha, 'hangs o'er our head'—

'Some woful song we have to sing,
In misery extreme. O never, never
Was my foreboding mind distress'd before
With such incessant pangs!'

"Oh! that it were no crime to quit this world like Faldoni and Teresa! and that we might be happy together in some other world, where gold and silver are unknown! By your hand I could even die with pleasure. I know I could. 'Insuperable reason!' Yes, my H., there is, and you force it from me. Yet better to tell you, than have you doubt my love; 'that love which is now my religion.' Know then, that if you were to marry me, you would marry some hundred pounds' worth of debts! and *that* you never shall do. Do you remember a solemn oath you took in one of your letters, when I was down at H.?

And how you told afterwards it *must* be so, because you had so solemnly sworn it? In the same solemn and dreadful words, I swear that I never will marry you, happy as it would make me, while I owe a shilling in the world. Jephtha's vow is past. What your letter says about my poor children made me weep ; but it shall not make me change my resolution. It is a further reason why I should not. 'If I do not marry you, I do not love you.' Gracious powers of love! Does my H. say so? My *not* marrying you is the strongest proof I can give you of my love. And Heaven, you know, has heard my vow. Do *you* respect it, and never tempt me to break it, for not even *you* will *ever* succeed. Till I have some better portion than debts, I *never* will be yours.

" While you are in Ireland—Yes, my love, in Ireland. Be ruled by me. You shall immediately join your regiment there. You know it is your duty. In the meantime something may happen. Heaven will not desert two faithful hearts that love like yours and mine. There are joys, there is happiness in store for us yet. While you are in Ireland, I'll write to you every post, twice by one post, and I'll think of you, and I'll dream of you, and I'll kiss your picture,—I'll wipe my eyes, and I'll kiss it again, and then I'll weep again. Be a man, join your regiment; and, as sure as I love you (nothing can be more sure), I will recall you from what will be banishment as much to me as to you, the first moment I can marry you with honour to myself, and happiness to you."

To Mr. H. ——

" A. 19 *March,* 1776.

" Why, why do you write to me so often ? Why do you see me so often, when you acknowledge the necessity of complying with my advice ? You tell me, if I bid you you'll go. I have bid you, begged you to go. I *do* bid you go. Go, I conjure you, go ! But let us not have any more partings. The last was too, too much. I did not recover myself all day. And your goodness to my little white haired boy ! He made me burst into tears this morning, by talking of the good natured gentleman, and producing your present.—Either stay, and let our affection discover and ruin us, or go. On the bended knees of love I entreat you, H., my dearest H., to go."

To Miss ——.

" Ireland, 26 *March,* 1776.

"Ireland—England—Good heavens, that M. should be in one part of the world, and her H. in another ; will not our destinies suffer us to breathe the same air ? Mine will not, I most firmly believe, let me rest, till they have hunted me to death.—But I will as you wisely advised, and kindly desire me, write on other subjects."

To Miss ——.

" Ireland, 8 *April,* 1776.

" In the hospitality of this country I was not deceived. They have a curse in their language, strongly descriptive of it—' May the grass grow at your door.' The women, if I knew not you, I should find sensible and pretty. But I am deaf, dumb, and blind, to everything, and to every person but you."

To Miss ——.

Ireland, 3 *May,* 1776.

" My last, I hope, did not offend you. The bank note I was obliged to return ; although I thank you for it, more than words can tell you.—Shall I, whom you will not marry because you will not load me with your debts, increase those debts ; at least prevent you from diminishing them, by robbing you of fifty pounds?—Be not anxious about me, talk not of the postage your dear letters cost me.   Will you refuse to make your H. happy? And think you I can pay too dear for happiness?—But you rave, I am rich—as rich as a Jew; and without taking into calculation the treasure I possess in your love.   Why, you talk of what I allow that relation, poor soul! that does not swallow up all my lands and hereditaments at Gosport.   Then there's my pay, and twenty other ways and means besides, I dare say, could I but recollect them.   Go to — I tell you I am rich.   Why, I can afford to go to plays, I saw Catley last night, in your favourite character.   By the way I'll tell you a story of her when she was on your side of the water.

" Names do not immortalize praiseworthy anecdotes, they immortalize names.   Some difference had arisen between Miss Catley and the managers concerning the terms upon which she was to be engaged for the season.   One of the managers called upon her, at her little lodgings in Drury-lane, to settle it.   The maid was going to show the gentleman up stairs, and to call her mistress.   'No, no,' cries the actress, who was in the kitchen, and heard the manager's voice, ' there's no occasion to show the gentleman to a room. I am busy below (to the manager), making apple-dumplings for my brats.   You know whether you have a mind to give me the money I ask, or not.   I am none of your fine ladies, who get a cold or toothache, and can't sing.   If you have a mind to give me the money, say so; my mouth shall not open for a farthing less.   So good morning to you —and don't keep the girl there in the passage ; for I want her to put the dumplings in the pot, while I nurse the child.'   The turnips of Fabricius, and Andrew Marvel's cold leg of mutton, are worthy to be served up on the same day with Nan Catley's apple-dumplings."

To Miss ——

" *Ireland*, 1 *July*, 1776.

" A friend of mine is going to England—(happy fellow I should think him, to be but in the same country with you)—he will call at the Cannon coffee house for me.   Do send me, thither, the French book you mention, *Werther*.   If you don't, I positively never will forgive you.   Nonsense, to say it will make me unhappy, or that I shan't be able to read it !   Must I pistol myself because a thick-blooded German has been fool enough to set the example, or because a German novelist has feigned such a story ?"

On the 20th of August, Miss Reay writes to Hackman, telling him that *Werther* was "just the only book he should never read."   She then goes on to express great anxiety on account of not having heard from him for some days, conjecturing that he might be ill ; and adding in a sort of postscript a request if her letter should fall into other hands to read than his, that a reply might be instantly returned to her, according to a particular address mentioned.   In fact, he had been unwell, but was nearly quite recovered again, so as to be able to answer her himself.   After a variety of tender sentiments, he went on to relate an anecdote, suggested by the idea of Miss Reay's epistle falling into the hands of strangers.   The anecdote is worth copying out.

" James Hirst, in the year 1711, lived servant with the Hon. Edward Wortley.   It happened, one day, in re-delivering a parcel of letters to his master, by mistake he gave him one which he had written to his sweetheart, and kept back one of Mr. Wortley's. He soon discovered the mistake, and hurried back to his master; but unfortunately for poor James, it happened to be the first which presented itself to Mr. Wortley, and, before James returned, he had given way to a curiosity which led him to open it, and read the love-told story of an enamoured footman.   It was in vain that James begged to have it returned. 'No,' says Mr. Wortley, ' James, you shall be a great man, this letter shall appear in the *Spectator*.' Mr. Wortley communicated the letter to his friend Sir Richard Steel. It was accordingly published in James's own words, and is that letter No. 71, volume the first of the *Spectator*, beginning *Dear Betty*. James found means to remove the unkindness of which he complains in his letter; but alas! before their wishes were completed, a speedy end was put to a passion which would not discredit much superior rank, by the unexpected death of Betty. James, out of the great regard and love he bore to Betty, after her death, married the sister. He died, not many years since, in the neighbourhood of Wortley, near Leeds, Yorkshire. To marry you is the utmost of my wishes; but, remember, I don't engage to marry your sister in case of your death.— Death! How can I think of such a thing, though it be but in joke?"

To Miss ——.

"*Ireland, 6 Feb.,* 1777.

"My last was merry, you know. I can't say so much for your last to-day. You must suffer me to indulge my present turn of mind in transcribing something which was left behind her by a Mrs. Dixon, who poisoned herself not long since at Inniskillen. It was communicated to me by a gentleman, after a dinner yesterday, who is come hither about business, and lives in the neighbourhood of Inniskillen.

" The unhappy woman was not above nineteen years of age. She had been married about two years, and lived with her husband all that time with seeming ease and cheerfulness. She was remarkably cheerful all the fatal day, had company to dine with her, made tea for them, in the evening set them down to cards, retired to her chamber, and drank her cup of arsenic. She left a writing on her table, in which is obscurely hinted the sad circumstance which urged her impatience to this desperate act. Enclosed is an exact copy :—

" 'This is to let all the world know that hears of me, that it is no crime I ever committed occasions this my untimely end ; but despair of ever being happy in this world, as I have sufficient reason to think so. I own 'tis a sinful remedy, and very uncertain to seek happiness, but I hope that God will forgive my poor soul; Lord have mercy on it! But all I beg is to let none reproach my friends with it, or suspect my virtue or my honour in the least, though I am no more. Comfort my poor unhappy mother, and brothers and sisters, and let all mothers take care, and never force a child as mine did me ; but I forgive her, and hopes God will forgive me, as I believe she meant my good by my marriage.—Oh! that unfortunate day I gave my hand to one, whilst my heart was another's, but hoping that time and prudence would at length return my former peace and tranquillity of mind, which I wanted for a long time; but oh! it grieves me to think of the length of eternity ; and the Lord save me from eternal damnation. Let no one blame Martin Dixon, (her husband), for he is in no fault of it. I have a few articles which I have a greater regard for than anything else that's mine, on account of him that gave them to me, but he is not to be mentioned ; and I have some well-wishers that I think proper to give them to.—First, to Betty Balfour, my silver buckles ; to Polly Deeryn, my diamond ring; to Betty Mulligan, my laced suit, cap, handkerchief, and ruffles; to Peggy Delap, a new muslin handkerchief not yet hemmed, which is in my drawer, and hope for my sake those persons will accept of these trifles, as a testimony of my regard for them. I would advise Jack Watson (her brother) to behave in an honest and obedient manner in respect to his mother and family, as he is all she has to depend upon now. I now g in God's name, though against his commands, without wrath or spleen to any one upon earth.   The very person I die for, I love him more than ever, and forgives him. May God grant him more content and happiness than he ever had, and hopes he will forgive me, only to remember such a one died for him.   There was, not long ago, some persons pleased to talk something against my reputation, as to a man in this town ; but now, when I ought to tell the truth, I may be believed ; if ever I knew him, or any other but my husband, may I never enter into glory ; and them I forgive who said so ; but let that man's wife take care of them that told her so ; for they meant her no good by it. With love to one, friendship to few, and goodwill to all the world, I die, saying, ' Lord have mercy on my soul ;' with an advice to all good people never to suffer a passion of any sort to command them as mine did in spite of me.   I pray God bless all my friends and acquaintance, and begs them all to comfort my mother, who is unhappy in having such a child as I, who is ashamed to subscribe myself an unworthy and disgraceful member of the Church of Scotland,   JANE WATSON, otherwise DIXON.'

"My pen shall not interrupt your meditations hereon, by making a single reflection. We both of us have made, I dare say, too many on it.   She too was *Jenny*, and had her Robin Gray."

At length Hackman returned to England.   He found that any preferment in the army was very uncertain and might not at all be realised ; and he determined to turn his thoughts to the church.   In pursuance of this design he made the requisite applications, took orders, and obtained the living of Wiverton, in Norfolk, sometime about the Christmas of 1778.   Shortly before his coming to his native country, Miss Reay had had a serious illness, his arrival in London having taken place about the beginning of May, 1777 ; for we find him writing from Cannon Coffee-house, Charing-cross, 4 May, 1777, in the following terms, to the object of his passion :—

" Did you get the incoherent scrawls I wrote you yesterday and the day before ? Yours I have this moment read and wept over.   Your feeble writing speaks you weaker than you own.   Heavens ! am I come hither only to find I must not see you ?   Better had I stayed in Ireland.   Yet now do I breathe the same air with you. Nothing but your note last night could have prevented me, at all hazards, from forcing my way to your bedside.   In vain did I watch the windows afterwards to gain information from the passing lights, whether you were better or worse."

How or where Mr. Hackman occupied himself during the period that elapsed between the spring of 1777 and that of 1779, we have not particularly ascertained ; but at last we can present one letter of his which will be read with the deepest interest, giving an account as it does of the death of Dr. Dodd, and some touches which have not been generally made public in any report of that unfortunate clergyman's tragic end.

TO MISS ———.

" *Cannon Coffee-house*, 27 *June*, 1777, 5 *o'clock.*

" As I want both appetite and spirits to touch my dinner, though it has been standing before me these ten minutes, I can claim no merit in writing to you.   May you enjoy that pleasure in your delightful situation on the banks of the Thames, which no situation, nothing on earth, can in your absence afford me.   Do you ask me what has lowered my spirits to day ? I'll tell you.   Don't be angry, but I have been to see the last of poor

Dodd. Yes, ' poor Dodd!' though his life was justly forfeited to the laws of his country. The scene was affecting—it was the first of the kind I had ever seen, and shall certainly be the last, though, had I been in England when Peter Toloso was deservedly executed in February, for killing Duarzey, a young Frenchwoman with whom he lived, I believe I should have attended the last moments of a man who could murder the object of his love. For the credit of my country (does he deserve the name of man ?) this man was a Spaniard.

"Do not think I want tenderness, because I was present this morning. Will you allow yourself to want tenderness, because you have been present at Lear's madness, or Ophelia's? Certainly not. Believe me (you *will* believe me, I am sure)—I do not make a profession of it like George S. Your H. is neither *artiste* nor *amateur*; nor do I, like Paoli's friend and historian, hire a window by the year, which looks upon the Grass-market at Edinburgh. Raynall's book you have read and admire. For its humanity it merits admiration. The abbe does not countenance an attendance in scenes of this sort by his writings, but he does by his conduct. And I would sooner take Practice's word than Theory's. Upon my honour Raynall and Charles Fox, notwithstanding the rain, beheld the whole from the top of an unfinished house, close by the stand in which I had a place.

"However meanly Dodd behaved formerly, in throwing the blame of his application to the chancellor on his wife, he certainly died with resolution. More than once to day I have heard that resolution ascribed to his hope that his friend Hawes, the humane founder of the Humane Society, would be able to restore him to life. But I give him more credit. Besides, Voltaire observes that the courage of a dying man is in proportion to the number of those who are present ; and St. Evremond, the friend of the French M.) discovered that *les Anglois surpassent toutes les nations a mourir.* Let me surpass all mankind in happiness, by possessing my *Ninon* for life, and I care not how I die.

"Some little circumstances struck me this morning, which, however you may refuse to forgive me for so spending my morning, I am sure you would not forgive me were I to omit. Before the melancholy procession arrived, a sow was driven into the place left for the sad ceremony, nor could the idea of the approaching scene which had brought the spectators together, prevent too many from laughing, and shouting, and enjoying the animal's distress, as if they had only come to Tyburn to see a sow baited.

"After the arrival of the procession, the preparation of the unhappy victim mixed something disagreeably ludicrous with the solemnity. The tenderest could not but feel it, though they might be sorry they did feel it. The poor man's wig was to be taken off, and the nightcap brought for the purpose was too little, and could not be pulled on without force. Valets de chambre are the greatest enemies to heroes. Every guinea in my pocket would I have given, that he had not worn a wig, or that (wearing one) the cap had been bigger.

"At last arrived the moment of death. The driving away of the cart was accompanied with a noise which best explained the feelings of the spectators for the sufferer. Did you never observe at the sight or the relation of anything shocking, that you closed your teeth hard, and drew in your breath hard through them, so as to make a sort of hissing sound ? This was done so universally at the fatal moment, that I am persuaded the noise might have been heard at a considerable distance. For my own part, I detected myself, in a certain manner, accompanying his body with the motion of my own ; as you have seen people writhing and twisting and biassing themselves, after a bowl which they have just delivered.

" Not all the resuscitating powers of Mr. Hawes, I fear, can have any effect; it was so long before the mob would suffer the hearse to drive away with the body.

" Thus ended the life of Dr. Dodd. How shocking that a man with whom I have eaten and drunk, should leave the world in such a manner! A manner which, from familiarity, has almost ceased to shock us, except when our attention is called to a Perreau or a Dodd. How many men, how many women, how many young, and, as they fancy, tender females, with all their sensibilities about them, hear the sounds by which at this moment I am disturbed, with as much indifference as they hear muffins and matches cried along the streets. *The last dying speech and confession, birth, parentage, and education·* Familiarity has even annexed a kind of humour to the cry. We forget that it always announces the death (and what a death!) of one fellow-being; sometimes of half a dozen, or even *more.*

" A lady talks with greater concern of cattle-day than of hanging-day. And her maid contemplates the mournful engraving at the top of a dying speech, with more indifference than she regards the honest tar hugging his sweetheart at the top of ' Black-eyed Susan.' All that strikes us is the ridiculous tone in which the halfpenny ballad singer chaunts the requiem. We little recollect that, while we are smiling at the voice of the charmer, wives or husbands (charm ye never so wisely), children, parents, and friends,—perhaps all these, and more than these,—as pure from crimes as we, and purer still, perhaps,— are weeping over the crime and punishment of the darling and support of their lives. Still less do we at the moment—(for the printer always gets the start of the hangman, and many a man has bought his own dying speech on his return to Newgate by virtue of a reprieve)—still less do we ask ourselves, whether the wretch, who, at the moment we hear this (which ought to strike us as an awful sound), finds the halter of death about his neck, and now takes the longing farewell, and now hears the horses whipped and encouraged to draw from under him for ever the cart which he now feels depart from his lingering feet—whether this wretch really deserved to die more than we. Alas! were no spectators to attend executions but those who deserve to live, Tyburn would be honoured with much thinner congregations."

Very much of the correspondence between Mr. Hackman and Miss Reay, so far as we know, does not exist; and even of that which is extant, we only present portions. We shall introduce only two more letters from the infatuated man and the object of his passion; the second being, as we have met with it, without a date, although it manifestly belongs to a period that approached very closely upon the *denouement* of the strange drama.

To Miss ——.

" 1 *March,* 1779.

" Though we meet to-morrow, I must write you two words to-night, just to say that I have all the hopes in the world, ten days at the utmost will complete the business. When that is done, your only objection is removed along with your debts; and we may, surely, then be happy, and be so *soon.* In a month, or *six weeks at farthest,* from this time, I might certainly call you mine. Only remember that my *character* now that I have taken orders makes expedition necessary. By to-night's post I shall write into Norfolk about the alterations at our parsonage. G.'s friendship is more than I can ever return."

" My dearest life!—I never think of you but with a pleasing pain, the consequence of that love, of which, I hope, I have given you every proof in my power. I never bring you to my recollection (which I almost continually do), but with inexpressible anxiety; for, while I know you are not wholly mine, so great is my misery that I cannot express it; which, added to the difficulty in which, at best, we have accomplished our meetings at Marylebone and other places, and the obstacle of Lord S—— between us, almost distracts me. You know my sufferings on your account are far from trifling. When, therefore, will you relieve them, and make that time happy which you only have hitherto rendered irksome and anxious to me? Having quitted the army by your advice, I am now wedded to the church, have lately been presented to a living in Norfolk, and require nothing now to complete my happiness, but to be wedded to you. In your own dear words, let us now be one. I know you have children, and I love them, because you are their mother. As the youngest is your particular favourite, and indulged with maternal fondness, I shall rejoice to have it with me when we are married. I know you are not fond of the follies and vanities of the town. How tranquil and agreeably, and with what uninterrupted felicity, unlike to anything we have yet enjoyed, shall we then wear our time away together on my living, and my estate at Gosport! We shall have near £200 a year from the one, and £100 a year from the other, which will be enough for us in a country life. And by all the vows you have made me, and by that stolen bliss we have known, I do now assure you, that dear as you are to me, and although parent of several children by Lord S——, if you are faithless enough to forsake me, and not embrace my offer, you'll feel for the despair it may occasion, when, perhaps, it will not be in my power to repeat that offer to you. O! thou dearer to me than life, because that life is thine! think of me and pity me. I have long been devoted to you; and yours, as I am, I hope either to die, or soon to be yours in marriage. For God's sake let me hear from you; and, as you love me, keep me no longer in suspense, since nothing can relieve me but death or you. Adieu!   " Your most humble and affectionate servant."

On his return from Ireland to London, Mr. Hackman had found Miss Reay confidentially connected with Signora Galli, an Italian singer, who had been engaged by Lord Sandwich to teach her in vocal music. She had come now to be very closely watched by his lordship, so that her passionate lover's access to her was difficult and dangerous. He had therefore to compass their meetings at great inconvenience and risk, through Signora Galli's means. This female, however, at length,—whether under the management and direction of the earl, or otherwise, we do not know,—announced to Hackman that all future intercourse with Miss Reay must be dispensed with, for that Lord Sandwich was resolved to bear with the clandestine amour no longer, and that indeed it would prove ruinous to the lady who was the object of it. In short, it was told to the passionate lover that she was tired of him, it being intimated, or insinuated at the same time, that she had given him up for the sake of another gentleman who had grown more dear to her, and who would in every respect be a preferable match.

Agitated by this sort of language, and the interruption he met with to his meeting Miss Reay as he before had done, the conflict of Mr. Hackman's mind was so great as not to escape the notice of his acquaintances. He became an altered man. While in the army, he was agreeable, affable, and sprightly; but on a sudden he now grew pensive, melancholy, and moody; the change, however, being to some extent accounted for, on the part of his friends, by his having made choice of a new and grave profession. Meanwhile his melancholy increased, being in reality attributable to his misery. He ceased not to brood on the altered, or supposed to be altered, state of the lady's feelings towards him; his condition was reaching to desperation; and had it been known to what a depth his wretchedness had sunk, and to what dreadful imaginations he was giving way, assuredly it would have been wise to guard him as an insane or frantic being. On the 20th of March, 1779, he thus wrote to a gentleman whom we find addressed as "Charles ————, Esq." :—

"Your coming to town, my dear friend, will answer no end. G. has been such a friend to me, it is not possible to doubt her information. What interest has she to serve? Certainly none. Look over the letters, with which I have so pestered you for these two years, about this business. Look at what I have written to you about G. since I returned from Ireland. She can only mean well to me. Be not apprehensive, your friend will take no step to disgrace himself. What I shall do I know not. Without her I do not think I can exist; yet I will be, you shall see, a *man*, as well as a lover. Should there be a rival, and should he merit chastisement, I know you'll be my friend. But I'll have ocular proof of everything before I believe.   " Yours ever."

To the Same.

"6 *April*, 1779.

"It signifies not; your reasoning I admit. Despair goads me on. Death can only relieve me. By what I wrote yesterday, you must see my resolution was taken. Often have I made use of my key to let myself into the A., that I might die at her feet. She gave it me as the key of love. Little did she think it would ever prove the key of death. But the loss of Lady H. keeps Lord S. within.

"My dear Charles, is it possible for me to doubt G.'s information? Even you were staggered by the account I gave you of what passed between us in the park. What then have I to do, who only lived when she loved me, but to cease to live now that she ceases to love? The propriety of suicide, its cowardice, its crime—I have nothing to do with them. All I pretend to prove or disprove is my misery, and the possibility of my existing under it. Enclosed are the last dying words and confession of poor Captain J., who destroyed himself not long ago. But these lines are not the things which have determined me. There are many defects in the reasoning of them, though none in the poetry. His motives are not mine, nor are his principles mine. His ills I could have borne. He told me of his inducements, poor fellow! But I refused to allow them. Little did I imagine that I should ever have inducements, as I now have, which I *must* allow. These extraordinary lines are said to be his; yet, from what I know of him, I am slow to believe it. They strike me as the production of abilities far superior to his; of abilities sent into the world for some particular purpose, and which Providence would not suffer to quit the world in such a manner.

"Till within this month, till G.'s information, I thought of self-murder as you think of it. But now nothing is left for me but to leap the world to come. If it be a crime, as I too much fear, and we are accountable for our passions, I must stand the trial and the punishment. My invention can paint no punishment equal to what I suffer here.

"Think of those passions, my friend,—those passions of which you have so often since I knew Miss ————, spoken to me and written to me. If you will not let me fly from misery, will you not let me fly from my passions? They are a pack of bloodhounds which will inevitably tear me to pieces. My carelessness has suffered them to overtake me, and now there is no possibility but this, of escaping them. The hand of nature heaped up every kind of combustible in my bosom. The torch of love has set the heap on fire. I must perish in the flames. At first I might perhaps have extinguished them, —now they rage too fiercely. If they can be smothered, they can never be got under. Suppose they should consume any other person besides myself! At present I am innocent."

It was next evening that Mr. Hackman wrote the following letter, addressed to his brother-in-law :—

"When this reaches you I shall be no more, but do not let my unhappy fate distress you too much. I have strove against it as long as possible, but it now overpowers me. You know where my affections were placed; my having by some means or other lost hers, (an idea which I could not support,) has driven me to madness. The world will condemn me, but your heart will pity me. God bless you, my dear Fred.; would I had a sum to leave you, to convince you of my great regard. You were my only friend. I have hid one circumstance from you which gives me great pain: I owe Mr. Wright, of Gosport, one hundred pounds, for which he has the writings of my houses; but I hope in God when they are sold, and all other matters collected, there will be nearly enough to settle our account. May Almighty God bless you and yours with comfort and happiness, and may you ever be a stranger to the pangs I now feel. May heaven protect my beloved woman, and forgive this act which alone could relieve me from a world of misery I have long endured. Oh! if it should be in your power to do her any act of friendship, remember your faithful friend, J. HACKMAN."

On the morning of the 17th of April, the unhappy writer of these latter epistles sat for a considerable time in his closet, reading "Blair's Sermons." In the afternoon he dined with his sister and brother-in-law, who had been married only five weeks. When he left their company, he promised to return to supper. He first went to the Admiralty after he had left his sister, where Lord Sandwich resided; and there seeing his lordship's carriage, he concluded that Miss Reay was going out in it, and would probably call on Signora Galli, at her lodgings in the Haymarket. To be satisfied herein, he walked up to the Cannon Coffee-house, Charing-cross, where he expected to see the lady pass, as she very soon did. He followed the carriage till it drove to Covent-garden theatre, where Miss Reay and Signora Galli alighted. He went into the theatre after them; and ere long observed a gentleman of handsome and elegant appearance, who, as afterwards came to light, was Lord Coleraine, speak to Miss Reay. The agitated lover instantly concluded that this was the person who now monopolised her affections, agreeably to the previous information of Signora Galli. No further evidence of infidelity was sought for; the maddened lover quitted the theatre, and furnished himself with a brace of pistols, resolved to fall by his own hands, and this too in the presence of the woman who had brought him to misery and despair. He returned to the theatre, with his weapons loaded, and when the play was over, he followed the object of his love and rage, in company with Signora Galli and Lord Coleraine, whom he had taken for his rival, into the lobby of the house, where he intended, and endeavoured to shoot himself; but the crowd preventing him, he kept Miss Reay in view, until she was under the piazza, in the way to her coach, which was called for by the name of Lady Sandwich's coach. Here he a second time attempted to kill himself, but a chairman running suddenly against him, nearly pushing him down, again balked his suicidal purpose. He recovered himself, and pursued Miss Reay to the door of the coach, in which Signora Galli was already seated. It was not, he afterwards persisted in declaring, till he had beheld her face at this instant, that he thought of murdering her; but all at once, alas! he said to himself it would be best for both to die together. He therefore took a pistol in each hand, although he had at first intended to use the second only against himself, if the other failed to take effect, and stepping between the ill-fated lady and her carriage, she being on his right hand,—she had accepted another gentleman's arm by this time, a Mr. Macnamara of Lincoln's Inn,— he discharged his right hand weapon at her first, and immediately after the left hand one at himself. Miss Reay was killed on the spot, the bullet having passed through her head; Hackman was only wounded and not mortally. He, however, fell; when, so fully bent was he on destroying himself, that he beat his head with the pistol, calling out, " kill me! kill me!"

The murdered lady's remains were then taken to the Shakspeare Tavern and her murderer also, the corpse having been deposited in a separate room. While the surgeons were dressing his wounds he inquired after her, and being told he had killed her, he would not believe it, saying, he was sure she was living, for that he only intended to destroy himself. —He freely gave his name, and who he was; and on being committed to prison, where he at length became in some measure composed, he failed not to reflect properly upon what he had done,—considering and contemplating not only the enormity of having made an attempt upon his own life, but of having robbed the being who was still far dearer to him of her existence.

During this most miserable man's confinement in Newgate, he was wonderfully tranquil for a person in his condition, yet always speaking of Miss Reay with rapture. He said often to his friends and relations who visited him, that life, since she was gone, would be to him a real punishment, and that death could only relieve him from a world in which he should consider himself lost, since the only object that was dear to him was out of it, and whom he was thwarted from wholly possessing when in it. To live, he declared, would be to him a living death; for which reason he proposed to plead guilty to the indictment that was to be preferred against him. When, however, he was asked whether he murdered Miss Reay with malice aforethought, and was told that the exact truth could only be made public by means of a regular trial and a statement in court of all the evidence for as well as against him, he consented to put himself on God and his country. At the same time he was resigned to the idea of being condemned to suffer, and so satisfied with the thought of dying, that before he was arraigned at the bar of the Old Bailey, he sent to the under- taker who buried Miss Reay, and after ascertaining that she had been decently interred, expressed his hope and desire soon to be laid near her, as a corpse, for that his life was hers, and the laws of the country demanded it from him.

In this manner he conducted himself, impatient to depart, and composed for encountering death, being only disturbed as concerned the present life, on account of a mother and sister, whom he knew he had plunged into misery; but otherwise declaring he was happier than for a long time he had been. Accordingly this poor morally diseased man, while striving to mitigate the anguish of others, proceeded calmly to prepare himself for meet- ing his judge and jury, void of every wish or hope of acquittal.

On the morning of his trial, he eat a hearty breakfast, his brother-in-law and some friends being with him. He was much agitated on his arraignment; but although wholly overcome by his feelings while the witnesses against him were giving their evidence of the deed he deplored—sighing and weeping in the most heart-rending manner,—his de- portment became noble, gaining him the admiration of the court, before the trial closed. The evidence for the prosecution having been gone through, he was asked whether he had anything to say in his defence. He now rose from the chair with which he had been indulged; he wiped away his tears, and after a deep sigh of such heavy woe as almost shook the court-room, he delivered the following speech with that power of expression, in a sonorous, although faltering voice, which wonderfully became him at the moment.

"My lord and gentlemen of the jury," said he, "I should not have troubled the court with an examination of witnesses to support the charge against me, had I not thought that pleading guilty to the indictment would give an indication of contemning death, not suitable to my present condition, and would, in some measure, make me accessory to a second peril of my life; and I likewise think that the justice of my country ought to be satisfied, by suffering my offence to be proved, and the fact to be established by evidence.

"I stand here this day the most wretched of human beings; I confess myself criminal in a high degree. Yet while I acknowledge with shame and repentance that my determination against my own life was formal and complete, I protest with the regard to truth which becomes my situation, that the will to destroy her who was ever dearer to me than life, was never mine till a momentary frenzy overcame me, and induced me to commit the deed I now deplore. The letter which I meant for my brother-in-law after my decease will have its due weight as to this point with good men.

"Before this dreadful act, I trust nothing will be found in the tenor of my life, which the common charity of mankind will not excuse. I have no wish to avoid the punishment which the laws of my country appoint for my crime; but being already too unhappy to feel a punishment in death or a satisfaction in life, I submit myself with penitence and patience to the disposal and judgment of the Almighty God, and to the consequences of this inquiry into my conduct and intentions."

This speech—not a question of it—was the transcript of the speaker's heart, and no wonder that it melted his auditory into sorrow and compassion. A brilliant and crowded assembly was deeply affected, even the members of the court participating in the emotions. —The letter which the prisoner referred to was then read, being the same that we have already presented, as having been written and intended for his brother-in-law on the evening of the day Mr. Hackman last dined with that gentleman at his private residence, which went to show that the writer had at the time he penned it, no forethought intent to destroy her who so shortly afterwards became his victim.—The jury had a plain and simple duty to perform, and accordingly they returned a verdict of guilty without quitting the box. The judge, Sir Wm. Blackstone, who in his summing up to the jury had complimented the prisoner's speech, then passed the awful sentence of the law; after which the prisoner, who had listened to his doom with resignation, was conveyed to his cell, where he employed the very short time then allowed murderers after conviction, in writing, and in repentance and prayer.—We now return to his letters and certain *notanda*, beginning with several that were penned almost immediately after the death of Miss Reay, but before the occurrence of the trial.

To CHARLES ———, ESQ.

"*Tothill-fields, 8th April.*

"I am alive, and she is dead; I shot her, and not myself. Some of her blood and brains is still upon my clothes. I don't ask you to speak to me—I don't ask you to look at me, only come hither, and bring me a little strong poison; such as is strong enough. Upon my knees I beg, if your friendship for me was sincere, do, *do*, bring me some poison."

To the Same.

"9th April.

"Your note just now, and the long letter I received the same time, which should have found me the day before yesterday, have changed my resolution. The promise you desire I most solemnly give you. I will make no attempt upon my life. Had I received your comfortable letter when you meant I should, I verily do think this would not have happened. Pardon what I wrote to you about the poison. Indeed, I am too composed for any such thing now. Nothing should tempt me. My death is all the recompense I can make to the laws of my country. Dr. V. has sent me some excellent advice, and Mr. H. has refuted all my false arguments. Even such a thing as I finds friends. Oh, that my feelings and his feeling would let me see my *dearest* friend. Then I would tell you how this happened."

To the Same.

"Newgate, 14th April.

"My best thanks for all your goodness since this day se'nnight. Oh! Charles, this is about the time. I cannot write."

What now follows was written after the unhappy man's conviction, the first letter being from Lord Sandwich, and occupied with a generous and noble intent.

"To Mr. Hackman, in Newgate.

"17th April, '79.

"If the murderer of Miss —— wishes to live, the man he has most injured will use his interest to procure his life."

"The Condemned Cell in Newgate, 17 April, 1779.

"The murderer of her whom he preferred, far preferred, to life, suspects the hand from which he has just received such an offer as he neither desires nor deserves. His wishes are for death, not for life. One wish he has. Could he be pardoned in this world by the man he has most injured—oh, my lord, when I meet her in another world, enable me to tell her (if departed spirits are not ignorant of earthly things) that you forgive us both, that you will be a father to her dear infants."

To Charles ——, Esq.

"Newgate, Saturday Night, 17th April, '79.

"My dear Charles—The clock has just struck eleven. All for some time has been quiet within this sad abode. Would that all were so within my sadder bosom! That gloominess of my favourite, Young's *Night Thoughts*, which was always so congenial to my soul, would have been still heightened, had he ever been wretched enough to hear St. Paul's clock thunder through the still ear of night, in the condemned walls of Newgate. The sound is truly solemn—it seems the sound of death. Oh that it were death's sound! How greedily would my ears devour it! And yet—but one day more. Rest, rest, perturbed spirit, till then. And then—

"My God, my Creator, my first Father! Thou who madest me as I am, with these feelings, these passions, this heart! Thou who art all might and all mercy! Well thou knowest that I did not, like too many of Thy creatures, persuade myself there was no God, before I persuaded myself I had a right over any life. O then, my Father, put me not eternally from Thy paternal presence! It is not punishments, nor pains, nor hells I fear: what man can bear I can. My fear is to be deemed ungrateful to Thy goodness, to be thought unworthy Thy presence, to be driven from the light of Thy countenance. Well thou knowest I could not brook the thoughts of wanting gratitude to things beneath me in Thy creation—to a dog, a horse; almost to things inanimate—a tree, a book. And thinkest thou that I could bear the charge of want of gratitude to Thee?

"And might—O might I resign the joys of the other world, which neither eye can see, nor tongue can speak, nor imagination dream, for an eternal existence of love and bliss with her, whom——Presumptuous murderer! the bliss you ask were paradise. My Father, who art in Heaven, I bow before Thy mercy, and patiently abide my sentence."

The poor maniac, at least in the matter of his passionate love for the murdered frail one, was certainly not well fitted for the office of that ministry, an important branch of whose office is that of directing and consoling the dying. And yet how affecting the outpourings of his labouring breast. We proceed to those *notanda* to which reference has already been made, and which he himself thus prefaced :—

"These papers, which will be delivered to you after my death, my dear friend, are not letters; nor know I what to call them. They, will exhibit, however, the picture of a heart which has ever been yours more than any other man's."

And what a striking and moving picture it is, interesting in the deepest manner one's heart in relation to the woe-worn writer.

"How have I seen," says he, to proceed in the order that he has himself recorded his sentiments and emotions when on the verge of the grave—when, as it were, at the foot of the fatal tree! "how have I seen the poor soul affected at that recitative of Iphis in her favourite Jephtha!

"' Ye sacred priests, whose hands ne'er yet were stained
With human blood!'

"To think that I should be her priest, her murderer! In one of her letters she tells me, I recollect, that she could die with pleasure by my hand, she is sure she could. Poor soul! little did she think—

"It is odd, but I know for a certainty that this recitative, and the air which follows it, 'Farewell,' &c., were the last words she ever sung. Now I say, and may say experimentally,—

"' Farewell, thou busy world, where reign
Short hours of joy, and years of pain!'

"I *may* not add,

"' Brighter scenes I seek above,
In the realms of peace and love.'

"Love! gracious God, this word in this place, at this time! Oh!"

"*Newgate, Sunday,* 18th *April,* 4 *in the morning.*

"Oh, Charles, Charles—torments, tortures! Hell, and worse than hell!

"When I had finished my last scrap of paper, I thought I felt myself composed, resigned. Indeed I was so—I am so now. I threw my wearied body—wearied, heaven knows, more than any labourer's, with the workings of my mind—upon the floor of my dungeon. Sleep came uncalled, but only came to make me more completely cursed. This world was gone, the next was come; but after that, no other world. All was revealed to me. My eternal sentence of mental misery (from which there was no flight), of banishment from the presence of my Father, of more than poetry e'er feigned or weakness feared was past, irrevocably past. Her verdict, too, of punishment, was pronounced. Charles! she—yes, she was punished; and by whose means punished? Even in her angel mind were failings, which it is not wonderful I never saw, since Omniscience, it seemed, could hardly discern them. O Charles, these foibles, so few, so undiscernable, were still, I thought in my dream, to be expiated; for my hand sent her to heaven before her time, with all her few follies on her head. Charles, I saw the expiation; these eyes beheld her undergo the heavenly punishment. That passed; she was called, I thought, to the reward of her ten thousand virtues. Then, in very deed, I began my hell, my worse than ever woman dreamed of hell. Charles, I saw her, as plainly as I see the bars of my dungeon, through which the eye of the day looks upon me now, for almost the last time. Her face, her person, were still more divine than when on earth,—they were cast anew in angel moulds. Her mind, too, I beheld as plainly as her face; and all its features. That was the same—that was not capable of alteration for the better. But what saw I else? That mind, that person, that face, that angel was in the bosom of another angel. Between us was a gulph—a gulph impassable! I could not go to her, neither could she come to me. No; nor did she wish. There was the curse. Charles, she saw me, where I was, steeped to the lip in misery. She saw me, but without a tear, without one sigh. One sigh from her, I thought, and I could have borne all my sufferings. A sigh, a tear! But no; she smiled at all my sufferings. Yes, she, even she enjoyed the tortures, the rackings of my soul. She bade her companion angel, too, enjoy them. She seemed to feast on my griefs, and only turned away her more than damning eyes, to turn them on her more than blest companion. Flames and brimstone—corporal sufferance—were paradise to such eternal mental hell as this. Oh! how I rejoiced, how I wept, sobbed with joy, when I awoke, and discovered it was only a dream, and found myself *in the condemned cell of Newgate!* "

"*Newgate, Sunday, 18th April, '79, 5 o'clock in the afternoon.*

"Since I wrote to you this morning I have more than once taken up my pen; for what can I do, which affords me more pleasure than writing to such a friend as you are, and have been to me? *Pleasure!* Alas! what business has such a wretch as I with such a word as that? However, pouring myself out to you thus upon paper is, in some measure, drawing off my sorrows. It is not thinking.—Cruel G.! and yet I can excuse her. She knew not of what materials I was made. Lord S. wished to procure a treasure which any one would have prized. G. was employed to preserve the treasure; and she suspected not that my soul, my existence, were wrapped up in it.

"Oh, my dear Charles, that you could prevail upon yourself to visit this sad place! And yet our mutual feelings would render the visit useless. So it is better thus. Now, perhaps you are enjoying a comfortable and happy meal. There, again, my misfortunes! Of happiness and comfort, for the present, I have robbed you. H. has murdered happiness. But this is the hour of dinner. How many are now comfortable and happy! while I ———. How many, again, with everything to make them otherwise, are, at this moment, miserable!—The meat is done too little, or too much———. (Should the pen of fancy ever take the trouble to invent letters for me, I should not be suffered to write to you thus, because it would seem *unnatural.* Alas! they know not how gladly a wretch like me forgets himself.)—The servant, I say, has broken something; some *friend* (as the phrase is) does not make his promised appearance, and consequently is not eye-witness of the unnecessary dishes which the family pretends to be able to afford; or some *friend* (again) drops in unexpectedly, and surprises the family with no more dishes on the table than are necessary.

"Ye home-made wretches, ye ingenious inventors of ills, before ye suffer yourselves to be soured and made miserable, for the whole remainder of this Sunday, by some trifle or another, which does not deserve the name of accident, look here, behold, indeed, that misery of which your discontentedness complains!

"Peep through the grate of this my only habitation, ye who have town-houses and country-houses. Look into my soul; recollect in how few hours I am to die—die in what manner—die for what offence!

"Now go,—be cross, and quarrel with your wives and husbands, or your children, or your guests; begin to curse and to swear, and call Almighty God to witness that you are the most miserable, unlucky wretches upon the face of the earth, because the meat is roasted half a dozen turns too much, or because your cooks have not put enough seasoning in your pies.

"I was obliged to lay down my pen; such a picture as this, in which I myself made the principal figure, was rather too much. Good God! to look back over the dreadful interval between to-day and last October two years. What a tale would it make of woe! Take warning from me, my fellow-creatures, and do not love like H.

"*Still Sunday, 7 o'Clock.*

"When these loose, incoherent papers come into your hands after my death, it will afford you some consolation to know my temper of mind at last. Charles, as the awful moment approaches, I feel myself more and more, and more composed, and calm, and resigned. It always, you know, was my opinion, that man could bear a great load of affliction better than a small one. I thought so then, now I am sure of it. This day sennight I was mad, perfectly mad. This afternoon I am all mildness. This day sennight! To look back is death—is hell. 'Tis almost worse than to look forward.

"Let me endeavour to get out of myself.

"In proof of that opinion which you always ridiculed—go to the gaming-table—observe that adventurer, who has come with the last fifty he can scrape together. See, how he gnashes his teeth, bites his fists, and works all his limbs. He has lost the last throw—his fifty are reduced to forty. Observe him now—with what composure his arms are wrapped about him. What a smooth calm has suddenly succeeded to that dreadful storm which so lately tore up his whole countenance! Whence the reason think you? Has fortune smiled on him? Directly the contrary. His forty are now dwindled to five. His all, nay more, his very existence, his resolution to live or die, depend upon this throw. Mark him—how calmly, how carelessly he eyes the box. I am not sure he does not almost wish to lose, that he may defy ill-luck, and tell her she has done her worst. See

> "'On a moment's point, th' important die
> Of life and death spins doubtful ere it falls,
> And turns up—death.'

"I'll surrender my opinion for untenable, if a common observer, from his countenance, would not rather point him out as the winner, than the agitated person yonder who really has

"Since I wrote what you last read, I caught myself marching up and down my cell with the step of haughtiness; hugging myself in my two arms, and muttering between my grating teeth, '*What a complete wretch I am!*'

"But I can now no longer fly from myself. In a few short hours the hand which is now writing to you, the hand which————

"I will not distress either you or myself. My life I owe to the laws of my country, and I will pay the debt. How I felt for poor Dodd! Well—you shall hear that I died like a man and a Christian. I cannot have a better trust than in the mercy of an All-just God. And, in your letters, when you shall these unhappy deeds relate, tell of me as I am. I forget the passage, 'tis in Othello.

"You must suffer me to mention the tenderness and greatness of mind of my dear B. The last moments of my life cannot be better spent than in recording this complicated act of friendship and humanity :—When we parted, a task too much for us both, he asked me if there was anything for which I wished to live. Upon his pressing me, I acknowledged I was uneasy, very uneasy, lest Lord S. might withdraw an allowance of fifty pounds a year, which I knew he made to her father. 'Then,' said B., squeezing my hands, bursting into tears, and hurrying out of the room, 'I will allow it him.' The affectionate manner in which he spoke of my S. would have charmed you. God for ever bless, bless and prosper him! and my S. and you, and————"(B. was Mr. Booth, Hackman's brother-in-law, and S. his sister.)

The note which follows, was written with a pencil. All that was legible is here preserved, though the sense is incomplete.

"*Tyburn.*

"My Dear Charles,—Farewell for ever in this world; I die a sincere Christian, and penitent, and everything, I hope, that you can wish me. Would it prevent my example's having any bad effect if the world should know how I abhor my former ideas of suicide, my crime, ... will be the best. Of her fame I charge you to be careful. My poor S. will . . . .   Your dying H."

During the procession to Tyburn the wretched man was much affected, and said but little. When he arrived at the fatal spot, and got out of the coach which had been provided for him, and mounted the cart, he took leave of Dr. Porter and the Ordinary in the most affectionate manner. Upon the whole, on the day of his death, his behaviour was composed and firm; he seemed to look upon his departure as welcome, and with pious resignation; or, at least, as of one who had survived everything that was worth living for, since the woman he adored to a degree of rage, despair, and madness, was dead. He was executed the 19th of April, 1779.

Executed! Sanguinary truly was the English criminal code. Surely some other course might well have been taken with this wretched man. Who can regard him as other than a maniac in the matter of his love? The very manner in which he occupied himself after his condemnation, and the things about which he continued to write, show that his mind was greatly unhinged.

XVII.—NICOL MUSCHET.

EVERY one will remember the introduction of the name of Nicol Muschet into the story of the Heart of Mid-Lothian, by the Great Northern Wizard, in connexion with a cairn, or rude pile of stones, situated near the foot of the Duke's Walk, within the King's Park, and no great distance from the palace of Holyrood House. Madge Wildfire, one of the characters of that beautiful tale, declares herself to have often held moonlight communion on that spot with the

shades of Nicol Muschet and his wife, who, though not buried there, had their earthly
fortunes lamentedly interwoven with the scene. To record the whole details of the career
of these persons, which used to form an Edinburgh fire-side story, would be almost an
outrage on good feeling, but the outline of the tragedy may be fitly presented to our
readers.

Nicol Muschet was the son of Mr. Muschet of Boghall, a small landed proprietor, and
was born at the close of the 17th century. The father of Nicol died when the lad was in
his boyhood, and left him under the charge of his mother, a woman of piety and virtue.
She gave her son a liberal collegiate education, and placed him under the care of Thomas
Napier, surgeon in Alloa, with the view of the young man being brought up to that profession. But after a time, Nicol returned to his mother's house, having found that the
Alloa surgeon had little or no business. In the year 1718, hearing of a dissection in
Edinburgh, a rare thing, seemingly, in that day, the young man went thither, and took
up his residence in the capital from that time. He appears to have engaged himself to
attend on a shop, but to have paid little attention to it, having fallen into the company of
loose-living young people. Whether of his own right, or through his mother's consent
and indulgence, he was liberally supplied with money, and this seems to have been one
of the chief causes of the youth's unhappy fate.

"One day," Nicol Muschet relates in his confession, "in the month of August, 1719,
accidentally walking to the Castle Hill, I saw a maid (servant) at the door of Adam Hall,
whom I never knew before, nor any pertaining to him. This maid shortly before had kept
a cellar near to the shop which I was in, and she, being acquaint with me, asked if I
would give her a choppin of ale? Which I granted; and when she and I had discoursed
some time, Adam Hall's daughter came to us; and the maid said, she, being throng
(busy), behoved to leave me, but that this young lady would willingly entertain me."
This was Muschet's first introduction to the daughter of Adam Hall, vintner on the Castle
Hill. Being at the period in want of lodgings, Muschet was directed by the young
woman Hall to the house of a friend of hers in the Anchor Close. Here he accordingly
took up his abode, and here Margaret Hall often visited him, under the plea of calling
on the landlady. Nicol Muschet declares that he never loved the girl, that he was
ashamed of her visits, and that he had heard unfavourable stories of her. But he did not
change his lodging, or go out of the way of her pursuit, while it was plain that Muschet's
fortune had led the Halls and their friends to look upon him as a most desirable match.
Out of simplicity, he says, and urged by Archibold Ure, goldsmith, an acquaintance of both
himself and the Halls, Nicol Muschet was finally married to the young woman Hall on
5th of September, after a three weeks' acquaintance between the parties.

The nuptials were scarcely solemnized, when the young husband repented of the contract.
but he stayed, nevertheless, till some time in November, in the house of his wife's father,
Nicol Muschet then went to the country, and there procured money and letters of recom-
mendation, with the view of going abroad to perfect himself as a surgeon. After returning to town, he met one James Campbell, formerly farmer in Burnbank, who suggested to
Muschet the possibility of getting rid of his wife by divorce. This was the first scheme
which Nicol Muschet entertained against his wife, and he was to give Campbell £50
sterling when that person could bring against the young wife evidence of infidelity
sufficient to authorise a separation. By introducing hired wretches to her company, and
drugging her liquor with laudanum, Campbell and his employer endeavoured, but in
vain, to accomplish their object. Then, moving onwards in villany, they thought of

cutting her off by poison, and with the assistance of James Muschet, periwig-maker, and his wife Grizzel, they contrived to give her corrosive sublimate in some sugar, which they mixed with brandy and hot water. This only caused severe vomitings and great suffering, however, which so little moved the heart of Nicol Muschet, that he gave her another dose of the same kind of poison, by means of a nutmeg-grater, into which he had introduced it. A third and a fourth time they repeated the dose, but the poor woman's constitution carried her through all these murderous efforts, without the loss of life, though at the expense of great torment.

Being continually supplied with money by Nicol Muschet, Campbell and James Muschet suggested plan after plan for despatching the unfortunate creature who was the object of the horrid conspiracy. It appeared, indeed, to have become the subject of daily and hourly deliberation between these callous villains. When poisoning failed, it was proposed to carry the unfortunate wife " to Leith, and to drink there till very late, and on their way home to drown her in a pond." This plan not seeming practicable, James Muschet said, "that he would, on pretence of kindness, take her to the west country with him on horseback, and have her pad so slackly tied, that he might easily throw her off in Kirk-liston water, by his checking the horse, which he was to do after much rain, so that the water might be big enough to carry her off." This scheme was also too difficult and too much dependent on chance to be long thought of, and it was finally resolved to " knock her on the head." The instrument selected for the purpose was a heavy hammer, and James Muschet was to use this for the reward of twenty guineas. The wife of James Muschet, as eager in the plot as her husband, agreed to keep Nicol's wife in her room in St. Mary's Wynd to a late hour, that James Muschet might have an opportunity of committing the murderous deed at the head of Dickson's Close, which his victim was to pass through on her way to her own house. " James Muschet and his wife were very careful for a while in observing all the foresaid proposals to get the design accomplished, always making it their business to invite her (the victim) to their room, and that never sooner than eight o'clock at night, lest she, coming too soon, might weary—and to keep her as late as possible; but always when he followed to give her the stroke in the dark close, somebody going up or down prevented him."

This barbarous design, so perseveringly and remorselessly followed up, was at length accomplished, yet that, in a measure, in an accidental way; in a way, at least, different from any that had been projected. On the morning of October the 17th, 1720, Nicol Muschet had occasion for a knife for some trifling purpose, and having lost his own, borrowed his landlady's, who desired him to keep it till he found the other. He declared that he had not thought at the time of applying the weapon to the object which it afterwards effected. On that same evening, after he and James Muschet had " diverted themselves with some company in the Canongate" till about seven o'clock, they came away to attempt once more the scheme of murder with the hammer. Leaving his accomplice watching for the chance, Nichol Muschet went into a house with his ill-fated wife, whose death was to be accomplished on her way home. But when Nicol and she came out of the house in question, " being now hardened and also desperate," he bethought himself that it was but a " light thing who was the executioner," and he resolved upon killing her himself. " I desired her," says he, " to go down the Canongate with me; and when she asked me on what account, I bade her ask no questions, but go along with me; and when we went the length of the Abbey, she asked whither I was going? I said she was not concerned to know, but only she behoved to go with me. And when we were going through St. Anne's Yards, she wept (oh, how does my heart bleed to think on it!) and prayed that Heaven might forgive me, if I was taking her to any mischief; and she desired to return. Then I said if she would return I was not to stop her, but I was going to Duddingstown, and if she would not go with me, she needed never expect to exchange one word with me after." By these arguments, Nicol Muschet prevailed upon the wretched woman to go as far as he thought convenient for the deed of blood, when he pulled out the knife and killed her. Her throat was the spot that received the mortal wound; and it adds to the horror of the crime, that the unhappy victim strove to avert her fate more by humble entreaties than by resistance; for the murderer admits, in his confession, that if she had chosen to struggle, he is confident he had not " got her overcome." Her piteous and fruitless cry was, " My love! my love! do not murther me!"

Having returned to the city, leaving the dead body where the crime was committed, Nicol Muschet immediately informed James Muschet and his wife of what had happened. These persons at once showed Nicol what use they would make of the mastery they had acquired over him, by demanding money from him, which he was compelled to grant. He then went to Leith, and came to Edinburgh again on the following night, when he saw James Muschet's wife, who declared that she and her husband intended " to perjure themselves for him." How little sincerity there was in this declaration, appeared on the following day, when the parties were examined, and revealed the whole affair. " They turned so inveterate against me, that, upon the Thursday night, the said Grizzel Muschet (notwithstanding her solemn protestations to the contrary, which I thought always made me secure against any danger) treacherously inquired for my quarters in Leith, on pretence of coming to me, and informing me how matters were going; which when she got notice of, she presently informed the magistrates of Edinburgh, and went along with a party of the city guards that same night; but they did not find me." They did find him, however, on the ensuing day, and their guide in the discovery was still Grizzel Muschet. Thus was Nichol Muschet fitly brought into the hands of justice by the agency of those very persons who had abetted his crimes and profited by them.

When first examined, the murderer denied the charge brought against him,—but he soon retracted his words, and confessed the whole. He was condemned to death, and was executed accordingly, in the beginning of January, 1721. His accomplices in plotting against the life of his luckless wife were also subjected to examination, but the evidence against them was not sufficient to make them partakers of his doom.

A cairn was placed near, but not quite close upon, the spot where the murder was perpetrated. The rude heap of stones was afterwards removed during the formation of a regular footpath through the park; but was again restored, where it remains to this hour. The precise spot where the crime was committed, is, according to Muschet's own account, close by the east end of the walk, which is near to the cairn.

This tale of crime was never told at the firesides of the ancestors of the present natives of Scotland's capital, without a moral being drawn from it, which moral, although void of novelty, is not unworthy of repetition, being to this effect, that Nicol Muschet presents a notable specimen of the consequences of a deliberated wickedness and the gradual familiarisation with criminal thoughts. A divorce was all that he contemplated and sought at first. By degrees, he listened to proposals for compassing his wife's death, by comparatively slow as well as hidden means, which were to be used by others. Ultimately, he himself became the murderer, and in a most savage as also regulated manner. Had he struggled earnestly against yielding to the first evil suggestion and cruel passion, he would not have died on the scaffold.

XVIII.—HENRY FAUNTLEROY.

THE trial of this gentleman for forgery took place on Saturday, the 30th of October, 1824. It was a case which, not only from the extent of the fraudulent transactions with which he was accused, but his rank in society, and the high respectability of the banking firm of which he was a partner, excited a very extraordinary degree of public interest. The death of a party, and the inquiries which were thereon instituted at the Bank of England relative to a large amount of stock, which it was then discovered had been drawn out by the prisoner, led at first to his apprehension.

At five minutes past ten o'clock on the day mentioned, Mr. Fauntleroy was conducted to the bar of the criminal court of the Old Bailey. He was dressed in a full suit of black, and appeared to be about forty-five years old, although his hair was unusually grey for a man of that age. The firmness which he had displayed at an earlier hour of the morning, seemed for a moment to desert him, when he was exposed to the gaze of the court. His step faltered, his visage was pale, and now much thinner than it had shortly before been; nor did he for a moment raise his head, but, placing his hands upon the front of the dock, he there stood with dejected mien, while the preliminary forms and business of the trial were gone through. He was arraigned upon seven different indictments, to each of which he pleaded Not Guilty, in a subdued tone of voice, and without lifting his eyes from the bar. A chair was now allowed him at the suggestion of his counsel, on the ground of indisposition.

The Attorney-General conducted the prosecution, confining himself to one of the seven indictments upon which the prisoner was arraigned, namely, that which charged him with fraudulently and wickedly forging and uttering a certain power of attorney for the transfer of certain stock in the Bank of England in the name of Miss Frances Young; and the facts of the case, as detailed in the evidence laid before the court, were succinctly these :—

The prisoner was well known as a partner in the banking establishment of Marsh, Sibald, and Co., of Berners-street, London, which had been established for about thirty years. His father, who died in 1807, had been a partner in the original firm, and his situation was immediately occupied by his son, the accused, upon whom also, for his practical knowledge of business, and the comparative superiority which he had in this respect over his co-partners, nearly the whole of the actual conduct of the bank devolved. In the year 1815, Miss Frances Young, of Chichester, became a customer to the firm, and had then entered in her name, at the Bank of England, the sum of £5,450 in the Three per Cent. Consols. She gave the firm of Marsh and Co. a power of attorney to receive the dividends in her name, but gave them no power to sell or otherwise to dispose of the principal. In May, 1815, however, an application was made at the Bank, and represented to have been so made in behalf of this lady, to sell, by her power of attorney, £5,000 of the stock.

With regard to the forms exacted by the Bank of England in transacting the business of such transfers, the following explanation may be sufficient :—The applicant goes to the Bank and obtains a slip of paper, which he fills up with the name of the party in whose behalf he applies; he describes the stock in the Bank, the amount and particulars required to be transferred, and the name and address of the person to whom the transfer is to be made. Upon receiving these instructions in the form inserted upon a slip of paper, the bank clerk, to whom it is delivered, hands over a power of attorney, which is to be transmitted to the person who is to make the transfer, for the purpose of receiving the requisite signature. It is customary at the Bank to preserve these slips of paper, but in the present case the particular slip had been lost, and therefore it could not be said to whom it was delivered, it being usual to endorse the name of the party on the slip. But the power of attorney, which was prepared according to the slip so made, is referred, with the necessary attestation of the witnesses. There must be to these powers of attorney two attesting witnesses, with the description of their respective names and addresses. The power of attorney purported to be signed by Frances Young, and that signature was proved to be a forgery. The attesting witnesses were John Watson and James Tyson, clerks in the bank of Marsh and Co., and their signatures were also forgeries; for they never had transacted any business with Miss Frances Young, and never executed any transfer of stock for her. In all such documents it is required by the Bank that the date be set forth in words at length. This was so done in the forged transfer in question, and was proved to be in the handwriting of Fauntleroy.

It was thus clear that the forgery had been committed either by the prisoner, or with his knowledge. The attesting witnesses were his clerks, men whose handwriting was well known to him, and a forgery of which he must have at once detected if brought to him by a third party. The practice at the bank was, that when these transfers, after being duly filed, were executed, they had to be deposited for twenty-four hours with the clerk, for the purpose of being compared with the books, and for such other inspection and precaution as might be deemed necessary on such occasions for the security of property, so far as time and circumstances allowed. After all these preliminary steps, the applicant is further called upon, before the instrument is completed, to write at the bottom these words, "I demand this power to be executed in my name," signed by the party. Now, Fauntleroy attended at the Bank in person, and had demanded in due form the execution of the said power of attorney. But sufficient as all these things were to prove the case, other evidence of his guilt, of an extraordinary nature, was adduced,—so singular indeed, and so complete in all its parts, as to leave no possible doubt that Fauntleroy had committed the offence. When he was taken into custody, in his counting-house, he, in the presence of the officer, locked his private desk, with a key which was then attached to his watch; that key was afterwards taken from him by the officer; and when the solicitor for the Bank of England went to search the house in Berners'-street for Fauntleroy's papers, to ascertain whatever particulars he could therein find respecting the forgeries, he found in one of the rooms of Marsh and Co's., bank, in which tin cases, containing title deeds of their customers were deposited, and on which the names of the owners were inscribed,—one tin box without a name. This led him to examine it. The key was found in Fauntleroy's private desk, which he had himself locked in the presence of the officer, and on opening this box was discovered a number of private papers belonging to the prisoner, and among them the remarkable document, in Fauntleroy's own handwriting, which here follows :—

"Consols, £11,151, standing in the name of my trusteeship; £3,000, E. W. Young; £6,000, Consols, General Young; £5,000, Long Annuities, Frances Young; another, £6,000. Lady Nelson, £11,595; Mrs. Ferrer, 20,000 Four per Cents; Earl of Ossory, £7,000; T. Owen, £9,400; J. W. Parkins, £4,000; Lord Aboyne, £6,000; P. Moore, and John Marsh, £21,000." This paper which contained a total of sums considerably exceeding £100,000, was all written in Fauntleroy's own hand; while these words, in the same hand, followed,

—"In order to keep up the credit of our house, I have forged powers of attorney, and have thereupon sold out all these sums, without the knowledge of any of my partners. I have given credit in the accounts for the interest when it became due.

"May, 7th 1816.   (signed)   HENRY FAUNTLEROY."

These other words followed the above amazing statement,—"The Bank began first to refuse our acceptances, and thereby to destroy the credit of our house: they shall therefore smart for it."

Surely, never had there been a record of a fraud that was more intelligible, and never one more negligently kept. The intention of Fauntleroy might be, when he drew up such a paper, to abscond, and thus to protect his partners from any suspicion of having participated in his acts. If such was the case, he had, however, afterwards altered his intention; and at all events, nothing but unaccountable negligence, or a judicial infatuation, could have prevented him from at length destroying the document. The Bank of England, in consequence of the astounding information which Fauntleroy's own record furnished them, beyond the suspicions and instructions they had at first acted upon, proceeded to examine the private accounts kept by the prisoner with his firm; and they there found that the accounts of the parties, whose moneys were fraudulently transferred, were regularly kept up, and the interest upon the dividends as regularly carried to them every half-year, as if the original stock had remained in being. In the particular case of forgery for which the prisoner was tried, his broker had sold out the stock in question to the amount of £2,950 2s 6d; this amount was paid over by the broker to the banking-house of Marten and Co., who transacted business for Marsh and Co., in the city, and was regularly noted in the day-book of the latter by a clerk, by whom the entry was made at the dictation of Fauntleroy. But, in the further management of the accounts, in passing from the day-book to the private ledger, this sum appeared to have been carried to the prisoner's private account. The general produce was, however, afterwards posted, so as to keep up the accounts according to the original amount intrusted to the Bank by the respective customers.

The surprise could not but be universal and great, how it came that, for a number of years, the dividends could have been so managed by the prisoner in his accounts, as to escape the detection of his partners. The explanation given was this, that Fauntleroy had the entire management for the firm of their stock-market business, and that he always so contrived to manage the entry in the books as to correspond with the nominal amount of stock intrusted to the firm by their customers, so as to keep up the delusion.

The evidence for the crown having been gone through, the accused, on being asked what he had to say in his defence, rose from the chair with which he had been accommodated, and, drawing a paper from his bosom, said, addressing himself to the judge, Mr. Justice Park, "My lord, I will trouble you with a few words." Then, wiping away a tear which forced itself down his pallid cheek, he proceeded, in a very low, and sometimes hardly audible voice, to state that, on joining the firm of Marsh and Co., in 1807, he found the concern deeply involved, in consequence of large advances to builders and others; that the house remained in embarrassments until 1810, when it met with an overwhelming loss from the failure of Breckwood and Co., for which concern they had accepted and discounted bills to the amount of £170,000. In 1814, 1815, and 1816, the firm was called upon, in consequence of the speculations in building, to produce £100,000. In 1819, the most responsible of the partners died, and the embarrassments of the house were increased by being called upon to refund his capital. During all this time the house was without resources, excepting such as he was now responsible for. He received no relief from his partners. Two had overdrawn £100,000. Having stated these circumstances at some length, he thus proceeded:—

"I alone have been doomed to suffer the stigma of all the transactions; but tortured as I have been, it now becomes an imperative duty to explain that the vile accusations heaped upon me, known to be utterly false by all those best acquainted with my private life and habits, have been so heaped upon me for the purpose of loading me with the whole of the obloquy of these transactions by which, and from which alone, my partners were preserved from bankruptcy. I have been accused of crimes I never even contemplated, and of acts of profligacy I never committed; and I appear at this bar with every prejudice against me, and almost prejudged. To suit the purposes of the persons to whom I allude, I have been represented as a man of prodigal extravagance. Prodigal indeed I must have been, had I expended those large sums which will hereafter be proved to have gone exclusively to support the credit of a tottering firm.

"I maintained but two establishments; one at Brighton, where my mother and my sister resided in the season, the expenses of which to me, exclusive of my wine, were within £400 per annum. One at Lambeth, where my two children lived, from its very nature private and inexpensive, to which I resorted for retirement, after many a day passed in devising means to avert the embarrassments of the banking-house. The dwelling-house in Berners-street belonged solely to my mother, with the exception of a library and a single bed-room. This was the extent of my expenditure, so far as domestic expenditure is concerned. I am next accused of being an habitual gambler, an accusation which, if true, might easily account for the diffusion of the property. I am, indeed, a member of two clubs, the Albion and the Stratford, but never in my life did I play in either at cards or dice, or any game of chance; this is well known to the gentlemen of the clubs; and my private friends, with whom I have more intimately associated, can equally assert my freedom from all habits or disposition to play. It has been as cruelly asserted that I fraudulently invested money in the funds to answer the payment of annuities, amounting to £2,200, settled upon females. I never did make any such investment; nor is there one shilling secretly deposited by me in the hands of any human being. Equally ungenerous, and equally untrue it is, to charge me with having lent to loose and disorderly persons large sums which never have and never will be repaid.' I lent no sums, but to a very trifling amount, and those were advanced to valued friends. I can, therefore, at this solemn moment declare most fervently, that I never had any advantage, beyond that in which all my partners participated, in any of the transactions which are now questioned. They, indeed, have considered themselves as partners only in the profits, and I am to be burthened with the whole of the opprobrium, that others may consider them the victims of extravagance. Frailties and errors enough have I to account for. I have sufferings enough, past, present, and in prospect; and if my life was all that was required of me, I might endure in silence, though I will not endure the odium on my memory of having sinned to pamper indulgences to which I never was addicted. This much has been extorted from me by the fabrications which have been cruelly spread amongst the public, that very public from whom the arbiters of my fate were to be selected. Perhaps, however, I ought to thank the enemy who besieged the prison with his slanders, that he did so while my life was spared to refute them, and that he waited not until the grave to which he would hurry me had closed at once upon my answer and my forgiveness."

No. 16.   R

The prisoner having concluded his address, sat down, exhausted by the effort and overcome by his feelings—weeping and deeply agitated. Sir Charles Forbes and fifteen other highly respectable witnesses attested their strong opinion of his honour, integrity, and goodness of disposition.

It was now the judge's turn to address the jury. In his charge he impartially recapitulated the evidence, which was so conclusive against the prisoner, alluding, at the commencement, to the prejudical reports of which the accused complained so much, and saying that he had allowed him to proceed with the complaint, although it had nothing at all to do with the question under consideration. With regard to Fauntleroy's alleged motive having been to support the credit of the partners, his lordship asked if any Christian or honest man could ever put the support of such credit into the balance with the misery which the atrocious conduct could not fail to produce ? It had been testified that the prisoner bore a very high character. The judge was glad to listen to such evidence. At the same time it was the misfortune that persons of high character were the very parties who had the opportunity of committing such frauds as were charged against the individual at the bar of the court,—no others could perpetrate them.

It was not long before the jury were prepared with their verdict, which, of course, was that of *Guilty*. The other indictments were consequently dropped, the prisoner meanwhile appearing to be absorbed in his anguish. He was, however, aroused by the judge rather abruptly saying, " Henry Fauntleroy," for he looked wildly at the bench and rose in expectation that judgment would immediately be pronounced upon him. The judge went on.—" Henry Fauntleroy, the learned Attorney-General does not feel it necessary, in the discharge of his public function, to proceed further with the other indictments which have been preferred against you ; nor is it any part of my painful duty to pronounce the awful sentence of the law, which must follow the verdict that has just been recorded. That unpleasing task will devolve on the learned Recorder, at the termination of the Sessions ; but it is a part of my duty as a Christian magistrate to implore you that you bethink yourself seriously of your latter end. (A convulsive sob from the wretched culprit was distinctly audible through the court at these words.) According to the constitution of this country, the prerogative of mercy is vested in the Crown.—With that I have nothing to do. I do not say that in your unhappy case the extension of mercy is impossible ; but I am afraid that, after the many serious acts which, under your own handwriting, have been proved against you, involving so many persons in ruin, you will only deceive yourself by indulging in any hope of mercy on this side of the grave.—Let me then beseech you to turn your heart to the contemplation of your awful situation, and, whilst it is yet in your power, use all your exertions to make your peace with God."

The wretched man was now quite overpowered ; he was barely able to raise up his hands, as if in the attitude of prayer, but without articulating a word. He was then removed, requiring support, to his prison.

Fauntleroy had been desirous, almost from the moment of his apprehension, to plead guilty, in order to spare himself the pain and mortification of being exposed for hours to the gaze of a crowded court, and compelled to hear the narrative of his many grave delinquencies ; but having become deeply annoyed by the reports which found speedy circulation and greedy acceptance, accusing him of grossest extravagances and numerous profligacies,—many of the reports being vile slanders, some of them associating his doings with those of the cold-blooded murderer Thurtell,—he became exceedingly nervous and distressed thereby, and was induced to put himself upon his trial. As soon as he somewhat rallied after having been reconducted to prison, he exclaimed, "Thank God, this trial is over." He was greatly exhausted, and some time elapsed before his spirits were sufficiently restored to enable him to take any refreshment. He was soon visited by his attorney and several friends, to whom he said he was satisfied with the trial, and that the jury could not have returned any other verdict than what they did. One of the jurors, it may be stated, wept very much, and several of them were greatly affected.

Fauntleroy slept some hours on the night succeeding his trial; and he attended Divine service next morning. The ordinary of the prison took for his text these words—"Believe in the Lord Jesus Christ and thou shalt be saved." The wretched man, during the service, looked like one who knew there was no hope on this side the grave for him, yet conducted himself devoutly and decorously. He was occasionally much affected, particularly after the chaplain called upon each and all of his audience, who had been already *convicted*, in these words, "Set thy house in order, for to-morrow thou shalt surely die."

Great exertions were employed to rescue the unhappy gentleman from the ignominious fate that hung over his head. A motion in arrest of judgment was made upon certain technical grounds and constructions of particular statutes; but without avail. Petitions numerously signed were forwarded to the Crown, recommending him to mercy; for a very deep sympathy was felt for the unhappy gentleman in many quarters. At the age of 15, when other youths were playing their gambols at school, he was introduced to the drudgery of a clerk in a banking establishment; and it was evident that he must have devoted great zeal and attention to the duties of his station, because, on the death of his father, when he was only 22, he was permitted to succeed him as a partner in the firm. His, however,—it came to be ascertained, independently of his earnest assertions and repeated declarations in his defence,—was no enviable situation; the capital of the concern was small; heavy losses brought on embarrassments; bankruptcy stared him in the face; and he ventured on an expedient,—most dangerous, ill-advised, and wrong, unquestionably,—to avert the ruin of the establishment, by obtaining, through the medium of forgery, those resources which could alone support the credit of the house, and prevent its failure. When he first deviated from rectitude, according to his own asseverations to his friends, which there is no ground for disbelieving, he merely intended to obtain temporary assistance, never for a moment contemplating fraud or injury to any one. Disaster, however, followed disaster in quick succession; the same means of relief were resorted to on each occasion, till the forgeries at last accumulated to such an enormous amount, that nothing less than a miracle could have relieved him. Every year increased the burdens and the difficulties; sums which had been sold out when the funds were extremely low, were occasionally obliged to be repurchased when the price of stock was enhanced; and as the dividends became payable, he was under the necessity of providing money to place to the credit of those individuals whose stock had been surreptitiously disposed of. Some notion may be formed of the extent of the sums obtained by forgeries, when it is stated, that the amount latterly required every quarter to supply the place of dividends, amounted to upwards of £4,000. Not only had Fauntleroy to manage the regular concerns of the house, but he had to keep correct accounts of all the sums drawn under forged letters of attorney, and every quarter to place to the customer the exact amount to which he would have been entitled if the stock had remained untouched. Besides this, when any death, marriage, or other occurrence took place which was likely to occasion a reference to the Bank of England, in these cases where the stock had been withdrawn, Fauntleroy was under the necessity of immediately replacing it, to prevent a discovery taking place.

What, therefore, must have been his feelings during the last fifteen or sixteen years of his life, knowing, as he could not fail to do, that the sword of justice was suspended over his head, as it were, by a single hair? Truly the way of transgressors is hard. His own words, when he was brought up to receive judgment, forcibly illustrate the torture he had endured. The following was the statement which he read at that awful moment:—

"My lord," said he, "I am well aware that no emergencies, however pressing,—that no embarrassments, however great, can be listened to as an excuse for the offence of which I have been found guilty; but I trust it may be considered as some palliation in a moral point of view, that a desire to preserve myself and others from bankruptcy, and not personal aggrandizement or selfish gratification alone, urged and impelled me to the acts I have committed; and when I first deviated from rectitude, it was owing to an acute, though I admit a mistaken feeling to obtain temporary relief, and not from any deliberate intention to defraud. God knows my heart and the truth of my present declaration, that I hoped and fully intended to make restitution immediately the expected prosperity of the house would have enabled me. This must, I think, my lord, appear evident, from my having frequently replaced the money withdrawn; and the bank books will prove, that many of the sums mentioned in the document written in 1816, have been since re-invested by me to the credit of the parties. That document, my lord, has been supposed to have been prepared in contemplation of flight. This idea is, however, erroneous, and is sufficiently refuted by my continuance at my residence and my business for years subsequently. The only object and intention of that paper was, in the event of sudden death, before the whole of the money should be re-invested, to absolve every one besides myself from suspicion. Unfortunately for me, a succession of adverse events, which I could neither avert nor control (and part of which I detailed at length on my trial), led on from one false step to another, until the affairs of the house became so involved that extrication was impossible. In these difficulties, I offered myself as the only sacrifice; and it is my duty as a man and as a Christian, to resign myself to my fate. For me, my lord, fallen and degraded as I am, life was no allurement; and a momentary pang will at once put an end to my mental agonies and to my earthly existence. But I have numerous relations—amongst them my dear and venerable mother,—whose feelings I reverence; and for their sakes, more than my own, I venture to supplicate that I may not be doomed to suffer a violent and ignominious death. If crime, my lord, can be atoned for by suffering, my offences, heavy as they are, have long since been expiated, not merely by the overwhelming embarrassments of the concern in which I was engaged, but by years of anxious terror and agonising apprehension; and if, my lord, the anguish of mind I have endured for the last sixteen years of my life, and the peculiar circumstances in which I have been placed ever since I arrived at man's estate could be made known to my most gracious Sovereign, I venture to hope that his Majesty's benevolent and feeling heart would be touched with compassion for my situation, and that I should not be considered an object wholly undeserving of the royal clemency. May I therefore, my lord, presume to solicit your lordship's humane interposition, to communicate, for his Majesty's merciful consideration, the circumstances to which I have alluded; and on behalf of my dearest relations I supplicate that the punishment of death may be remitted."

This appeal, like all the other efforts used to save his life, proved unavailing. The hour and moment arrived when the unhappy man was to be made acquainted with the absolute determination of his fate. His brother and son were with him at the time, but the former of these attached ones feeling himself too nervous to support himself through the trial, retired, leaving only the youth with his father.

The Rev. Dr. Cotton, the ordinary, dressed in his black gown, with the death warrant in his hand, entered the apartment of the prisoner, and found him engaged in reading the Prayer Book. Fauntleroy instantly rose from his seat, and approaching the reverend gentleman said, "Ah! Mr. Cotton, you are come; I see how it is." The doctor was unable to speak for some moments; but he presented the black seal of the Recorder, which rendered further explanation unnecessary. The prisoner then said, "I expected nothing less than death, and, thanks be to God, I am resigned to my fate." "Yes," said the Ordinary, "the report is fatal to you, and I trust and believe you are prepared." "It is very extraordinary," observed Mr. Fauntleroy, with a smile, "that I should have opened the Prayer Book at the very spot in which the culprit prays to God for power to bear the last extremity. I looked into it for comfort, and the comfort it gave me was in turning my thoughts to the grave." Dr. Cotton said he was rejoiced to see him in so tranquil and resigned a state of mind. "Yes," said he, "I have gained by your excellent advice, and I learn those things without fear or trembling. When am I to suffer?" (It was on a Wednesday that this solemn interview took place.) The Ordinary told him that Tuesday next was the day appointed for his execution. "Very well," said he, "I shall be ready. It is very odd, that when I opened that book of prayers which you gave to me, no doubt for the purpose of keeping my thoughts upon a separation from this life, I exactly hit upon the words, 'Almighty God, give me grace and strength to spend the short time I have to live as it is meet, and make me acceptable to Thee, for Christ's sake.'"

On the next interview which the Ordinary had with the unhappy gentleman, he said, in rather a cheerful tone, "It is better that I should die, than that I should have escaped to another country. Had I gone to America, as some of my friends appeared to have wished had been the case, although I solemnly declare I never had any such intention, every bit of bread I should have swallowed would have been as poison to me; I never could have enjoyed another happy hour. I had, I will acknowledge, some flattering hope,—it was merely a flattering hope,—but still it was hope.". Dr. Cotton said, "My dear Sir, I cautioned you against giving way to hope,—I told you there was no chance." "Yes," replied Mr. Fauntleroy, "you prevented me from encouraging that dangerous hope, the disappointment of which would have been intolerable; but still it broke in upon me in some shape or other from the first. But it is well that I am to die. Oh! Mr. Cotton, I have one great consolation in leaving the world—I have got the assurance of a most virtuous and estimable friend, that my poor boy and my two other children shall be taken care of; and I go out of life without any fears about them. Indeed, my son has now before him the prospect of a prosperous course; he will fare better than he would if I had been merely an exile. I hope my calamity of itself will operate in making him virtuous."

Various most affecting scenes occurred between the prisoner and those with whom he had been the more nearly connected in past years; because it is not to be left out of consideration that Mrs. Fauntleroy was alive and had interviews with him at Newgate,— her son having been the first to communicate to her the dreadful intelligence of his father's fate. This was not all; for the infatuated man's misconduct had in other respects than that of acting foully in money matters, been treasuring up guilt, terrible responsibility, and anguish for himself. There was a female who had been living with him, with her two babes, that had to take a final farewell of the criminal, which took place on the Friday prior to his execution. The details of these mournful occurrences shall here be passed over, however, that we may hasten to the concluding scene of all.

On the day of his execution, Mr. Fauntleroy showed himself to becoming advantage, as indeed he had done ever since his apprehension, being woe struck, yet firm and composed. He was dressed in black, and appeared a well made man. His hair, though grey, was quite thick, and lay smooth over his forehead. His countenance had the aspect of a regulated and subdued resignation. The impression which his appearance altogether was calculated to make at the time he was pinioned was that of profoundest commisseration, unmixed with the slightest degree of the unfavourable sensations excited by unmanly fear of dying on the one side, or ruffian fool-hardiness on the other. On his way to the scaffold, though successfully endeavouring to retain his erect posture and measured step, he gradually became exhausted. He took his station immediately under the rope, with his clasped hands projected before him, and his head elevated, but with a perfectly unmoved countenance. He seemed quite unconscious of the surrounding multitude, and calmly awaited the closing of the scene. He continued immovable throughout the last awful preparations of the executioner, and in the attitude already mentioned. While the service was still reading the platform dropped, so steadily and sudden, indeed, that the body was not agitated by it, the executioner, as usual, instantly hanging by the legs, to hasten death.

The Ordinary declared, after the execution, that he had scarcely ever witnessed so much firmness. Mr. Fauntleroy's hand, it was also remarked, when he was upon the scaffold, had been as warm as that of a person under ordinary circumstances. The hands of most of those who are upon the point of execution are cold and clammy.

XIX.—WILLIAM CORDER.

THE trial of William Corder for the murder of Maria Marten, excited an extraordinary share of public concern,—lament for the unhappy victim, and abhorrence of the ruthless monster, who put an end to the life of one whom he had contributed to delude and to disgrace by a death that allowed not a moment for repentance. Indeed, it would be difficult to point out a parallel or a precedent for the enormity and heinous conduct of the miscreant in the whole criminal records of England.

There were some circumstances connected with this appalling case, and the conduct of the accused, which lent it a peculiar interest. Several months prior to the trial, and also a very considerable period after the murder, Corder advertised for a wife in the columns of the *Morning Herald* and of the *Sunday Times*. The following is the statement he put forth in the former of these papers, the 13th of November, 1827 :—

" MATRIMONY.—A private gentleman, aged 24, entirely independent, whose disposition is not to be exceeded, has lately lost the chief of his family by the hand of Providence, which has occasioned discord among the remainder, under circumstances most disagreeable to relate. To any female of respectability, who would study for domestic comfort, and willing to confide her future happiness in one every way qualified to render the marriage state desirable, the opportunity is good, as the advertiser is in affluence; the lady must have the power of some property, which may remain in her own possession.

(The notice of property was omitted in the advertisement as it appeared in the *Sunday Times*.)　Many very happy marriages have taken place through means similar to this now resorted to, and it is hoped no one will answer this through impertinent curiosity ; but should this meet the eye of any respectable lady, who feels desirous of meeting with a sociable, tender, kind, and sympathising companion, they will find this advertisement worthy of notice.　Honour and secrecy may be relied on.　As some little security against all applications, it is requested that letters may be addressed (post paid) to A. Z., care of Mr. Foster, stationer, Leadenhall-street, which will meet with the most respectful attention.''

Now, the number of answers which were promptly returned to this matrimonial scheme, was not only very great, but Mr. Foster published above *fifty* of them, without giving their signatures, of course, but it is impossible to peruse the documents without perceiving that they were, one and all of them, written by persons who could readily make a good use of their pen, not a few of them besides evincing polish and refinement. Many more were received than were thus made public, a multitude having been handed to Corder on his calling for them ; but as he seems to have given over making further application for answers, the moment he fixed on a marrying partner, Mr. Foster at length felt himself entitled to make free with the strange kind of literary property which he afterwards printed.

Advertisements from men wanting wives, have almost always, it is believed, been the productions of persons who wished to try the force of credulity in the fair sex, and whether it was possible that any females, except of the lowest order, destitute of native modesty to protect, or of friends to advise, could so far forget what is owing to themselves, and the delicacy of their sex, as to present themselves for wedlock to men of whom they could have no knowledge, and who might, for aught they were aware of, commence in this way a system of seduction.　Surely, few could have imagined that, in answer to Corder's advertisement, above a hundred letters should speedily be returned by as many females, stating their fitness to supply the advertiser with a wife, suited to his pretended character and expectation.　And yet the scheme so far succeeded, that he obtained a wife through its means,—a female of respectable character, who kept a boarding school near Ealing, answering the advertisement, and becoming soon afterwards his spouse.　He was living, in fact, with his wife and in her house, at the time when he was taken into custody.

It was on the 7th of August, 1828, that the trial of Corder commenced ; the event taking place at Bury St. Edmunds, Suffolk, before Chief Baron Alexander.　The accused was the son of respectable parents, living at Polstead, in that county. His father had been dead some time, having been a farmer in that parish ; but after his decease, the land was held by the widow, first with assistance of her eldest son, and next of the prisoner himself.　Maria Marten was the daughter of parents in a humble sphere of life, residing in the same parish, and had been personally known to Corder for a considerable period, especially from about a year prior to the 18th of May, 1827.　At that date, an intimacy of a close nature took place between the parties, and an illegitimate child was the fruit of it.　She was not delivered of the child at her father's house, but returned with the infant about six weeks before the 18th of May mentioned, Corder owning himself to be the father of the baby.　In about a fortnight more the child died.　During this period, he was several times heard to say to Maria that the parish thought of having her taken up for another bastard child of which she had been delivered ; intimating that after having a second one illegitimately, there was the greater likelihood of the threat being put into execution. They were likewise heard quarrelling more than once regarding a *five pound* note, which was mentioned between them. On one occasion the young woman was heard to say to him, "if I go to gaol, you shall go too." During the same period of their acquaintance, Corder repeatedly said that it was his intention to make her his wife. On the Sunday immediately before the 18th of May,—which fell upon a Friday,—Maria Marten went to his mother's house, he having first been on that day to her father's cottage. It was there agreed that they should go next day to Ipswich to get married. They did not however fulfil the purpose. They then arranged that they should go on the next Thursday; but that arrangement was not carried into effect; nor indeed does it ever seem to have been meant by the villain. On the 18th, about the middle of the day, Corder was again at the dwelling of Maria's father. On this occasion she was up stairs with her step-mother. He desired her to make herself ready and go along with him. She said that she could not go then. He replied, you have been disappointed several times, and you must go now."

It was upon this agreed that she should in a measure disguise herself in order to escape observation; and that she should put on a man's dress,—Corder undertaking to carry her female attire to a place called the Red Barn, which was on his mother's farm, where Maria was to redress herself in her proper clothes. Thence they were to proceed to Ipswich to be married. The young woman put into a large bag a certain quantity of her apparel, and also a small basket, which contained a black velvet reticule, retaining on her person, a flannel petticoat, a pair of stays and a jean busk. She had also combs in her hair, and earrings in her ears, and a green handkerchief about her neck. The two went out of Marten's house at the same time, but by different doors, yet both taking the direction of the Red Barn. Corder professed that he was anxious to avoid Maria being recognized, saying that none of the workmen on the farm were in the way at the time, and that the course was clear. He also assigned as a reason for going to Ipswich on that day, that John Balm, the constable, had come to him in the morning to the stable, saying, he had got a letter from London, enclosing a warrant to take Maria and prosecute her for her bastard children; a statement which was afterwards found false. From that period, none of her friends ever saw the victim alive again. Alas! when she quitted her father's cottage for the last time, "she was crying and low spirited."

On the following Sunday morning it was that the step-mother next spoke to him at her own house, saying, "William, what have you done with Maria?" He answered, "I have left her at Ipswich, where I have got her a comfortable place, to go down with Miss Roland to the waterside." On asking how she was to do for clothes, he said Miss Roland had plenty for her, and would not let him provide any. He also said he had got a license, but that it would have to be sent to London to be signed, and that they could not be married under a month or six weeks.

On a subsequent day in the same week the stepmother had another interview with Corder, and she then told him that her son had seen him on the Friday previously near the Red Barn, with a pick-axe on his shoulder. To this he replied, "It could not be me that he saw; it must have been Acres, who was employed that day in stubbing trees near the barn." From this period to the discovery of Maria's body, the accused saw the father and stepmother of the unfortunate young woman very frequently. At one period he was absent from Polstead for some time; and on his return he gave accounts of Maria's living with some relations of his at Yarmouth. When inquiry was made by the Martens' after her health, he said she was very well; and when asked why she did not write, he answered that she had a sore on the back of her hand, which disabled her from moving her fingers.

In the interval between the 18th of May and harvest time, Corder had several conversations with other individuals respecting Maria Marten, and to these persons he gave a different account of her from that which he had made to her father and relations. He told one person that she had gone by the steam-packet to France, and another person that she was living at no great distance from them. He had a very particular conversation on the subject with a woman of the name of Stow. In the course of their talk, she asked him whether Maria was likely to have any more children; to which he answered, " No, she is not. Maria Marten will have no more children." Mrs. Stow immediately said, " Why not; she is still a very young woman." He replied. " No; believe me, she will have no more ; she has had her number." Mrs. Stow then said, " If you are married, why don't you live with her ?" " Oh, no," was his reply, " for I can go to her any day in the year, just when 1 like." " Perhaps you are rather jealous of her,' observed Mrs. Stow ; " and when you are not with her, you think somebody else is." " Oh, no," said he; " when I am not with her, I am sure nobody is." From Mrs. Stow, who belonged to Polstead, Corder about the period in question borrowed a spade.

We pass on now to the month of September, 1827, when Corder was engaged in directing the workmen to get in the harvest. For some time before the 18th May, the barn had been empty, except so far as the floor was covered with old litter. When the wheat was cut, he gave orders that the corn should be laid in the upper bay of the barn. He was present when the first and second loads were taken in, and superintended the operation. The keys of the barn were always kept in his mother's house, and the barn was, besides, not easy of entrance, as it was surrounded by a sort of outhouses, and was only approached by a gate, which was seven feet high. After the corn had been got into the barn, Corder left Polstead. He was driven on that occasion to Colchester by a man of the name of Bright. To that person he gave a different account of Maria Marten from what he had given to any other, for he said he had not seen her from the May preceding. And yet before he left Polstead on this occasion, Corder told Maria's father that he should have the pleasure of seeing his daughter soon. He also told him that he had bought a new suit of clothes in which he intended to be married to her.

About the middle of October, old Marten received a letter from Corder, bearing the London postmark, in which he declared he had made Maria his wife. He also expressed his surprise that the father had not answered the letter which he said Maria had written home upon her marriage, informing the father that Miss Roland acted as bridesmaid. He desired that the old man would answer his communication immediately, and told him to address his reply under certain initials, to a certain place in the city. The father wrote in answer, to say that no such letter as Corder had described had ever been received. The villain then sent back another communication, stating that he had made inquiry in the Post Office respecting the loss of the alleged letter, and that he attributed the accident to its having had to cross the sea, Maria having been in the Isle of Wight at the time when it was sent off.

Some time further elapsed without the Martens hearing anything satisfactory about Maria; and in consequence they grew more and more anxious and suspicious concerning her. Their solicitude and fears increased daily, at length assuming a definite shape. Meanwhile Corder's scheme of advertising for a wife had been adopted, having—let it be particularly observed—been resolved upon nearly about the date that he wrote the two letters from London to his wretched victim's parent, declaring that he had got married to the daughter, and that his happiness was now secured, with many other atrocious falsehoods, presenting a species and system of villany which has seldom been equalled. It ought also here to be remarked, that if the smallest pains which common prudence might suggest had at this period been taken to inquire into Corder's character, near the place to which he belonged, an end would have been at once not only put to his matrimonial speculation in the way of advertising, but the discovery made by the parents of the poor deluded Maria Marten, that Corder had been deceiving them by the most barefaced lies from the day of the murder. It is indeed an astonishing instance of that infatuation which often characterises the conduct of murderers, that this man should have supposed it possible for him to go on in making the friends of his victim believe that she was still alive, and his lawful wife.

At last the suspicions of the poor people were directed to the Red Barn. The father of the victim became anxious to examine the place. Accordingly, in the April of 1828, he went to the building and searched. The corn was then thrashed out, but the old litter still remained there. They examined two or three places, and at length in the upper bay, they met with a spot where the floor did not appear so firm and consistent as the other parts of the ground in the barn. The part was immediately taken up, when, within a foot and a half from the surface they found the body of a female, having on parts of a woman's dress, corresponding with what Maria's stepmother had seen or helped to put on Maria on the 18th of May. Around the neck, for example, was the green silk handkerchief before mentioned. In short, there was such an identification made, notwithstanding that decomposition had taken place to a considerable extent, that strong suspicion immediately attached to Corder, information of the facts being speedily forwarded to London. Prudently the body was allowed to remain as found in the barn until it was inspected by a surgeon. As this gentleman's testimony was highly important, and is extremely interesting, its more remarkable portions are here given :—

It was, said Mr. Lawton, a female body, a full grown young woman, that they showed to him in the hole in the barn. He examined the face; it was in a very bad state, and there was an appearance of blood about it. The green handkerchief round the neck was tied in the usual way, but drawn extremely tight, so as to form a complete groove round the neck. It was apparently done for the purpose, as if it had been pulled so by some person. It was sufficiently tight to produce strangulation. There was also in the neck an appearance of a stab, about an inch and a half in length, and perpendicular, extending deep into the neck. There was the appearance of an injury having been done to the right eye, and the right side of the face ; seeming as if something had passed into the eye, deep into the orbit, injuring the bone and the nose. It seemed to have been done in two ways ; by something passing in at the left cheek, and then out of the right orbit ; and there was a stab also. It appeared as if a ball had passed through the left cheek, removing the two last grinders. He did not think that a ball so passing through would, of itself, cause death ; but with the strangulation, and the stab in the neck, it would have been sufficient, with the ball, to produce death. There had also something penetrated between the 5th and 6th ribs, and there was a stab in the heart which corresponded with the opening in the ribs. It appeared to have been done with a sharp instrument. A sword produced appeared to fit the wound through the opening in the shift and the ribs. It is not difficult to distinguish between a wound made during life, and one after death ; in the first the edges gape open, in the other instance, a wound gapes very little. Could speak with certainty that the ball came out at the eye, from the manner in which the bones were driven in. Had no doubt it was done by a bullet at some time or other.—Other medical testimony was adduced corroborative of the above.

Information of the finding of the body in the barn, &c. having been forwarded to London, an intelligent police officer was employed to apprehend Corder, who was found at Ealing. The officer on first seeing the accused, told him that he had come to apprehend him upon a very serious charge,—for nothing less than the murder of Maria Marten, asking Corder if he had known such a female. The answer was in the negative, having been repeated more than once,—the accused at last adding "You must be mistaken in the person you are come to apprehend." The officer returned, "No, I am not mistaken as to the person; your name is Corder, I believe;" and had for answer "it was."

At the time of the apprehension of Corder, the officer searched the house in which the accused was living, viz., that which was the wife's, and in one of the rooms he found a small black velvet bag, which was identified on the trial to have belonged to Maria Marten. In that bag was a brace of pistols, there was also a sword found which belonged, as well as the pistols, to the accused. It was also proved that he had gone some few days before the 18th of May to a cutler, who had sharpened the sword according to the orders he then received.

These and other corroborative facts were elicited from the witnesses on the trial, several of the Martens having been amongst the first examined. During the interrogatories which were put to the stepmother of the murdered young woman, the prisoner put on his spectacles,—for his sight was otherwise imperfect,—took out a red morocco pocket-book, in which he commenced writing, and looked steadfastly at the witness. She was a decently dressed country woman; she never returned Corder's glance. The trial had commenced at twenty minutes before ten o'clock, and about two he ate and drank with seeming appetite. He was at the time twenty-five years of age, was of middle height, of a fair and healthy complexion, large mouth, turn up nose, large eyes, which had a fixed and glazed aspect, and his features bore rather a smile than any other expression. He was dressed in a dark-coloured frock-coat, with velvet collar, black waistcoat, and blue trousers. The trial extended to a second day, the prisoner being put to the bar a little before 9 o'clock; and although he looked around him at times with seeming cheerfulness, he was manifestly not so much at his ease as on the previous day. During the examination of Mr. Lawton, the surgeon, who produced the skull of the deceased, he looked attentively at the spectacle,—inclining his body forward so as to command a full view of it. But, as if the effort to sustain this attitude, and evince this expression, had become too great for his nerves, he suddenly flung his back against the pillar, hastily drew off his spectacles, and evidently laboured under the strongest emotion.

The evidence having been concluded on the part of the prosecution, the prisoner was called on for his defence. Upon this, Corder advanced to the front of the bar, took out his papers, and read as follows with a tremulous voice:—"I am informed that, by the law of England, the counsel for a prisoner is not allowed to address the jury, though the counsel for the Crown is allowed that privilege. (Such was the law at the period of the trial, but happily there has been a change in that particular.) While I deplore as much as any human being can, the event which has caused this inquiry, let me entreat you to dismiss from your minds the publications of the public press, from the time of its promulgation to this hour; let me entreat you, let me dissuade you, if I can, from being influenced by the horrid and disgusting details which have for months issued from the public press—a powerful engine for fixing the opinions of large classes of the community, but which is too often I fear, though unintentionally, the cause of affixing slander upon innocence. I have been described as a monster, who, while meditating becoming the husband of this girl to whom I was evincing an affectionate attachment, was actually premeditating and plotting the perpetration of the horrid crime. With such misrepresentations it was natural, perhaps, to expect that an unfavourable impression should have been created against me, and the more so when the accusation went beyond the present case, and was connected with other crimes well calculated to excite prejudice against me. It is natural you should come to this trial with feelings of prejudice, but as you expect peace and serenity of mind at home, I implore you to banish from your minds all the horrible accusations which have been promulgated, and give your verdict on the evidence alone. Consider, gentlemen, that the attorney for the prosecution, is also the coroner before whom the inquest was taken; and his conduct in refusing my being present at the inquest, is conduct which you cannot approve. (This fact had been urged by Corder's counsel at the commencement of the trial.) Since my committal the coroner has been again at Polstead—has got up additional evidence. My solicitor pressed for a copy of the depositions, which were refused in consequence of these unjust proceedings. I never heard one of the witnesses examined, and cannot therefore have come prepared as I ought to be. The coroner thus acting in his double capacity, was likely enough, when meditating to act as attorney for the prosecution, to have entertained impressions inconsistent for the fit discharge of his inquisitorial inquiry; and again, as attorney for the prosecution, he was liable to be diverted from the fulfilment of his duties as coroner, so that I was in this respect, on the threshold of inquiry, exposed to disadvantages from which I ought to have been saved. This, however, was not all: my solicitor remonstrated; he was not only refused copies of the depositions, but the attorney for the prosecution, without any notice to me, has visited Polstead and taken examination upon oath of the different witnesses, and come to this trial prepared with evidence taken behind my back, and pruned down to suit the exaggerations of this case. I therefore am brought to be tried for my life without any fair knowledge of the evidence against me. In consequence of this unjust proceeding on the part of the coroner, how can I controvert, as I might have done, were I allowed to hear the witnesses, equivocal facts and highly coloured statements, of which I am for the first time informed when brought to trial for my life.

"It has been well observed that truth is sometimes stranger than fiction. Never was this assertion better exemplified than in this hapless instance. In a few short months I have been deprived of all my brothers, and my father recently before that period. I have heard the evidence and am free to say that, unexplained, it may cause great suspicion, but you will allow me to explain it. Proceeding, my lord and gentlemen, to the real facts of the case, I admit that there is evidence calculated to excite suspicion, but these facts are capable of explanation; and convinced as I am of my entire innocence, I have to entreat you to listen to my true and simple detail of the real facts of the death of this unfortunate woman. I was myself so stupefied and overwhelmed with the strange and disastrous circumstance, and on that account so unhappily driven to the necessity of immediate decision, that I acted with fear instead of judgment, and I did that which any innocent man might have done under such unhappy circumstances. I concealed the appalling occurrence, and was, as is the misfortune of such errors, subsequently driven to sustain the first falsehood by others, and to persevere in a system of delusion, which furnished the facts concealed for a long time. At first I gave a false account of the death of the unfortunate Maria. I am now resolved to disclose the truth, regardless of the consequences.

"To conceal her pregnancy from my mother, I took lodgings at Sudbury. She was delivered of a male child, which died in a fortnight in the arms of Mrs. Marten, although the papers have so perverted that fact; and it was agreed between Mrs. Marten, Maria, and me, that the child should be buried in the fields. There was a pair of small pistols in the bed-room, Maria knew they were there. I had often showed them to her. Maria took them away from me. I had some reason to suspect she had some correspondence with a gentleman, by whom she had a child, in London. Though her conduct was not free from blemish, I at length yielded to her entreaties, and agreed to marry her, and it was arranged we should go to Ipswich, and procure a license, and marry. Whether I said there was a warrant out against her I know not. It has been proved that we had many words, and that she was crying when she left the house. Gentlemen, this was the origin of the fatal occurrence. I gently rebuked her; we reached the barn; while changing her dress she flew into a passion, upbraiding me with not having so much re-gard for her as the gentleman before alluded to. Feeling myself in this manner so much insulted and irritated, when I was about to perform] every kindness and reparation, I said, 'Maria, if you go on in this way before marriage, what have I to expect after? I shall, therefore, stop when I can, I will return straight home, and you can do what you like, and act just as you think proper.' I said I would not marry her. In consequence of this I retired from her, when I immediately heard the report of a gun or pistol, and returning back, I found the unhappy girl weltering on the ground. Recovering from my stupor, I thought to have left the spot; I endeavoured to raise her from the ground, but found her entirely lifeless. To my horror I discovered the pistol was one of my own she had privately taken from my bed-room. There she lay, killed by one of my own pistols, and I the only being by! My faculties were suspended. I knew not what to do. The instant the mischief happened I thought to have made it public, but this would have added to the suspicion, and I then resolved to conceal her death! I then buried her in the best way I could. I tried to conceal the fact as well as I could, giving sometimes one reason for her absence, and sometimes another. It may be said, why not prove this by witnesses? Alas! how can I? How can I offer any direct proof how she possessed herself of my pistols, for I found the other in her reticule. That she obtained them can-not be doubted. All I can say as to the stabs is, that I never saw one, and I believe the only reasons for the surgeon's talking about them is, that a sword was found in my pos-session! I can only account for them by supposing that the spade penetrated the body when they searched for the body in the barn. This I know, that neither from me, nor from herself did she get any stab of this description. I always treated her with kind-ness, and had intended to marry her. What motive, then, can be suggested for my taking her life? I could have easily gotten over the promise of marriage. Is it possible I could have intended her destruction in this manner? We went in the middle of the day to a place surrounded by cottages. Would this have been the case had I intended to have murdered her? Should I have myself furnished the strongest evidence that has been adduced against me? I might, were I a guilty man, have suppressed the time and place of her death, but my plain and unconcealed actions, because they were guiltless, supplied both. Had I intended to perpetrate so dreadful a crime, would I have kept about me some of the articles which were known to be Maria's? Had I sought her life, could I have acted in such a manner? Had I, I would have chosen another time and place. Look at my conduct since. Did I run away? No! I lived months and months with my mother. I left Polstead in consequence of my family afflictions. I went to the Isle of Wight. It is said that the passport was obtained to enable me to leave England at any time. No, it was to enable me to visit some friends of my wife in Paris. Should I have kept her property, had I anything to fear from their detection? In December last, I advertised in the *Times* newspaper the sale of my house, and gave my name and address at full length. Did this look like concealment? You will consider any man innocent till his guilt is fully proved. It now rests with you to restore me to society, or to an ignominious death. To the former I feel I am entitled—against the latter I appeal to your justice and humanity. I have nothing more to add, but that I leave my life in your hands, aware that you will give me the humane benefit of the law in cases of doubt, and that your lordship will take a compassionate view of the melancholy situation in which my misfortunes have placed me."

This address was delivered, in many parts, in a feeble and tremulous tone of voice, and under considerable emotion, which were natural enough circumstances whether the prisoner was innocent or guilty. It was clear, at the same time, however, from the pronunciation of particular words and the manner of the accused, that he was not a person of any very considerable education. He read from a copy-book, and whether from the composition not being wholly his own, or from his near-sightedness, he stammered sometimes over words, and infringed the order of the sentences. He was, of course, heard with the utmost silence and attention by the court and jury, and he occasionally drew his eyes from the book and fixed them on the jurymen, as if to ascertain the impression he had made. Towards the close of his address his voice faltered, so as in particular passages to be nearly unintelligible.

Several witnesses were called for the defence, the points they principally spoke to being his apparent kindness to Maria Marten about the period she was delivered of the child that he acknowledged as his own, while the young woman was absent from her father's; and also that he appeared to be a very kind and good-natured young man. The summing up of the case by the Lord Chief Baron next took place; the following being some of its more important passages:—

Before he entered upon the details, his lordship adverted to what had been said relative to the prejudices which had been raised against the prisoner by means of the press and otherwise. It was unfortunate, extremely unfortunate, whenever such prejudices were raised; for they placed the life of the prisoner more in jeopardy than the ordinary circumstances of the case against him. Sorry, indeed, was he to say, that, as society was constituted at present, these prejudices could not be avoided. Accounts of the transaction had got into the newspapers. These accounts only related to the charge at the commencement of the business: they contained an *ex parte* statement of it, without giving the prisoner an opportunity of urging anything in his defence against it; and that was certainly a mischief, and an injury to him. The jury, however, had a more important task to perform: they had to decide this issue by hearing the evidence on both sides, whereas the public had heard only one side. (At an early period of the trial, the conduct of the coroner, who also acted as the solicitor in the prosecution, did not pass without remark and animadversion.) " We have also been told," said the judge, " that drawings and placards have been dispersed, not only in the neighbourhood of this town, but also in the immediate neighbourhood of this very hall, tending to the manifest detriment of the prisoner at the bar. Such a practice is so indecorous and so unjust, that I can with difficulty bring myself to believe that any person, even in the very lowest class, will so far degrade himself as to think of deriving gain from the exhibition of this melancholy transaction. Another circumstance, to which the prisoner has alluded, and which, I trust, for the sake of religion itself, is a mistake—another circumstance which I feel myself bound to notice, is the assertion that a minister of the Gospel, quitting the place where he usually performed divine worship, and erecting his pulpit near the very scene of this terrible tragedy, had there endeavoured to inflame the passions and to excite the resentment of the populace against the prisoner, when he knew nothing upon proper proof of the prisoner's having had any share in it, and only from rumour, thus inflaming them against a crime which was not then known to have been committed, and exciting their resentment against an individual who was not proved to have committed it. I cannot conceive of any act more contrary to the spirit and principles of that religion of which he professes himself a minister; and if we have been rightly informed of his conduct, the man who could commit such an act deserves the most severe reprobation. I do not know who the individual is who is stated to have misconducted himself so much. I hope we are all labouring under some mistake on this point, and that this outrage upon decency has not been perpetrated."

The venerable judge next went on to say, that the course which the defence had taken saved him from the necessity of going over the evidence which was adduced to prove that the body which had been found in the Red Barn was the body of Maria Marten. The prisoner had admitted that he buried her mortal remains there. "The next part of the evidence," continued his lordship, "to which I call the attention of the jury, is that which regards the different accounts which Corder gave, after the disappearance of Maria Marten, of the various places at which she was living; for those accounts have some bearing upon his defence. I might, perhaps, be relieved from the necessity of alluding to that part of the evidence altogether; but the manner of the prisoner's avowal may, when closely considered, be of some avail in enabling us to discover the truth of his statement, that her death was occasioned by a voluntary act of suicide on her part. I shall not omit reading any of the evidence which has reference to this point, unless you, gentlemen, state to me that in your opinion it is unnecessary for me to read it." The learned judge then proceeded to read the evidence of Mrs. Marten, the step-mother of the young woman: when he came to that part of it in which the witness swore that Corder said, "Mrs. Marten, the reason I go to Ipswich to-day is because John Balam, the constable, came into the stable this morning, and informed me that he had got a letter from Mr. Whitmore, of London, and that in that letter there was a warrant to have Maria taken up to be prosecuted for her bastard children;" the judge observed that this was very important evidence, as it bore directly upon the prisoner's defence; it showed that he was endeavouring to seduce her away from her home by holding out to her a terror which had no existence in reality. The jury would consider how far this was, or was not evidence to contradict the statement of the prisoner. It appeared also from the evidence of Mrs. Marten, that Maria Marten was very low-spirited on setting out for the Red Barn, and had been so for some time previously. That circumstance ought not by any means to be forgotten by the jury.

With regard to the prisoner's defence, his lordship also remarked, that it was very extraordinary, if the statement in it was true, that he had not said a syllable about it to the police officer at the time he was apprehended; but that he had repeatedly asserted he never knew anything of any such person as Maria Marten, though he was then formally informed that he was expressly accused of having murdered her. On coming to the evidence of Lawton, the surgeon, he particularly called the attention of the jury to the evidence which that gentleman had given relative to the fracture of the skull by a ball, respecting the wounds in her neck, heart and ribs, by a sharp instrument, and also regarding the possibility of her having died by strangulation from the tightness of the handkerchief round her neck. They had heard it that day asserted that the poor woman had committed suicide; but even according to the story they had heard, it was very strange that immediately on being left alone she should use such weapons to destroy herself; for it appeared in the first place, that she must have fired a pistol at herself, and then, either before or after firing it, have given herself certain stabs in different parts of her body. With regard to the character given in defence to the prisoner, the judge said, that in opposition to direct evidence as to facts, if such evidence existed according to the judgment of the jury, the general character of humanity and good-nature was of no avail, for that it was only when the balance of evidence seemed equal that it could reasonably prove of service to an accused person. The real question for the jury's decision was, are the representations by the prisoner true or false? If they should be of opinion that they were true, then Corder was entitled to an acquittal. His representation was that the deceased had shot herself with his pistols, which she had got into her possession. The prisoner wished to have it supposed that she had carried his pistols to the Red Barn in her pocket. Now, Corder had seen the stepmother and sister of Maria Marten in the witness-box, and he might have cross-examined them upon that point. But no one question had been put to them to show that the deceased had those pistols previously to leaving her father's cottage. So far as they had any evidence at all respecting such weapons, they appeared to have been in the prisoner's possession, and not in hers, for he had been seen snapping them. What had struck him (the judge), from the beginning of the defence to the end as the most extraordinary feature in it, was the manner in which the alleged suicide was committed. It often happened that these poor girls, when disappointed in their expectations, did lay hands on themselves; but then the mode of their death was in general very simple. In the present case, if they were to credit the evidence of the surgeons, the wounds inflicted on the body of Maria Marten were of a double description. There were first, the wounds in the eye, and in the cheek, inflicted by a bullet; and next the wounds applied with a sharp instrument on the heart and ribs, and the wound on the vertebræ of the neck behind the skull. It was extraordinary that instead of hanging herself upon a tree, as poor girls usually did in such circumstances, or drowning herself, she should have used two different means to destroy herself,—the one by shooting herself with a pistol, which was a very unusual weapon for a woman to wield, and the other by stabbing herself. The jury must decide on the credibility of the medical witnesses, who ventured to speak as to these two distinct causes of Maria Marten's death, independently of the third mode of death by strangulation; and then they must come to a conclusion how far it was possible that such multifarious wounds and means could be the work of her own hands.

The jury retired to deliberate concerning the verdict they should return, and after an absence of fully half an hour, they returned with that of *Guilty*. Sentence of death speedily followed.

Corder during the earlier part of the summing up of the judge paid the most eager attention, listening to the burthen of the indictment as given by his lordship, and the necessity the law imposed of proving to the satisfaction of the jury, that the death of the person had been occasioned by one of the means stated; but ere long he seemed to be overcome by stupor. At that part where Mrs. Stow's account of her conversation with him was gone over, with regard to Maria Marten having had her fated number of children, that he could at any time he pleased go to her, and that when he was not with her nobody else was, a fainting seemed nearly to overcome him,—a transient paleness was in his countenance, his eyes rolled in their sockets, he heaved deep sighs, and laid his head on the bar against which he had been previously leaning. He was also much agitated when the evidence of the police-officer was read as to his denying all knowledge of such a person as Maria Marten, and the remarks of the judge about his not at once, on being told that her body was found in the barn, confessing that he knew her and that she had destroyed herself, and had been buried there, instead of denying any acquaintanceship with her, caused a momentary faintness and swimming of his eyes.—During the reading of the evidence of the surgeons, he moved uneasily from side to side, seemingly unable to maintain his self-possession without continual change of position. In short, till he was removed to his cell, the alternations between complete prostration of mind and forced rallyings were manifest to the spectators, affording an instance in which guilty remorse, hopelessness, and despair were fearfully depicted,—something almost too fearful and awful to contemplate. It was understood that he expected the judge would dwell at length upon his defence, and that he had prepared himself for a vigorous effort to attend to the remarks he imagined would be made on the subject. When, however, the Chief Baron passed over his story by a bare statement of its principal points, and made not a single remark on it at that part of the summing up, but proceeded to the business of weighing the testimonies as a whole, he relapsed into a depression which he never surmounted to the end of the charge. As the jurymen passed him to deliberate, he cast upon them a piercing look of the most intense solicitude. During the time of their absence, nothing could be more disconsolate and desponding than his appearance. On their return he once more resumed his standing posture. At last, on hearing the word *Guilty*, he raised his hand slowly to his forehead, pressed it for a moment, and then dropped it, as one utterly dejected and forlorn,—his head falling droopingly upon his bosom. By the time the sentence was pronounced he would have sunk to the floor, had he not been prevented by the attention of the governor of the gaol. He then sobbed loudly and convulsively, and was almost carried out helplessly to that chamber which he was never again to quit finally, but to be led to the scaffold.

It was a singular feature in the origin of the inquiry into the disappearance and absence of Maria Marten, that her stepmother persisted before the Grand Jury in the story of the dream which had two or three times haunted her, that the poor young woman's body would be found in Corder's barn. The natural solution of this impression on the mind of Mrs. Marten may be traced to her anxiety and the frequent conversations which no doubt occupied the family regarding the girl's fate, coupled with the prisoner himself, which, preying upon the feelings of a person in her situation, must have been calculated to lead to many suggestions, conjectures, and speculations,—to inspire such apprehensions as would find expression even in midnight dreams. The *Red Barn* could scarcely fail of being the theme of most anxious cogitation as the exact spot towards which the weeping and spirit-broken victim of murder set out when last she had been seen alive, although the journey was taken in hopes of being wedded to him in whom all reliance was put. The counsel on neither side alluded to this remarkable operation of mind which had been spoken to before the Grand Jury by the affected stepmother; not wishing, it may be presumed, to lend encouragement to superstitious notions, in a case which was too pregnant with strong facts and abounded too fully in real circumstances to admit of any doubt as to arriving at a just and safe conclusion.

Corder did make a confession of his dreadful crime, shortly before the time of his execution: it was in these words:—

"I acknowledge being guilty of the death of poor Maria Marten, by shooting her with a pistol. The particulars are as follows:—When we left her father's house, we began quarrelling about the burial of the child, she apprehending that the place where it was deposited would be found out. The quarrel continued for about three quarters of an hour upon this and about other subjects. A scuffle ensued, and during the scuffle, and at the time I think that she had hold of me, I took the pistol from the side-pocket of my velveteen jacket, and fired. She fell, and died in an instant. I never saw even a struggle. I was overwhelmed with agitation and dismay. The body fell near the front doors on the floor of the barn. A vast quantity of blood issued from the wound, and ran on to the floor and through the crevices. Having determined to bury the body in the barn (about two hours after she was dead), I went and borrowed a spade of Mrs. Stow; but before I went there, I dragged the body from the barn into the chaff-house, and locked up the barn. I returned again to the barn and began to dig the hole; but the spade being a bad one, and the earth firm and hard, I was obliged to go home for a pick-axe and a better spade, with which I dug the hole, and then buried the body. I think I dragged the body by the handkerchief that was tied about her neck—it was dark when I finished covering up the body. I went the next day, and washed the blood from off the barn floor. I declare to Almighty God, I had no sharp instrument about me, and that no other wound but the one made by the pistol was inflicted by me. I have been guilty of great idleness, and at times led a dissolute life, but I hope through the mercy of God to be forgiven." In answer to a question from the under sheriff, he said, "that he thought the ball had entered the right eye." Mr. Orridge, the governor of the gaol, had wished to have further explanations on several points, but felt that in the circumstances of the condemned he could not press him, especially as the wretched criminal said to him on more than one occasion, "Spare me upon that point—I have confessed all that is sufficient for public justice."

At 10 minutes before 12 o'clock, on the day of execution, Corder was brought from his own cell, which was on a second story of the prison, to a cell on the basement story. He was there pinioned by the executioner. He appeared resigned to his fate, though he sighed heavily at intervals. After his arms were fastened, he would have fallen to the ground, had it not been for the support afforded him by one of the constables. He recovered after a moment from the faintness which had overcome him, and kept ejaculating in an under-tone, "May God forgive me! Lord receive my soul!" The executioner was then going to put the cap upon the prisoner's face, when Mr. Orridge interfered, and said that the time was not yet come. He was then led by his own desire around the different wards of the prison, and shook hands with the different prisoners, who were assembled at the doors entering into them. As a proof that he was at that time perfectly conscious of what he was doing, he singled out a prisoner of the name of Nunn, shook hands with him as well as his pinioned condition would allow, saying, "Nunn, God Almighty bless you." In another ward he supplicated the same blessing on two prisoners.

After he had gone round the entrance to the different wards of the prison, which were ranged around the governor's house, he proceeded to the entrance to the debtor's yard, where he bade farewell to three individuals who came to the gate to shake hands with him. After this,—Mr. Orridge thinking that such an affecting visit might prove beneficial to the juvenile offenders in the prison,—the procession to the scaffold was formed in the usual manner. The Rev. W. Stocking, for whose attentions Corder expressed himself most grateful, led the way, reading the commencement of the burial service,—" I am the resurrection and the life, whosoever believeth in me shall not die, but have everlasting life." In a few minutes afterwards the procession reached the door-way which opened to the scaffold, and Corder was placed upon the floor which, when withdrawn, was to plunge him into eternity. After he was brought under the fatal beam, Mr. Orridge approached him, and asked him whether he wished to address the multitude. He gave some answer, and Mr. Orridge immediately said to the crowd, in a loud voice, " He acknowledges the justice of his sentence, and dies in peace with all mankind." The executioner then drew the cap over his face. The officer who supported him said that Corder added, when quite unable to stand, " I deserve my fate: I have offended my God. May he have mercy on my soul!" Within a minute afterwards, the deadly bolt was withdrawn, and William Corder was cut off from the number of the living.

Corder's wife visited him after his condemnation, and conducted herself towards the wretched man not only with great tenderness and affection, but with a remarkable firmness and prudence. Shortly before he was executed he wrote a feeling letter to her.

On speaking on the subject of a confession, it was said that Corder had on one occasion asked an attendant in his cell, in what way it could contribute to the salvation of his soul to tell of the follies of his life to the world, or what other effect it would have than to cast needless disgrace on his family. And yet it was reported that the following conversation passed between him and one of the prison officers :—

" Pray, Mr. Corder, is it true that it was by an advertisement you were first introduced to Mrs. Corder ? "

" Indeed it was."

" Had you many answers to it ? "

" I had forty-five. Some from ladies in their carriages ! "

" Well, that surprises me."

" Surprise you, so it may, as it did myself; but I missed of a good thing."

" How was that ? "

" Why, then I will tell you. One of the answers which I received required that I should be at a certain church, on an appointed day, dressed in a particular manner, and I should meet a lady, also dressed in a particular way, and both understanding what we came about, no further introduction was necessary."

" But how could you know her? There might be another lady dressed in the same way."

"Oh! to guard against a mistake, she desired that I should wear a black handkerchief round my neck, and have my left arm in a sling; and in case I should not observe her, she would discover and introduce herself."

" And did you meet her ? "

" No, I did not; I went, but not in time, as the service was over when I got there."

" Then when you did not meet with her, how do you know that she was respectable ? "

" Because the pew-opener told me that such a lady was inquiring for a gentleman of my description ; and she came in an elegant carriage, and was a young woman of fortune."

"Then you never saw her afterwards?"

"No, never; but I found out where she lived and who she was, and would have had an interview with her, had it not been that I became acquainted with Mrs. Corder, from whom I was not a day absent until we were married."

"Was that long after your acquaintance?"

"About a week."

Two specimens from the *Fifty letters* which Mr. Foster published of those which had been directed to his care for Corder, in answer to the matrimonial advertisement, are here added, these being pretty much in the style and wording to the tenour of the majority of the communications.

"Sir, as I am not in the habit of trumpeting forth my own praises, I can say little on the subject of merits or personal charms; but if I may give credit to the opinions of friends, I am possessed of those requisites so essentially necessary to constitute the happiness of the married state. You, however, I trust, if serious, may have an opportunity, if you think proper, to judge for yourself. If you have not made your choice, I shall be happy to hear from you immediately."

"*Dec. 1st*, 1827.

"A young lady, who is desirous of settling in a respectable situation of life, has seen A. Z.'s advertisement, but previous to giving her name, would be glad to hear from him, stating whether he is still entirely disengaged, as the advertisement has been out several days. The lady thinks it rather unreasonable on the part of A. Z. to expect 'the real name and address,' at the same time withholding his own, as he must be aware that considerations of delicacy have, or ought to have, more weight with the female than the male part of the creation. The advertiser may feel assured that this letter is not written from impertinent motives, as the writer is really desirous of giving up the state of 'single blessedness.' She is under his own age, possesses some accomplishments, has moved in a genteel sphere of life, with an irreproachable reputation, and is generally considered of an amiable disposition. Having been thus explicit, the lady thinks herself entitled to ask some further particulars of A. Z., who may, if he thinks proper to continue this correspondence, address a letter to L. G."

XX.—JOAN PERRY, AND HER TWO SONS.

In the interesting collection of papers made by Harley, Earl of Oxford, and well known under the title of "The Harleian Miscellany," a pamphlet, of date September, 1676, is found, containing an account of the mysterious disappearance of a man named William Harrison, and the unhappy consequences that resulted therefrom. The narrative is authenticated by the name of the writer, Sir Thomas Overbury, nephew of the ill-fated gentleman of the same appellation, who was so barbarously destroyed in the Tower, in the year 1613. We here give the details of this most remarkable case, which were derived by Sir Thomas from minute inquiries made on the scene of the occurrence; Overbury having been a magistrate resident in the neighbourhood of the particular spot. Sir Thomas's letter to Dr. Shirley, who was physician to Charles II., authenticating the account, and published along with it, is as follows:—

"Sir,—It has not been any forgetfulness in me, you have no sooner heard from me;

but my unhappy distemper seizing on my right hand, soon after coming down into the country, so that till now I have been wholly deprived the use of it. I have herewith sent you a short narrative of that no less strange than unhappy business which some years since happened in my neighbourhood; the truth of every particular whereof I am able to attest, but I think it may very well be reckoned amongst the most remarkable occurrences of this age; you may dispose of it as you please, and, in whatever else I can serve you, you may freely command me, as,

" Sir,

" Your most affectionate kinsman and humble servant,

"Burton, Aug. 23, 1676."   THOMAS OVERBURY."

Now comes the original history :—" Upon Thursday the 16th day of August, 1660, William Harrison, steward to the Lady Viscountess Campden, at Campden, in Gloucestershire, being about seventy years of age, walked from Campden aforesaid to Charringworth, about two miles from thence, to receive his lady's rent; and, not returning so early as formerly, his wife, Mrs. Harrison, between 8 and 9 of the clock that evening, sent her servant, John Perry, to meet his master on the way from Charringworth; but neither Mr. Harrison, nor his servant, John Perry, returning that night, the next morning early Edward Harrison, William's son, went towards Charringworth, to inquire after his father; when, on the way, meeting Perry coming thence, and being informed by him he was not there, they went together to Ebrington, a village between Charringworth and Campden, where they were told, by one Daniel, that Mr. Harrison called at his house the evening before, in his return from Charringworth, but staid not; they then went to Paxford, about half a mile thence, where, hearing nothing of Mr. Harrison, they returned towards Campden; and in the way, hearing of a hat, band, and comb, taken up in the highway, between Ebrington and Campden, by a poor woman then leesing in the field, they sought her out, with whom they found the hat, band, and comb, which they knew to be Mr. Harrison's; and being brought by the woman to the place where she found the same, in the highway, between Ebrington and Campden, near unto a great furze brake, they there searched for Mr. Harrison, supposing he had been murdered, the hat and comb being hacked and cut, and the band bloody; but nothing more could be there found. The news hereof, coming to Campden, so alarmed the town, that men, women, and children hasted thence in multitudes, to search for Mr. Harrison's supposed dead body, but all in vain.

" Mrs. Harrison's fears for her husband being great, were now much increased; and having sent her servant Perry the evening before to meet his master, and he not returning that night, caused a suspicion that he had robbed and murdered him; and thereupon the said John Perry was the next day brought before a justice of peace, by whom being examined concerning his master's absence, and his own staying out the night he went to meet him, he gave this account of himself:—that, his mistress sending him to meet his master between 8 and 9 of the clock in the evening, he went down Campden-field towards Charringworth, about a lane's length, where meeting one William Reed, of Campden, he acquainted him with his errand; and further told him that, it growing dark, he was afraid to go forwards, and would therefore return, and fetch his young master's horse, and return with him; he did so to Mr. Harrison's court-gate, where they parted, and he staid still; one Pierce coming by, he went again with him about a bow's-shot into the fields, and returned with him likewise to his master's gate, where they also parted; and then he, the said John Perry, saith he went into his master's hen-roost, where he lay about an hour, but slept not; and, when the clock struck twelve, rose and went towards Charringworth, till, a great mist arising, he lost his way, and so lay the rest of the night under a hedge; and at day-break on Friday morning went to Charringworth, where he inquired for his master of one Edward Plaisterer, who told him he had been with him the afternoon before, and received three and twenty pounds of him, but staid not long with him: he then went to William Curtis, of the same town, who likewise told him he heard his master was at his house the day before, but, being not at home, did not see him; after which he saith he returned homeward, it being about 5 of the clock in the morning, when, on the way, he met his master's son, with whom he went to Ebrington and Paxford, &c., as hath been related.

"Reed, Pierce, Plaisterer, and Curtis being examined, affirmed what Perry had said, concerning them, to be true.

"Perry being asked by the justice of peace, how he, who was afraid to go to Charringworth at 9 of the clock, became so bold as to go thither at 12 ? Answered, that at 9 of the clock it was dark, but at 12 the moon shone.

"Being further asked, why, returning twice home, after his mistress had sent him to meet his master, and staying till 12 of the clock, he went not into the house to know whether his master were come home, before he went a third time, at that time of night, to look after him? Answered, that he knew his master was not come home, because he saw light in his chamber-window, which never used to be there so late when he was at home.

"Yet, notwithstanding this, that Perry had said for his staying forth that night, it was not thought fit to discharge him till further inquiry were made after Mr. Harrison, and accordingly he continued in custody at Campden, sometimes in an inn there, and sometimes in the common prison, from Saturday, August the 18th, unto the Friday following; during which time he was again examined at Campden, by the aforesaid justice of peace, but confessed nothing more than before; nor at any time could any further discovery be made what was become of Mr. Harrison. But it hath been said that, during his restraint at Campden, he told some, who pressed him to confess what he knew concerning his master, that a tinker had killed him; and to others he said, a gentleman's servant of the neighbourhood had robbed and murdered him; and others, again, he told that he was murdered, and hid in a bean-rick at Campden, where search was in vain made for him: at length he gave out that, were he again carried before the justice, he would discover that to him he would discover to nobody else; and thereupon he was, Friday, August the 24th, again brought before the justice of peace who first examined him, and be asking him whether he would yet confess what was become of his master, he answered, he was murdered, but not by him; the justice of peace then telling him that, if he knew him to be murdered, he knew likewise by whom he was; so he acknowledged he did; and, being urged to confess what he knew concerning it, affirmed that it was his mother and his brother that had murdered his master. The justice of peace then advised him to consider what he said, telling him, that he feared he might be guilty of his master's death, and that he should not draw more innocent blood upon his own head; for what he now charged his mother and brother with might cost them their lives; but he affirming he spoke nothing but the truth, and that if he were immediately to die he would justify it, the justice desired him to declare how and when they did it.

"He then told him, that his mother and his brother had lain at him, ever since he came into his master's service, to help them to money, telling him how poor they were, and that it-was in his power to relieve them, by giving them notice when his master went to receive his lady's rents; for they would then way-lay and rob him; and further said that, upon the Thursday morning his master went to Charringworth, going of an errand into the town, he met his brother in the street, whom he then told whither his master was going, and, if he way-laid him, he might have his money : and further said, that in the evening his mistress sent him to meet his master, he met his brother in the street, before his master's gate, going, as he said, to meet his master, and so they went together to the churchyard, about a stone's throw from Mr. Harrison's gate, where they parted, he going the foot-way, cross the churchyard, and his brother keeping the great road, round the church; but in the highway, beyond the church, met again, and so went together, the way leading to Charringworth, till they came to a gate about a bow's shot from Camp-den Church, that goes into a ground of the Lady Campden's, called the conygee (which, to those who have a key to go through the garden, is the nearest way from that place to Mr. Harrison's house); when they came near unto that gate, he, the said John Perry, saith, he told his brother, he believed his master was just gone into the conygee (for it was then so dark they could not discern any man so as to know him), but perceiving one to go into that ground, and knowing there was no way, but for those that had a key through the gardens, concluded it was his master; and so told his brother if he followed him, he might have his money, and he, in the meantime would walk a turn in the fields, which accordingly he did; and then, following his brother about the middle of the conygee, found his master on the ground, his brother upon him, and his mother standing by ; and being asked, whether his master was then dead? answered no, for that, after he came up his master cried, ' Ah, rogues ! you will kill me,' at which he told his brother he hoped he would not kill his master; who replied, ' Peace, peace, you're a fool,' and so stran-gled him ; which having done he took a bag of money out of his pocket, and threw it into his mother's lap, and then he and his brother carried his master's dead body into the garden, adjoining to the conygee, where they consulted what to do with it, and, at length, agreed to throw it into the great sink by Wallington's mill, behind the garden; but said, his mother and brother bade him go up to the court, next the house, to hearken if any one were stirring, and they would throw the body into the sink; and being asked whe-ther it were there, he said he knew not, for that he left it in the garden; but his mother and brother said they would throw it there, and if it were not there, he knew not where it was, for that he returned no more to them, but went into the court-gate, which goes into the town, where he met with John Pierce, with whom he went into the field, and again returned with him to his master's gate; after which he went into the hen-roost, where he lay till 12 of the clock that night, but slept not; and having, when he came from his mother and brother, brought with him his master's hat, band, and comb, and threw them, after he had given three or four cuts with his knife, in the highway, where they were found : and being asked what he intended by so doing ? said he did it, that it might be believed his master had been robbed and murdered ; and having thus disposed of his hat, band, and comb, he went towards Charringworth, &c., as hath been related.

"Upon this confession and accusation, the justice of peace gave order for the appre-hending of Joan and Richard Perry, the mother and brother of John Perry, and for searching the sink where Mr. Harrison's body was said to be thrown, which was accordingly done, but nothing of him could be there found ; the fish-ponds likewise, in Campden, were drawn and searched, but nothing could be there found neither; so that some were of opinion, the body might be hid in the ruins of Campden-house, burnt in the late wars, and not unfit for such a concealment, where was likewise search m ..e, but all in vain.

"Saturday, August 25th, Joan and Richard Perry, together with John Perry, were brought before the justice of peace, who acquainting the said Joan and Richard with what John had laid to their charge, they denied all, with many imprecations on themselves, if they were in the least guilty of anything of which they were accused; but John, on the other side, affirmed to their faces, that he had spoken nothing but the truth, and that they had murdered his master; further telling them that he could never be at quiet for them since he came into his master's service, being continually followed by them, to help them to money, which they told him he might do by giving them notice when his master went to receive his lady's rents; and that he, meeting his brother Richard in Campden-town, the Thursday morning his master went to Charringworth, told him whither he was going, and upon what errand. Richard confessed he met his brother that morning and spoke to him, but nothing passed between them to that purpose; and both he and his mother told John he was a villain to accuse them wrongfully, as he had done; but John, on the other side, affirmed that he had spoken nothing but the truth, and would justify it to his death.

"One remarkable occurrence happened on these prisoners' return from the justice of peace's house to Campden, viz., Richard Perry following a good distance behind his brother John, pulling a clout out of his pocket, dropped a ball of inkle, which one of his guard taking up, he desired him to restore, saying, it was only his wife's hair-lace; but the party opening it, and finding a slip-knot at the end, went and showed it to John, who was then a good distance before, and knew nothing of the dropping and picking up of this inkle; but being showed it and asked whether he knew it, he shook his head and said, yea, to his sorrow, for that was the string his brother strangled his master with. This was sworn upon the evidence at their trial.

"The morrow being the Lord's day, they remained at Campden, where the minister of the place deigning to speak to them (if possible to persuade them to repentance, and a further confession) they were brought to church; and in their way thither, passing Richard's house, two of his children meeting him, he took the lesser in his arms, leading the other in his hand; when, on a sudden, both their noses fell bleeding, which was looked upon as ominous.

"Here it will be no impertinent digression, to tell you, the year before, Mr. Harrison had his house broken open, between 11 and 12 of the clock at noon, upon Campden market-day, whilst himself and his whole family were at the lecture; a ladder being set up to a window of the second story, and an iron-bar wrenched thence with a ploughshare, which was left in the room, and seven score pounds in money carried away, the authors of which robbery could never be found.

"After this, and not many weeks before Mr. Harrison's absence, his servant, Perry, one evening, in Campden garden, made a hideous outcry; whereat some who heard it, coming in, met him running, and seemingly frightened, with a sheep-pick in his hand, to whom he told a formal story, how he had been set upon by two men in white, with naked swords, and how he defended himself with his sheep-pick; the handle whereof was cut in several places, and likewise a key in his pocket, which, he said, was done with one of their swords.

"These passages the justice of peace having before heard, and calling to mind, upon Perry's confession, asked him first concerning the robbery, when his master lost seven score pounds out of his house, at noonday,—whether he knew who did it? Who answered, yes, it was his brother. And being further asked whether he were then with him? He answered no, he was then at church; but that he gave him notice of the money, and told him in which room it was, and where he might have a ladder that would reach the window; and that his brother after told him he had the money, and had buried it in his garden, and that they were at Michaelmas next to have divided it; whereupon search was made in the garden, but no money could be there found.

"And being further asked concerning that other passage of his being assaulted in the garden, he confessed it was all a fiction, and that, having a design to rob his master, he did it, that, rogues being believed to haunt the place, when his master was robbed, they might be thought to have done it.

"At the next assizes, which were held in September following, John, Joan, and Richard Perry had two indictments found against them; one for breaking into William Harrison's house and robbing him of £140 in the year 1659; and the other for robbing and murdering of the said William Harrison, the 16th of August, 1660. Upon the last indictment, the then judge of assize, Sir C. T., would not try them, because the body was not found; but they were then tried upon the other indictment for robbery, to which they pleaded not guilty; but some whispering behind them, they soon after pleaded guilty, humbly begging the benefit of his majesty's pardon and act of oblivion, which was granted them.

"But though they pleaded guilty to this indictment, being thereunto prompted, as is probable, by some who were unwilling to lose time, and trouble the court with their trial, in regard the act of oblivion pardoned them; yet they all afterwards denied that they were guilty of that robbery, or that they knew who did it.

"Yet at this assize, as several credible persons have affirmed, John Perry still persisted in his story, that his mother and brother had murdered his master; and further added, that they had attempted to poison him in the jail, so that he durst neither eat nor drink with them.

"At the next assizes, which were the spring following, John, Joan, and Richard Perry were, by the then judge of assize, Sir B. H., tried upon the indictment of murder, and pleaded thereunto, severally, not guilty; and when John's confession, before the justice, was proved, *viva voce*, by several witnesses who heard the same, he told them he was then mad and knew not what he said.

"The other two, Richard and Joan Perry, said they were wholly innocent of what they were accused; and that they knew nothing of Mr. Harrison's death, nor what was become of him; and Richard said that his brother had accused others, as well as him, to have murdered his master; which the judge bidding him prove, he said that most of those that had given evidence against him knew it; but naming none, not any spoke to it, and so the jury found them all three guilty.

"Some few days after, being brought to the place of execution, which was on Broadway-hill, in sight of Campden, the mother (being a reputed witch, and to have so bewitched her sons they could confess nothing, while she lived), was first executed; after which, Richard, being upon the ladder, professed, as he had done all along, that he was wholly innocent of the fact for which he was then to die, and that he knew nothing of Mr. Harrison's death, nor what was become of him; and did, with great earnestness, beg and beseech his brother, for the satisfaction of the whole world and his own conscience, to declare what he knew concerning him; but he, with a dogged and surly carriage, told the people he was not obliged to confess to them; yet, immediately before his death, said he knew nothing of his master's death, nor what was become of him, but they might perhaps possibly hear."

The story of John Perry, whereby he not only accused his mother and his brother, but himself, as having been guilty of robbing and murdering his master, turned out to be utterly false,—the discovery, lamentable to tell, coming too late to rectify the terrible wrong and error, William Harrison returning to Campden about two years after his disappearance. His written statement to Sir Thomas Overbury accounted for his mysterious removal in the following manner :—

"Honoured Sir,—In obedience to your commands, I give you this true account of my being carried away beyond the seas, my continuance there, and return home. On a Thursday, in the afternoon, in the time of harvest, I went to Charringworth, to demand rents due to my Lady Campden, at which time the tenants were busy in the fields, and late before they came home, which occasioned my stay there till the close of the evening. I expected a considerable sum, but received only three and twenty pounds, and no more. In my return home, in the narrow passage amongst Ebrington Furzes, there met me one horseman, and said, 'Art thou there?' and I, fearing that he would have rid over me, struck his horse over the nose; whereupon he struck at me with his sword several blows, and run it into my side, while I, with my little cane, made my defence as well as I could; at last another came behind me, run me into the thigh, laid hold on the collar of my doublet, and drew me to a hedge, near to the plain; then came in another: they did not take my money, but mounted me behind one of them, drew my arms about his middle, and fastened my wrists together with something that had a spring lock, as I conceived, by hearing it give a snap as they put it on; then they drew a great cloak over me, and carried me away: in the night they alighted at a hay-stack, which stood near to a stone-pit by a wall side, where they took away my money. About two hours before day, as I heard one of them tell the other he thought it to be then, they tumbled me into the stone-pit; they staid, as I thought, about an hour at the hay-rick, when they took horse again; one of them bade me come out of the pit; I answered they had my money already, and asked what they would do with me; whereupon he struck me again, drew me out, and put a great quantity of money into my pockets, and mounted me again after the same manner; and on the Friday, about sun-setting, they brought me to a lone house upon a heath, by a thicket of bushes, where they took me down almost dead, being sorely bruised with the carriage of the money. When the woman of the house saw that I could neither stand nor speak, she asked them whether or no they had brought a dead man; they answered no, but a friend that was hurt, and they were carrying him to a surgeon; she answered if they did not make haste, their friend would be dead before they could bring him to one. There they laid me on cushions, and suffered none to come into the room but a little girl; there we staid all night, they giving me some broth and strong waters: in the morning very early, they mounted me as before; and on Saturday night they brought me to a place where were two or three houses, in one of which I lay all night, on cushions, by their bedside. On Sunday morning they carried me from thence, and, about three or four o'clock, they brought me to a place by the sea-side called Deal, where they laid me down on the ground; and, one of them staying by me, the other two walked a little off, to meet a man, with whom they talked; and, in their discourse, I heard them mention seven pounds; after which they went away together; and about half an hour after returned. The man (whose name, as I after heard, was Wrenshaw), said he feared I would die before he could get me on shipboard, where my wounds were dressed. I remained in the ship, as near as I could reckon, about six weeks, in which time I was indifferently recovered of my wounds and weakness. Then the master of the ship came and told me, and the rest who were in the same condition, that he discovered three Turkish ships; we all offered to fight in defence of the ship and ourselves; but he commanded us to keep close, and said he would deal with them well enough; a little while after he called us up, and when we came on deck, we saw two Turkish ships close by us; into one of them we were put, and placed in a dark hole, where, how long we continued, before we landed, I know not; when we were landed, they led us two days journey, and put us into a great house, or prison, where we remained four days and a half; and then came to us eight men to view us, who seemed to be officers; they called us, and examined us of our trades and callings, which every one answered; one said he was a surgeon, another that he was a broad-cloth weaver, and I, after two or three demands, said I had some skill in physic. We three were set by, and taken by three of those eight men that came to view us; it was my chance to be chosen by a grave physician of eighty-seven years of age, who lived near Smyrna, who had formerly been in England, and knew Crowland, in Lincolnshire, which he preferred before all other places in England; he employed me to keep his still-house, and gave me a silver bowl, double gilt, to drink in; my business was most in that place; but once he set me to gather cotton-wool, which I not doing to his mind, he struck me down to the ground, and after drew his stiletto to stab me, but I holding up my hand to him, he gave a stamp, and turned from me, for which I render thanks to my Lord and Saviour Jesus Christ, who staid his hand and preserved me. I was there about a year and three quarters, and then my master fell sick, on a Thursday, and sent for me; and calling me, as he used, by the name of Boll, told me he should die, and bade me shift for myself; he died on Saturday following, and I presently hastened with my bowl to a port, almost a day's journey distant; the way to which place I knew, having been twice there employed, by my master, about the carriage of his cotton-wool; when I came thither, I addressed myself to two men, who came out of a ship of Hamborough, which, as they said, was bound for Portugal within three or four days; I inquired of them for an English ship, they answered there was none; I entreated them to take me into their ship, they answered they durst not, for fear of being discovered by the searchers, which might occasion the forfeiture, not only of their goods, but also of their lives; I was very importunate with them, but could not prevail; they left me to wait on Providence, which, at length brought another out of the same ship, to whom I made known my condition, craving his assistance for my transportation; he made me the like answer as the former, and was as stiff in his denial, till the sight of my bowl put him to a pause: he returned to the ship, and, after half an hour's space, he came back again accompanied with another seaman, and for my bowl undertook to transport me; but told me I must be contented to lie down in the keel, and endure much hardship; which I was content to do, to gain my liberty. So they took me aboard, and placed me below in the vessel, in a very uneasy place, and obscured me with boards and other things, where I lay undiscovered, notwithstanding the strict watch that was made in the vessel; my two chapmen, who had my bowl, honestly furnished me with victuals daily, until we arrived at Lisbon, in Portugal; where, as soon as the master had left the ship, and was gone into the city, they set me on shore moneyless, to shift for myself. I knew not what course to take, but, as Providence led me, I went up into the city, and came into a fair street; and, being weary, I turned my back to a wall, and leaned upon my staff; over against me were four gentlemen discoursing together; after a while one of them came to me, and spoke to me in a language I knew not. I told him I was an Englishman, and understood not what he spoke; he answered me in plain English, that he understood me, and was himself born near Wisbeach, in Lincolnshire; then I related to him my sad condition, and he, taking compassion on me, took me with him, provided for me lodging and diet, and, by his interest with a master of a ship bound for England, procured my passage; and bringing me on shipboard, he bestowed wine and strong waters on me, and, at his return, gave me eight stivers, and recommended me to the care of the master of the ship, who landed me safe at Dover, from whence I made shift to London, where being furnished with necessaries, I came into the country.

"Thus, honoured sir, I have given you a true account of my great sufferings and happy deliverance, by the mercy and goodness of God, my most gracious Father in Jesus Christ, my Saviour and my Redeemer; to whose name be ascribed all honour, praise, and glory. I conclude, and rest,　　　　　　　Your Worship's

　　　　　　　　　　　In all dutiful respects,

　　　　　　　　　　　　WILLIAM HARRISON."

To the preceding narrative the following observations are appended in the original publication :—" Many question the truth of this account Mr. Harrison gives of himself and his transportation, believing he was never out of England; but there is no question of Perry's telling a formal false story to hang himself, his mother, and brother; and since this, of which we are assured, is no less incredible than that of which we doubt, it may induce us to suspend hard thoughts of Mr. Harrison, till time, the great discoverer of truth, shall bring to light this dark and mysterious business. That Mr. Harrison was absent from his habitation, employment, and relations, two years, is certain; and, if not carried away (as he affirms), no probable reason can be given for his absence; he living plentifully and happily in the service of that honourable family, to which he had been then related above fifty years, with the reputation of a just and faithful servant; and having all his days been a man of sober life and conversation, cannot now reasonably be thought in his old age, so far to have misbehaved himself, as in such a manner voluntarily to have forsaken his wife, his children, and his stewardship, and to leave behind him, as he then did, a considerable sum of his lady's money in his house. We cannot, therefore, in reason or charity, but believe that Mr. Harrison was forcibly carried away; but by whom, or by whose procurement, is the question. Those, who he affirms did it, he withal affirms never before to have been seen; and that he saw not his servant Perry, nor his mother, nor his brother, the evening he was carried away; that he was spirited, as some are said to have been, is no ways probable, in respect he was an old and infirm man, and taken from the most inland part of the nation; and, if sold, as himself apprehends he was, for seven pounds, would not recompense the trouble and charge of his conveyance to the sea-side.

The conduct of John Perry in some measure justified the extremity to which the law proceeded against himself, his brother, and his mother; at least, one feels little sympathy for such a wretch, unless, indeed, instead of having been actuated by motives of revenge against those so nearly allied to him, he was the subject of insanity, as he himself declared. Happily, now-a-days, the production of the body would be demanded by the law in a similar case, in the absence of sufficient direct ocular testimony, ere criminality could be decisively assumed.